I0762967

How the Story Goes

How the Story Goes

A Novel

Andrew Forrester

An Imprint of HarperCollins*Publishers*

This is a work of fiction. Names, characters, places, and incidents are products of the author's imagination or are used fictitiously and are not to be construed as real. Any resemblance to actual events, locales, organizations, or persons, living or dead, is entirely coincidental.

HarperCollins books may be purchased for educational, business, or sales promotional use. For information, please email the Special Markets Department at SPsales@harpercollins.com.

hc.com

FIRST EDITION

Interior text design by Diahann Sturge-Campbell

Library of Congress Cataloging-in-Publication Data has been applied for.

ISBN 978-0-06-345213-8

Printed in the United States of America

26 27 28 29 30 LBC 5 4 3 2 1

For Meg

How the Story Goes

CHAPTER ONE

If Whit Longacre could have chosen the background music for his current existential crisis, it most likely would have been something from the sad dad-rock category. He would not have chosen the soundtrack to the latest Disney movie, but that was where things stood: Annie in the backseat, obliviously belting out every part, changing her voice as she changed roles, and Whit in the driver's seat, feeling, as he often felt these days, on the brink of nervous collapse.

His task, always at hand, was colossal. It was usually soul-crushing, and when it wasn't soul-crushing, it just hung there, at the edges of his awareness, like a fine, anxiety-inducing mist. Like the technique sound designers use in horror movies, playing inaudible but unsettling noises that fill theatergoers with a dread they might not even be able to name. In Whit's mind, his dread *did* have a name: the Monumental Task.

"Are you ready for school today?" he asked, shouting over a solo about a family who just doesn't understand as he glanced in the rearview mirror.

Annie waited for a break in the lyrics, grinning and dancing, and then yelled back, "*Yes!*" She jumped in again on the next verse, and Whit's separate worries seemed momentarily less significant, like a leashed lion. Still there, but not going to devour him just yet. Annie was ready for school. That was good. And he had managed to get her out of the house today with her auburn hair looking less child-of-a-widower chic and more like it had looked when Helen was here. Annie's clothes matched; she had what she needed for the day, a healthy lunch packed into her padded lunch box. Those things were good, and the Monumental Task could be ignored for a time.

The road was wet and black, the trees on either side highlighted with tufts of the first fall foliage. As he rounded the corner, slowing into the creep of the carpool line, his eyes fell on the brown paper package in the passenger seat. That was another issue. The Task was almost all-consuming, yes, but there was this, too. One of those small unbearable things, the sort people make jokes about: *I can't believe I did what I'd been putting off for two months and it only took two minutes*. How many minutes, days, had this thing ridden around with him? Someday Annie was going to be big enough to ride in the front seat, and she was going to say, *Hmm, Dad, what is this package with Mom's handwriting on it, and don't you think she hoped it would be delivered within a hundred years of her death?*

Whit pulled into the main drop-off lane of the Foothills School, a small private school Helen had liked far more than he had, though that was out of his hands now: when Helen died, they'd renamed the library after her. She had also asked, toward the end, that money be put aside for a scholarship fund, so he and Annie were really stuck. Anyway, Annie liked it here. As a third-grader, she'd been attending the school for a few years already, so the stability was good, especially these days. And of course, there were so many parents who knew them, knew their story, and were eager to help Whit out with single-dad life.

So many parents.

The door opened for Annie, and she had hardly disappeared amid their duet of goodbyes and *I-love-you*'s when another head poked into the backseat, mostly bald, with hexagonal glasses and a theatrically wide grin that reeked of manipulation.

"Knock, knock!"

Whit expelled a laugh, like someone passing a kidney stone.

"You didn't knock," he said through a strained smile, as if he were making a joke. He wasn't.

"Oh, ha-ha," Noel Pendergrass said. He actually enunciated the two *ha*'s like a robot reading a text message transcript. "I guess I assumed you had an *open-door* policy."

Whit was having to contort himself to look back at Noel, and cool air was seeping in from the outside, and while Noel, the impassioned chairperson of the Carpool Committee, was dressed for carpool duty in New England in October, Whit was dressed for sitting in the front seat of a warm Range Rover.

"I guess you could say that." Whit was still smiling like he had a dental cheek retractor in his mouth. "Did you need something, Noel?"

"Well, as a matter of fact, I do need help. With *carpoooooool dutyyyyy*."

He said it in that specific Oprah Winfrey way, dragging out the second syllable as if the word were a celebrity or a prize and not the single least appealing volunteer opportunity Whit could think of. Not because he disliked the cold or early mornings, but because he disliked Noel, who had, on more than one occasion, uttered sentences that began, "Now that your wife has passed on to the Great Beyond . . ."

The Great Beyond. Like she was the cat at the end of *CATS!* and not his wife of ten years.

"I have a proposition," Noel said, "and I really think it might be good for you, as a way of getting involved again. It's been over a year since Helen pa—"

Whit faked a coughing fit, and Noel paused.

"Anyway, mind if we make a quick loop? I can just—"

The man was actually lowering himself into the backseat, making an effort to crawl his way into the warm car, which suddenly felt to Whit like a very sacred space.

"Oh, I wish," Whit said, more frantic than he would have liked, "but I can't talk just now. I'm dropping this off at the library, and Mrs. Pryor has a meeting first thing."

He held up the package from the front seat, freezing Noel into a position halfway through the "March of Progress" evolutionary chart, his long-limbed body crouched and curling over Annie's seat. His eyes, though, were filled with a *Homo sapiens* yearning to know what the package held.

"Ah," Noel said, through an even brighter grin. "Well, then, some other time."

"Mm-hmm."

Whit released his foot off the brake. The car lurched slightly, and Noel pulled back, startled.

"Whoops," Whit said, not looking back.

"Ha-ha!" Noel called, closing the door.

A minute later, idling in his parking spot, Whit looked at himself in the rearview mirror.

"Well."

He looked at the package still in his hand.

"I guess today's the day."

CHAPTER TWO

The lower campus of the Foothills School was tucked into an actual forested foothill. Trees grew right up to the edge of the dark wooden buildings, cresting over their huge windows and green metal roofs, and there were large glacial rocks out front, near the flagpoles. Whit liked those parts of the school. He liked moving from walkway to covered walkway to reach the front-office building. The school was an open, modular space, and the thought of Annie spending much of her day outside, navigating the green gaps between buildings with her teachers, classmates, and friends, made him happy.

Chiefly, it was the school-obsessed parent community that bothered him. People like Noel, who devoted their lives to knowing the latest updates to the school handbook and memorizing the state of every school-related relationship, performance review, and curriculum change. Also, there were the receptionists.

Whit knew the two women who worked the front desk by sight, but he could never remember their names. He thought of them as Wet-Looking Curly Hair Woman and Woman with the Extensive Neck Scarf Collection. But beyond the always lacquered hair and the scarves (today's was houndstooth), what had stood out to him for the last year were their sad eyes. These ladies were longing, deep within their bones, to drop a pity casserole off at his house. They leered at him like he needed to be cared for in some way that blurred the lines between the maternal and the sensual, and it gave Whit the creeps.

"Hello, Mr. Longacre," Wet-Looking Curly Hair Woman

said, and he nodded in greeting. "It's been a while since we've seen you up here. Not writing today?"

"Well," Whit said, more easily polite with her than he was with Noel, "I'm hoping to, but you never know when the Muse will strike."

Whit dug his left thumb into his thigh while the ladies chuckled. There was no Muse, and he hated perpetuating the myth that writers were mystics who communed with some great, invisible, story-breathing force. He wrote in a cramped, ground-level office surrounded by piles of books and notepads and dirty mugs. And yes, sometimes on days like this—when his window fogged over and the lamps were shining their orange light against it—he imagined that from the outside his space looked like a lantern glowing in the woods. But an ivory tower it wasn't. That was Helen's office, the third-floor room where she wrote her novels, looking out over the trees on one side and a sliver of the sea on the other. He liked his little room, he did, but the ease with which he could make something symbolic of this arrangement was not lost on him.

"Well, how can we help you?" Woman with the Extensive Neck Scarf Collection asked.

"I need to drop this off," he said, holding up the package, "in the library."

"Would you like us to put it in Mrs. Pryor's box?"

Whit repressed a sigh. He could see where this was heading.

"No, I'd like to give it to her myself."

The ladies made similarly perplexed faces.

"Well, I'm afraid Mrs. Pryor is—"

He cut them off.

"Please, I'm under strict orders to hand-deliver it there."

"Orders from—?"

"Helen," he said, flatly but truthfully. There had been a sticky note and everything.

The ladies cocked their heads to opposite sides, and he could almost see the ingredients for baked ziti combining behind their eyes. He knew how they saw him, and he knew he wasn't doing himself any favors in the sad writerly widower department: the sandy beard, the sage cable-knit cardigan, the dark blue eyes that looked either weepy or just tired. (And on really special days, both!)

"Anyway," he said.

"Yes, of course," said Woman with the Extensive Neck Scarf Collection. She shrugged, and immediately a visitor pass materialized. She slid it over the desk to him and very possibly gave him a wink.

"You have a good day now," one of them was saying as he turned to leave. Whit waved without looking back, trying not to run like someone who had just narrowly escaped the clutches of predatory sympathy.

*

The walls of the building were paneled in a wood that resembled the interior of a stately lake house. He walked down a hall lined on one side with picture windows and on the other with student art, occasionally broken up by doors to teacher classrooms and posters about inclusivity and anti-bullying. The school felt pleasantly alive. Distant voices formed a constant hum, which reminded Whit of walking through a movie theater hallway, and the occasional loud cheers or bangs of who knows what only added to the sensation. He did have to hand it to Helen: this place, with its scent of cedarwood and lavender and lemon, smelled a hundred times better than any movie theater or school he'd ever walked through.

The double doors to the Helen Albright Longacre Library were open, and on the other side of the threshold was the room in this school that Whit thought was most worth the price of tuition. In the middle of the library, a cartoony, handcrafted tree with construction paper bark and felt leaves the size of dinner plates stretched toward the ceiling, where it bloomed outwards like an umbrella. Floor pillows and large, comfy-looking beanbag chairs were scattered around it like dropped seedpods; vines and glowing Christmas lights grew out from it and crisscrossed half the shelves. Paper lanterns hung from the ceiling, interlaced with *papel picado* and strings of dangling, glittering golden stars. In one corner was a large claw-foot bathtub filled with blue cushions and a sign that said, "*Water* you waiting for? *Dive* into a good book!" A Narnian lamppost stood tall in the FICTION section, and two suits of armor—one Japanese and one ambiguously European—watched over the history books. Whit spotted a dozen stuffed animals in various alcoves, and there were at least three reading nooks that he, at thirty-seven years old, would have been happy to curl up in for the rest of the day. It was a magical space, and Mrs. Pryor, the librarian, was a magical, grandmotherly kind of woman. But she was nowhere to be seen.

Whit approached the checkout desk, eyes darting over the various trinkets, including a set of figurines from *The Wind in the Willows* having a delicious afternoon tea and a Dog Man made from painted cardboard. There was a bell, too, like at the front desk of a hotel, but ringing it seemed tacky in a space like this. He wouldn't treat Mrs. Pryor like a hotel clerk, not for a million bucks. Anyway, the woman could probably sense that he had entered her enchanted realm; at any moment, she would materialize in fairy godmother fashion, bursting forth from blue flames or floating over to him in a large pink bubble.

"Can I help you?" a voice asked from somewhere unseen, and Whit almost laughed. Mrs. Pryor *was* magic.

But the voice was wrong—lower, younger, a bit more *direct*

than the librarian's had ever been. When he craned all the way over the desk, he saw her: a woman about his age on all fours, rummaging for something in the bottom cabinet of the desk. From above, he saw that she wore a deep purple sweater and jeans with duck boots, and she had wavy, sable-colored hair to her shoulders. When she did not look up, Whit leaned back to stand straight.

"Um," he said to the vacuum of space above the desk, "I was hoping to leave something with Mrs. Pryor—"

"She's out sick today. I'm subbing for her."

"Oh, okay." Whit felt like he was talking to a ghost. He prayed that the front-desk women weren't on their way to check on him. He couldn't bear to be seen standing here, delusionally holding court with the empty air. And—*oh*—the realization suddenly hit him that they'd been trying to save him from this awkward interaction, trying to tell him Mrs. Pryor was out today, and he had ignored them.

"Well," he said, defeated, "I'll just come back."

"No," the disembodied voice said, "don't go to the trouble. I can take whatever it is—I'll see her later today."

Whit waited, but the rummaging continued.

"I'm actually under strict orders to hand-deliver it to her," he explained, beginning to hate this moment and this interaction. He was tempted to turn and leave, hoping the substitute librarian would be too slow standing up to catch him. But then he thought of the front-office ladies again, and their unbearable, hungry pity—how they seemed to imagine he was too enfeebled by grief to have a normal human interaction. No, thank you.

"I'm telling you," the voice said, "whatever it is, I'll get it to her."

"I really can't—"

There was a great *bang* below the desk, followed by a creak and a noise like whimpering wood.

"Everything okay down there?" Whit asked the disembodied voice, bewildered and embarrassed as he stared instead at the nearest dangling star.

"No," the voice moaned, and then it broke into a bevy of words like a roller coaster slowly cresting a hill before barreling forward. "These kids just cram books in here, but it's not really their fault, because the book drop is narrower than you'd expect, and kids' books can be so weirdly shaped. I mean, I'm looking at a picture book about root systems that is the size of a cafeteria tray, and I'm just wondering, which teacher allowed their student to shove this enormous book through the book slot?"

Another bang, a crack, and the sound of many books sliding over one another, followed by another, more human thud. Whit stretched over the desk again, and now the woman was on her back, laughing with her head awkwardly plonked against the back wall. She held the root systems book high.

"Got it," she said, more to herself than Whit. Then she saw him and seemed to remember she had been speaking to someone just ten seconds before.

"Are you all right?" he asked as she straightened up into a sitting position and then stood. She had green-framed glasses and the kind of sloping bangs Whit had always liked, and he was just noticing her wide hips and thinking that this was the first time he'd talked to an unfamiliar woman this close to his age in he didn't know how long, when he noticed the lanyard around her neck dotted with a few pins. One was a kestrel with a spoon in its beak. Ah. So she was a fan of Helen's books.

"I'm fine," she said eventually, as she placed the large book on the desk in front of her and began fiddling with the computer, presumably to check it back in.

"Now," she said to the computer, "tell me about this mysterious package only my mother can receive."

"Oh. Your mother." Something about that made sense. This

woman did not look like Mrs. Pryor, and she certainly didn't dress like the older woman, who was always draped in shawls and long beaded necklaces like a retired soprano. But there was something about her, a kind of quietly frenetic energy. Like her mother, she didn't seem obnoxious or loud, but you got the sense she could perform, in some necessary way, at a moment's notice.

"Yes," she said, looking at him for the first time, "my mother. I just moved to town, and already she has me subbing for her. Child labor."

She said it lightly, like a joke her mother could actually hear. Then her eyes were back on the computer again, and Whit felt like the least interesting person in the world.

"So you see," she continued, "whatever it is, you really can give it to me."

Whit passed the package from one hand to the next. He moved his booted feet up and down, up and down. Helen would never know, of course. And this woman—her name tag said MS. PRYOR, SUBSTITUTE—was a very close second to her mother, who was out sick for who knew how long. Whit certainly wasn't going to ask.

"Okay," he said finally. "Well. It's—here it is. She thought . . ."

He trailed off, placing the package gingerly before him on the desk and patting it once with his hand. Then, after bringing his interlocked fingers to rest at his waist, he thought better of it and slid the package all the way across the desk to Ms. Pryor.

She looked at him like he had just performed the macarena sans accompaniment. "Thank you," she said, repressing a laugh.

"It's a gift from my wife. She thought the library might like to have it, display it somewhere."

Ms. Pryor was still watching him, nodding and smiling like a babysitter humoring a talkative child.

"Okay," he said again, turning to leave. "But, oh," he added, raising a finger and turning back as he remembered Helen's other proviso, "she was totally okay with the school selling it or putting it up for auction or whatever, if they needed money for, I don't know, a new gym. But surely there are other ways to make money at a place like this, right? And come to think of it, a gym would be sort of depressing. A new art room, maybe. An orchestra room. Orchestra hall? You get it."

He was babbling now, and whatever Ms. Pryor had been doing before, going on about the books in the book drop, that was different. Those were her inner thoughts, articulated like a soliloquy for whichever audience happened to hear it. His rambles, Whit knew, were more like the nervous ravings of a sad widower: a character he did not enjoy playing and one that, for some reason he couldn't understand, felt particularly disagreeable to him now.

"All right," Ms. Pryor said, and it was then that she finally looked down at the package. He knew the words she was reading, because they had ridden around in his front seat for months: *For the most magical library there is, with all my affection and appreciation. Cheers, Helen.*

The substitute librarian slowly began to unwrap the package, her short fingers treating it with delicacy and care, like she was someone who handled books (it *was* a book) reverently and often.

From the front cover, it looked unremarkable. It was simply a first edition of the first book in the Greenwood Castle Saga: *The Door in the Garden Wall.* But then Ms. Pryor turned to the title page, which was signed:

Helen Albright Longacre

She looked up at him, her mouth just slightly open and her eyes newly narrowed.

"There's more," Whit said, indicating with his hand that she should continue turning pages.

She did, her eyes widening behind her green glasses as she looked through page after page of handwritten annotations, all inscribed by one of the English-speaking world's most prominent children's fantasy writers.

"But how did she—?"

Ms. Pryor looked up at him again, and Whit surprised himself by laughing.

"What? How did she get this? She made it. She wrote it."

Ms. Pryor looked down at the book again, then up once more. "She—?"

"She wrote the inscription and annotations herself. And the book."

A realization washed over Ms. Pryor's face: that his wife was the author of the Greenwood Castle books, Helen Albright Longacre, who had died a little over a year ago in that most quotidian way—undetected Stage 4 cancer. Which made him the bereaved husband who was giving her librarian mother a precious gift.

Her eyes took on a liveliness different from that of the front-office ladies. To Whit, they seemed to convey genuine compassion, but then she set her face once more and whipped her eyes back to the book.

"But this is amazing," she said. "This is . . ."

She ended with an awed sigh. Whit shrugged. How did you respond to that?

"Well," he said, realizing that Ms. Pryor the fan would probably enjoy sifting through the annotations without the late author's husband watching her do it. "Please make sure your mom knows about it as soon as possible. Helen thought she'd be excited."

"Are you kidding? She'll die."

Whit smiled softly, and then Ms. Pryor realized what she'd said, and then Whit realized what she'd said. She looked ready to apologize, but she stopped herself, and Whit, for some reason, liked that.

"All right," he said. "Thank you. I hope you have a good day."

"Thank *you*," Ms. Pryor said, and then she was lost to the notes

Helen had written from her chemo chair about such-and-such elf and such-and-such warlock, and Whit rallied himself to once again face *it*, the monumental, all-consuming task he'd successfully avoided thinking about for the last hour, which was a much longer break than usual. But first, there were the front-office ladies to deal with and the unexpected thought that maybe a steaming baked ziti on the doorstep wouldn't be so bad after all.

CHAPTER THREE

Tuesdays were writing group days, which were at turns wonderful and excruciating. Wonderful, of course, because writing is a solitary art, and joining with one's peers—particularly peers who wrote in different fields and therefore were not competitors but fellow creators—was life-giving to Whit. But writing group days were also terrible, horrible, because they meant sharing a bit about what you'd written since the last meeting and what your goals were for the day. Then they would write together, and lately, for Whit, that meant staring at his blank computer screen while his writing partner tap-tap-tapped away next to him.

As Whit walked toward Carafe, the coffee shop where the group met, he made his mental lists:

What I've Written Since Last Time:

1. Nothing.

Goals for Today:

1. Avoid being crushed beneath the monumental weight of potential failure, the possibility I may never write anything worthwhile again, the reverberating notion that maybe I should have learned a real trade, the not-terribly-slim chance my agent and/or publisher will drop me, all made exponentially worse by my wife's death and everything that comes with *that*.
2. Respond to emails.

He'd start with number 2.

Carafe was located on Cork Street, which was not technically the main street of Whelk Harbor, though everyone in town treated it that way. This came down to cuteness. The brick sidewalks were lined with beech trees, and in about a month the street would be decorated with multicolored Christmas lights and coniferous greenery. Red bows would be wrapped around lampposts, arranged in arches over doorframes, and perched in the display windows of the boutique, the bakery, the bookstore, the bistro, and the ice cream shop, all of which had taken over the white colonial-style buildings with black roofs. The church and the town hall, as well as the bank and a real estate agency, backed up to Cork Street, which was a favorite spot for wintry strolls (a paper cup of hot cocoa in hand) or, in summer, swimsuited bike rides (towels draped over necks and hanging from beach bags). Today the trees were shifting, in a gentle October way, from green to orange, yellow, and red, and every doorstep and staircase was crowded with warty pumpkins and elongated gourds.

Carafe even had a scarecrow out front. The shop, a relatively new addition to town, had taken over a former sunglasses store, which had taken over a former video rental store, which had once, somewhere far down the line, belonged to a blacksmith. There was some talk at first, among the locals, about how a coffee shop was simply an attempt to please tourists, how the bistro and bakery already functioned in much the same way that a coffee shop would. The town's first selectman had even tried to mount a protest at the grand opening, but the owners, who turned out to be lovely, lifelong New Englanders, provided the paltry group of activists with coffee as well as scones sourced from the bakery and breakfast sandwiches from the bistro, all gratis. Needless to say, the protest ended in a lot of well-fed, contented sighs. And now, with its flagstone floors and ever-warm fireplace, its constant hum of Chet Baker standbys and the orderly shelves of small-batch single-origin offerings, the coffee shop had become a symbiotic partner in the town's ecosystem.

Willa was waiting for Whit at the banquette in their usual corner, wearing a thick turtleneck sweaterdress the color of burlap, with her dark hair in Bantu knots. Their writing group had gotten smaller and smaller over the years, until just the two of them remained.

"Hello, Whitacre," she said, using a nickname he hated. His full name was Whitman, not Whitacre, *obviously*, he would say, because could you imagine? Whit*acre* Long*acre*?

He nodded at the barista, who knew him and would soon pop over with his usual drink. Whit squeezed in across from Willa.

"Hello, Wilhelmina," he said, using her actual full name, which she also hated. "How's it going?"

"Oh, you know," she said, lifting her fingers from her laptop to stretch them, interlocked, high above her head. "It's torturous and bleak, and I feel as if I have never written anything good in my life and never will again. So, the usual."

She smiled. Willa had won many awards for her literary fiction. She was both critically and financially more successful than Whit had ever been. But it was nice to know they both struggled, even if her struggles apparently ended with six-figure book deals and second editions bearing shiny medallions on their front covers while his struggles just . . . kept on.

Whit opened his laptop and logged in. But when he saw that the number of unread emails in his inbox was closer to his age than his shoe size, he reached up and closed it immediately. Willa laughed.

"Emails?"

"Emails," Whit sighed, dragging his hand through his beard, "and emails and emails."

"Helen's people or yours?"

Whit laughed.

“Helen’s, of course.” Her agent, her editor, even superfans, whose devotion to Helen bordered on the obsessive and deranged.

“Did you take your email off your website yet?”

“I did, but the fans are still emailing. I’m worried it’s on Reddit or something.” Whit sighed.

Helen’s fans were very kind usually, and very sad. Most of them were still sending condolences, but some of them did a thing Whit found repellant: implicitly comparing their grief to his.

“I don’t usually mind. It’s just when they act like we’ve both experienced the same level of loss—as if reading some books is the same thing as really knowing someone.”

Whit heard the words coming out and was surprised by how clinical they sounded and felt. No breaking down today—that was good.

Willa nodded. She had heard him say this before.

Whit shrugged in acknowledgment. It was nice to be understood.

“And what do the publishing people want?”

Whit closed his eyes. “What else?”

“An ETA on the book?”

“Always the book.”

After she died, Helen had shocked everyone, including Whit, by “leaving” her book to him, if it could be called that, in her will. It was one of her last wishes (alongside the scholarship fund for the Foothills School) that Whit be the one to finish the fifth and final book in her famous series. Helen’s books were fantasies set in a complex, diverse world full of magic and palace intrigue. Whit was a mystery novelist; the closest thing to fantasy in his books was the high success rate of his detective. Helen’s books were about three half-magical children: a half-elf, a half-giant, and a half-fairy. The children in Whit’s books were usually murder victims.

That Whit would be the executor of Helen’s will had been a

given, and he'd expected its contents to be standard, unexciting. They'd agreed long ago to keep their wills and bank accounts separate, because they were practical and because things like copyrights could get complicated. But they'd also agreed that Helen would get all of Whit's assets and vice versa. In any case, reading a will whose contents he already more or less knew had not been top of mind in the days after losing Helen.

Annie had wanted to return to school as soon as possible, and so Whit had been in the car after dropping her off, driving like an automaton following its programming. He'd been listening to Steely Dan on the satellite radio and thinking of nothing—he'd been thinking of nothing for what seemed like forever—and the call had startled him. It was Helen's lawyer, asking him to stop by when he got the chance.

He drove straight there, and the details of the meeting were hazy now. He remembered being walked through his duties with the scholarship fund and a financial gift for the MFA program where they'd met. The annotated book wasn't mentioned, having been a spur-of-the-moment idea from Helen's hospital bed. And when the lawyer finally said the words "literary estate," Whit had not expected much beyond details of royalties and who held what copyright. But there had been a bombshell. In the early days of Helen's sickness, she had amended her publishing contract so that it said, in legalese, that the fifth book would be written by Helen if she were able, and that her estate would decide her successor if she were not.

She had not been able to complete the book, and Whit knew this, of course he did. But he knew it in the same way he'd known she wouldn't be able to see Annie graduate, or to celebrate their twentieth anniversary. It had not been something he could fix, but then here came the will, where it was mentioned alongside the ring she'd left to Whit's sister and the heirlooms she'd left to her cousins: *I leave the completion of the fifth and final novel in the*

Greenwood Castle Saga to my husband, Whitman Howard Longacre, using whatever means he deems necessary and appropriate.

After that, it seemed to Whit that he had teleported from the office to the car, and he suddenly found himself back on the road home, pulling into a grassy alcove in the trees used mostly as a parking lot for hikers and mountain bikers. His clearest memory was the way his head fell to the steering wheel of its own accord, and how all of it—the grief of Helen's absence, the crushing heaviness and total exhaustion of single parenting, and now this new thing—seemed to pull him downwards, like a million tiny weights eager to drag him through the floor of the car and into the soil below.

This was the Monumental Task that weighed on him, at all times and in all places. It was up to him to finish a beloved series that he had had no hand in writing; it was his job now to surprise, delight, and satisfy millions of readers, sticking an impossible-to-stick landing, for the sake of the fans, yes, but for Helen, too. Helen's editor would send him overly enthusiastic, carefully worded emails asking about his "progress" and his "vision," using words like "endgame." Her agent was kinder, though she did continually offer to connect him with "the Tolkien people," meaning whoever was left of the people who'd helped Christopher Tolkien with the completion of his father's Middle-Earth books.

But it wasn't as though Whit only needed a little mentoring or guidance. He needed someone to teach him how to write again. In the time since Helen had gotten sick, he'd started three separate mysteries of his own—two attempts at sequels and one stand-alone—and all of it had been derivative, lifeless garbage. Even he didn't care who had done the murders. He tried a contemporary literary thing without any bloodshed, but it was about a widower and his daughter and every word he typed nauseated him.

Far worse than failing at his own writing, though, was the experience of sitting himself down to work on Helen's book. Both cognitive and fine motor function left his body. He couldn't type. He could remember nothing about the first four books in the series, despite having read them all. There was just so much *stuff* in them; each was nearly twice as long as his longest novel, and each relied on a complex magic system and an arcane class structure, with continual nods to Helen's novellas and her fans' theories. And beneath all of that was the sense that Helen had known, since page 1 of book 1, how the saga would end.

He had found a few charts and a half-erased whiteboard in her office, but the truly shocking thing, what no one could believe, including the editor, the agent, and Whit himself, was this: nowhere had she written down the hard-and-fast ending of the years-long tale. Helen hadn't discussed it with the publishing people, so implicit was their trust in her and so private her writing process. He had searched her computer, the drawers in her office, her car, her bedside table, and found nothing. Whit didn't even have a title to go by.

"Didn't she ever mention . . ." the editor, Shreya, would start on their occasional phone calls.

"No," Whit would sigh. "She was very tight-lipped during the actual drafting. It was usually only after the first go-round was completed that we'd talk about it at all."

But even in those conversations, he and Helen hadn't gone into much detail. They worked in different literary worlds: he wrote for adults, she for children and teenagers (and, she always reminded him, women in their twenties and thirties). Scratch that, she wrote for *everyone*, and he wrote for people who had opinions about *Masterpiece Theatre* and for the one woman at the *Los Angeles Review of Books* who usually liked his stuff okay. Helen's worlds were infused with a cozy kind of magic, a dark but defeatable evil, and a unique lightning-in-a-bottle Greenwood Castle sensibility, while Whit's books were grim and rainy. Sometimes the mystery was solved only after someone beloved died, and a few times it wasn't solved at all.

So why him? That was what really ate at him. Apart from the fact that they were married, and that they had loved each other, once very powerfully, he could think of no good reason why she had left him with this task. He was baffled, and beneath that, if he could manage to crack the shell that usually kept his own emotions concealed from view, he also felt a steely anger. How could she do this? Why hadn't she told him? Why had she been so withholding about so many things?

Willa coughed and drew Whit's attention from his closed laptop to her wary eyes.

"Hi," she said. "Can I ask you a terrible question?"

Whit's stomach dropped like it did when he knew someone was about to mention Helen. But he only said, "Of course."

"How's the actual writing going?"

Relieved, Whit mimed getting shot. Willa smiled.

"It isn't going," he admitted. Once again. "Days and days of blank documents."

"Have you tried writing by hand?"

"Yes."

"Writing in different places?"

"Yes."

"Changing the time of day? Writing in the evening instead of the morning, that kind of thing?"

"Yes, Willa."

She nodded, thinking. "I have a friend who lights a candle whenever she's ready to write. She says it sets the tone and tells your brain you've entered 'the writing space.'"

"That is very woo-woo of you."

"Not me," Willa corrected, raising a finger. "My friend. Have you tried typing in Comic Sans?"

Annoyance crept into Whit's voice for the first time. "Have I *what*?"

She shrugged. "It's a thing. People on the internet say it makes them type faster."

Whit breathed deeply into tented hands.

"I don't think we're that desperate yet."

Willa made a face that said, *I think we are very close to being that desperate.*

The coffee shop inhaled a cold breath as the front door opened, and Willa's insightful look turned to one of dread.

"Incoming."

Whit's irritation spiked. He knew before turning to look that it would be Ian Hoult. Ian the Terrible. The man's eyes searched the room lazily before landing on Willa and Whit, and then he made a show of reluctantly walking their way, as if they were waving him over against his will rather than trying not to make eye contact.

Whelk Harbor was a small town with a high number of writers per capita. Ian was the third of three (formerly four) members of the writing group, and Whit had more than once fantasized about going head to head with him on the National Book Award shortlist, beating him, and then stabbing him with the pointy end of that exhaust pipe–shaped trophy. Never would Whit speak this fantasy out loud, not only because of the daydream's violent nature, but also because he and Ian both knew who would actually win in such a showdown. If one of them was the critical darling, it was not the mystery writer but the author of heavily researched novels in which famous and friendless figures did ambiguous and/or ruthless things for three hundred pages.

Once upon a time, the writing group had consisted of Whit, Willa, Helen, and Ian. For a while, it felt like the four of them were struggling side by side, and even when they got agents and book deals, they had been in it together. Ian was unassumingly smart, as if he was used to being overlooked, and it had given him a kind of lovable snarkiness. But then his second novel, a literary historical volume called *And Now We Must Say Farewell*, had won the PEN/Faulkner, and there had been a big book tour and the obligation to "do press," as Ian had told them over and over, each time as if he regretted it. As a consequence, Ian had started missing their weekly meetings, and though the other three had feigned disappointment, in fact they were relieved. Success had not agreed with the man.

Ian reached their table now and shrugged with his whole body, because his life had become one of faux apology. He had started dressing as if he'd read the definition of *unkempt* and taken it as a costuming guideline for day-to-day living. His linen shirt looked as though he'd been practicing sailing knots with it; his brown jeans were stained in two places, and his shoes were horrible closed-toe Birkenstocks. His brown beaded bracelet and longish hair, dark and wild, were so at odds with his ever-increasing vanity that the man radiated pretense.

"Here you are," Ian said in his lazy way, "my fellow writers in arms. The life of the mind."

After this non sequitur, he did a painful show of solidarity with two raised fists.

"How are the '*lyrical marvels*' going?"

He quoted these words at Willa often, hardly masking his jealousy. They were taken from a review of one of her early novels, and he somehow made them sound like ironic curse words.

Willa gave him a bland smile. "Oh, you know."

"Ah. And Whit, how are the wizards?"

Helen's book was not about wizards, and Whit was never quite sure whether this was an inexpert attempt at teasing or a real display of Ian's ignorance.

"They're just fine."

Ian raised his cheeks in something smile-adjacent and waited, completely comfortable with the silence. Finally, after an excruciating fifteen seconds:

"And what about Detective Fraulein Maria? I hope she hasn't returned to the convent indefinitely. She doesn't seem the type to be satisfied with a cloistered existence."

Ian laughed so loudly at his own joke that people from other tables looked their way.

Whit gripped the leg of the table. His "Sister Marguerite" books riffed on that strange phenomenon in detective fiction, where members of the clergy, usually British, stumble into solving crimes in tiny hamlets with as many murders a year as there are beads in the rosary. Whit's books were cozy mysteries with diminished coziness. They were serious (he hoped) and compelling (he hoped) and surprising (please, God), and they turned the genre on its head in welcome, unexpected ways (surely they at least did that).

Whit clinched his teeth and smiled. "Not indefinitely, no. She's just on hiatus while I finish the book for Helen."

Something about the direct answer—the acknowledgment of Helen and her absence—seemed to disarm or confuse Ian, who looked away. But still he stood, waiting, and finally Willa let her compulsion to be polite win out.

"What about you, Ian? What are you working on?"

"Oh, well, there's the new book, of course, if I can ever get to it. I'm calling it *Standard Deviations*, it's about mathematicians. I'm trying to trace a line from Ada Lovelace to Sofya Kovalevskaya to Benoit Mandelbrot."

He had delighted in perfectly pronouncing *Kovalevskaya* and now waved a hand like this was all probably too complicated for Whit and Willa to follow.

"But *The Atlantic* wants me to write something about the class I'm teaching at Plymouth College this semester, and it's taking up all my time."

He seemed to pause for a show of praise or awe, but this time even Willa refused to take the bait.

"Right now," he said, entirely unfazed, "I'm grabbing a cuppa on my way out to visit a creative writing class at the high school. I wish I'd said no, but the teacher's an old friend of my mother's, and well, duty calls."

"Oh, how fun," Willa said, presumably in an effort to move things along. "Well, enjoy. And good luck with all that."

"Yes, thank you. Well." Another long, oblivious pause, and then, at long last: "Happy writing, friends."

"You too," Willa said, before sighing in relief as the man walked away.

Whit laughed, but mostly he was thinking of how Helen would have said just the right thing to put Ian in his place. She had always been better with words.

CHAPTER FOUR

When the library phone rang at the end of the school day, Merritt Pryor knew it would be her mother, Kathleen, checking in to see how substituting had gone. The day before, Kathleen had texted her daughter regularly, because she was bored at home and hated being away from school. So Merritt had sent back occasional updates about particular class visits, a few questions about the online catalog, and some small bits of juicy schoolroom gossip. *(Mr. Llewellyn tried to print out invitations for a Halloween party to which no faculty or staff were invited and had been found out when the copier jammed; a fourth grader got stuck in a bathroom stall with his shoes two stalls over.)* But today her mother's texts went ignored. She had been busy. Very busy.

"You didn't text me back," Kathleen said, her voice full of feigned offense.

"I know, I'm sorry," Merritt said, moving her belongings from the checkout desk into a public radio tote. "I'll be home in a few minutes."

"I was hoping you'd pick up some things for dinner on the way."

"Of course," Merritt said, and then listened as her mother went over the qualities of the savoy cabbage she should look for and the brand of lentils she preferred. She was about to hang up when the question jumped out of Merritt's mouth.

"Mom, do you know Whit Longacre?"

Now and then since he left, Merritt had been trying to remember what she knew about the man. She had been aware of his existence, in the way she knew that Dolly Parton once had a very nice husband somewhere in the background. She knew that Helen Albright Longacre was married to a mystery writer, but that his books were more literary and experimental than your standard Agatha Christies. When Kathleen mentioned to Merritt that the Longacre child had arrived at the Foothills School, Whit's name, of course, had come up again, but Merritt had only been interested in the undisputed star of the bestseller lists. What was Helen Albright Longacre like? Was she "normal"? Did she ever drop any writing tips? Kathleen had only said, again and again, that the woman was generous but private about her work. And then she was gone, and while the world grieved the loss of an author, the Foothills School grieved the loss of a community member. Helen.

Eventually, there'd been the press release from her publisher assuring the public that the final book in her beloved series was soon to be ready for publication, thanks to the careful stewardship of her husband, in whose capable hands she'd left the completion of the work. Merritt hadn't cared who polished up the manuscript, as long as it eventually saw the light of day and brought a story she had loved to a close.

Then today Whit had come into the library and ignited Merritt's interest, though she spent most of the day absorbed in *The Door in the Garden Wall* for what was probably the fourth time.

She loved the Greenwood Castle books, unabashedly. It had been this series that convinced her to get an MFA specializing in creative writing. She had read them all in a heady sprint, here in this very town, sitting by her parents' fireplace when she wasn't in her father's hospital room, and they had been a lifeline for her, a rope dangling into the cavern of post-college life. Her father was dying, and her future was a cloudy, terrifying mystery, but what if, she had wondered, she could make something like *this*? And then, years later, she had dropped out of the MFA program before eventually landing here, living with her mother in a town where she knew no one, subbing and working part-time. But at least today she had gotten to read this book again.

And this read-through was different. This read-through had *handwritten notes*. From the *author*. Notes about which characters had different names at first and side stories she had mapped out and then abandoned. There was a recipe for the signature cake that appeared at every feast. (Merritt took a picture on her phone.) A handful of magical symbols described in the text were drawn in detail, and there was a pretty decent sketch of the main character's famous amulet on one of the endpapers. It was an encyclopedia of wonderment.

"Oh, that poor man," Kathleen said now. "To lose your wife so young, and then with poor Annie, too."

"Annie?"

"His daughter. Third-grader?"

"Oh, yes," Merritt said, pretending to know which child she was talking about, and then something shifted between her ribs. Oh. She had spent the day delighted by what she was having the chance to read, never once slowing to acknowledge how this book had landed in her lap: a student at this school had lost her mother, and now her father had delivered a rare artifact, all in memory of the late woman.

"Merritt, it was so sad when she died. Annie was just about to start second grade, and the two years before had been this big thing, of course, because of who her mom was, and we'd all heard so much about her, but then she turned out to be so lovely and funny and down to earth, and she was so giving with her time and money. And then this diagnosis, and suddenly she was gone. There were the news stories and things, of course, but poor little Annie and Mr. Longacre, I just think about how they were dealing with something really personal that was separate from all of that."

"That's awful," Merritt said, meaning it.

"Yes, truly. Why do you ask?"

"Well, he came by today," Merritt explained, and then went on to tell her about the book.

"Oh my word!" Kathleen said, and Merritt could tell she was smiling. "That's just wonderful."

"It really is," Merritt agreed, moving to turn out the various strands of twinkle lights. She told Kathleen about reading it, and about the details she'd learned, and then somehow, as she locked the door to the library (leaving the book safely inside), they landed back on Whit.

"How did he seem?"

"Oh, I don't know." Merritt tried to remember as she moved down the hallway toward the front doors. He had looked a bit frumpy, a bit sleepy perhaps, and certainly some people would have said his beard could use a trim, but she liked a beard, and anyway, he looked like a parent, really, and maybe a writer.

"He looked like a writer."

Kathleen laughed. "Yes, that sounds right. But you know what I mean. Did he seem sad? Mournful?"

Merritt waved at the last remaining office lady, noticing that the hair she'd thought was shower-wet that morning was actually some sort of mousse situation. Interesting.

"He did not seem mournful," she said, outside now. The landscape before her was still mostly green and misty, making only the most implicit nods toward the approaching fall days. The air shared the pleasant coolness of a pillow's underside, and Merritt was thankful for her sweater. "Or maybe a little mournful. But mostly he seemed, I don't know, a little odd, and a little hesitant to say who he was, his relation to his wife. His beard looked a little scraggly, I guess."

"His beard?" her mother said, surprised.

"Yes, his beard, but he didn't look disheveled or anything like that. Just shy, or maybe sort of modest. He probably thought I was a little odd though, too. I was on my hands and knees digging through the returns bin when he showed up—you really need a sign about where to put oversized books, Mom, because—"

"There was a sign!" Kathleen interrupted. "I had to take it down because someone drew *breasts* on it, and my money is on Preston Benson, who is, I'm sorry to say, a little shit."

Merritt smiled. "I'll make you a new sign tomorrow."

*

Merritt's mother recovered quickly from her illness, primarily because the illness had actually been a minor eye surgery Kathleen insisted on keeping quiet. Merritt, who'd once fielded questions about her scoliosis for a full two months of wearing a back brace (in middle school, just imagine), understood: the Pryors were private people when it came to physical ailments and bodily functions.

Now, though, it was back to business as usual, which in Merritt's case was anything but. She had moved to Whelk Harbor a month before with absolutely no prospects other than her mother's insistence that Goodenough Books, the bookstore on Cork Street, would hire her because they would hire anyone who, like Merritt, was willing to be paid essentially nothing. Kathleen had been right, thankfully, and today, on her way to work, Merritt was walking the brick-lined sidewalks of this absurdly appealing street, coffee tumbler in hand, earbuds in her ears, thinking that maybe this life detour wasn't such a bad one. Sure, it had meant the end of all her hopes and dreams, the absolute, unresuscitable demise of all her ambitions, but at least this street was cute. And at least she finally had a reason to wear her deep indigo fall coat, which felt like something Little Red Riding Hood would have graduated into wearing as an adult. The MFA program she'd dropped out of in Texas had been a good one, but there were no seasons there, only whiplash shifts from surface-of-the-sun hot to below-freezing temperatures. The trees in Texas seemed to shed all their leaves at once, and on the rare occasion that it snowed, people acted as though Jesus himself was returning on his white horse to end the world as we knew it. In Whelk Harbor, people knew how to drive on snowy roads.

Merritt walked through the windowed door of the bookstore, its charming bell tinkling overhead, and then made her way to the back room, where a work apron and Huong waited for her. Ten years younger than Merritt and twenty times cooler, Huong had just graduated from the college down the coast. She was staying with her parents and working at Goodenough Books while she "figured things out." On day one, Huong, with her bobbed black hair, a fuzzy white sweater, and possibly ironic cargo pants, told her this in a bored-teenager voice while they stood together in the stockroom. Merritt had said, "Me too," and the two women had formed an immediate if not quite warm connection.

It was the truth. Merritt was herself trying to figure things out, and, depressingly, she had also moved in with a parent. She had tried something in Texas, and it hadn't worked out, and now she was living with her mom in a small New England town. The only thing that kept this whole situation from dipping into Hallmark Christmas movie territory was that Whelk Harbor was not her hometown, but the place her parents had moved to from Virginia a decade ago to look after Merritt's grandfather. But her grandfather had died, and then her father, too, and well, Hallmark movies didn't usually deliver such a ruthless one-two punch.

"Morning," Huong said without looking up from her phone as she sat on a stack of boxes. Today she was wearing wide-legged jeans and an oversized flannel, and Merritt hated, *hated*, that she felt uncool, that she could even care about being uncool at her age.

"Hi," Merritt said lightly, smoothing the front of her chunky beige sweater and trying not to think about her own jeans. *No*, she thought, *I like this sweater. I am not a wide-legged-pants person. I do not need to wear anything ironically ever again.*

"Is it just us today?"

"Yes," Merritt answered, and though Huong didn't say it, they were both thinking the same thing: the training wheels were off. The store's owner was a woman named Diana, who shirked the normal uniform of New England women in Whelk Harbor—unflashy but quality clothing that would protect them from surprise bad weather in a pinch—in favor of cashmere sweater sets and trench coats and the occasional floral scarf over her nearly white shoulder-length hair. Merritt had replaced a former morning shift manager, and Diana had been eager to relinquish the day-to-day duties to her new employee. She continually swatted away Merritt's hesitations like they were persistent bees. *You'll be fine. You're a grown-up, aren't you?*

"Well," Huong said, glancing up at last, "let's see how this goes."

"As long as we don't set the building on fire, I think Diana will call it a success."

"A high bar," Huong said, standing up with a short laugh, "but I think we can manage."

Whatever catastrophes the two women had been imagining did not come to pass. Huong handled the register, and Merritt walked around tidying things, giving suggestions to the occasional patron, changing the soundtrack from jazz classics to coffee shop acoustic and then back to jazz. The bell tinkled, and locals came in looking for gifts or a current bestseller called *How to Kick Ass Like a Girl*. Had she read it? No, she had not, not really a fan of self-help, if you could believe it. Four separate women came in looking for a novel about a pregnant and possibly mentally unwell ex-nurse on bedrest who is sure her rich neighbor has stabbed the gardener with a pair of pruning shears—a book club pick. When the bell over the door rang out once again, Merritt almost didn't turn around, determined to force the admirably indifferent Huong to do the greeting song-and-dance for once. But then she did take a look, and it was him. Whit Longacre, formerly the husband of Helen Albright Longacre.

"Oh, it's you," she said, and he looked at her like he recognized her and was surprised to be recognized back. Fair. It had been several days, and she had been a little preoccupied with his gift the last time they met.

"It's me," he said, his smile not unkind but also not enthusiastic. He had trimmed his beard, she noticed, and he wore a beige fisherman's turtleneck and greenish pants. "Oh, gosh."

She followed his eyes as they moved down her body, and something twisted up her spine. Was he checking her out?

"We match," he said, laughing now. It was true, right down to the green pants.

"Oh God," she laughed back. "I don't know which of us should be more embarrassed."

"Neither. We look great."

His voice had a certain edge to it—a half-rasp, perhaps. Why did noting that make her face feel warm?

"We," she said, holding out the *e*, "look like the kind of people who take color-coordinated family photos on the beach."

"Oh, so you've met my mother."

Merritt laughed. "You actually have met mine, and it won't surprise you to learn that our family pictures are all a little bit blurry, not a coordinated outfit in sight."

"I'd actually like to see those."

Her face was really warm now, but Merritt was smiling when she said, "How can I help you, Mr. Longacre?"

He held up a hand. "Whit. And I have a bit of a strange question."

"Okay?"

Whit looked embarrassed. He glanced at Huong, who was doing a sudoku on the register computer. He cast his eyes quickly over the room, taking in the exposed beams above, the Persian rugs below, the high shelves, the mishmash of chairs and couches (wingback, Louis XVI, a few fragile-looking wooden ones), the fairy lights. As Merritt stood at the top of a small slope in the warped floor, their eyes were almost even. She saw that his gray-blue irises looked self-conscious today, and hesitant, rather than sad.

"I need to see what Greenwood Castle books you have."

"Don't you have them all?" Merritt asked, before immediately wishing to take the words back.

Whit shrugged. "You would think so, and yet—I think we must be missing one of the stand-alones. You know, one of the ones that's not technically part of the main story, but . . ."

He trailed off.

"Yes. There are three novellas. I believe."

Merritt added the "I believe" at the last moment, hoping to suggest that this was just casual knowledge for her, the sort of thing a bookseller and ad hoc school librarian had bouncing around in her head. But the truth was that she knew everything there was to know about the books of Helen Albright Longacre.

She walked toward the children's section, Whit following behind at a polite distance. "So," she said, as they reached the shelves in the corner, a snug nook with extra fairy lights and cut-out letters that said, "Reading Is Magical." "There are the standard books in the series here. And here are the companion things. There's the collection of fairy tales"—she pulled it off the shelf—"and the villain origin story one"—she added it to her pile—"and the one about the missing unicorn that turns out to be a dream sequence. People were mad about that one."

Merritt stood straight and handed all three to Whit, who looked somewhere between guilty and confused. "We have all these," he laughed.

"What?"

He shrugged. "We have these. Multiple copies. It's silly, but I have this vague memory of another short story, even though I'm certain these are the only ones."

Merritt eyed him for a second. How could this man not know his own wife's work better than this?

"I know she appears in two anthologies—"

Whit interrupted. "The Christmas one," he said, nodding, "and the one about 'magical' summer nights. I checked those."

"Oh," she said, called up short. So he did know *that*.

Whit seemed to search his mind for a second before speaking again.

"But is there something somewhere about a giant baby, or a baby giant, or—"

"Oh!" A firework laced through her brain, and Whit's confusion suddenly made sense. "Yes! I know exactly what you're looking for."

His eyebrows rose, and a smile that was hardly a smile grew above the sand-stubbled chin on his square jaw.

But then, just as quickly, Merritt felt herself making her own guilty face.

"Okay, but there's bad news."

She watched as the man in front of her seemed to tire in place.

"There's only one copy."

He narrowed his eyes. "That sounds fake."

"It's real."

"Can we steal it? Do the *National Treasure* of children's books?"

She smiled. "It's less exciting than that, sadly. The book was a tiny little novella, and it was written," she said, intentionally using the passive voice to avoid making his late wife into a subject, "for a charity thing. She, your wife . . ." Well, there went the passive voice. The English language had its limits. "She wrote it to be auctioned off, and as far as I know, she *hand*-wrote it. The thing they bought, whoever bought it, was just, like, a Moleskine notebook."

"Oh." Whit looked out across the shelves, then nodded to himself. "I remember that. Or I remember the auction part. But that would mean no one has read it, right? Other than whoever bought it."

"Right." Then, after a moment's thought, Merritt added, "Should we find out who that was, and maybe what they did with it?"

Whit nodded, and again he followed her across the store, this time to the register.

"Sorry, Huong, can I use the computer?"

The young woman glanced up, then clocked that Merritt was not alone. She looked at Whit, then back at Merritt, and widened her eyes just slightly. Merritt rolled hers.

At the computer, she started googling.

"How's your mom?"

Merritt smiled at him, touched. "She's all back to normal."

"So no more double duty then."

"No, thank God. If you haven't noticed, it's much quieter here."

"No snotty kids shoving oversized books into the book drop."

"No book drop at all. It's bliss," she said. "Oh, here it is . . . well, that's depressing."

Whit leaned onto the counter, and Merritt turned the screen so they could both see it. "A billionaire," she said. "Some tech person. He bought it for nearly a million dollars. And it says here he keeps it in a display case in his home office. Perfect for a heist, if you're in the mood for a little . . ."

"Where did the auction money go?" he asked rather than playing along.

"A children's, uh, cancer thing."

"Well," he said, clearing his throat. "Well, that's good. That's good."

He looked like he was watching a video replay in front of him, maybe trying to piece the memory of these events back together.

"Why do you need the book?" Merritt asked after a moment.

"Oh, I don't think I do anymore, not if no one's read it. But I'm . . . well, I'm writing the book for her. For Helen. The last book in the series. And I saw this Post-it note in her office the last time I was in there that said something like 'giant baby story important question mark,' and I could only just remember that she *had* written another thing about a giant—anyway, I suppose it's *not* important, so that's good."

This was a lot to process, but Merritt just nodded and tried to make her face more neutral than her brain. The series *wasn't* already finished? The press releases had made it sound like Helen's husband was merely editing a pristine, preexisting manuscript, but this question about the baby giant, and that statement—"I'm *writing* the book for her"—these things did not sound like the words of a man putting the finishing touches on an extant masterpiece.

Merritt forced herself to say something.

"Well then, I guess no heist. Which is a shame."

"A real shame," he agreed. "You seem like you're good in high-pressure scenarios. Anyway, thank you for your help."

She looked at him, standing there in the sweater and pants that matched her own, and she thought he did look sad, and yes, tired, but there was something else there, too. He seemed thoughtful and observant and determined. But, she wondered, did he seem like a man who could successfully land this literary plane he'd been tasked with piloting?

"You're welcome." She smiled softly. "Let me know if there's anything else I can do."

He nodded at her. "I will. Truly, I might have more questions, and you seem like you might know the answers. Thanks again."

The bell tinkled a second time, but the door didn't close.

"Oh, and . . ." Whit said, turning back to look at her with one hand on the frame.

"Yes?" she called from across the store.

"What's your name?"

The question caught her off guard, so much so that she paused, giving Whit room to explain himself. "I can't keep calling you 'Ms. Pryor' in my head."

She laughed at that. "Please don't. It's Merritt."

He nodded once, his mouth in another almost-smile. "Well. Goodbye, Merritt."

"Goodbye."

The door closed, and from somewhere in PERSONAL GROWTH, Huong let out a long *hmm*.

"Don't start," Merritt said as she watched Whit walk down the windy street.

*

One of the things Merritt missed about Texas was all the driving. She made it through so many audiobooks and podcasts just commuting back and forth between her apartment and campus, and she became one of those people who could guess different NPR newscasters before they'd said their names. *Lakshmi Singh!* she would recite to herself in her beat-up Nissan Versa. *Korva Coleman!*

So on days like this, when she found herself missing, if not the commute itself, the *sounds* of the commute, she'd put her earbuds in and pull up the local public radio station, which, she admitted only to herself, was not as good as the one she'd grown to love back in Texas.

As she walked, indigo coat pulled tight around her, cool wind blowing her hair back, Merritt listened to a woman describe recent depressing arguments before the Supreme Court.

"*Nina Totenberg!*" Merritt said aloud to herself.

The streetlights were just coming on as the autumn twilight stretched itself thin, and the white wooden buildings on either side of the road glowed like jack-o'-lanterns. Someone somewhere was burning leaves, perfuming the breeze with that familiar toastiness. She definitely did not miss the Texas commute.

The Supreme Court story ended—it *was* Nina Totenberg—and a new one started, with someone reading what sounded like a piece of fiction. The writing was crisp, somehow both direct and expressive, and its simpleness felt powerfully raw and compelling. It was an uncut diamond of prose, and its description of a woman—a bespectacled graduate student—caused her pulse to quicken.

"Those are the first words spoken by the narrator, known only as 'the Professor,' in Graydon Lyons's highly anticipated new novel, *Serious Games*."

Merritt froze. It felt like someone had pulled the emergency brake on her body. The wind was suddenly icy, and a sick feeling leapt from the soles of her feet up to her shoulders. The tips of her fingers buzzed, and her earbuds were megaphones, too loud, too loud, too much pressure in her skull. She wanted to yank them out, and she wanted to throw up, but instead, she listened because she had to listen. There was no other option.

"The campus novel marks a departure for the author and is the first time Lyons, a creative writing professor himself, has waded into a contemporary setting: this time, that of higher education. Its subject matter—an affair gone wrong between a married professor and his student—is raising some eyebrows. But this is no surprise to Lyons."

And then there it was, crystal clear, his voice in her ears, all the way up here on this New England street.

"Of course, every book I've written holds up a mirror to myself. This one is set in a world with which I am intimately familiar, and I always expected that readers would try to draw connections to my personal life. Odd as it may seem, there's less of myself in this story than in my works of historical fiction. But ambiance and tone, the sense of place—well, it would be impossible to avoid commentary on modern academic life in a story like this one, and I'm not going to shy away from that."

Merritt realized she was walking again only because she was now stopping, lowering herself to a bench. She yanked the earbuds out and shoved them into her bag, their case forgotten.

Oh my God. Oh my God, oh my God.

Oh my God.

He had actually done it.

CHAPTER FIVE

It was a Thursday. Meaning that Monday, Tuesday, and Wednesday had all ambled past Whit with nothing to show for themselves. Just a blank Word doc and a blinking cursor and, yet again, the sense that Helen had made a horrible mistake. It wasn't just that she should have left the completion of her series to another children's fantasy author; she should have left it to someone who, at the very least, *knew how to write a damn book*.

The failed giant-baby escapade had been discouraging. It was Whit's most proactive undertaking in weeks, and it had amounted to nothing beyond proving to him once and for all that he was not cut out for this—not if people like Merritt Pryor had better recall of the minutiae of Helen's publication history than he could ever dream of having.

And then today had been especially demoralizing. After dropping Annie off at school, he returned home to his little writing room, which just now felt less cozy, more cramped, more farcical. It was like a set piece for a play about a failed writer where you could knock on the bookshelf, the desk, Whit's cranium, and they would all ring hollow. He had sat in his chair, aimless, for a quarter of an hour; then he had done a truly terrible thing and gotten on YouTube. He felt himself falling deeper and deeper into a hole of Amateur Singers Surprising Competition Show Judges with Their Unexpected Talent videos, but he did not resist.

An *hour and a half later*, with a gasp like an unfortunate *Titanic* passenger breaching the ocean's surface, he pulled himself back into the real world. He did the brave thing then and actually tried handwriting something, anything (his own work, the beginning of Helen's), and found himself doodling like a bored teenager in chem class. He went for a walk in the woods behind his stone-walled, ivy-covered house.

There was a lot of woods to walk in. The house, along with the family Range Rover, had been bought after the astronomical success of Helen's first two books. They had drastically remodeled the home's interior, and when the land bordering the back of their property went on the market, Helen snatched it up, lest it become a shopping center or data farm or something equally depressing. Now there were twenty-five acres of woods and hills to roam in, and Whit paid for a monthly service that maintained miles of trails and mended fence lines. This was one of the perks of being married to a queen of kid lit that Whit particularly enjoyed, especially when he needed a long, long walk. He had felt that need more frequently in the months since Helen's death—and especially as the burden of the Monumental Task and his potential failure to accomplish it had grown more onerous and frightening.

The long walk—which, he told himself, would "get the juices flowing" and "help the gears start to turn"—had simply made him thirsty, hungry, and listless. Once back, he made tea, then ate a whole sleeve of Milano cookies from the bag while leaning over the sink. He emptied all the trash cans and started a load of laundry. When he was standing at the stove with a stiff brush in hand, ready to tackle a particularly stubborn bit of charred spaghetti sauce, the phone rang.

It was Joan Eaton, Helen's literary agent, whom he resented a little because he heard from her twice as often as he spoke with the woman who represented his own books. He groaned and stared at the phone and groaned again, and then decided to get the hard part over with now, because at least that was easier than going back to his study.

"Hello."

"Whit, hi. What are you up to?"

He glanced at the hardened black tomatoey scab. "I'm writing."

"Ohh, that's what we like to hear," Joan said, her voice low and drawn out, like the voice people use to speak to an especially old person or a friend's nervous pet.

Whit twisted the brush in his hand. "Yup," he said, trying to rush through the small talk to get to what was surely next: the inevitable flurry of questions, the patronizing encouragements. The word "progress."

"And how are things? How's Annie?"

"Oh, she's good, I think, as far as I can tell. Kids, you know."

"Yes, yes."

What were they even saying? *Kids, you know*? Get on with it.

There was a pause, during which Whit began scrubbing, and then:

"So, listen."

Here it was.

"I'm just going to cut to the chase. The publisher is getting antsy. Every day we're fielding questions about when the new book is coming out, yada yada. And they're prepared to put a rush on things, once the draft is completed, but—well, Whit, the problem is that it's *not* completed. Right?"

Whit did not answer. The tomato stain did not budge.

"I mean, we just haven't made much *progress*, have we? Realistically?"

Progress. We.

"So anyway, here's the unpleasant part. They're having the lawyers look into the contract. Helen's contract. The idea is that we're in danger of breaching the agreed-upon terms."

Whit stilled. He waited.

"They're saying," Joan explained, her voice growing lower and slower and losing all of its brashness, "well, they're basically saying that they can *legally* get someone else to finish the book. If you, um, don't."

Something small unspooled within him. A fleeting hope. Was this a way out? But no. *No.* How could he even want that? Helen had laid this task at his feet, and he'd be damned if he would fail to pick it up and carry it all the way through. He didn't understand it, but then there had been a lot about Helen he'd never understood, and still she had trusted him. She had seen something in him (who knew what?) and trusted that he could do this, and to let her down in this favor, the final favor he'd ever do for her, wouldn't just mean failing her scores and scores of fans; it wouldn't even just mean failing Helen. It would be like giving up on their memory, their commitment to and belief in each other. He had to do this for both of them.

"They can't do that."

Joan waited.

"I mean, they can't do that to Helen. They wouldn't do that to her, would they?"

"Well, Whit, I really think they would. If it were any other book . . . But I'm guessing, and this is just a guess, I'm guessing they'll try to leverage the drop-dead deadline—the if-everything-goes-wrong one that Helen agreed to—and they'll use it against you. If you aren't finished by then, you—Helen's estate—and, by proxy, Helen will have technically broken the deal, freeing them up considerably."

Whit wondered if Joan even heard herself. *Drop dead. If everything goes wrong.* Helen did. Everything had. A sick part of him wanted to laugh at Joan before hanging up dramatically—*Drop dead yourself, you monster!*

But Joan wasn't a monster, and Whit didn't have the energy to do anything dramatically. He took a deep breath. Maybe this was a bluff. Whit had met Joan in person a few times, at various dinners and readings and conferences. She had always seemed like the embodiment of kindness and wisdom. Like a coach who knew that the way to get your best out of you was through gentle encouragement and a light but steady hand. He could see her now, with her ear-length black hair and the spectacular mole on her left cheek, cradling the phone with her shoulder while typing away on her computer at his imagined version of an agent's desk, crossing her fingers and hoping her gambit paid off. If coddling and encouraging and all but wrapping Whit in a warm blanket hadn't worked, maybe she was shifting to tough love and fearmongering.

The chances of that seemed low. Whit knew she was right: if it were any other book, things would probably look different. But this book was a guaranteed cash cow. Even if the final product was garbage, even if Whit just copied and pasted one of the more popular fanfics into the manuscript, the books would fly off the shelves and into the hands of costumed people at midnight parties. Delivery trucks weighted down solely by boxes of these books would encircle the globe. For all the publisher cared, the book didn't have to be good. It just had to be finished. It just had to exist.

"So," Whit said, brush discarded as he attacked the sauce stain with his fingernail, "when exactly is *that* deadline?"

He could hear Joan sigh into the mouthpiece.

"Oh, Whit. They want a draft by January."

They let a pause settle over them.

January. So, four months. Four months to fulfill the last thing Helen had asked of him. God, he felt so ashamed when he thought of her, of how she had entrusted her magnum opus to him, placing it in his deeply incapable hands. He was not what she had imagined him to be, and that knowledge hung on him now like a suit of rusting armor.

Whit had four months to achieve what he hadn't been able to do over the last twelve. The thought of navigating these treacherous waters—filled with sharkishly rabid fans and a decade's worth of lore, backstories, and who knew how many little Easter eggs just waiting to pay off in some flashy way—had overwhelmed him from the moment he'd learned of Helen's plans for him. Now he felt virtually immobilized.

He gave the burnt spaghetti sauce one final scrape, and up it popped, like the tab on a can of soda.

"Well then," he said, in a confident voice that was utterly fake, "I guess I'll have it for you in January."

When he hung up the phone, Whit leaned on the stove again, feeling almost dizzy. Then he turned around and lowered himself to the floor, his back against the oven door, his legs splayed across the cold stone tile.

The Task was monumental. He needed help.

*

The fireplace at Goodenough Books was a fixture of the store, and except during the hottest parts of the summer, Diana, the owner, had told Merritt, it was to always be crackling with a fire made with fragrant wood from nearby forests. It burned now, and Merritt sat before it on a lumpy red leather armchair, drinking her tea and willing the bell over the door to stay silent. Huong was in the back, breaking down cardboard boxes for the recycling, and Merritt only barely had the energy to worry that her coworker would come out and see her still here in this spot, thinking and staring at the lava-like embers beneath a glowing block of pine.

Graydon Lyons had done what the two of them had joked about a year ago in his lake house. He had written a book about them. *Serious Games*, which sounded too much like *Dangerous Liaisons* or *Fatal Attraction*, though no one at NPR or in the interviews she'd read seemed to care. All of them, too, seemed to buy his repeated statement that it wasn't autobiographical. *Any resemblance to actual persons, living or dead, events, or locales is entirely coincidental.* Sure.

Merritt might have bought it, too, except that last March, Bebe, her closest friend from the MFA program, had told her over drinks that Graydon had shared something in a class workshop that sounded a lot like Merritt. He was writing about a character, an ambitious young woman named Isabel Abbott, interested in writing children's literature, who had caught the eye of her professor—or, in his version, wheedled her way into the professor's orbit. Everyone in the class, Bebe said, had looked uncomfortable, all of them being aware, in a small program, of Graydon and Merritt's recent breakup. All of them were also smart enough to make the jump from "Pryor" to "Prior" to "Abbott." Apparently, the class's response to the character had been awkward and tepid, and surely, Merritt had told herself, Graydon was just getting something out of his system. Surely he wouldn't actually *do* anything with the character. Since then, in an act of self-preservation, Merritt had blocked the memory of this conversation with Bebe from her mind.

Her hopes had been foolish. This book, too, focused on an ambitious young woman named Isabel, and the critics praised Graydon's "nuanced" and "complicated" treatment of her (*The New Republic*). She was the story's focus, while the narrator-professor was intentionally obscured, little more than a lens through which to observe this star on the rise. According to critics, Graydon, who was known for his alternative histories, was "doing something new and vital and compelling here" (*The New York Review of Books*). He was commenting on the campus novel trope—younger student meets older professor—with "reënergizing force" (*The New Yorker*). The one exception to all this praise came from a woman writing in the *Los Angeles Review of Books*, who called the book "at turns dull for the sake of dullness and crass for the sake of crassness"; Merritt immediately followed her online in solidarity. The horrible thing, though, was that the majority of these reviewers were probably right. Graydon's writing was always surprising and hard to put down. He insisted that his students subvert expectations. "If the signs point right, don't even think about going right. And for God's sake, don't go left, either. Go up, go down, go backwards. Just don't be boring." He had said this, proclaimed it, really, in a class she audited early on, and Merritt had dutifully written down this advice, captivated by Graydon's vitality and self-assurance.

But now here was his book. Younger student meets older professor, and whatever he wrote in that story, and however well he did it, Merritt knew that Graydon had *lived* that trope more than once. Was it really that inventive when you and your ex-girlfriend were the source text for your novel?

The reviews described the character Isabel (almost certainly named in an ironic nod to the Henry James heroine) as a pastiche of competing feminist archetypes: driven and rebellious and calculating. As the novel progresses, through a series of deft twists and reveals, she becomes a sort of empress-with-a-knife-but-no-clothes—someone who perfunctorily checks the boxes when it comes to intelligence and scholarship and self-actualization but hides dark secrets and even darker urges.

"Darker urges"? *Whatever*, Merritt thought. That was patently fictional. But the other things. The ambition that falters and deflates; the emptiness beneath Isabel's skill. It made her sick to think about. That must be what Graydon thought of her; now he had turned that version of her into something to be observed—and because of who he was, people would be clamoring to do just that. People would read this book and discuss it over coffee and at dinner parties like the one where she'd first met Graydon. Academics would smash this character between two glass slides and shove her beneath their microscopes in order to expose all her ghastly defects, cobbling them together in order to say something esoteric about post-postmodernism or neoliberalism, or, if they really figured things out, autofiction, God help her. Overnight, actual graduate students who studied Don DeLillo, Ben Lerner, and Rachel Cusk would be adding *Serious Games* to their exams lists, digging through Merritt's insides and splashing her guts across the pages of their dissertations, all in hopes of landing tenure-track jobs like the one occupied by Graydon Lyons, PhD.

Merritt took a sip of her now-cold tea and thought about when she first met the man who would eventually do this to her. Graydon was a professor in the creative writing program. Not her professor, but he was a known and treasured presence in the department, just like the other novelists, poets, and memoirists whose books either sold well or garnered positive reviews. As a writer whose works did both, Graydon was revered by every category of person associated with the school.

Twenty years older than her, he had crossed the room at a party to speak to her. It was a dinner thing at the bungalow of another professor to honor a Pulitzer Prize winner who'd come to give a talk. Graydon knew the woman—knew her well in fact, and had blurbed her books and appeared alongside her in anthologies and essay collections—but he had looked across the room, set his wineglass down on a credenza, and walked. Away from the Pulitzer Prize winner and over to Merritt.

She had been talking to Bebe about something stupid—food Instagram accounts they both followed, probably—and then Bebe had squeezed her arm as if to keep her from falling overboard. She looked meaningfully over Merritt's shoulder, and when Merritt turned, she saw him, first just looking at her, and then, out of nowhere, moving her way.

"You're Merritt Pryor," he said, and his voice was smooth and refined, like a well-tuned viola. He had carefully sculpted salt-and-pepper hair that was mostly pepper, and a jawline like an action figure. His eyes were that same otherworldly blue seen in sled dogs. But first and foremost, he had done what she longed to do more than anything: he was a writer and a damn good one.

And he knew her name?

"Mary Anne showed me your story about the school play gone wrong. I liked it very much."

She hadn't realized professors were passing students' work around. The school play piece was one of the first things she turned in that first semester. Merritt had wanted to write about the kids themselves, but her inner critic led her to tell the story from the music teacher's perspective instead.

"Thank you," she said, hoping he'd attribute her reddening face to the wine.

She was wearing a short black dress, had worn it on purpose because it looked quite good on her, and he was in a blue suit with a white shirt, no tie, and he had crossed a room to speak with her about her work.

"I'd love to talk to you about it. I'm going outside for a smoke."

"I don't smoke," she said as Bebe disappeared somewhere.

He smirked. "It's never too late to start."

"I feel like anytime after the 1960s might have been too late to start."

The words slipped out of her, as jokes often did when she was sparring with an equal or, in this case, a superior.

Graydon covered his heart. "Are you calling me old?"

She could remember everything about this moment so clearly. This *exact* moment in the space between his question and her answer. Music was playing—some obscure soul singer from the seventies—the walls were wine red, and people were talking in the elevated, academic language of these parties. She remembered thinking that, because it was the fall and the windows were open, this was the rare event where she wasn't sweating her brains out, and then, in this moment, a breeze blew through the room and the tenor of the evening seemed to shift in one great swing. She had felt like she was standing on the deck of a boat as it crested a wave.

"I think I'm just expressing concern for you, for your lungs," she said, feeling like the answer was a subpar parry, beneath the standards of whatever this was that they were doing.

Graydon raised his thick eyebrows and twisted his mouth, like someone using their tongue to push something from one cheek to the other. To her relief, it was a look of amusement.

"Oh, I think the old boys are doing just fine." He rapped at his chest with the knuckles of one hand. "But I'm sure my undergrads are praying I get emphysema after I made them listen to me read aloud from Pynchon."

"Well," she said, smiling now herself, "it would be wrong to disappoint your students."

She had joined him for a cigarette and then joined him at his loft and then joined him on trips to art exhibits and to conferences where he was the plenary speaker. They had gone together on long drives in the country to search for antique end tables and cloudy Venetian mirrors, and she had been his date at dinners with other professors and at book launches with bigwig publishing people in New York and LA and, once, London.

The next summer she had joined him at his lake house, where he'd joked with her, saying that she'd be a compelling main character in a book, if he wrote that sort of thing. He was always saying things like that, as if he'd been studying her, trying unsuccessfully to figure her out but enjoying himself nonetheless.

"You wouldn't actually, though, right?" she'd said back. "Put me in a book? I'm too complex to be contained on the page anyway."

He had smiled and said, no, of course he wouldn't. Lying next to him on the swinging porch bed—an absolute luxury to her mind—she had said, "Promise?" And he had actually crossed his heart with a finger; they had interlocked their pinkies, laughing at the silly solemnity of the act. Then they had kissed and drunk the best wine of her life and spent the evening watching the rain fall around them, the watery smell blanketing the house, until the lightning came, and the thunder rumbled so loudly that it shook the porch, and they ran inside giggling like teenagers.

Thinking of it now, she felt something flicker and crackle beneath her skin. It had been cute—the finger-over-heart pantomime—and unusually sweet. Then they had broken up, and he had broken his little promise. Worse, she realized now, he had probably started writing before their relationship had even ended, if the book was already out in the world. And here she was, in front of this fire, feeling like a deflated pool float. She hadn't been able to stay at the program after she and Graydon ended things. It hadn't helped that he'd moved on, quite quickly. Or rather, he had moved backward, since he had gone back to seeing his ex-wife, a professor of religious studies who specialized in American fundamentalisms. It was only then that Merritt had learned this was something of a pattern between them: they would break up, they would date other people (he skewed younger, she skewed older), and then they would reunite, until they broke up again.

This revelation made her feel cheap and stupid, but it hadn't been enough to make her leave school. She left because she realized that Graydon had changed her, and she hated that. She hated that she had let herself get caught up in the headiness of who he was and that she had taken the reflected glory of a writer like him and let it *do* something to her. Before Graydon, when she was surrounded by people like herself, for whom writing was compulsive, a necessity, she had been, if not happy, at least *certain*. It was the closest thing to team sports she'd ever experienced. It was like summer camp all the time, and she knew, at the molecular level, that she was where she should be, doing what she should be doing. More than that, she was, well, in her element. No one else in the program was receiving the same kind of consistently positive feedback, from students and professors both. And no one wrote as much or as quickly as Merritt. Within months, she knew she was the envy of every first-year student.

And then came Graydon and the whirlwind of his glamour and intellect. She would think to herself things like, *I am sleeping in Graydon Lyons's bed*, and, *Graydon Lyons is holding my hand on the way to the National Book Critics Circle Awards.* Worse, she would think, without having yet proven herself in any meaningful way, *I deserve to be here*. She had cheated herself, she realized in hindsight, because maybe she did deserve to be there, or would in time, but Graydon had offered her a shortcut and she'd taken it. She believed that a man like him would only be with a person like her, a real writer, but who knew what that actually meant? What kind of writer was she? What kind of person was she?

And then things were over with Graydon, and the white-hot fire that had fueled her belief in herself and her work for as long as she could remember sputtered, snuffed out in what felt like an instant. Her writing suffered. Her professors had granted her leeway when her excuse for missed work or a skipped workshop was "I was a plus-one at the Kirkus Prize awards"; they were less lenient when she stopped being able to explain herself. By April in her second year, two months after the breakup, she knew she couldn't possibly catch up on all she'd missed, forgotten, or simply ignored, and when her director suggested she take an incomplete, she politely declined. She didn't have the money to stick around in Texas and do an extra year of the program, and worse, she didn't know if she had the *ability*.

She dropped out. What had felt like an early leg up the ladder with Graydon had actually been a self-betrayal, and now that spark, that thing, the stupid fucking Muse, whatever you called it, was lost. There was the hope that she could find it again, but for now she was wandering through the woods alone, with only a nub of a candle and a room at her mom's house and a job selling books. The job part, at least, was good. It was a welcome distraction.

The bell tinkled, and she nodded to herself. Yes. A welcome distraction.

She placed her mug on a side table, allowed herself one deep, centering breath, and stood, turning around as she did.

"How can I— Oh, it's you."

Whit stood in the doorway, his hair and beard wet from the misty afternoon. His flannel work shirt looked like it was made for woodsmen, not writers, and that almost made her laugh. Except he kind of did look like a woodsman. The flannel was unbuttoned, and his heather gray T-shirt beneath clung, slightly damp, to his chest. The dew that made his hair hang in his eyes could have very well been the sweat from a hard day leveling trees, and if she had to, she'd guess that this man had chopped his fair share of firewood—

Stop it, Merritt.

"It's me," he said. He bit one half of his lower lip and waited there at the front of the store, almost like a child afraid to ask his parents for some vital thing.

"Are you okay?" she asked, surprised by the question and the fact that she meant it.

"Yes," he said, nodding deliberately, as if deciding in the moment that he was in fact okay. "But I do think I need your help."

"Okay," she said slowly, placing a steadying hand on the back of the chair.

He watched her for a moment longer, then shrugged before asking the last question she'd expected to hear.

"Have you ever wanted," he said, "to write a book?"

CHAPTER SIX

It was that no-man's-land time between lunch and dinner, so the bistro was relatively empty. Merritt had never been there, and on another day she would have been more conscious of its weathered brick walls, its rattan chairs, and the broad picture windows so unlike those of the other buildings on the street; there were hanging plants and creeping vines and, along one wall, a shelf filled with orchids. Here, too, a fire crackled in the grate, and each table was butcher-block thick. Merritt noticed none of it.

Whit Longacre was staring at her from across a menu, just waiting . . . and waiting. She realized she was looking at his beard, surprised by its fullness, and avoiding his eyes. She looked further down to his chest, where hair poked out slightly from the top of his T-shirt, but then she shifted her gaze to the eyes once more, and, well, she was back where she started.

"I'm sorry," she said, "but what makes you think I could help you finish it?"

It. The novel. The final novel of his wife's series, which he had asked Merritt to help him with in the bookstore. They had walked almost in silence to the bistro, waiting to go over the details until they sat down.

"You wouldn't be helping me finish it," he said now, "so much as helping me start *and* finish it."

"Wait, what?"

Her suspicions from the week before were confirmed in a flash. The book wasn't finished. *I'm writing the book for her*, he had said, and he had meant it.

Whit glanced down to the menu for a moment, stalling probably, then drew his eyes back to her with some determination. "I haven't written much at all."

"What *have* you written?"

Whit held his mouth open for several seconds, as if he were hoping words would teleport into it. Then, finally, he spoke, wincing as he did.

"'Once upon a time.'"

Merritt physically recoiled.

"'Once upon a time'?"

He shrugged apologetically.

"'Once upon a time'?" she said again. Her voice was flat.

"Yes."

"Like the beginning of a fairy tale?"

"Yes."

"So," she started, feeling winded by this information. "So . . ."

He laughed a miserable laugh.

"So, that's not . . ."

"It's not great, no."

"It's really not."

More shrugging. Merritt's eyes wandered away from Whit's face, staring at nothing as her brain did some literary calculus. "It's also what you say at the *beginning* of a story. We're *four* books in here—"

"I know!" Whit said, guilty, and then he looked relieved when a white-haired waitress appeared, wearing a denim shirt and a khaki apron tied at the waist.

"What can I get you two to drink?"

"A beer, please. Whatever IPA you have on tap is fine."

Merritt recoiled again. Blech.

"And you?"

"Just a water, please."

"I'm paying," Whit half-whispered.

"And a cabernet," she said immediately. The words "Once upon a time" were still ringing in her brain and she needed to rinse them out.

The waitress smiled. "I'll have them right out, and I'll bring some bread for the table."

When she was out of earshot, Merritt leaned forward. "So, you have written—I'm sorry to be blunt—but you have written essentially nothing."

"Correct."

"For a whole year."

"Yes."

"What have you been *doing* for the last twelve months?"

"Well," he said, dropping his eyes to the menu again, "grieving the loss of my wife and adjusting to the reality of a world without her."

Oh, shit. Shit shit shit. This was the second time she had said something like this to him. The second time she had alluded, accidentally but still very insensitively, to his wife's death. The first time, in the library, when she so casually suggested that her mother would *die* to read the annotated copy of *The Door in the Garden Wall*, she had decided not to apologize, believing that it was more respectful to treat Whit as a mature person who understood how idioms worked. But now . . .

"Of course. Of course you have . . . I'm so sorry."

He rubbed a flat hand over the paper menu, drawing and redrawing a large, meaningless *L*. But then he lifted his eyes, smiled, and laughed the barest zephyr of a laugh.

"It's okay. That's not fair of me to do."

"No—"

"I mean, it's not like that's *all* I was doing. I got very into ordering different kinds of loose-leaf teas through various subscription services, and an embarrassingly large portion of my year involved binge-watching *Vanderpump Rules*, the—"

"*Real Housewives* spin-off?"

"Yes, exactly," he said matter-of-factly, before continuing. "And there was also a fair amount of walking and some attempts at a spin class, which did not help my depression—"

"Wait, I'm sorry," she said, holding up a hand. "I'm not sure I'm really ready to move on from *Vanderpump Rules*."

"That's fair," he said, amused.

"I need you to tell me how this happened. Are you all caught up?"

"I've watched every season, yes."

There had been very few times in Merritt's life when her jaw actually dropped, but this was one of them. "Every season."

"Listen, I'm not proud of it, but—"

"How?" she demanded. "I mean, how did this happen . . . to you?"

"You make it sound like an affliction."

She didn't answer but gave him a pointed look.

He smiled again. "Fine. One day I was trying to write. But I was feeling sad—about Helen, yes, but also just that sort of, you know, the mindless sadness that creeps in from time to time."

Merritt nodded, grateful that the mention of Helen had been quick and straightforward. Grateful that leading him to another unhappy acknowledgment had been relatively painless this time around. But beyond that, she was grateful that she understood him. Mindless, unasked for, unexplainable sadness was not unfamiliar to her, but no one she knew seemed to talk about it like that. She didn't think it was depression. Just a day or week of feeling sad, sad, sad.

"Anyway, I decided to give myself a break, and I did something I never do, which is to turn on the TV in the middle of the day. And I landed on this show where these people, whom I now know are named Jax and Stassi—that's Stassi like *mossy*, not Stacey like *Macy*—they were arguing in a club in Las Vegas during a birthday party, and then in an instant Jax was in the parking lot physically fighting Stassi's boyfriend, both of them inexplicably shirtless. And that episode rolled immediately into another episode, and then another, and I became obsessed."

Merritt waited, thinking about how this man was a published author of books that were considered cultured and literary, but saying nothing.

"I could not look away from these people who essentially talk about *absolutely nothing* in hour-long increments. It was the most wonderful gift. A true brain-cell-eradicating time suck. Which is what I needed then, I think, to get through the days. I didn't want to be thinking or feeling. I wanted to be watching every episode of *Vanderpump Rules* in which Stassi has a dramatic birthday party, which happens astonishingly often. It is a terrible show, and it is very dear to me."

The drinks came, and Merritt stared at Whit as he accepted the beer and bread, and then they ordered some food, and she watched again as Whit thanked the waitress kindly, genuinely. She took a sip of her wine, then shook her head. Somehow, *somehow*, he had made this shocking confession into something sweet and understandable. Somehow she was identifying with a man who had binge-watched *Vanderpump Rules*.

"That's a lot to share with someone who is basically a stranger," he said, after a long pull from his glass. "But that's what I was doing instead of writing."

*

Whit watched the woman across from him, this woman whom he did not know, the recipient of his foolhardy proposal. She was eyeing the basket between them, overflowing with sliced sourdough, the tiny ramekin of honeyed butter at the edge of its gingham blanket hanging on for dear life.

She held up a piece of bread and examined it as she spoke. "So my question, again, is why do you think I'm the one who can help you with this?"

Whit felt sheepish in a way he typically associated with middle school.

"I googled you," he admitted. "Eventually. I saw that you did an MFA at a good program, so I know you can at least put pen to paper, and you've been so helpful, so knowledgeable about the books."

He fidgeted with the silverware, dropping his eyes for a moment. He felt a little like he was trying to keep a skittish woodland animal calm until help arrived.

"I dunno," he said. "I just have this sense that you're the right person to help me."

When Whit looked up and saw her blank face, a hole opened up beneath him, and he fell into it. Was he crazy? Was he doing a crazy thing? Every further explanation he could think of seemed thin. He had no solution to his problems, he was as lost as he'd ever been, and Helen was gone. He couldn't ask for her help or have her unsolicited feedback laid on him. He had hated that, the way she'd given advice when he hadn't asked for it, but now he would give everything to hear her opinion on anything at all. He would give everything to hear her voice, and he longed to find another of her long red hairs threaded through his shirt. He was so lost.

And that's why he'd reached out for help. But he wasn't a drowning man grabbing whatever passed by him. He knew that he could have asked someone he knew personally. He was friendly with so many writers, far beyond the bounds of the Whelk Harbor set. But those writers had also been, to a person, friendly with Helen, and he realized, only now as he considered it after the fact, that he didn't need more help thinking about what Helen-the-person would do. He needed someone who knew Helen-the-writer. He needed someone new.

There were a dozen other reasons he'd asked Merritt for help, beyond the MFA. Some were circumstantial—she lived close by, and she liked books. Some of his reasons were more pointed, like seeing the pin on her lanyard, the kestrel and the spoon, a symbol from the second book that fans were constantly having tattooed on themselves. (Did Merritt have a tattoo?) But the real reason he'd asked her could not really be articulated. On those singing competition shows he often found himself watching on YouTube (did he have a reality TV addiction?) they would call it the X factor. Whatever it was, Merritt seemed to have it. He felt that he could trust her, and that she would care about the work. But one could not say such things out loud.

"And I saw your pin," he said instead, "that day at the library. The kestrel one."

"The Sign of the Scout?"

Oh, yeah. That's what it was called.

"Yes."

"You did know it was called that, right?"

She was testing him, and for some reason, it amused him. "Are you accusing me of not knowing my wife's books?"

Merritt waited for a long moment before speaking. "No," she said, still thinking. "No, I don't think so. I think you've read them. I'm sure you're familiar with them, but I'm not sure you . . . well, I'm not sure you actually *like* them."

Whit couldn't help it. His half-smirk grew into a full grin. He laughed, took a sip of his beer, and then held it up, as if to tap it against her wineglass.

"That is really funny," he said, and Merritt looked confused.

"What?"

"You're the only person who's ever said that to me."

"Okay?"

"And you're absolutely right."

Merritt's jaw dropped for the second time that afternoon. "You're joking."

He held up his hands. "I am not joking. Or, okay, I'm exaggerating a bit, maybe. I don't *not* enjoy them. They are excellent books, and I am fully aware of their virtues, without any caveats. They're just . . . not for me."

Merritt shook her head, wide-eyed and ready to speak, and Whit held a hand out over the bread to slow her.

"But," he said, "before you decide I'm a horrible person, I should tell you . . . Helen truly, genuinely hated everything I ever wrote."

Merritt, who was raising her wine to drink, set the glass down once more.

"What? What is wrong with you people?"

Whit grinned again. "I know. Trust me, I know. I should be clear that she never said she hated it. She wouldn't have done that."

A memory of her face after reading *The Vow of Obedience*, the last book he published before she got sick, washed over him, and he paused for a moment to remember it. They were in the living room; it was afternoon. She set the book down beside her and grinned at him proudly. She could be very gentle to him.

"But there was just something about the way she talked about it, I knew. I knew my work wasn't just *not* for her, but she actively disliked it. And we never spoke of it, not in those terms. We would say, though, on occasion, that we were each other's biggest fans when it came to our success, and nowhere near each other's biggest fans when it came to reading our actual books."

Whit watched Merritt think for a moment as she ate her bread in a protracted, three-chews-a-minute way, and then she asked exactly what he expected her to ask.

"So she knew that about how you felt, but she still asked you to finish the series?"

Whit shook his head, mouth open in bemused agreement. "I know."

"And you asked *me* because of my pin."

"And you know the books."

She narrowed her brown eyes at him, and a single wrinkle appeared at the center of her brow. "Why do you say that?"

"Oh, come on," he said. "You put on a nice show the other day at the bookstore, but I could tell you were ready to explode from all the pent-up knowledge in your brain. I have a feeling you know every book in the series, frontwards and backwards, and every novella, and I would not be surprised if you had written some fan fiction here and there."

She let out a scoffing noise and looked away, surveying the wall of orchids. Not, Whit noted, a denial.

"But mostly," Whit lied, "because of your MFA."

Merritt exhaled and moved her head around like a limited-edition Major League Baseball bobblehead. "Well."

"What?" Whit asked.

She wavered a moment longer before explaining, "Technically, I did *half* of an MFA."

They paused, and Whit tried to stop himself, but he couldn't. "Half?" he said at last.

"Half." Then, after another, shorter pause: "Bad breakup."

Whit forced himself to nod, as if unfazed, though he regretted pushing her into revealing this information.

"I'm sorry," he said, feeling like that was insufficient, and she nodded, too.

"It happens. Does that change your opinion of me?"

"No," Whit said, with what felt like too much speed. Then, as if more talking would somehow make things better, he added, "You got in, didn't you?"

"And I got out."

Whit laughed. "Right, well . . . MFAs aren't . . . they're not the only way to . . . I don't think it matters one way or another. I know you can write."

Mercifully, the waitress returned with their food—a Romaine salad with goat cheese, almonds, and strawberries to split, roast chicken for him, and a brie and apple panini for her—and then Whit waited.

"And," he said finally, after they'd each had a few silent bites, "on top of all that, there's just . . ."

He stopped himself. He had explicitly decided *not* to say this, and now he was saying it. Could not, it turned out, *stop* saying things.

"There's just something about you," he said, moving his fork in the air in an abstract circle.

Merritt paused, her panini floating above her plate. She chewed her last bite, slowly again, as she thought. Then she spoke.

"Okay."

"Okay what?"

Merritt shrugged, then waved her panini in one hand before holding it up as he had earlier with the beer. "Okay, I'll do it."

"You'll do it?"

"Yes, Whit," she said, almost irritably, and the way she said his name sent a bubble through his lungs that emerged in a laugh.

"And you know I'm going to pay you, right?"

"Oh," she said, through a mouthful of panini, her face almost incredulous. "Obviously. I want a contract, an advance, a royalties agreement, the whole shebang."

"Of course," Whit said, looking down to cut his chicken. "We'll get it all down on paper."

When he looked up again, Merritt was looking around the space, smiling to herself, and Whit found that he couldn't help doing the same.

CHAPTER SEVEN

Merritt opened the front door to the yellow Victorian on the outer rim of town to find her mother in her natural state: curled up in the oversized easy chair in the corner of the living room–turned–personal library. Stepping into the space felt like stepping into the branches of a lit Christmas tree, with its little fireplace and scattered lamps illumining a small forest of houseplants, all hanging from wall-to-wall bookshelves. And there was Kathleen, like a favorite family ornament. She was in what Merritt thought of as her nighttime uniform: a tan sweatsuit from her alma mater, with her copious gray-brown hair twisted into a sloppy bun. Tonight she was wrapped in a quilt Merritt's grandmother had made, with her reading glasses perched at the tip of her nose, just inches above what looked to be one of Anthony Trollope's Palliser novels. Verdi played from a speaker hidden somewhere on the shelves.

"Hi, Mom. What are you reading?"

"Oh, *Can You Forgive Her?* And I have to say, at this point, I'm not sure I can."

Kathleen looked up.

"Well, look at you."

"What?" Merritt said, touching her face absent-mindedly.

"You looked pleased as punch."

"I do?"

"You do. What's happened to you?"

"Nothing," Merritt lied. She was immediately unsure of her reason for doing so. What did she have to hide? Whit had asked her to keep things quiet until they worked out the terms of their agreement with his lawyer brother-in-law, but surely that didn't include her own mother.

Why didn't she tell Kathleen? This was good news. A new job on top of her shifts at the bookstore. But more than that, she was bursting with hope—she was going to be a writer! Again! A ghostwriter, sure, but a writer nonetheless, and for a series of books that had meant so much to her. Surely this had to count as part of a dream, partly come true. Perhaps the curse was ending—perhaps she could track down the missing spark and shove it back into her chest. And then maybe this would be the beginning of her real life, her writing life, a life without Graydon or an MFA and all the better for it.

But it did feel, too, like she had done something crazy in agreeing to help this man she hardly knew on a stratospherically huge project. The question was whether it was Steve-Jobs-in-a-California-garage-with-a-dream crazy, or just *crazy* crazy.

And of course, there was no guarantee that ghostwriting would lead to more writing—her own writing. But she had tried not to think about that. First, they talked about money, which always made her feel awkward, but less so now because this was *real* money. The advance alone would more than triple what she'd make at the bookshop in the same time frame. She could pay off her student loans from the failed MFA, and if she were a little braver, or a little more settled in Whelk Harbor for the long term, she could use it for an apartment or a duplex—but that was not something to worry about now. For now, she had a book to think about writing, and her agreement to do so had made Whit smile in a way she'd never seen him do before. He had kept smiling, actually, as they ate their dinner, even as Merritt needled him for more information on *Vanderpump Rules*.

Now, staring at her mother, she imagined herself saying these things, and her face fell. Whatever joy Kathleen had seen was leaving her body in real time. These days, Merritt knew better than to let herself be an optimist.

"Nothing's happened," Merritt said again. "I just had a nice day."

That, at least, was true.

*

Annie Longacre had *not* had a nice day. Something had happened, Whit could tell, but she wouldn't say what. Not on the car ride home, not as Whit plied her with snacks and helped her with homework, not over dinner.

Often he wondered who he had to blame for his daughter's sporadic bouts of emotional unavailability: himself or Helen. Whereas Whit was often out of touch with his own feelings, Helen had been mysterious and, it seemed to him, intentionally reticent. Early in their relationship, it had frustrated him. The woman had thoughts and feelings—why wouldn't she just share them? Just say what the problem was? But as with other early annoyances—Whit's too-loud crunching, Helen's tendency to sigh forcefully but over nothing—it became something to get used to. She had her private, sometimes inaccessible interior world, and, it seemed, so did their daughter.

At bedtime, Whit had read aloud from an old favorite—the trippy, delightful *Dory Fantasmagory*—and Annie had hardly listened. Normally she was in stitches, laughing away while Dory pretended to be a dog or at the novel's every mention of a toilet monster, but tonight she lay passively in her bed. When Whit finished a chapter, he looked down to see her asleep already, and far worse, evidence of tears in her eyes.

He closed his own eyes for a moment, though the pink of Annie's nightlight impeded his efforts at achieving a mind-clearing darkness. For all her personal reserve, Helen would have noticed the tears. Helen would have been able to convince Annie to talk without grilling her.

Whit looked around the room. It was all his late wife's doing, in partnership with their daughter. The walls were a lavender color, Annie's choice, and he had resisted it, until Helen convinced him to "let her be little." There were framed illustrations from *Anne of Green Gables* and *Heidi* and the cover image from *Esperanza Rising*, round paper lanterns hung from the ceiling, and the bed where he sat now was draped with a gauzy white canopy. A large dollhouse sat in one corner (Helen's from childhood), and there was an old rocking horse that, to Whit's knowledge, Annie had never played with, as well as a toy chest that had belonged to Whit's sister Evie. The other furniture was all antique and utterly charming. Whit's favorite piece was an old Larkin drop-front secretary desk that he and Helen had found together at an estate sale when Helen was pregnant. "We'll give it to her," she had said, "when she's old enough to use it," and they had.

Now, alongside many books, Annie had made it into a sort of shrine to her mother, dotted with things Helen had given Annie, as well as things Annie had taken for herself in the last year, with Whit's permission. "Whatever you see that's hers, it's yours. She would want you to have it."

Annie had loved that, but she had been remarkably reserved, gathering only things that seemed really special to her. Along the top two shelves, she'd placed a photograph of Helen, young and vibrant and passionate, in her student union shirt from college; a porcelain ring holder shaped like a swan stretching its neck; a dried hydrangea from Helen's wedding bouquet; a Madame Alexander doll with one missing shoe; and an empty, quartz-colored perfume bottle with a crystal topper and a vivid pink pump.

Whit stood, walked over to the desk, and put his nose to the bottle, which smelled of roses and something somehow green beneath. His heart ached—a physical thing—not just for himself, and not for Helen, but for the little girl who had only these things left of her mother.

He looked back at her now, fast asleep as she clutched a stuffed Totoro doll atop her comforter. He walked over, lifted her eight-year-old frame in his arms, and used his hands, awkwardly, to pull down the blanket. As he set her back down, she stirred, her eyes fluttering a bit as she took him in.

"I love you, Annie girl," he whispered. "More than ice cream."

She smirked at their old joke, her eyes already half-closed again.

"I love you, too, Dad," she said, dazed, before immediately dipping back into sleep.

Well, that wasn't nothing.

*

The next morning, a Saturday, Merritt decided to go for a hike. She had let Kathleen force various articles of clothing on her, including hiking boots, a red flannel shirt, an army green puffy vest, and a navy puffy jacket on top. She felt like an extra in *A River Runs Through It*, a movie that, she reminded her mother, featured only male fishermen.

"First of all," Kathleen said, adjusting Merritt's collar at the door and forcing a full canteen of water into her hands, "you look adorable. And secondly, living here is all about dressing in layers. You never know when the wind will pick up or a rainstorm might come in, especially out in the woods and hills, where the weather gets wackier."

Merritt rolled her eyes, good-naturedly.

"I'll probably walk a mile or two at most, Mom. And I'm going to stay on the path."

"That's a good plan, novice that you are. But it's always better to be prepared. There's no such thing as bad weather, only bad clothing."

It was not the time to say so, but Merritt was never not struck by her mother's fortitude. When her father had died, Kathleen grieved, as anyone would. But she remained her same caring, capable, occasionally acerbic self. She laughed and read and worked a job she loved, and Merritt found herself thinking that people did, in fact, keep moving forward after great losses.

"Thanks, Mom," was all she said now. She trudged down the front steps into a mist that made her grateful for Kathleen's fussiness.

Merritt made her way to her Nissan, turned it on, and immediately swatted the radio off. She would not have her walk sullied by another NPR sneak attack from Graydon Lyons.

On her mother's advice, she had chosen a nearby trail, one that started and ended on the opposite edge of town and was therefore hard to get lost on. After leaving her car in a small dirt parking lot, she began to walk. Merritt enjoyed walking, which had never felt quite as true to her in Texas. Here, it took only a few steps to leave Whelk Harbor behind and feel like she was out in the world, in capital-*N* Nature. Even as her feet padded along packed-dirt paths, and even in the presence of multiple elderly couples wearing unstylish sunglasses and walking with those ski pole–looking things, she was a woman of the woods out here, a natural woman, whatever. She liked it.

For a while as she walked she thought about Whit and their plan, willing the excitement she had felt last night to return in full force, but then her mind wandered. She wondered what Graydon would think (if he ever heard about what she was doing), and she began mounting a defense against him, preparing talking points about the value of children's literature and the particular skills it required of its authors . . . This walk, she realized, was doing the exact opposite of what she'd wanted from it. In fact, it was making her more anxious, less settled, less connected to Mother Earth, and then—

And then she found herself staring at a small pond, slate gray against the morning sunrise. Mist was tucked into its edges like dust along baseboards, and the low winter light was bisected and trisected by the orange- and red-leafed trees. Something about the sight made her think, *I am going to be a writer.* Moments like this one were what she wanted to put on paper. Not what it looked like specifically—she hardly got jazzed about setting—but the thing she felt in her ribs as she looked out on the milky pink and stark gray scene. She wanted to put it down in words—this yearning, this hope, this connection to the world. A sense of both aloneness and togetherness as she walked in the crisp air, her hair damp in places, her cheeks cool and rosy. *I am going to be a writer.*

*

Whit had tried every strategy in his repertoire for getting Annie to open up. First, on Saturday, he'd gone with Helen's tried-and-true method of quality time plus patience. Whit had told himself, in Helen's voice, that Annie would talk when she was ready. She was apparently not ready: not at the library, or when they went out for ice cream, not while they watched *Mary Poppins*, not for the whole of Sunday. And so, this morning on the drive to school, he'd tried the direct route of asking, "Is everything okay, Annie?" and been told "Yes?" the question mark making his daughter sound more like a teen than a third-grader. "What about Friday night?" he'd hazarded, but Annie seemed to have developed short-term memory loss. "I don't know what you're talking about." Whit had given up and then spent the morning speculating about the right thing to do, wishing Helen were here to help, missing her all over again, and then realizing, with a start, that he was hungry.

He threw together a Croque Monsieur, something Helen had

introduced him to on their honeymoon, when they had stayed in her great-aunt's home in the south of France. It had taken some convincing, since, as a rule, Whit was opposed to ham sandwiches, but Helen had spoken with such confidence, quoting chefs who'd said things about its merits as the perfect lunch and so on, and he'd been persuaded by her warm, commanding assurance. He'd ordered one alongside her, and they ate them at a table looking out over the beach, where women in broad hats and men in speedos sunbathed, swam, and laughed. Helen had been right, of course, and since then they had kept a ready supply of Gruyère and Parmesan, thickly sliced white bread, grainy Dijon mustard, and French ham. Whit had kept up the habit after Helen died, and the sandwich always made him think of the Riviera in the summer.

He was allowing himself to rest in this memory—blue-striped umbrellas and shores covered in pebbles and people with fewer qualms about beachside nudity—because it was easier than thinking about Annie or the fact that (1) he had written nothing all morning, and (2) in a matter of minutes Merritt would arrive for their first day of work. He had spent Sunday sublimating his nerves by giving most of the house its first good cleaning in days, and then today, after dropping Annie off at school, he'd passed the morning in his study, swiveling around in his chair and listening to a BBC history podcast about the Tang Dynasty.

He felt the oven-baked cheese crack under his teeth. Maybe this was a mistake. Or worse, a betrayal. What would Helen think of Whit bringing in someone else to help him finish her masterpiece? Another woman, an attractive woman, and one whom he hardly knew, who had been only too eager to jump in and help?

Whit felt a burst of guilt but was spared from having to come up with an answer when he heard someone rapping at the front door, and of course it was Merritt.

"Hello."

"Hello." Merritt's smile was broad. She wore a purplish coat, the cut of which reminded Whit ever so slightly of something owned by a suitor in a Jane Austen novel.

"I like your coat," he said, which was not exactly true, but it was what came out.

"Oh, thank you," she said, still standing on the small, covered porch. She had a brown leather backpack over one shoulder and a tote bag in her opposite hand. Her green-framed glasses had little flecks of water on the lenses.

"Is it raining?"

"It's just misty."

"Did you walk here?"

"No," she said, leaning to one side so he could see a silver Nissan Versa on the country road past the gate.

"Oh. You could have parked on the drive. I'll write down the gate code."

He sort of hated the gate code. A relic of Helen's fame.

"Oh, okay," Merritt said. "Next time."

Her smile was beginning to look strained. This was awkward—why was this awkward? Could she sense his hesitance? Maybe his worries about Helen were seeping out of him, sabotaging this partnership before they could even give it a shot. Or did she sense Helen's absence like a distant ghost?

"Well, can I come in?"

Oh God, what was happening to him? Was the part of his brain that navigated human interactions taking a nap? Was he unwittingly slipping into sociopathy?

"Gosh, yes, please."

Merritt laughed, not unkindly, and followed him in, taking the liberty of hanging her coat on the coatrack, presumably because she doubted Whit's ability to accomplish something requiring such elevated social *savoir faire*.

"So this is your house," she said, standing in the foyer in a black sweater, black pants, and black lace-up boots, the one pop of color a short, silky gold scarf knotted at her neck. "It's very . . . cozy."

The pause, he knew, had been necessary while Merritt searched for a word other than "big." Oddly enough, "cozy" worked. Under the watchful eyes of Helen and a legion of contractors and interior designers, the big stone, English-style house had been transformed from a picturesque but musty money pit into something airy and spacious, lit by dozens of warm and fuzzy lamps and beeswax candles. There were flagstones in the entryway and kitchen and charmingly uneven, pristinely restored wood floors everywhere else. Thick Persian rugs filled every space where they made sense; ancient, exposed oak beams arched over whitewashed walls and walls papered in soothing deep blue and green patterns. The huge space had once crackled with the energies of a famously social Victorian judge's family. He'd brought his wife and their army of children across the sea from Scotland and built a house that could stave off their homesickness. But over the centuries it had grown derelict and damp. Until Helen.

Whit sometimes bristled at the bigness of it all. He had not been used to obvious displays of wealth, and he'd been surprised by how easily his wife slipped into a new kind of elegance when the book money started pouring in. But the piles of throw pillows and endless baskets of blankets, the art and the antique furniture, the multiple fireplaces and the sheer oldness of the place, made him feel like he was safe and warm in the Cotswolds or on a Brontë sister's favorite misty moor. It was Helen's gift to herself and to him and Annie, and Whit was deeply grateful for the home she had left behind.

"It's a two-hundred-year-old historical stone house," he said to Merritt now, "remodeled within an inch of its life, but it still gets *cold*, so please let me know if you need the heat turned up while you're here."

He was borrowing these lines, verbatim, from Helen. It was what she had said to guests, and now he was repeating the words like flight attendants on a weekly flight from Tampa to Raleigh.

Get it together, Whit.

"Can I get you something to drink? Water? Tea?"

"I'd accept tea."

Merritt followed him to the kitchen. Everyone who'd been in his house for the last year had been there before: his sister, his mother, Willa, some of his and Helen's couple friends who'd checked in on him early on, then came around less and less frequently. Merritt was the first guest in who knew how long to see the place with fresh eyes. He didn't look back as they walked, but he wondered what she saw: The sad remnants of a concluded marriage? A bachelor's hovel? Or something else?

"I love this house," she said once they were in the wide-open kitchen. When he turned to look at her, he decided she meant it. Thank God he had cleaned up.

"Thank you. It feels like home."

She nodded, then leaned against the counter that ran beneath a long window, her backpack still on.

"Sorry," he said, filling the kettle at the farm sink. He popped it onto the stove, lit one of the eight burners, and turned to her. "Let me take your bags to my study."

She was distracted. "You have one of those things."

Whit followed her gaze to the pot filler faucet over the stove.

"Oh, right," he laughed. "I always forget."

Merritt looked at him as if she were trying to crack an interesting, somewhat amusing code. It made Whit's face burn slightly.

"Your things?" he said, and she shook herself out of her musings to hand over her bags. Whit left her in the kitchen, then took the walk down the hallway as an opportunity to do some deep breathing exercises. Why, he could not say. He was not a deep breather. But this was turning into one of the more awkward encounters of his life, despite the early ease he'd felt with Merritt at the bookstore and the bistro. He could not make heads or tails of that, and now here he was, standing in his study, trying to remember whether you were supposed to breathe in for three seconds or five seconds and what came after that.

"Enough," he said aloud after a moment, giving himself two small slaps on one cheek. "Be normal."

When he got back to the kitchen, Merritt was examining the fridge display. Annie's schoolwork and artwork and a single photo from a trip to Niagara Falls, the three of them in yellow ponchos on a boat amid the spume, laughing and hugging and happy.

Merritt turned, and Whit felt his hackles rise reflexively in preparation for the pitying smile she would lay on him. Instead, she offered him a genuine grin and said, "Your daughter's such an artist."

"Oh, Annie?" he said, because of course he did, because the two slaps to the face had not been enough to remind him how many children he had. "Yes, it seems like it comes really naturally to her. And she didn't get it from her parents, I can tell you that much."

"I can hardly draw stick figures," Merritt said.

"For some reason, I doubt that."

They stared at each other for a second, both of them trying to figure out what he meant, until the kettle started whistling. After a painfully protracted discussion of the teas Whit had available, they settled on a pot of green, which Whit privately disliked. When they moved to the study, Whit saw it, too, through Merritt's eyes, realizing for the first time that his deep clean had not quite extended this far. Once, he had watched a video online about Roald Dahl's writing cottage, in which old Roald said the only time he'd ever vacuumed the space was when a goat broke in and pooped everywhere. Unfortunately, Whit had unconsciously taken this is as writing advice from a master, and, well, now the desk against the window and the shelves against the walls were covered with piles of loose paper and manila folders and several empty or half-empty coffee mugs. There were books open everywhere, and the armchair by the space heater was sagging beneath the weight of a year's worth of unread magazines, which he only now realized was probably an extreme fire hazard. And why had he never listened to Helen and had this ghastly green rug replaced with something less like the top of a pool table?

"Okay, well . . ." he said. He looked at Merritt to see if she appeared to be making an escape plan, but she was just smiling kindly, and yes, perhaps a smidge pityingly.

"Well," she said gamely, "can you show me what you have so far?"

"I'm afraid not much has changed since we last spoke."

Merritt laughed.

"Sure, but I just mean your notes and outlines, that sort of thing?"

Whit's face remained unchanged as he waited and a pit in his stomach opened.

"Oh," Merritt said, reading the signs. "So . . . really, *nothing*?"

"Please don't mock me, I will cry."

It was a joke, but Merritt looked horrified. "I wasn't mocking—"

"No, no," Whit laughed, "I'm joking. But I do need this to be a judgment-free zone."

Merritt held her hands up and nodded. "Roger that."

She transformed her face into the picture of understanding, but still, something was happening that Whit did not like. Their awkwardness had been excusable at first; to an outside observer, it might even have been endearing. But now it was merely uncomfortable, and the fault lay with him. He had invited this woman into his home—had essentially asked her to come in and judge him—and only now was that fact really dawning on him.

There was a pause, and then Merritt spoke again.

"What about in Helen's office? Is there anything of value there?"

Whit bit his lip. He did not want to go there. He did not want to bring someone there. That felt . . . no. They would not be doing that today.

"I really don't think so," he said.

Merritt narrowed her eyes, blatantly reading him, then smiled again.

"Okay then. *I* have some notes."

"*You* do?"

"I do."

She opened one of her bags on the side table where they rested, slipped a single file folder from it, and waved it as evidence.

"Just a few of these and—"

"A *few*? You've been on the job five minutes and already you've written exponentially more than I have over the last year?"

Merritt shrugged. "They're just ideas."

"Well, let's see them."

Whit's torso expanded, making room for an unfamiliar sensation of hope. Maybe this would work. Maybe this would really work.

"Okay," Merritt said, biting her own lip.

She waited again, then spoke all at once, as if the words had been Heimliched out of her: "*Ijustgotnervous.*"

"You what?"

She shrugged. "Suddenly, I am spine-chillingly nervous. What if you hate it all?"

"I will not hate it."

"You could."

"Merritt," Whit said, stepping toward her. He stopped himself just before his raised, conciliatory hand would have touched her shoulder. "I could not possibly hate whatever you have come up with more than I've hated *my* inability to write anything at all."

Slowly, she eased her teeth out of her bottom lip.

"Okay," she said again, half-laughing. She looked around the room. "I hate to say this, but I think we might need to move back to the kitchen."

Whit looked around, too. Clearly, she was right. What had he imagined? That the two of them would share the chair at his desk like kids who'd snuck into a crowded movie?

What was he thinking?

*

The man was in shambles, that much was obvious. But it was a charming degree of shambles, and Merritt's repeated thought had been *I am going to be a writer.* Though things felt immediately strained between them, the upper hand, it had seemed, was hers, because she was the one behaving so totally normal. Until this moment, when the two of them sat at the blocky wooden kitchen table, a steaming mug of tea apiece, her laptop freed from the tote bag and open in front of her, the backpack at her feet.

"So," she said, hearing an unsteadiness in her voice that she hoped Whit, in his sudden-onset kookiness, had missed. "I've written out briefs for each of the main characters."

She opened the file folder and began arranging printed sheets of paper in a grid before the two of them.

"There's concrete stuff like where we last saw them, or where we can expect them to be at the beginning of the story, and there's more abstract stuff, too, like where they are on their character arc and the state of their relationships with the rest of the cast of people."

Merritt glanced at Whit, who had gone bug-eyed. Oh God, what did that mean? Quickly, she began explaining herself.

"This is all just my interpretation, of course, and we can discuss everything, and maybe you have a different sense of things, and that's fine, of course, it's your baby. Or your, what, half-baby? Step-baby? This is not helpful, we can cease and desist with the baby metaphors."

Whit waved a hand for her to stop.

"You did *all* this?"

Merritt took a deep breath, ashamed of her presumption.

"Yes. I'm sorry."

"You're what?"

"Sorry."

Whit lowered his head all the way to the table. She had killed him. He'd died, clearly, of incredulity. But then he raised up again, a grin shining on his face like a neon marquee. He shook his head with a different kind of incredulity than she had expected.

"This is amazing—*you're* amazing."

Merritt felt the words in her throat. No one had told her she was amazing for a long time. Since before she started apologizing all the time. Since before dropping out, before Graydon.

Whit scanned the papers, touching them as if they were priceless treasures, as if to make sure they were really there. He held one up and began to speed-read it with fluttering lips before slapping it down on the table.

"I . . ." He shrugged. "I can't believe it. Incredible."

Merritt's own grin was threatening to go supernova, and though containing it made her cheeks feel like they were lifting weights, she managed by returning her attention to the backpack.

"Well," she said, clearing her throat. "There's more."

As she pulled two more file folders from the bag, she shot a glance back at Whit, whose eyes had once again gone praying mantis–shape.

"*What?*"

She shrugged.

"I had a light day at work yesterday."

Whit put both hands on his head and said, eyes closed, "You're a wonder, Merritt Pryor."

He opened them.

"A true wonder."

Something about those words said by this man, from that mouth, while those eyes looked at her—this man who was sitting before her, appreciating the work she had done and the brain she had done them with . . .

Oh no, Merritt thought, in response to the egg-like thing that had just cracked open in her chest.

Oh no, oh no, oh no.

CHAPTER EIGHT

Growing up, Merritt had been a teacher's pet, though not by choice. People were just constantly making her into one. She excelled at school and was well mannered and always game for a class discussion, and teachers loved that sort of thing. It had not been good, at first, for Merritt's ability to do hard work, because every time she stood at the front of the room to give a book report on her most recent Madeleine L'Engle experience or explain the primary imports and exports of Brazil, her teacher would breathe a sigh of relief, immediately committed to being impressed by whatever it was she had to offer.

This moment with Whit felt a bit like that. He was dazzled by her preparedness, which in his eyes constituted quite a bit of work. The truth was, for a Greenwood Castle fan like herself, these documents essentially wrote themselves. She knew this world like she knew the complete lore of the Baby-Sitters Club, the history of most American Girl dolls, and the comprehensive soundtracks of the movie musicals she'd grown up loving: she had immediate, encyclopedic recall when it came to these imaginary people, places, and things. All she'd had to do was write it all down.

And now Whit was looking at her like that, like she was something special, and she was desperate for him to look absolutely anywhere else.

"So I think we should make an outline—do you outline?"

"I outline," he said, and she nodded, and then that's what they did. They talked about possibilities for the ending of this final installment, what it would need, what people were expecting, what they were not expecting but might appreciate, what could be surprising but still satisfying. They talked about the beginning, and then the middle, and . . . some more on the middle . . . still talking about the middle . . .

"Maybe we should take a break on the middle," Merritt said, and Whit agreed immediately.

"It's almost time for me to pick up Annie from our nanny share, anyway."

Merritt's primary feeling at these words was relief. She felt like she'd been running a marathon where the mile markers had labels like HAVE IMPRESSIVE IDEAS and PROJECT CONFIDENCE and BE NORMAL. But there was the barest wisp of regret, too. She scolded herself. What had she imagined? That after a hard day's work they would pop open a bottle of champagne to celebrate?

"But here, hold on a second." Whit disappeared again into his sad what-the-cops-would-find-on-a-welfare-check study and returned with a piece of paper.

"My brother-in-law is a lawyer, and he drew this up for us."

He slid the paper across the table and then collected their empty tea mugs, politely busying himself in the kitchen while she looked it over.

"If anything seems off or unfair or one-sided, just let me know," he was saying, but she wasn't really listening. "And of course feel free to have your own lawyer review it."

The deal was this: she would be an uncredited ghostwriter, which she was not to publicize. Fine. But the money. Half of the advance was to be paid out to her in installments while they wrote, with the second half paid out in full on the completion of the manuscript, plus 10 percent of the estate's royalties on the book.

She sat in silence for so long that Whit started wiping down the counters with a spray bottle and towel.

"Does it look okay?" he said eventually, with some of the same sheepishness he'd shown in the bistro.

Merritt was staring at the largest sum of money that she had ever been offered in any context.

"I'll let you know."

Whit smiled from behind the counter. "Great, look it over and bring it back next time with any notes."

She agreed, trying not to look like she was rapidly ticking off items on a list of things she would do with the money. Pay off student loans, fix the rattly sound in her car, quit her job at the bookstore (once the manuscript was finished). Be an adult.

She packed her things, hardly noticing their weight in her various bags, and Whit led her out.

"Thank you," he said, from the front door, looking out at her on the gravel path. "Really can't believe how much we did today. I could never have . . . just, thank you."

"We've hardly started," she said, almost harshly, because he was getting earnest, and that was puncturing her daydream of a Scrooge McDuck money swimming pool.

"Exactly," Whit said with a shrug. "Imagine where I'd be without you."

Merritt touched her neck.

"Okay then," she said. "Same time tomorrow?"

"Well, Tuesdays I have writing group."

Merritt waited, a sharp hope piercing her chest at the thought that he might invite her. Then he looked apologetic.

"So Wednesday?" he said.

Merritt smiled widely, maniacally. "Yes! Wednesday. See you then."

Back in her car, Merritt stared at the old gray stone house where her life was going to change. It was encircled by a farm fence and shadowed on three sides by a wooded hill, on the other side of which was the sea.

"No," she said aloud to herself.

She had been here before.

"No," she said again. She would do her job, she would make some money, and she would use this experience as a stepping-stone to writing again. That was it.

She turned on the car. The brassy theme song for *All Things Considered* was playing on the radio. She slapped at the dial and drove home to her mother's in silence.

*

Whit walked into writing group that Tuesday like a man on a red carpet. He was *this* close to shielding his eyes from imaginary camera flashes and waving magnanimously at imaginary fans. Because he had written. Or prewritten. Outlined, if he were splitting hairs. But that was semantics and beside the point: he had *something* to report, something to celebrate. He had made *progress*, and a *vision* had begun to take shape, and if he opened his inbox today to a flurry of emails from Joan the agent and Shreya the editor, then his and Merritt's skeleton of an outline would be enough to stand between him and despair like Gandalf on that tiny rock bridge in the dwarf caves.

See? He was even thinking in fantasy terms now. That was progress, and there was no other word for it.

"Well, you're looking very smirky today," Willa said as he settled down next to her.

"I should be. You are looking at someone who *wrote*."

Her face opened up in a look of real surprise that he could have taken offense to. But he was too relieved at having put words down on paper to be hurt.

"Your own work," Willa asked, "or Helen's?"

"Helen's."

He grinned, really satisfied.

"That's great," Willa said in a relieved way just this side of patronizing. Still, Whit didn't care. The Monumental Task was at least an inch less monumental.

Willa closed her laptop to give Whit her full attention. "What changed?"

Whit's mouth hung open, and for a moment, he considered keeping Merritt a secret. The contract had stated that they would not publicize their arrangement, but this was his friend—his closest writerly confidant. And still . . .

"I asked someone for help," he said, all vagueness.

"That's very mature of you."

"Well, when you've exhausted all your options—staring at the computer screen, deep-cleaning the house, et cetera."

"As one does," Willa said with a laugh. "Who'd you ask?"

Whit gripped the chair below him as he spoke, unable to name the reason for his timidity.

"Merritt Pryor. Kathleen—"

"Kathleen Pryor's daughter?" Willa interrupted. Her son was a middle schooler at the Foothills School.

"Yeah. You know her?"

"No, but Kathleen always updates me on her when I volunteer in the library. I thought she was in Texas getting an MFA?"

Whit nodded. "She was."

He hesitated. Dropping out was Merritt's story to tell, and she hadn't even told *him*. The silence was heavy, and it needed to be addressed, but after a moment of nodding and thinking, Willa spoke first.

"You know, her mother did say she was having a hard time last year. Some boyfriend she didn't like the sound of. She was a little worried this would happen."

Why did Whit feel nervous?

"What would happen?" he asked.

"That she would drop out. *Is* that what happened?"

"I really don't know the details . . ."

"She was at Barton, wasn't she? The same school as Graydon Lyons? He has that new book coming out."

Whit considered this. Graydon Lyons was a big deal. He had the sort of story people told when Whit was in his own MFA program: Lyons had been mentored by Philip Roth, had a short story explode in *The New Yorker*, and burst onto the national scene with his first novel, which imagined what would have happened had Texas not lost the Battle of the Alamo in 1836. His works were lauded for their progressive themes, their complex female characters, and their unflinching critiques of American exceptionalism. Just last year he'd been asked to write the preface to a new edition of *A Connecticut Yankee in King Arthur's Court*, which Whit had read and enjoyed.

"Was she one of his students?" Willa asked.

"I don't know," Whit said again.

She raised a single finger. "I think I remember Kathleen mentioning that she was— Oh goodness."

She placed her hand on the table.

"Merritt wasn't the one in his new book, was she?"

Whit looked hard at her hazel eyes, searching for meaning. "I don't know what you're talking about?"

Willa laughed. "I forgot you live under a rock."

He bristled but pushed it down.

Willa continued. "Lyons's new book. It's 'new ground' for him." She rolled her eyes and did ironic air quotes. "It's about a grad student in a creative writing program, and everyone is speculating it's autofiction, or at least *semi*-autofiction."

"They always say that."

She shrugged. "Sure, but how often do creative writing professors write about creative writing students who fall in love with creative writing professors?"

Whit shrugged back and looked away, as if suddenly interested in the chalkboard menu across the room.

"Well, I highly doubt it's about her. Or anyone else for that matter. It's fiction."

He cleared his throat.

"Right," Willa said, nodding. "There are some psychological thriller elements, I think, as the book goes on and the relationship gets more twisted. Probably too crazy to be anything *real*."

Bad breakup, Merritt had said.

If Merritt *was* the inspiration, then her ex-boyfriend was a prick—and, unfortunately, the kind of prick who ended up on NPR's "Books We Love" list. Oh, poor Merritt.

Or maybe not poor Merritt. He didn't know. He supposed he could always ask.

Whit almost laughed out loud. The man could hardly offer Merritt a cup of tea without saying something crushingly stupid. He would not be asking her if her ex-boyfriend had written an unflattering, sure-to-be-critically-acclaimed novel about their life together.

But that didn't mean he'd stop thinking about it.

*

New books come out on Tuesdays. This is something all booksellers know, and Merritt was now a bookseller. Her more senior bookseller, Diana of the Sweater Sets, had come in that morning before opening with the sole purpose of telling Merritt which displays should be set up where. She wanted a Halloween table with spooky stories old and new; she wanted a selection of books by writers from New England; there was to be an endcap display of autumnal texts ("think *beach reads* but to be perused in a bed of leaves"); and she asked for a small dais at the center of the new-release table dedicated to Graydon Lyons's newest book, *Serious Games.*

"Why?" Merritt had asked, and Diana had looked at her the way George W. Bush looked at that man who threw the shoe.

"Why?" Diana repeated. "Because it's all the rage. It's going to fly off the shelves in the cities, and I have a feeling it might not do too badly here, either."

Now the display was all but finished, and the empty dais stared back at her. It was made to look like a Grecian column that had been sawn down to the size of a serving platter. The crate full of copies of *Serious Games* sat at her feet, and when Merritt finally leaned over to lift it, she felt like she might die. She plopped the box atop the newest Colson Whiteheads and Elizabeth Strouts and slowly reached for the box cutter in her apron pocket. As she clicked the blade up a few notches, she had a vision of herself stabbing the box, using the same the force with which Norman Bates would approach shower curtains. *Oops, Diana,* she would say, *something must have happened in transit.*

Instead, Merritt gently pierced the packing tape and slid the knife across the length of the box. When the folds opened, she saw, beneath slips of paper and bubble wrap, a cover of royal blue. It was simple and sleek, unadorned but for the words SERIOUS GAMES in a sensible white font and, only slightly smaller, the words GRAYDON LYONS and A NOVEL. She lifted a copy from the box and cringed. It had that sandpapery texture that made her skin crawl.

She stared for a long time before managing to turn it over. The back was covered with "Advanced Praise" from writers whom she knew to be Graydon's friends: people she had met at his side while attending parties and readings, and one token woman who had once joined them with her husband for a weekend at Graydon's lake house. "A stunning, unflinching, often hilarious portrait of modern academic life," she called the book, and Merritt deeply wished that she had not been so humiliatingly polite to her in all those conversations on the boat dock and around the kitchen island. Merritt had pretended to care about that woman's bichon frise, enduring dozens of cell-phone photos of the thing with pink bows on its ears, and now that woman was treating this book as if it weren't a send-up of someone she knew. What horrible things had she read and possibly believed before blurbing this book?

The worst part was that Merritt could find out if she wanted. She could crack the thing open and discover the answer herself, and she wouldn't even have to worry about padding Graydon's pockets with her own money, because here she was with the book in hand. She could read it during her breaks. Hell, she could steal a copy if she really wanted to—and she did want to, with the same desire you can have to touch something that might burn you.

Merritt placed the book on the dais, keeping it closed. Then she placed another on top of it, and another on top of that one, until she had succeeded in creating the least appealing display in the store.

She walked back to the cash register. The books watched her from their toddlerish pile.

"Dammit," she muttered as she walked back to the table to arrange it properly.

Well, at least *she* wasn't petty.

CHAPTER NINE

Merritt stared at the radio dial in her car, fully aware that she was being ridiculous. How many NPR stories about one measly novel could there be? She jammed her finger into the button and waited, defiance keeping her body rigid. It was just the normal hourly newsbreak stories. Increasingly bleak political news, a merger of two media conglomerates, and a natural disaster in Kentucky—all were more important than her own personal calamity. And now here came *Krys Boyd!*, talking to a musician who had released a critically acclaimed country music album. Merritt did not care, but it felt like a victory that she had turned on the radio at all, and it took her mind off Graydon Lyons as she drove to Whit's house.

She had worked out a new schedule with Diana, having alluded to a second part-time job that she took pains to make sound a lot like copywriting. On days when she wrote with Whit, she would spend the mornings at Goodenough Books, leave at lunch, and then return to the store to close when needed. She had sold only one copy of *Serious Games* today, to Ian Hoult. He was one of the local authors and someone she had pretended to like back in grad school, when she felt compelled to care about such things. This morning she pretended not to recognize him.

Merritt tossed her head a bit to rid it of these thoughts. It was time to transition to ghostwriter mode. She had ideas for Whit, and she was determined, now more than ever, to execute them with glorious precision.

Merritt had carefully planned things so that she would arrive early at Whit's. She pulled out a large thermos of her mother's chicken soup with leeks and rice and tried not to feel like a schoolgirl with a packed lunch as she ate it there in the front seat. With each spoonful, she added a bullet point to her checklist for the afternoon: she had ideas for the outline and for a potential new character, and a theory she'd been working on, since long before Whit came into her life, about the half-fairy and an allusion to Sleeping Beauty was gaining steam in her brain. She was waving her spoon in the air—a quirk of hers when she got a good bite or a good idea—when a knock on her window nearly sent her soup flying.

It was Whit, of course. She rolled down the window.

"Hi," she said, embarrassed.

Whit looked like he was trying not to laugh. "What are you doing?"

"Eating my lunch."

"Out here?"

She shrugged. "I don't like eating in front of people."

"You ate at the bistro."

"You were eating, too, that's different."

She could see Whit's breath. He held himself by the elbows, which were covered by a tan Carhartt that (*just face it*, *Merritt*) looked quite good on him, showing off his sturdy arms and broad shoulders.

"Will you just come inside? It's cold out here."

"*I'm* warm," she joked.

He had already turned around to walk in.

"Come inside," he called without looking back.

As she screwed the thermos lid back on, Merritt let herself smile.

*

"So," Merritt said, as she removed her coat, "I have some more ideas."

"Me too," Whit said, trying not to sound too excited by this fact.

"And I have this."

Merritt pulled the signed contract from her tote.

"Everything look okay?"

Merritt made a show of pretending to think.

"Yeah," she said eventually, flatly. "It's . . . yeah. Everything looks shipshape."

Whit laughed and carefully avoided her fingers as he grabbed the paper.

"Good. You eat, and I'll make tea."

Whit reviewed his other plans for the day as they headed for the kitchen. He was a great outliner himself, so he knew there was no chance of them completing their full blueprint today. That took patience and extreme care for a book like this one, with its four previous installments and its ravenous, critical fans. But he had spent the night before looking over Merritt's work, which she'd left behind.

He had already read Helen's books, and he'd reread them this last year as he tried to find the gumption to write the next one. But last night had been different. Reading Merritt's character briefs was like encountering a piece of really good literary criticism: it unlocked something for him. He was understanding these characters now as fully realized individuals with years of history and central experiences, with quirks, fears, strengths, and, most importantly, desires. He felt a now-familiar burst of shame at the realization that it had taken Merritt to stir this appreciation in him. He wished he'd been able to feel it when Helen had been here and to praise what she'd made more openly and honestly.

The truth was, he had needed Merritt's insights. For the first time, he knew, consciously, what Helen's characters wanted—he *got* it. It made sense. *They* made sense in a way they never had before. By the time he finished reading Merritt's briefs, he felt more confidence in the success of this project than he had yet.

"Your notes are wonderful," he told her now as he put the kettle on and Merritt finished her soup at the table.

"Oh," she said, her spoon inches from her face. "Thank you."

"You sound surprised."

She shrugged. "I am."

"You really get these books, you know? You're helping me get them."

Whit spotted the barest trace of redness in her cheeks before Merritt dropped her face to stare at her soup.

"And anyway," he continued, "I think we should start with Ursula, the half-fairy."

"What do you mean?"

"We talked about the middle, right?" he said, aware of the heightened energy in his voice. "How it's a bit murky and all, but I think that's fine. We have a sense of the beginning, and the end is taking shape, and what needs to happen now, I think, is that we focus on our three protagonists and their arcs. The middle should naturally fill in that way, and Ursula seems like a good place to start."

"Why her?" Merritt asked, covering her mouth and trying unsuccessfully to mask a slurping sound. Whit hardly noticed.

"Because of what you said." He waved his hand enthusiastically before picking up a stack of papers on the counter. "In here. How she's been steady and diligent and all those things for three and a half books, and how it was only in book 4 that we really saw her start putting her own story first. So let's do it, too. Let's put her story first."

"Are you sure you should be drinking caffeinated tea?" Merritt asked.

Whit moved his eyes from the papers he still held aloft to the mugs and teabags in front of him.

"I'm fine," he said eventually. "I'm just excited."

Merritt smiled at him. "So am I. I have some ideas I want to talk about, too, but let's do your thing first."

"What ideas?"

She shook her head, still smirking. "Nope. I don't think we should let whatever this is"—she gestured to his entire body—"go to waste."

"Fair," he said, laughing to himself as he let the boiling water tumble into the mugs. "Let's go in here."

Merritt followed him into the living room, where logs crackled in the grate. He sat in one squishy armchair and gestured to its companion on the other side of the fire.

Whit had made the barest sketch of an outline, based on his and Merritt's conversations about beginnings, middles, and endings. Now, showing it to Merritt, he tried not to be too self-congratulatory about this rare feat of *actually doing work*, but Merritt sensed it.

"You did this on your own?" she asked, clearly fighting a smile.

"Yes, in fact I did," Whit laughed. "All by myself."

She was nodding her head slowly, pursing her lips into a frown like someone highly impressed. "*Wow.*"

Whit rolled his eyes good-naturedly. "No autographs, please."

After talking for a bit about how to flesh out this outline, they eventually developed a system that felt intuitive to them. Merritt would dump information and insights about the various characters and their motivations, and Whit would suggest bullet points of plot to get them from point A to point B to point C, which Merritt would rearrange before Whit went back through once more with his mystery novelist's eye for things like pacing and probability.

Then they started and, to Whit's delight, it *worked*. They were a symbiotic, self-perpetuating machine that relentlessly churned through chapters and plot points in a way Whit found both wildly unfamiliar and deeply thrilling.

They continued this process for an hour or so, sitting in their chairs until Merritt got down on the floor to spread out her various printed materials. Whit felt awkward sitting above her, so he joined her there.

"More tea?" he asked after another half hour. His body had begun to ache in embarrassing ways, and he needed to stand for a bit.

"Sure," she said. "Let me just finish this one thing."

In the kitchen on his own, Whit found himself grinning, really grinning, and he was so taken aback that he actually touched his mouth with his fingers like he did after getting numbed at the dentist.

What was going on?

He knew what was going on: they were writing. He and Merritt were actually writing, and it was going really well, and when he'd thought about the Task over the last few days, he hardly even used the word "Monumental" because they were sharing the load and it was, unbelievably, quite bearable. That was why he was grinning.

Except.

Except that he and Merritt were *sharing the load.* The phrase lingered in his brain. Had this been what Helen had in mind when she left the book to him? Who knew? A surge of frustration welled up in him, a streak of defensiveness toward Helen and her enigmatic, secretive ways. What else was he supposed to do? Whit had been so painfully out of his depth before Merritt came along. He had needed someone to save him from the weight of inaction, and it was starting to look like Merritt had been the perfect choice. He should not feel like he needed to apologize for doing the savvy thing required to save the Greenwood Castle series.

Still, when he'd felt his mouth turned up in that unrelenting grin, guilt had shot through him, intermixed with worry. Would Helen have hated this? Would she have hated to see Whit giving away even a piece of her book to another person, a fan whom he'd hardly known at first? Inviting her into their home, sharing their thoughts and theories? Sharing the load?

Helen had been a writer. That was a dumb thing to think, because of course she had been a writer. What he meant, as he riffled through the cabinet for a tea option he wasn't bored with, was that surely Helen would get it. Writing was so difficult at times, and if he'd asked Helen to produce one of the Sister Marguerite mysteries for him, he was sure that she, too, would have needed help.

That was one of the things about being with another writer. They got it. Most of the time.

When Merritt came in, the kettle was boiling, and he was still thinking about writers being with writers. Whit was fairly certain that Merritt had some experience in this. This was the moment he could ask her about Graydon Lyons and the book and the real reason she'd left grad school.

He had seriously considered it when he was talking to Willa in the coffee shop. *I'll just ask her*, he had thought, because it seemed the respectful thing to do, rather than nursing this possibly false idea of Merritt, which felt strangely sexist ("the scorned ex") as well as oddly voyeuristic.

But glancing at her now as she looked through the windows over the sink, taking in the little meadow with the firepit and the rows of hydrangeas and the tree line beyond, he realized he'd been wrong. How would he even begin? *So, have any critically acclaimed books of literary fiction been written about you lately?*

"It's beautiful out there," she said, shooting him a smile before returning her eyes to the window. "How long have you lived here?"

"A little over eight years. We bought it with the advance of the second book."

Whit had not grown up around rich people. His parents' divorce was partially prompted by a series of bad investments on his father's part, and he'd grown up with a mother who worked for the local botanical garden. He always felt a little embarrassed driving the Range Rover around town or accidentally letting a comment slip about "having land." The parents at Annie's school talked constantly about remodels and second homes, and Whit and Helen had pledged, early on, to never become like that. Still, the house existed. It had been remodeled. Before Helen's sickness, they'd talked about a lake house and a New York apartment. But living that way was not his norm, and for some reason he wanted Merritt to know that.

"It was kind of weird honestly. All this."

He pointed around vaguely.

She leaned against the counter while she sipped her tea. "What do you mean?"

Whit thought for a moment. "Neither of us came from money. She had a rich great-aunt, but that was it. Our parents were middle-class and making it, and I'd say mine were *just* making it. And then she got a lot of cash all at once, more than I ever will, which is itself weird . . ."

"Because she's a woman and you're a man?"

Whit rolled his eyes. "No. I don't care about that."

"Really?" she said, more curious than skeptical. "You never cared she was making more money than you?"

"Fine, I cared, but not because she was a woman, and not because she was my wife. It was because it made my own writing feel . . . sort of small. Insignificant by comparison."

Whit had never said that out loud before. He looked at his tea.

"But that's not true," Merritt said, using her mug to point at him in a way that drew his eyes back up. "Lots of people read your books."

"Do you?"

He meant it as a joke, but it felt like a cheap shot as it left his mouth.

Except Merritt didn't seem all that vulnerable to cheap shots.

"No," she said immediately, unapologetically, "but I've been seriously considering it. I think it might help me understand you better, write with you better. What?"

Whit must have been making a face. He tried to go neutral.

"Don't you think your books will give me some insight into your psyche? Your *way of being*?"

She said the last part with exaggerated air quotes, and Whit laughed.

"I don't know," he said. "I really don't know what my books say about me. All I meant was that millions of people have read Helen's books, in so many languages, and that can be weird to witness but never experience yourself. I'm not saying a million people would even *like* my books, just that the difference in scale is . . . I don't know, it's something."

"I think I get it," Merritt said, walking over to the sink to rinse her mug.

"I'll do that." She brushed him off.

"There's a girl from my grad program," she said, once again looking out the windows as she rinsed, "and I mean that, she's a *girl*, and she was churning out these edgy, esoteric short stories for our workshops—really bizarro stuff—and then suddenly she landed a six-figure book deal for one of those sexy romantasy novels before she even graduated. Jessica Brittany."

"Two first names."

Merritt nodded. "She made me feel . . ."

"Small," Whit said again, filling in her pause.

"No," she said, surprising him. "It made me hungry, I guess, to write *my* thing. But I think I know what you mean anyway—that kind of success makes you look at your own work differently, when all you should really be doing is thinking about the writing itself, in its own little bubble of creativity."

Whit nodded, though he was sure he had never once entered into anything remotely resembling a "bubble of creativity."

"What were we talking about in the first place?" he asked.

"Money. Comparison."

"Comparison." He nodded, then put a hand to his chest, miming a blow there. "That's what we were really talking about. You don't seem like you compare yourself to people, though."

"I just told you about Jessica Brittany!"

By now she was finished with the mug, but she still stood looking back at him from the sink. The afternoon sun was turning the trees a goldish color that made Merritt's hair look like warm brass.

Whit laughed.

"Sure, but do you spend hours thinking about how you'll never measure up to Jessica Brittany? Is that a pen name, by the way?"

Merritt let a puff of a laugh leave her nose and rolled her eyes.

"It is not, if you can believe it. And no. You're right. I don't think about *her* very often."

She paused, letting her mouth hang open, and Whit could almost swear he saw the words forming there. She didn't think about this Jessica Brittany, didn't compare herself to her, but perhaps to a certain celebrated author and creative writing professor . . .

But then she clapped her hands once. "Okay. Enough of that. Noses to the grindstone?"

Whit's eyes dropped back to his tea for a moment; then he looked at her framed against that window one more time, longing to ask her why she really dropped out, but not certain why it mattered.

"Back to it," was all he said, and he let her lead the way back to their warren of papers by the fireplace.

CHAPTER TEN

Merritt was enjoying her routine. She spent the mornings at work avoiding the gaze of Graydon's books and speculating with Huong about what kind of life Diana must be living. ("I bet she is really into reformer Pilates," Huong had suggested. "The fancy kind, with the special rolling bed." "And complaining about other members of the Junior League" was Merritt's reply.) One small joy was that Diana had been wrong: despite its popularity elsewhere, *Serious Games* was decidedly not flying off the shelves at Goodenough Books, and not just because Merritt never recommended it. More than once, she watched as patrons picked up the novel, read the inside flap, and set it back on the dais. She loved seeing that, and then she would scold herself for caring, and then she would remind herself that a horrible man had written an almost certainly unflattering book about her and of course she cared.

When she left the bookstore, always mumbling something about her "other gig," she would drive a circuitous route to Whit's for lunch, taking care to maintain the secrecy of their arrangement.

After Whit found her a second time in her car eating lunch, a tomato and farro salad, he had essentially dragged her inside by the ear. So now she sat at his table and they talked while she lunched, and he did her the kindness of mostly not watching her in the physical act of chewing and swallowing. Then they would write. The basic outline took a little over a week, which Whit insisted was actually very fast-moving for him; now it was time, they agreed, to have a go at the first chapter.

"We can toss this out if it's bad," Whit said when they sat down at the kitchen table to really, finally, start writing. "I think we have more planning to do, if I'm honest, but I always find that writing the first chapter gets my head in the right space. Do you feel that way?"

Merritt considered lying, but she was not a liar.

"I don't know," she said honestly. "I've only written one book, and I didn't finish it. And it might be terrible."

"I'm sure it's not terrible."

She shrugged and pulled her laptop closer, watching Whit's cursor move across their shared document to type the words "Chapter One."

"It might be," she said again, filling the silence.

Whit stopped typing and looked at her over the top of his laptop. "Why don't I read it?"

"What? *No.*"

The words somersaulted out of Merritt, which was sort of surprising. A black hole seemed to have opened in her chest, out of which nothing, not even words, should have been allowed to escape.

"Sure, why not? Let me read it, and I'll tell you, honestly, if it's terrible."

"I can't let you do that," Merritt managed to say. It was at that moment she realized she was sweating. Clad in a dove gray sweater that had suddenly decided to go full tilt into its job description, her skin was getting itchy and she was desperate to strip down to her T-shirt and step outside so the cool air could cover her.

"Of course you can let me read it," Whit said.

"Of course I cannot. You are an actual, real novelist—"

"So were your professors at your MFA, right?"

Graydon was not her professor, but his face flashed across her mind.

"They were," she admitted flatly. "And also, they were paid to read my stuff. And also I dropped out. So."

"*So*, you've had a novelist read your work before. How about one who's also a *friend*?"

He seemed to put all his weight into the cheesiness of that sentence, but she was not swayed.

"That's even worse!" Merritt insisted. She closed her laptop and looked at Whit, willing him to understand.

"I don't understand," he said, reading her thoughts. "You want to write, don't you?"

"I think so. Yes. And speaking of, we should really get to it with—"

"No," Whit said, holding up a hand in a gesture that would have been condescending coming from someone else—coming from Graydon, if she were being honest—but Whit filled it with surprising gentleness. "You want to write, I know you do. And part of writing is being read. I would never make anyone share their work before they were ready, but the offer stands. I'd love to read it one day, once you get there."

He held her gaze with his dark blue eyes, and Merritt tried to look as though that word—*love*—hadn't set her whole brain spinning like a gyroscope. Would he really *love* to read it? Or was that just something people said?

"What's it about, by the way?"

"*No*," Merritt said with an unexpected laugh.

He furrowed his eyebrows at her in a mock threat. "Come on. You can at least tell me that."

Merritt gripped the seat of the kitchen chair and tried to decide whether the gurgling in her stomach was something excited or just pre-vomitous. This was a not-unfamiliar feeling, in two senses. First, of course she had done all this before: talked about her work, read her work aloud, had her work mercilessly critiqued with a metaphorical comb that was less fine-toothed, more Bond-villain instrument of torture. But second, she had felt this same way for the last several days. Being with Whit, doing the job of an author with someone who had done it all before, had been quietly electrifying. She was doing something, really doing it, and she was being useful and creative, and Whit kept looking at her like she was well and truly saving his life one Greenwood Castle fact at a time. She loved every part of it: the outlining, the brainstorming, the breaks for tea. It felt more real than anything she'd done since leaving grad school, and possibly even before, and now here was this man, whom she only barely knew, asking her about a silly little story she had made up in her head and then had the audacity to try putting down on paper.

"Fine," she said, exhaling. "It's a take on the Narnia books, and books like them. But no one does those anymore—portal stories, about kids slipping into little pre–Modern European worlds, and this isn't that, either. It's about what it would be like to live in Narnia, or wherever, when these outsider kids stumble in like little accidental colonizers and suddenly they're the kings and queens. What would that feel like to the Narnians, and so on."

Whit's eyebrows stretched upward. "So it's an anti-colonial, anti-imperialist *children's* novel?"

"Yes, exactly."

"Can you do that?"

Merritt laughed. "Children's lit isn't what it was when we were growing up."

"Sure," Whit said, joining in the laugh. "Do you know, I read *Charlie and the Chocolate Factory* with Annie, and there's a whole weird white savior thing with Willy Wonka and the Oompa Loompas. I did a lot of impromptu editing."

Merritt nodded. "Makes sense. It's everywhere. The Babar books are about an elephant going to Europe and then coming back to Africa 'civilized.' Then there's the sexist stuff—don't get me started on *The Giving Tree*."

"*The Giving Tree*?" Whit said, looking genuinely distraught. "But that book's so sweet."

"Oh, Whit," Merritt said, putting her hand on the table like she was about to deliver bad news. "When was the last time you read it?"

"I don't know. We didn't read it to Annie when she was little. Must have been when I was a kid."

"Mm-hmm," Merritt said, feigning solemnity.

"What? *What?*"

"The book is about a tree that gives herself away until she's nothing but a stump." Merritt raised her hands slightly, as if to say, *Can't you see?* "And it's all to support an ungrateful little boy and his big dreams, and that makes her happy—giving herself away. Being the giving tree. And the boy grows up and he's wretched, he's this greedy old man and he's never fulfilled by any of it, but the tree, which again, is now a stump, is *happy*. Happy to be a stump! What a joke."

Whit scratched the side of his head. "And that's sexist."

It wasn't a question, but it wasn't *not* a question.

"Whit," Merritt said flatly. "Yes."

"But she's a tree."

Merritt pulled her head back. "I thought you were a writer. She's not just a tree, obviously, and Shel Silverstein goes out of his way to make her a *female* tree, whatever that means, and it's just . . . I really can't believe you can't see how gross that is?"

Whit's face was still somewhere between distraught and confused. "Isn't it possible she—the tree—is just being, like, a really good mother? Don't you think all women, I mean *mothers*, should be—"

Suddenly, his face cracked into the beginnings of a grin, and he stifled a laugh.

"What?" Merritt asked, something hot flashing across her shoulders. "What? Are you messing with me? You're messing with me, aren't you?"

"I am messing with you," Whit said, the grin now complete

and very puckish. He had good teeth. "I never read that book growing up, but Helen banned it from the house. Someone gave it to us at a baby shower, and she threw it away. Wouldn't even donate it to a Little Free Library."

The heat in Merritt's torso had moved to her face, but it began to subside as Whit spoke. "I knew I liked her," she said, now able to smile, if just softly.

Whit gave a half-shrug, dropping his eyes slightly. "I did, too."

Merritt felt the familiar pang of regret, having somehow forced Whit into facing his wife's death yet again, but she decided that Whit wasn't allowed to make her feel that way, not even unintentionally, after tricking her into delivering what might uncharitably be called a rant. Well, some things were worth ranting about, and exploitative anti-mother propaganda for children was one of them.

"Don't mess with me like that," she said after a moment, her tone that of a woman occupying the high ground. "I won't apologize for being right about a bad book."

Whit nodded, smiling with his eyes. "You shouldn't. I'm very sorry for tricking you into demonstrating your obviously good and noble qualities."

Why, *why* did her face go hot again at that?

"Whatever," she said, feeling like a teenager in a '90s movie. "We really should start this chapter."

She felt him watching her as she opened her laptop again.

"You're right," he said. "That would make me, like the tree . . . *happy*."

"Oh, shut up," Merritt said, staring once again at the shared document. She bit her cheek to keep from giving him the satisfaction of a smile.

CHAPTER ELEVEN

Diana was in today, floating between the various displays in a pea green sweater set and pearls. Occasionally she would click her tongue before adjusting a book here and there, but mostly she waved both of her arms over Merritt's handiwork and nodded approvingly.

"*This* . . . is very good, Merritt. You may have a future in book staging."

"Thanks," Merritt said, holding back her sarcasm as she manned the register. "Huong helped."

"Yes, and good for her," she called to the MEMOIR section, where Huong was reshelving go-backs. Diana tended to treat Huong, a twenty-two-year-old college graduate, like a child learning to ride a bike. *She's doing great*, Diana mouthed, and Merritt nodded, smiling in a way that genuinely pained her jaw.

Diana joined Merritt at the desk, raising reading glasses on a pearled string to her eyes and wiggling her fingers to indicate that Merritt should slide down and relinquish the computer. While Diana began working at a rate of one click or *hmm* every ten seconds, Merritt set about applying a large rubber stamp to the brown paper totes they gave out as shopping bags.

"I really thought we'd be moving more of those Graydon Lyons books," Diana said, causing Merritt to fumble the stamp and drawing Diana's eyes her way. "Oh, do that one again, dear."

"What do you mean?"

"It looks like a kindergartener did it with her eyes closed."

Merritt assessed the bag and found Diana's characterization unduly harsh, but that wasn't the point. "I meant about the books."

"Oh, just look at that pile—a very good pile, by the way. *Brava*."

"But how many have we sold?"

"All right, nosy little you," Diana laughed. Merritt's skin rankled as the older woman clicked and tapped away. "None today, one yesterday, and . . . two over the past week. I have a crateful in the back that the publisher will be none too happy to see again. I just can't believe more people aren't reading it."

"Like, in the world?"

"What?" Diana asked, moving her glasses back to their resting place on her chest.

"Aren't people reading it?"

Merritt had refused to google *Serious Games* and had avoided her mother's copy of *The New York Times Book Review* on Sunday. A hope crept into her chest that maybe the novel's performance at Goodenough Books was representative of a national trend—

"Oh yes," Diana said, cutting that hope in two. "It's on all the bestseller lists. Just not in Whelk Harbor. Odd, isn't it?"

"So odd."

"Well, now that one looks like someone's bled all over the bag, dear. Perhaps you should take a break."

"I think I will, thanks."

Merritt went to the back room and slumped into a chair. She was tired of this—the way the book seemed to haunt her and weigh her down. Either she needed to give it up and read the thing or she needed to move on.

Okay, she decided. *I will let myself feel however it is I feel about this thing for five more minutes. And then I will move on. Graydon Lyons does not get to have a hold over me anymore. Do you hear that, Graydon? I relinquish you.*

*

Ten minutes later, Merritt stood by the NEW RELEASES display, holding the book in her hand, thinking that maybe reading just the first chapter wouldn't be a total rejection of her principles, when the bell over the door rang. It was Moishe, a kindly bald man Diana's age who worked the afternoon shift. It was time for Merritt to leave.

"Hello, Diana, hello, Merritt. *Don't* read that, Merritt, it's just dour and self-serious, and I wasted my weekend on it."

Moishe's literary frame of reference was mostly gay historical romance, but Merritt still fell a little bit in love with him for a moment.

"Noted." She smiled, and then she set about gathering her things.

In her parked car, Merritt ticked boxes in her head, making sure she remembered where she and Whit had left off so she could spend the drive going over her plans for the day. How quickly she was able to mentally leave behind the bookstore and Diana and Graydon and jump back into it with Whit. She had even begun humming a self-satisfied, ad-libbed tune . . . until her car refused to start.

She sat listening for anything happening under the hood—as if she would know what that meant. After about two minutes of sitting and thinking, the door to the bookstore opened. Huong walked out and came over to peer through the windshield. Merritt stepped out of the car.

"I thought you might have died," Huong said as she stood there in her oversized cardigan covered in comically large crocheted daisies.

"I did not die," Merritt groaned, "but my car did. Do you think you could give me a jump?"

"Do you know how to jump a car?"

Curses.

"No," Merritt sighed. "Do you?"

Huong made a face of such pure incredulity that Merritt thought she might really believe Merritt had lost her mind.

"Message received," she said, angry at herself for being the kind of person who hated all *car stuff.*

The door opened again, and Moishe and Diana wandered out.

"What's wrong?" Moishe asked.

"Her car is dead, and she has no idea how to jump it."

"Thank you, Huong," Merritt sighed. "Moishe, can you . . . ?"

"I'm afraid I don't drive," Moishe said, genuinely apologetic.

"No problem. I can always walk."

She typed Whit's address into the phone, remembering that he seemed to have walked to the bookstore the first time she saw him there.

The house was five miles away.

"*Jesus,*" she said under her breath.

"Where are you walking?" Diana asked.

Merritt sighed. "Nowhere, apparently."

"Where *were* you going to walk? I'm just leaving. I'll give you a ride."

Merritt had carefully avoided going into much detail as to why she needed afternoons off. She squeezed her hands into fists as she spoke.

"I'm going to Whit Longacre's house."

"On a *date*?" Huong spat out with something like violence.

"*No,*" Merritt said quickly. "God, Huong. I'm helping him with some things. Purely business."

Huong's face did not change.

"Well," Diana said through a lofty smile Merritt would have enjoyed flicking with her finger, "look at *you.* I can take you, but let's be quick. I have to be at the salon at two."

Diana escorted her farther down the brick-paved road to her car, a tricked-out silver Lexus sports car that confirmed Merritt's suspicion that the bookstore was more of a passion project for Diana than a required source of income.

"So what is it exactly that you're working on with Whit Longacre?" Diana asked, pulling the car out of its spot against the curb.

Merritt clenched her teeth, frustrated with herself for not coming up with a lie before now.

"Just some . . . copy," she said lamely. "Paperwork stuff. Pretty boring."

"Oh, I'm sure," Diana said, and Merritt had no idea if she was being sarcastic. "How did you get connected with him? He's become very reclusive."

"Well, his wife died," Merritt said, unable to stop herself. But Diana looked unfazed.

"Yes, well," she said as she signaled, "still, he wasted no time hiring himself a young, *attractive* woman to help. Despite having been an author for years, writing all those books as *solo affairs*."

"Oh, gross, Diana."

The woman laughed, enjoying Merritt's forthrightness.

"It's been a year. And anyway, it's not like that."

At a stoplight, Diana gave her a look. "It is not gross. You can't be that far apart in age."

Merritt was thirty. Whit was thirty-seven. She had looked this up sometime last week, trying to figure out how old he and Helen had been when they had Annie, since they both seemed young to have had an eight-year-old. In an interview Merritt skimmed, Helen spoke about getting pregnant unexpectedly at twenty-eight, sooner than she'd planned and right in the middle of writing the first Greenwood Castle book—but this was all far more information than Merritt would ever admit to knowing.

"It's not like that," she said again, trying to blot out the words "young, attractive woman" from her memory.

*

The writing was going well for Whit. He was reminded of the time he'd switched from using a handheld can opener to an automated one—a wedding present. The difference between the jagged grinding via hand crank and the smooth, automatic slice of the machine was astounding, and he couldn't believe he'd been opening cans any other way up until then. He imagined making this comparison to Merritt and laughed at the thought of her reaction to being associated with something used to unseal baked beans and Spaghetti-O's. She was funny and clever and so capable, and in short, Whit couldn't believe he'd been trying for a full year to write this thing without someone like her.

He found himself waiting for Merritt to arrive in the space between dropping Annie off at school and lunchtime, and it took a lot of effort to keep from opening the front door at the first sight of her car. Sometimes he would imagine Helen seeing him like this, and he'd feel a dagger of embarrassment, but then the door would open and he'd be swept into the whirlwind of their writing.

Today, when a Lexus pulled down the drive, he did let himself get the door. He was about to call out to ask if she'd gotten a new car when Merritt exited the passenger side.

"Thank you," she said in a hurried voice. "See you at the store."

She slammed the door shut and began tramping quickly toward him before waiting for an answer, but the window was already rolling down on the driver's side.

"*Hi* there," an older woman's voice came from across the lawn. Then, to Merritt, "Let me know if you need a ride home, dear."

"I'll manage," she said, climbing the steps at a brisk pace, her face knotted up in a get-inside-quickly look that drew a stifled laugh from Whit.

"What was all that about?" he asked a moment later, back at the tea kettle.

Merritt finished chewing her sandwich before speaking from her usual place at the kitchen table. "That was my boss, Diana. From the bookstore. My car died after work, and no one knew how to jump it, so she dropped me off."

"Oh yeah, I know her a bit," Whit said before registering the words. *Diana. Bookstore. Dropping Merritt off.*

"She's *fine*," Merritt continued, giving the word a different thrust than he'd ever heard someone give it. "Just patronizing and a little nosy."

"Ah." Whit was trying to play it cool, but there were precious few things Diana might be as curious about as why Merritt was visiting Whit Longacre.

Merritt dropped her half-eaten sandwich onto her crumpled lunch sack and held up her hands. "Don't worry," she said quickly. "I didn't tell her anything really."

"What does 'really' mean?"

Merritt gave him a look informing him that his tone had shifted.

"I told her just enough to make it clear that a ride was necessary."

Whit tried, really tried, to look neutral and understanding, but he was thinking, again, of what Helen would say about all this. Wondering if he was doing something wrong by her, or something stupid in the grander scheme of the series and this book's existence. If Diana found out that Merritt was helping Whit on the book, and if she realized how long this help was taking and put two and two together . . . It was not outside the realm of possibility that a woman who owned a bookstore would have connections in the broader literary world. If the rumor mill got to churning—*Whit Longacre spends his days with a lovely younger woman writing his late wife's last novel from scratch*—well, the fans could be ruthless, and the longevity of the Greenwood Castle franchise, as Joan was fond of reminding him, was tied up in this novel's success. Whit sighed despite himself.

Merritt crossed her arms. "What?"

"Nothing," he said, hollowly.

"No, it's not nothing."

Whit opened his mouth, but he had difficulty finding words that didn't sound like he thought she was careless, indiscreet, stupid—

"Whit, do you think I'm stupid? I understand the deal. I signed the contract. I'm a grown-up."

He laughed, not because it was funny, but because he felt caught. He started blindly into the next sentence. "No, I just worry—"

"You worry that I'll give the game away and screw everything up."

He lowered himself into a chair in a way that felt like a full-body shrug.

Merritt stared at him, not letting him off the hook. He wanted to close his eyes to hide from the glare, but he wanted to stand firm, too. He did believe in Merritt, but there was a lot riding on this.

"Just what did you tell her?"

Merritt dropped her head backwards, clearly annoyed, but after a moment she straightened back up.

"I told her I was helping you with copy. I kept it very vague."

Whit considered this with squinted eyes, talking as he thought. "So I, who have written several books on my own, suddenly need to hire someone to do some sort of copy—"

"Oh stop," Merritt said, standing up. "That's basically what she said, too."

Whit had never seen her like this. *Miffed* was the word that came to mind, and he understood, but still, he needed this to all work out.

"We'll just workshop the line," he said eventually, "and work on your, uh, *mediocre* lying skills."

To his surprise, and clearly despite her best efforts, Merritt laughed.

"Shut up, please."

Whit nodded, and Merritt sat again, this time sideways in her chair.

"And please trust me, Whit," she added. "I won't mess this up."

Whit nodded. "I believe you," he said, and he really wanted to mean it.

They started writing soon after, in the living room with the fireplace going. They were in it now, writing what could eventually become the first few chapters of Helen's book. Merritt had an uncanny knack for imitating the narrative voice, and she knew the characters like they were her own inventions. But Whit was an experienced novelist, and he had a better handle on plot, suspense, stakes, satisfying revelations. He did a lot of concurrent editing of Merritt's words, cutting here or asking her to elaborate there, occasionally suggesting something that Merritt would then acknowledge good-naturedly but unenthusiastically. Only once, days ago, had she outright laughed at his ignorance: he'd suggested that they bring in a character who had famously died a tragic death in book 3.

"She *could* come back," he had said, laughing as well, despite himself. "It's a magic world, isn't it?"

"Yes," Merritt had said, rubbing her eyes, "in which one of the three primary and oft-repeated rules is that no one *ever* returns from the dead."

"Oh, shut up."

Today they were more in the zone than usual, keeping their side conversations to a minimum as Merritt researched an allusion in book 4 that she thought might be worth capitalizing on in book 5; Whit was doing his thing, reading and rereading what they'd already written, cutting and condensing here, pushing for more there, and adding to or adjusting their copious outline in an effort to give the story all of the thrust and inevitability and occasional surprise of a good mystery novel.

Still, Whit kept feeling antsy, thinking about Diana and the tiff with Merritt and, beneath all that, worrying again that he was somehow doing something wrong. He had to keep telling himself to sit on his hands, to refrain from suggesting they take a break fifteen minutes in, then thirty minutes in. Finally, the hour mark rolled around.

"Break?" he said, cutting Merritt off midsentence. "I mean . . . sorry. Should we break in a minute? It's been an hour."

Merritt glanced at the clock on her phone. "Yeah, sure," she said, clearly surprised.

"Actually, do you think we could go on a walk or something? I've got all this nervous energy for some reason, and I think I need to get rid of it."

"A walk? It's freezing."

"Maybe for Texas," he joked, "but in New England this is basically spring. Come on, I'll show you my favorite trail. It's where I go when I have writer's block."

"Do you have writer's block right now?"

"No."

Merritt considered this, then shrugged. "Sure, fine."

"What?"

"It's just . . ." Merritt paused and searched the ceiling with her eyes. "I'm starting to see why you haven't written very much. All these breaks you take."

She smiled in a prodding way, and Whit smiled back, shaking his head as if she had disappointed him.

"Breaks are good for your brain, Merritt. It's been proven."

"Where exactly?" she asked, standing up from her chair.

"I don't know. Studies. Science. I was an English major, don't ask me."

"You're lucky I was an English major, too."

The two of them put their coats on. There was a door in the kitchen that led to the yard, which Whit held open for Merritt before following her out.

"What were you planning to do with that English major?" he asked as he began to lead her on the trail into the woods to the right of the house. "Write?"

"Not originally," she said from behind him. "I didn't know what to do really. My first job out of school was a horrible fundraising job in elementary schools, where I'd beg kids to sell wrapping paper and buckets of popcorn, which was not quite what I'd dreamed of back in class reading Toni Morrison and George Eliot."

"And you gave all that up," Whit asked without looking back, "for grad school?"

A sniff of a laugh behind him, then: "Kind of. I got a technical writing job eventually, doing instructional materials and trouble-shooting guidelines for a software company—really grim stuff. And then my dad got sick."

Merritt's pause let Whit know, somehow, that her father had not gotten better.

"So I came here for a bit, and then, after—well, after, I started the MFA program."

"I'm sorry," Whit said.

"Me, too, sometimes. Two years and nothing to show for it—"

"No," Whit interrupted, "I mean about your dad."

"Oh."

He turned to look at Merritt. Her indigo coat stood out against the yellows, oranges, reds, and greens of the trees around them.

"What was his name?"

Whit had read somewhere that this was a kind thing to ask, though in his case, with Helen, it hadn't often been necessary. It turned out to be true, however, because Merritt's face brightened.

"Barry," she said, almost laughing. "A very dad name."

Whit smiled and nodded, and then turned to walk. They

passed the next few minutes quietly, listening to the wind and the crunch of leaves punctuated by occasional animal sounds, until Merritt spoke.

"By the way, did you walk the five miles to the bookstore that day you came in about the baby-giant thing?"

Something hot filled Whit's face. He glanced back at her.

"You're looking at me like that's crazy," he told her.

She smirked at him. "It is a little crazy."

He shrugged. "*That* day I definitely did have writer's block. But then, I had writer's block basically every day before we started working together."

Merritt looked down, rubbing her arm absent-mindedly, and Whit realized he had probably sounded embarrassingly desperate. To move on, he started walking again, then stopped to point at something to their right.

"There, that stream there is what Helen based the one in the book off of."

"The Brook of Lost Memory?" Merritt asked, stopping to stand at his shoulder.

"Yeah, that."

Merritt made a noise of amusement at his persistent ignorance, then *hmm*-ed. "I can see it, I think. Yeah, that's sort of how I imagined it."

Whit shrugged, lost in a thought that felt like a sense memory. It wasn't often that Helen had joined him on his walks, but there was one fall day, like this one, when the two of them had come out here. Annie had been small enough for them to take turns wearing the front-facing baby carrier.

"Maybe," Helen had said, out of nowhere, in her ever-calm voice, "it's a water thing."

"What?" he'd asked, squeezing Annie's cold hands in each of his. Then he saw Helen's face and knew what was happening, because it often happened to him. She was in the world of her books, working out questions as she walked, and the nearby stream had provided an answer to one of them.

"I need a way for Ursula to remember something she's forgotten. Maybe she has to bathe in a brook or something to get the memory back."

This was after the second book had sold but just before the series had become a global phenomenon. Whit had just published his first book in the Sister Marguerite series, and though they had more money than they'd ever had, the future remained murky, and it felt like the two of them were still just trying to make it as writers.

"Sort of like Achilles," Helen continued.

"Or a backwards Lethe," Whit had put in, offering another Greek myth.

"Exactly," Helen said, presenting him with a shining grin that communicated pure gratefulness. "A backwards Lethe, exactly."

There were so few moments like that, times when they had felt like two writers side by side, and remembering it now felt like a blow to the chin.

"Whit?" Merritt said, for what he realized was the second time. "You okay?"

"What? Yes, sorry. I zoned out there for a second. What were you saying?"

"I was asking if any of this is in *your* books."

She waved her hands before her at the tall green spruces and firs, the more festal beeches and maples, the wet rocks and their overcoat of moss.

"My books?" Whit said, caught off guard.

"Yes?"

Whit thought for a moment, then smiled, surprised at himself. "You know, I suppose it is. There's a Sister Marguerite book where they stumble onto a corpse while making a pilgrimage to a holy tree in Italy that supposedly grew from a seed dropped by Saint Paul."

"Okay . . ."

Whit shrugged. "A lot of that book takes place in a forest, and, well, I've never been to an Italian forest. It's just these woods reimagined, though I never realized that until now."

Merritt nodded, interested. "Well, I look forward to that one. I'm liking *The Hour of Matins* so far."

"You what?" Whit said in a voice that was half-gulp. Something electric had raced through him, which didn't make sense. People did, in fact, read his books, and he had been the one to give Merritt the speech about writers writing for an audience. Still, the knowledge that Merritt was reading his book—his *first* book—had caused an internal frisson, a second, different blow to his body.

"I'm liking it," she said, casting her eyes around the trees in a way he found suddenly maddening.

"Oh, please don't start with *that* one."

"Of course I started with that one, what do you mean? Should I start in the middle of the series?"

"Yes. I promise, it gets better. I'll catch you up on the important plot points."

"Okay, that's absurd. I'm a completist. And anyway, I said I'm enjoying it."

"Don't say I didn't warn you." Whit turned and began walking in the direction of the house. The old story slithered through his brain as they walked: Sister Marguerite, the Anglican novitiate and amateur detective who investigates the mysterious death of a fellow nun during their morning devotions. He liked his novels, truly, and he thought they did the things he wanted them to do—did them well. They were murder mysteries, but they were also ruminations on faith, doubt, and duty, on wanting to believe in goodness and not always being able to. And he did *believe* in being read by people. But, with the exception of Helen, Willa, and, for a time, Ian Hoult, his readership had always been distant and sort of imaginary. They existed, but somewhere else. He didn't see them, and he only very rarely heard their opinions on his work.

The idea of Merritt reading his books, though . . . he didn't know what exactly that felt like (beyond the sudden squirminess in his stomach). (Where had that come from?) But it definitely felt like *something*.

CHAPTER TWELVE

After their walk, Merritt and Whit returned to writing, once again falling into a groove they both felt was especially productive. For Merritt, it was thrilling, a kind of pleasant fugue state in which the words fell onto the page like perfectly placed darts on a dartboard. She was making notes about her fairy tale theory, building her ideas out into a plausible arc that could fit within the outline they'd already crafted before sharing them with Whit. She felt like a detective building a case until she was finally ready to speak.

"I think there's something here."

They were at the kitchen table now, with their teas, and Whit looked up from his.

"There are lots and lots of fan theories about Christabel and the story of Sleeping Beauty."

"I thought elves *didn't* sleep?"

"Correct," Merritt said, with a faux-impressed nod. "But she's half-human, so I suppose it's possible. Anyway, there are all these little things that could be clues strewn throughout the books. Her elf father's estate is called Briar House. The family crest has a rose on it. We know she's cursed at the very end of book 4, and some magic force is making her sluggish, and there's a throwaway moment at the beginning of that book where she pricks her finger—"

"I don't think so."

Whit's voice was so clipped, so direct, that she felt called up short.

"You don't think what?"

Whit's face was solemn and self-assured.

"I don't think she would purposefully be doing a Sleeping Beauty thing."

"What do you mean?" Merritt said, a little incredulous at this sudden snag in what had felt like a surefire discovery. She decided to defend herself. "It's all there: Christabel can finally fall asleep somewhere around the midpoint of our book, which means Ursula and Rupert need to awaken her."

Whit's face was unmoved. She went on.

"Helen's done this before, with the Robin Hood imagery in book 2, and the arrow in the stone instead of a sword in the stone in book 1. It's exactly the kind of thing people look for."

Merritt was right about this, she was sure, and yet here was Whit smiling with a sudden calm confidence.

He adjusted how he was sitting, pressed his hands together as if in prayer, then rubbed both index fingers across his mouth. He was *really* giving his next words a good once-over before uttering them aloud.

Then he looked at Merritt, almost apologetic.

"It might be something people think Helen the *author* would do, but it's decidedly *not* something Helen the *person* would do."

Oh.

"She hated those old princess-y fairy tales. She would let Annie watch the movies, *Sleeping Beauty*, *Snow White*, *Cinderella*, but she would explain the whole time what was wrong with them, how those boys shouldn't have kissed sleeping girls without their permission, and how Cinderella really should've gotten to know Prince Charming a little better first."

Though he was looking at the window, he was really looking at the memory, his lips still turned up at their corners.

"I agreed, but we would get in little arguments about it, because Annie was four or five, and couldn't Helen just let her enjoy the movie, blah blah."

He paused and thought and smiled again. Merritt nodded, ignoring a feeling akin to dread that had lodged in her stomach.

"Her whole thing was, why even give the bad stuff airtime when there were so many better stories for girls out there?"

Now Whit looked at Merritt like he was grateful for the memory.

"So," he continued, "she might have been doing something like that unconsciously, but—" He laughed. "She would *hate* to be accused of that, and I can pretty much guarantee it wouldn't be a major plot point in this book."

"I'm sorry," Merritt said immediately, feeling suddenly stupid. "I wasn't trying to *accuse* her of anything, I just—"

Whit waved his hands quickly, kindly. "Of course you weren't! You were following a lead. It's all we have, leads. We have to use them where we can."

Merritt nodded, but inside, something felt wrong. Like a sweater twisted into a knot by the washing machine. She knew she should be compassionate toward this man who sat before her, remembering his wife with warmth and certainty. And of course Whit knew Helen better than she ever could. But what he'd said about Helen the writer and Helen the person . . . weren't they concerning themselves explicitly with Helen the writer? Wasn't that why Merritt was here? Because *she* was the expert when it came to Helen's work?

And she had worked on this idea, had been working on it for a long time, even before taking this job to help this man who didn't know which way was up when it came to the Greenwood Castle books. But now Whit had summarily dismissed her idea—her *good* idea, she knew it was good—and he'd wrapped it in a bow of gentleness and understanding that made her feel like there was nothing she could do about it.

She wanted to speak up for herself and her instincts, to talk about how events in fiction aren't necessarily always in keeping with one's moral compulsions—didn't he, the mystery novelist, *know* this?—and she wanted to suggest that maybe Helen was going to do something subversive with this allusion, that they could be subversive, too. She sat there with the words forming between her teeth, and then Whit's phone buzzed.

"Crap," he said after reading a message. "That's the nanny from the nanny share. She's sick in bed."

Something about this information seemed to weary Whit, right before her eyes, and she remembered that he was a tired, grieving father who no longer had a wife with whom he could share the load. This was a bitter pill that seemed to undermine her justifiable defensiveness, and for the second time in as many minutes she felt called up short.

"I need to pick up Annie from school in a bit."

Whit blinked it slow motion. He was clearly exhausted.

She swallowed the pill and felt its bitterness gradually fade.

"Can I drop you off somewhere on the way?" he asked. "Or if you prefer to call Diana—"

"God, please no," Merritt interrupted, drawing a laugh from Whit. "I mean yes. You can drop me off."

Whit scratched the back of his head, thinking and feeling but keeping it to himself. Then he nodded to her, as if he'd built the resolution needed to do the next thing, small as it was, and pick up his daughter from school.

"Splendid," he said. "Let's get going."

*

In the garage, she saw a silver Audi Q4 Sportback next to a surprisingly tall, faded blue jeep with a hard-shell top that could be removed in warm weather. Whit opened the garage and started walking toward the Range Rover parked behind them in the driveway. He paused when Merritt didn't follow him right away.

"What?"

Was she gawking?

"Nothing," she said. "You just didn't strike me as a three-cars-one-of-which-is-for-joyriding kind of person."

He smiled.

"I used to just drive the jeep, if you can believe it. I've had it for years, and I love it, but then . . ." He paused again, almost certainly avoiding saying something akin to *we got rich*. "The Audi was Helen's idea. It's electric and just more sensible, especially with all the cold weather we get here. Less—"

"College frat boy?" she said before she could stop herself. It felt good, after Sleeping Beauty, to get a little dig in.

"*Wow*," Whit said, making a look of mock disappointment, as if she'd crossed a line.

"Too far?"

He shook his head slowly. "Just, wow."

Then they both laughed. The bitterness was almost undetectable now.

"But I've been driving her old car. The Range Rover. I get the feeling Annie likes it."

Minutes later, Merritt could see why. They were warm in the spacious SUV with its legroom and couchlike comfort, driving back to town on a side road she hadn't known about. She wondered if the lemon and lavender scent was from a car wash, or an air freshener, or if it was the last lingering vestige of the woman who'd once driven this car.

"*Eleanor Beardsley*," Merritt muttered to herself.

"What's that?"

"Nothing, just talking to myself."

"Are you guessing the NPR correspondent—"

"Before they say their names, yes."

"Oh. Neat."

She gave his shoulder a shove. He smiled to himself, and they drove on, quiet for a moment. Out of the corner of her eye, she watched the way his thumb rubbed the steering wheel. She hated that the word *caress* came to mind, but it did, and part of her wondered whether his reasons for driving this car went beyond his daughter's preferences.

Whit's phone rang, and he ignored it, but not before the words EVIE LONGACRE—MOBILE flashed across the car's head unit.

"Your mom?"

"My sister."

"Ah."

A sister. She knew he had a brother-in-law but hadn't worked out whether that man was Helen's brother or his sister's husband. Whit had seemed like an island to her, but of course he had a family before Annie and Helen.

"Are you close?"

He nodded. "Yeah. But she calls a lot more since Helen died. She worries."

Merritt shrugged and nodded, just barely managing to stop herself from saying that her mother had done that when she and Graydon broke up. It was not the same thing.

"Is it just the two of you?"

"My parents, but they're divorced. And then Evie lives in New York with her husband, Édouard Marchand. He's French Canadian, a former pro hockey player turned lawyer. We have him to thank for our contract. Extremely fashionable and a bit of a jock. I love him."

Merritt laughed.

"What about you?"

She shrugged. "Just me and my mom now."

Whit nodded. "Helen loved your mom. I mean, I love your mom, too, but Helen really loved her. And Annie does, too."

"That's sweet," Merritt said and, feeling immediately that the words sounded dismissive, added, “She had nice things to say about you and Helen and Annie, too.”

Her eyes widened as she realized what she’d just revealed, and though she refused to even glance Whit’s way, she was sure he had looked at her then. *You’ve been talking about me*, his energy seemed to say.

“When I told her about the job,” Merritt added, after far too long a delay. “I told her about the job, is that okay?”

Now he definitely looked at her. “Your mom? Of course you can tell your *mom*. I think I trust her more than Diana.”

“Don’t bring up Diana anymore, please.”

Whit laughed.

“But if your mom tells anyone, it’s curtains for her.”

Merritt sensed a tiny edge of seriousness there, but she smiled at the joke.

“Curtains? Are you a 1920s mobster? Anyway, Kathleen Pryor is a locked box, and you are not allowed to threaten her.”

“If she tells anyone, she’s sleeping with the fishes.”

“Please, stop, you’re making it worse.”

“She tells anyone . . . we’re going to the mattresses,” he said.

“Leave the gun,” she said in a bad Italian accent, “take the cannoli.”

He gave her a look.

“What? I’ve seen *The Godfather*.” She smirked. “I definitely don’t just know those lines from *You’ve Got Mail*.”

He grinned. “I love that movie.”

“Now you’re mocking me.”

“No,” he said, actually pointing a finger at her. “I never joke about Nora Ephron.”

Merritt leaned back against the cool window, evaluating him. A playful smile pushed his cheeks up toward his eyes, making them into joyful little half-moons.

"Fine," Merritt said. "On three, the best Nora Ephron movie is, one . . . two . . . three—"

"*When Harry Met Sally*," he said, and she shook her head.

"No. That was a test. It's still *You've Got Mail*."

Whit gave an exaggerated eye roll, but then stopped halfway through.

"Crap."

"What?" Merritt said, following his eyeline. "Oh."

They were not back in town, but instead in a line of cars leading to what looked to be a school.

"Muscle memory—I just drove straight here. I'm sorry. I'll turn around."

Merritt watched as he glanced at the clock.

"Will you be able to drop me off and make it back in time to pick up Annie?"

"I'll just be a little late," he said, beginning to fiddle with the gear shift.

Merritt imagined Annie waiting for her dad as the line of cars slowly came to an end, and the image almost broke her heart. She placed her hand on Whit's but drew it back when she felt his eyes on her once again.

"Don't do that," she said, as if it hadn't happened. "We can just get her and then drop me off on the way back home."

Whit thought this over, but only briefly. "Okay," he said, relieved but not exactly settled.

"What?"

He shrugged.

"I don't know, it's . . . it's just a small school and people are weird."

She laughed to cover up the blush spreading across her face.

"You think people will talk about . . . us?"

He shrugged.

"Do you want me to hide in the back?"

He paused for just an instant too long.

"Oh my God, you considered it."

"*No*," he said quickly, half-laughing. "No. I just, I don't know, I'll—"

"I will behave myself," she said, performing confidence to cover her awkwardness. "Everyone will know that this is purely professional."

This, she thought to herself. *Us. Purely professional.* As if it would be anything else.

God, she could die. And Whit looked as if he was considering swerving into oncoming traffic. She pushed her cheek into the glass of the window to cool her burning face.

"Oh!" Whit said abruptly, pulling her head back up.

"What?"

He turned the volume dial slightly and a man's voice filled the car.

"*Scott Horsley*," he said, triumphant.

Merritt threw her head back against the car seat headrest.

"Dammit," she groaned, "I didn't know we were playing."

"From this moment forward, we are officially keeping score."

They waited in line after that, and Merritt focused all her attention on listening to a story about the latest stunts of extremist congresspeople jockeying for power and then one about a girl in Tuscaloosa whose lemonade stand had raised over $700,000 for MS research.

"That's nice—"

"—Oh *fuck* me."

"*Whoa*," she said, genuinely surprised. "What's wrong?"

Whit was clenching his jaw and shaking his head as if he were in some sort of psychic pain.

"I just cannot stand this guy."

He nodded at a bald man with hexagonal glasses wearing a bright neon safety vest and a cheerful smile.

"He looks . . . nice," Merritt said tentatively, surprised by Whit's sudden vitriol.

"Just wait," Whit said, pulling to a stop as the drivers in front of them had their doors opened so their kids could pile in. Merritt watched as Whit's face shifted only slightly—from murderous to willing-to-seriously-maim—and then was surprised when the stranger tapped on her window.

"Oh," she said.

"Mm-hmm," was Whit's response, in an I-told-you-so voice. He rolled the window down. "Hello, Noel."

"Hello, Whit," the man beamed, placing his hands on the open window and leaning forward, far too close for Merritt's comfort. "We don't usually see you for pickup. And who is this?"

His tone, Merritt noticed, was akin to that of a grandmother asking after a college kid's plus-one at a family wedding.

Okay, she thought, *I'm starting to get it.*

"I'm Merritt," she said, so Whit didn't have to go into details.

"I *see*."

Noel winked visibly at Whit, whom Merritt felt tense next to her.

"I work with Whit," she explained. She wanted to add more, but then that felt suspicious, like she needed to give a reason for being in his car, as if it were *shady* or *fishy* or any of those words that mean *untoward*, when in fact, it was entirely *toward* that she was here. It was!

"Mm-hmm. Well, as much as I'd love to chat," Noel said, as if he weren't the one leaning through the car window, "I have a job to do." Another wink. "But I did want to ask if you've given any more thought to—"

Whit cut him off. "Carpool duty. Yes."

Noel's eyes went big. "*Yes?*"

"Yes, I've given it more thought, and no, I won't be volunteering. Would you mind sending Annie this way? The line is starting to back up."

Merritt tried not to laugh at the positively affronted look on Noel's face. In response, the man seemed to grip the car door more tightly as he actually lowered himself to be eye level with Whit, as if Merritt were invisible between them.

"You know, Whit," he said, his tone more serious now, "I've told you that I think it would be good for you, now that Helen has passed on to the Great Beyond—"

Merritt stifled a gasp at his absurd word choice. Whit cleared his throat as if to interrupt, but Noel barreled forth.

"—but I also think it's worth reminding you that we parents are expected to demonstrate a certain level of commitment to this school. It's in the handbook that each of us signs during the enrollment process every year."

Noel shrugged, as if offering this reminder was just an unfortunate duty. Merritt waited, training her eyes on the windshield before her. She wanted, desperately, to look at Whit. She could feel him radiating angry heat and the potential energy that would precede a punch to the face.

"You know what, Noel," Whit said after a pause, in a low voice Merritt had never heard him use before, "you're right. You're totally right. I think I'll call the head of school and ask when she thinks the goodwill should run out from the *million-dollar* scholarship fund established in Helen's name."

Noel pulled back slightly, but Whit continued.

"As *soon* as it does, and I mean the *minute* the required sympathy for my wife—who is *dead*, by the way, Noel, not in 'the Great Beyond'—the minute that sympathy runs dry, you can expect a call from me, just begging to throw on a high-viz vest and open car doors under your distinguished leadership. Does that sound like a deal?"

Merritt stared at Noel then—she couldn't resist. And to her pleasure, he looked as though he had been slapped.

"It does indeed." His voice was an enfeebled murmur. "I'll fetch Annie."

Merritt watched him go, enjoying the way even his gait seemed deflated and embarrassed.

"I'm so sorry," Whit said behind her, his voice entirely different now.

She turned to look at him, unable to keep from grinning. "Are you joking? That was . . . masterful. And it serves him right. *The Great Beyond*? Are you kidding me?"

"I *know*!" He leaned forward and gave Merritt's arm a single squeeze, clearly compelled by the relief of someone whose disdain is suddenly justified. The warmth of his touch was momentary and entirely chaste, but Merritt felt as if it traveled down her arm, through her shoulder, and straight into her chest.

She smiled, then masked the crackling feeling in her body with the words, "What a creep."

"Indeed," Whit said, as the back door opened to reveal a little girl with reddish hair in pigtails, wearing dark green corduroy overalls beneath a puffy lavender jacket.

Annie. Her pigtails were twisted imperfectly but thoroughly into endearing braids, and Merritt wondered whether Whit had done them.

"Hi, sweetheart," he said, as Annie climbed into the car, obviously tentative and confused. "This is my friend Merritt. She's the one who's helping me do some writing, and she needed a ride."

Annie closed the door, and Merritt turned around to face her, hyper-aware that the feeling in her body had shifted into a different kind of nervousness at meeting this girl—but she tamped it down, as she'd done with her desire to explain things to Noel. There was nothing untoward here, either.

"Hi, Annie," Merritt said, hoping her voice sounded kind but not condescending. "Do you mind if your dad takes me home on the way to your house?"

Annie shook her head no, her lips forming a weak smile that was undoubtedly powered by good manners. Merritt felt a surge of affection for this girl, and for her father, and for her mother, and then for Annie again, who had lost that mother so young but shared her hair and, Merritt suspected, still acted in accordance with what Helen had taught her about politeness to others.

"Thanks," she said, and she sent the word out like a hug.

*

Whit watched Annie in the rearview mirror as they drove.

"How was school?"

She was looking out the window. What was she thinking about all this? Annie was eight years old and smart. The mother of her closest friend, Liza, had remarried after a divorce, so Annie knew about stepfathers and stepmothers and parents with girlfriends and boyfriends, and God, why was Whit thinking about that now? That's not what this was, and he hoped Annie knew that.

"It was good," she told the window. "It was library day."

Merritt and Whit looked at each other, as if Annie were a comedian onstage who'd just said something that resonated with them both. Whit chuckled as Merritt turned around in her seat again—she was going to pull a muscle—to talk to Annie.

"You know, Mrs. Pryor is my mom."

Annie's eyes lit up in the mirror.

"She is?"

"She is. Did she read to your class today?"

Annie nodded. "She's been reading a chapter book to us about Gooney, um . . ."

"*Gooney Bird Greene*?" Merritt offered, and Annie's already gleaming eyes gleamed more.

"*Yes.*"

"I love those books. She used to read them to me, too. Lois Lowry, the author, is one of my favorites."

"Mine too," Annie said, and Whit bit his lip, positive that Annie had never read another book by Lois Lowry.

The remainder of the drive was filled with the two of them talking books and Merritt generously answering a series of questions about her mother ("Does she knit? I feel like she knits." "Does she have a TV?" "How many sweaters does she have?").

Whit felt what he often felt when he saw Annie just *being okay.* Warmth, like a candle in his ribs. Annie was okay. She was smiling. She was laughing. And Merritt was the one making her do it.

She really was a wonder.

CHAPTER THIRTEEN

That night Willa dropped off dinner. She had been doing so once a week since Helen died and still managed to be less annoying about it than Whit's sister had been, with her equally sympathy-driven phone calls. Actually, Willa's gesture was not annoying at all, owing to her frank, no-nonsense way and the fact that she removed all opportunities for resistance from Whit. She informed him that a weekly dinner was just something he would to have to get used to until she stopped enjoying cooking or the two of them had a dramatic falling-out.

Now her drop-offs served as weekly check-ins, away from Carafe and the threat of Ian Hoult bursting through the door, looking bedraggled and put upon by all his literary and commercial success.

"Hi," she said now as she walked into the kitchen where Whit was washing dishes. She never knocked. "Ramen tonight—homemade and, it must be said, very good."

She placed a large Dutch oven on the counter, then dug through the tote on her shoulder to retrieve four brown orbs.

"Soft-boiled eggs. Just made, still warm, I don't know how she does it. Peel them, cut them in half, and place them elegantly in each bowl of soup. Perfect for posting photos of your meals online, if you're into that sort of thing."

Whit must have made a face because she laughed and held up a hand.

"Which, I know you're not. I'm just saying, it's going to be a picture-perfect meal, and you're welcome."

Whit finished drying his hands and felt his face fall into a look of genuine gratitude.

"Thank you, Willa, as always."

She held up her hand again. "*Tsh.*"

"Willa!" Annie said from the doorway.

Willa turned and lowered herself so the eight-year-old could embrace her.

"You act like you're surprised to see me."

"No," Annie said, giving her another squeeze, "just happy."

Willa stood up, keeping a hand on Annie's shoulder.

"Stay close," she said, "because your dad still has not RSVPed to our Halloween party this weekend, and I need you to help me guilt him into going."

Annie looked horrified. "We're *not* going?"

Whit laughed, rubbing his forehead with a sink-warm hand. "Who said that?"

Annie looked at Willa, then back to Whit and waited. "We *are* going?"

He shrugged. Parties had always exhausted him. Now there was an added layer of discomfort from being out of practice, thanks to a year of social avoidance. But Willa's plan was working, of course. He wouldn't say no to Annie, not on Halloween.

"Sure," he said. "But I am not wearing a costume."

"I'm afraid costumes are required for entry when it comes to adults," Willa said. She turned to Annie. "*You* wear whatever you want. And there will be kids from school there, so bring a friend if you like."

She looked pointedly at Whit. "Same goes for you. I heard you had a friend with you at pickup recently."

Whit almost growled.

"If you say you heard that from Noel, I swear to God I'll—"

"I heard that from Noel."

Now he did growl.

"And I told him to stop talking nonsense. But . . ."

She faded out, and Whit shook his head, pressing both hands against his suddenly hot ears.

"No buts."

"I'm just saying, Merritt sounds like a nice *friend*, and Adrienne and I would love to meet her."

"Willa—"

"Really, I'm not saying *anything*, just that you should invite her. Shouldn't he, Annie?"

"Oh," she said, joining Willa in the Looking at Whit Intently Club. "Yeah, probably."

What was Annie thinking?

Willa gave him a wicked smile from above his daughter's head. He supposed that was settled then, too.

When Willa was gone, he sent Merritt a text.

Would you be interested in coming to a Halloween party with my writing group friend this weekend? Costumes, I regret to inform you, are required.

Merritt texted back almost immediately.

Oh, fun! I think I should be free. I'll check and get back to you.

Well. He'd better start figuring out what to wear.

*

When Whit's text came through, Merritt was lying on top of her bed with her jeans still on, scrolling through her socials on her phone. This was dangerous business. Two of the bookish accounts she followed had posted about *Serious Games*, earning an immediate, knee-jerk block. She had then gone back and unblocked them, on the off chance that these posters had seen some deep flaw in the book—she was begging for just one person to find some deep flaw—but no, they too were fawning about its smart critique of sexual politics and power dynamics in modern academia. Then Whit had texted, saving her from herself.

Sure! she had typed, before immediately deleting it in favor of Oh, sounds fun. Maybe! But then that sounded too cavalier.

Let me check my schedule.

Too uninterested.

I think I should be free! I'll check and get back to you!

Did she sound like a seventeen-year-old? So many exclamation marks.

I think I should be free. I'll check and get back to you.

Now *that* sounded like a man writing an email that did not need to be a reply-all.

Oh, fun! I think I should be free. I'll check and get back to you.

What—seriously *what* was wrong with her?

She sent it, and then waited an hour, hoping to give the appearance that her social calendar was not depressingly vacant, before texting to say she'd be there.

"It's not a date," she had told herself, out loud as she lay in bed that night. But even her own voice had sounded unconvinced.

Now, two days later, she was walking from her mother's house toward the home of the Barrett-Linds, which was located on Cork Street, like Goodenough Books and Carafe but on the other side of the village green. It was the residential side, made up of large, mostly whitewashed Victorians as well as traditional New England saltbox colonials.

As usual, Merritt was enjoying her walk, with the autumnal trees and autumnal breeze and the seemingly endless series of pumpkins: squat ones in muted oranges and whites that looked as if they'd been sat on, zucchini-ish oblongs that curved at the end like swans' necks, the bright bursts of almost sensually vivid red pumpkins, and the occasional verrucose gray oval ones. She carried a bottle of wine in one hand and had to hold her top hat to her head with the other because the breeze was picking up. But she didn't mind. In fact, Merritt felt especially at home beneath her indigo coat, in her sheer black cape and bell sleeves. She was proud of her costume, which was fun but not too over the top. She had spent the day trying to guess what the *vibe* would be, hating herself a little bit for caring and for continually thinking the word *vibe*, and eventually she decided on something that could be dressed down if the party turned out to be more of a masquerade-mask-slash-animal-ears-and-a-T-shirt event.

She arrived at the house that both the map on her phone and the collection of parked cars confirmed to be Willa's. It was one of the white Victorians—a Queen Anne, she thought—with a wraparound porch, a balcony above, and a pencil-shaped tower at one corner. Merritt opened the low wrought-iron gate and walked up the red-brick path to a porch lit by two fire lanterns.

She stood there for a moment. Merritt never felt nervous about social gatherings—being good at parties was secretly a point of pride for her. She liked to say that she had an introvert's brain in an extrovert's body, which wasn't exactly what she meant (what kind of body would that be?), but it made sense enough to her.

Why, then, did she feel a tremble in her throat? Why was the thought of meeting Whit's friends and their kids and whoever else might be here making her wish she'd said no to his text?

She knew why.

The door opened, exhaling a wave of mulling spices and citrus. It revealed a Black woman, shorter than Merritt and dressed in a baggy white wind-suit with three-quarter sleeves and a red stripe across the chest. In an arch over her short, curly hair was a thick white headband that covered both ears, except for a silver cross earring dangling from her right side.

"*Whitney Houston at the Super Bowl*," Merritt gushed, thrilled by the choice.

The woman's face broke into a brilliant smile.

"Yes!"

"Incredible," Merritt said, pulling her coat open slightly. "I'm—"

"*Stevie Nicks?*"

"*Yes!*"

Oh, she liked this woman.

"Two icons."

Merritt smiled. "Great minds."

"You look wonderful. Merritt?"

She nodded.

"I'm Willa. So glad you could make it."

"Thanks for having me," Merritt said, holding up the wine.

"Too kind." Willa took the bottle in two hands and nodded Merritt inside, closing the door behind her.

"I'm a big fan of your mom, by the way."

"Oh, me too," Merritt said. It was her usual joke response, because most people in this town seemed to love Kathleen Pryor.

Merritt looked around at the narrow, wood-floored entryway wallpapered in a blue William Morris pattern that she recognized from her undergraduate art history class. One child was chasing another up the stairs leading to the second story, and in the rooms beyond, she heard jazz standards and the jovial voices of a party in full swing. Candles were lit here and there, and the house was pleasantly warm, in contrast to the bluster outside. Willa's hand at her elbow offered its own warmth.

"Let me take your coat."

"Great, thanks," Merritt said, shrugging it off. She was trying to look furtively into the dining room and study on either side of her, listening for Whit's familiar voice, but apparently not furtively enough.

"Whit and Annie aren't here yet," Willa explained as she folded Merritt's coat over itself, "but if you'll let me put this away, I'll introduce you to Adrienne, and to Albie, if he hasn't run off too far with his friends."

When Willa returned, she led Merritt through the house, which was comfortably cluttered in the style of an English country house, and, less comfortably, crowded with people she did not know. In the kitchen—a pleasant sage-and-white affair—several people were gathered around a massive cheeseboard, admiring the food as well as the tastefully arranged pumpkins, candelabra, and mercury glass skulls. A stout white woman stood by the stove, ladling a plum-colored liquid into clear glass mugs.

"Adrienne," Willa called, and her wife looked up. She was older than Willa, and wearing a pitch-perfect Rockford Peaches costume, though the red baseball cap was tucked into the pocket of the apron she wore around her waist. She wiped a strand of straw-colored hair from her face and gave Merritt a soft smile that, in the glow of the kitchen and steam of the stove, made her look momentarily like a woman from an oil painting.

"This is Merritt."

"Hi," Adrienne said, reaching over a narrow wood-topped island on wheels.

"I love your costume," Merritt said.

"Can you tell what I am even without the hat? It itches, and I've been mentally composing a letter to the costume shop about it for the last half hour."

"Of course. You look amazing."

Adrienne did a mock curtsy, but she looked happy.

"Thank you. You're Whit's friend?"

Something prickled across Merritt's skin at the words. A disagreeable sensation. She knew what these women must think, and it embarrassed her. Was that it? Was she embarrassed that Willa and Adrienne thought—she might as well give it words—there was something between her and Whit?

There was *something*, of course, because here she was at this party, but in what capacity? Whit had texted to invite her (hardly a grand gesture), and he'd suggested they meet here (the opposite of romance), and he was bringing his daughter with him. Plus, he wasn't even here yet.

"I am," she said, answering Adrienne's question. "His friend and faithful servant."

"Friend and *savior*, it sounds like," Willa said with a pantomime of exaggerated relief.

Merritt laughed, gratified that Whit had evidently spoken well of her, or at least of the work they had done together.

"Well, he's saving me a bit, too. It's been inspiring me to write again."

"What do you write?" Adrienne asked, moving to the stove for a moment before turning back with mugs for Merritt and Willa as well as one for herself.

Merritt took hers gratefully and immediately sipped to stall.

"*Careful—*"

Merritt winced.

Adrienne laughed.

"—it's very hot."

"So I see," Merritt said, smiling through the sting. "I'm writing something for kids. Middle grade, I think. Or at least I'm trying."

"It sounds like you're on the road to doing it," Adrienne said, holding up her mug for Merritt to clink.

"I guess so."

Willa's hand found her elbow again. "You are."

She dropped her hand, but the kindness of it and of Adrienne's words lingered. Merritt brought her mug up to Adrienne's. Willa joined.

"Cheers."

"Already drinking without me?" someone said behind her.

Whit.

Merritt turned, trying not to smile, and had to stifle a gasp. The man had shaved. But not entirely.

"Nice mustache," Willa said, clearly meaning the exact opposite.

"Thank you," he said brightly, as if he didn't catch her tone.

"I think I made it pretty clear this was a costume-only event . . ."

"You did indeed," he said, nodding and holding his arms out in a pose. He was in a good mood.

"Gray pants, a mustache, and a green sweater with a pink button-down is hardly a costume, Whitacre."

"*Au contraire*," he said, looking at Merritt for the first time. His eyes shone like gray-blue river stones, and then he pulled a falsely disappointed face. "Though I'm guessing Merritt doesn't get it, either."

"I was going to say you look like Ned Flanders, but—"

He beamed.

"That's because I *am* Ned Flanders. See?" he said, turning to Adrienne and Willa, arms still raised.

"I didn't peg you for a *Simpsons* fan," Merritt said.

"Well, when one is confronted with draconian party rules—"

Willa let out a huff. Whit grinned.

"—it's an easy costume. But I did have a phase. And apparently, you did, too?"

She shrugged. "I contain multitudes."

He nodded, his eyes holding her in them.

"Yes, you do."

She cracked.

"But you're right. I've seen probably one, maybe two episodes."

Whit pretended to be shocked. "That's a pretty big gap in your pop culture knowledge."

"Don't worry. I've filled it with hours and hours of only the highest-quality reality television."

His grin shifted into something more subtle, more private—a joke for just the two of them.

"Where's Annie?" Willa asked, like a voice from another world.

"Oh, she ran upstairs as soon as she got here. I guess she thought that's where the kids were."

Why was Whit still looking at her?

"She was right."

"Mulled wine?" Adrienne offered.

"Please."

He broke his stare to take the glass mug. The four of them stood in a loose circle. Willa raised her drink again to toast.

"To . . ."

Willa trailed off, in thought.

"New friends," Adrienne said, with a firm nod in Merritt's direction, "and old ones."

Merritt couldn't help glancing at Whit, who was looking at her again, and who pursed his lips at her in what Merritt considered to be the world's first non-annoying example of the action.

The four of them clinked glasses, and then the air shifted in the way it does when a door opens.

"More guests," Willa said, heading that direction as Adrienne turned her attention to one of the couples at the cheeseboard.

"Do you want to—?" Whit asked with a nod in the direction of the living room.

Merritt nodded back, following him from the kitchen, which was getting steamy, into a well-appointed space that combined the same English-country-house style of furniture with splashy modern paintings and unusual light fixtures.

"Hi," Whit said, turning to look at her near the piano. She had never seen him grin like this before.

"Hi. Did you pre-party?"

"Did I what?"

Merritt gave him a look. "You're very smiley."

Whit put a hand on his chest. "I'm allowed to smile."

She waited.

The smile grew.

"But yes, we stopped at Annie's friend Liza's house before we came so they could put on their matching costumes. And the stepdad made me an old-fashioned. And then another. It's my first party in a while."

"And then you *drove* here?"

"The dad drove my car," he said, with a cheerful shrug, as if this fact was somehow delightful.

"You're tipsy."

"You're Stevie Nicks."

She bit her lip, pleased. "I am. Should you slow down on the mulled wine?"

"Should *you* slow down on the judgmental tone?"

They laughed. What was this? What were they doing?

Whit looked around the room for a moment. Merritt searched for a new topic. When she could no longer pretend to be taking a record-breakingly long sip of wine, she said, "Willa seems great. And Adrienne, too."

"They're the best. Truly. I think I would have died without them last year."

Merritt didn't know what to say to that.

"Do you know other people here?"

Whit looked at the current population of the living room, then back to her.

"Liza's parents are here somewhere. And there will be a few other parents from Annie's school—their son Albie goes there—but other than that . . ."

The front door opened again, and a man's voice said "Willa, *hello*." Whit's eyebrows rocketed so far up his forehead that it must have been painful.

"What?"

"She couldn't have," he said to himself, peeking around Merritt's shoulder, presumably trying to catch a glimpse of the entryway. Merritt looked, too, in time to see Willa hurrying toward them.

"So," she said, "I meant to tell you that—"

"Willa, you didn't."

She winced. "I did."

Whit's fingers flew to his hair like claws.

"Willa."

"I know."

"*Willa.*"

"I *know*," she said, throwing her hands up in defeat. "Trust me, I know, but I was at the store yesterday, buying *multiple* crates of wine, and he was there—"

"Probably because he wants to drink himself into some delusional Hemingwayesque state," Whit interrupted, before turning to Merritt in anticipation of the pot-calling-kettle-black look she was in fact giving him. *Don't*, he mouthed to her, almost laughing in spite of his obvious dismay.

"I don't know why he was there, Whit, but he saw me, and he said, 'Looks like you're getting ready for a party,' and I said, 'I am,' and then he just waited, and suddenly I was explaining myself to him. And before I knew it, I had invited him. I'm sorry for being polite. I never thought he'd actually *come*."

"*Of course he would come*," Whit hissed. "The man loves the sound of his own voice and forcing stories in which he is the hero onto unsuspecting bystanders, and where better to do that than—oh, hi, Ian. I didn't know you were coming tonight."

Merritt looked past Willa to see an almost comically frowzy man. Threadbare corduroys, a pilled navy sweater, and a navy duffle coat. He had an unlit pipe in his mouth and an oversized sailor hat on his head. Oh, *that* Ian. Ian Hoult.

"Call me Ishmael," he said with both hands against his chest, just enormously self-satisfied.

He looked ready to hug Whit, which apparently drove the latter to offer Merritt as a sacrifice. He grabbed her by the elbow and pulled her in front of him.

"This is Merritt Pryor."

Ian made a face of unvarnished delight, but it was impossible to tell whether it was directed at just her or at her proximity to Whit. He certainly didn't recognize her from the time she'd checked him out at the bookstore.

"Do I know you?"

Okay, so she had registered as a person with a pulse, but whatever validation she might have felt was undermined by the man's flirtatious eyes, as if the two of them had shared a secret. It was the way boys looked at girls in college, when they couldn't be certain whether they had drunkenly hooked up in the past. Merritt recoiled.

"I don't think so."

Whit realized his mistake and spoke again before Ian could.

"How's the *Atlantic* piece going?"

She could hear the pain in his voice at having to ask this and almost laughed. First Carpool Guy, now this. How many more men in this town had earned Whit's utter disdain?

Ian was evidently thrilled to have the subject raised and launched into a speech about how he couldn't believe *The Atlantic* continued to be interested in hearing from him. Whit caught her eye and she had to physically restrain herself from smiling.

"But now," Ian said eventually, "they want me to write something about this new Graydon Lyons novel."

Instant lightheadedness. Immediate shortness of breath. The words were a blow.

"I mentioned on a podcast recently that I was planning to teach it in my Life Writing and Autofiction course next semester at Plymouth College—they're having me back—and I suppose that ruffled some feathers, because, you know, Lyons is going out of his way to say it's neither of those things. But then, as I'll explain in the piece, that's *why* I'm teaching it. Beyond the fact that it's my prerogative as a professor—"

"Visiting professor," Whit interrupted.

Ian almost scowled but kept his cool.

"Indeed. But when it comes to what counts as autofiction, it's a game of inferences, and those inferences don't really include what Graydon Lyons has to say. Once a book is published, I don't actually care whether an author believes he's written something personal or not—that's for us to determine. And I'm fairly certain this thematic departure for Lyons has to do more with his own proclivities than it does with a desire to reinvent himself."

This second speech was accompanied by more hand flourishes than Merritt thought strictly appropriate for anyone who was not a nineteenth-century British dandy. The half of her brain that was not melting down like a nuclear reactor watched Whit as it was delivered, and her only source of comfort in this wretched moment was the way his eyes turned shark-dead as the skin around his mouth grew more and more taut. He was melting down, too, but while hers was a cold-sweat situation, Whit looked to be experiencing whatever emotions precede a *Dateline*-style crime of passion.

"That's really interesting, Ian," he said, in a voice that might have come from a text-to-speech phone app. Ian seemed to have sobered him up.

Sensing that Whit was about to make an excuse to get away from the man, Merritt heard herself asking, against her better judgment, "What makes you so sure it's autofiction?"

Ian seemed surprised that she was capable of further speech, much less apprised of the definition of *autofiction*. He looked at her again in the way you might look at a precocious child, and Merritt clenched her jaw.

"Have you read it?"

The words were saturated in condescension.

"Not yet."

Ian took a breath as if he were humoring her.

"Well, are you familiar with his work?"

"Yes," Merritt said. She wanted to stop there—this man didn't deserve her explanation—but she couldn't resist. "I've read everything else he's written."

His eyes widened, and his lips formed a smile that seemed to suggest she had passed some sort of test.

"Oh, well then. A true fan, I see."

"Well," was all Merritt could say, and when she looked at Whit, something passed between them. A sad sort of understanding, perhaps. Had he figured it out? Was this what dying felt like?

"Well," Ian said back, "then you know, I'm sure, that the man is a creative writing professor, like the man in the book. And after a truly negligible amount of snooping, I've learned that this supposed champion of progressivism *also* has a history of—how do I put this delicately?—unscrupulous behavior. He likes to *sample the merchandise* his university offers."

Whit laughed humorlessly. "He what?"

Ian looked at him. His face was suddenly prudish and disapproving. "You know."

"He *samples* the university's merchandise?"

"*Yes.*" Ian's posture was pure superiority, as though he would never stoop so low.

"So in this scenario," Whit continued, "the university is selling something that Graydon Lyons samples?"

Ian opened his mouth, his forehead crinkled.

"Well—"

Whit laughed again. Merritt wanted to hug him.

"So, what, Graydon Lyons likes to audit classes? Borrow T-shirts from the spirit shop? That doesn't sound as nefarious as all that eyebrow work you're doing would suggest."

Ian's hand went instinctively to the brows in question.

"No, you're overcomplicating it, I was just saying—"

"We know what you were saying, Ian," Whit interrupted, his voice now flat. "You're just not saying it very well. The metaphor seems to have gotten away from—"

"He fucks his grad students, how's that?"

Like Whit, Ian's voice had lost all traces of amusement, but Merritt hardly noticed as she absorbed the sheer forcefulness, the harshness, of the verb. Sweat spread across her body like sudden condensation. Her stomach felt as if she were looking over the edge of a sharp precipice.

"As I said, Ian, we get the picture." Whit turned his whole body to look at Merritt, positioning himself between Ian and herself. "Would you like to get some air?"

"Yes, please," she said, her voice faint.

Whit's eyes filled with an empathy that was equally comforting and mortifying.

"The back porch is that way," he said, taking her empty glass mug. The fingers of that hand brushed hers as his other palm came to rest, just briefly, on her elbow. "I'll get us refills and meet you there."

He held her eyes in his for a moment, then nodded once and walked toward the kitchen, and she watched him go.

"It was nice seeing you, Ian," he said without looking back.

Behind her, Ian scoffed. She looked at him, almost against her will.

"He's been like this since his wife passed," he sighed, shaking his head. "Prickly. Sad how grief changes people."

Fuck you, she wanted to say.

Get a fucking life, she wanted to say.

"I guess so," she said instead. "Nice meeting you."

"You too. I'm sure I'll see you around."

He did something with his eyes that wasn't quite winking, then left.

There wasn't space in her brain for much besides *he fucks his grad students*, but there was space enough to hate herself for not being the first one to walk away.

CHAPTER FOURTEEN

"Where's Merritt?"

Whit looked up from the pot of mulled wine. Willa was leaning on the counter in her impeccable Whitney Houston costume. Behind her, a woman in a devil suit chatted with a man who was dressed as either Jennifer Lopez or someone from *Drag Race*, or perhaps both.

"She's on the porch, recovering from an Ian Hoult encounter."

He set his jaw to keep from elaborating on his suspicions.

Willa made a not-surprised face, then said, "It's pretty cold out there."

"I'm bringing her a hot beverage."

He looked at Willa, who nodded and then waited.

Whit set two full mugs on the white countertop.

Willa was still waiting.

"What?" he said with an impatient sigh.

She raised her eyebrows. Whit lowered his.

"What are you trying to say?"

"I'm not saying anything."

"But you are."

"Whit, you've been grinning like the Cheshire Cat from the time you opened my front door all the way until you had to speak with my worst-ever party guest."

He bit his lip now at what felt like a smile threatening to return. Willa was right. He'd been grinning since he got here, but his brain hadn't yet worked out why. With some effort, he forced his face into something neutral.

"Oh, Whit," Willa said. She shrugged. "You should probably go check on her."

Willa gave him a closed-mouth smile, and as she turned to speak to the man with enormous fake breasts, something happened in Whit's brain. It was like ice shifting in a cocktail glass or a log settling in the fireplace.

Oh, Whit.

*

Merritt was sitting on the steps, her coat tucked beneath her to form a barrier between the frigid stone and her body. The cold front was blowing in at full force, making her hair whiz around her head. Who knew where the top hat had gone. Her breath puffed out before her, making her yearn for a cigarette, a feeling she immediately found repulsive because she had only ever smoked with Graydon.

He fucks his grad students.

The words were dehumanizing, yes, but it was more than that. It was that people, even this man Ian Hoult, thousands of miles away, seemed to know and be disgusted by this fact. It was that she was just one of the grad students, one face in a series of who knew how many. She knew this, she had known this, had learned this was his pattern. None of it was a surprise . . . and yet. *He fucks his grad students.*

How long would she feel this way? It wasn't as if she was sitting around grieving. She wouldn't even describe what she was feeling as missing him, now that she knew what he was. Graydon Lyons had been endlessly captivating, and he had made her feel smart and interesting. She had seen things with him—the world behind the curtain that separated writers like him from everyone else—and she had loved that. She had loved him. But Graydon Lyons was also a miserable, emotionally stunted narcissist, and she was glad to be free of him.

No, what she felt was some mixture of shame and self-loathing. If people knew she was not only one of the grad students but also *the* grad student from the book . . . God, she could die. She no longer felt that her stomach was going to expel its contents but just the opposite—as if her stomach were a great, yawning ravine she herself was in danger of falling into.

"Hi."

She turned to look at Whit, framed by the glowing white shape of the house behind him and the dangling café-style bulbs above. The mugs in his hands were overflowing with steam, and she took one gladly as he lowered himself to sit by her on the steps.

"Jeez, it got cold."

"Oh. Yeah." Merritt took a heartening sip.

She looked at Whit, who seemed tentative, careful. Was he embarrassed, too, now that he had figured her out? She was almost certain he had figured it out.

"It's me."

Saying it felt like passing a kidney stone. She had to get it out.

Merritt turned her head from Whit to stare across the shadowy yard as she spoke.

"The Graydon Lyons book. It's about me."

She felt him waiting next to her.

"You knew, didn't you?"

Whit shifted positions. "I had an inkling. With where you went to school and that stuff about the bad breakup. And then when Ian brought it up, I could just tell . . ."

Merritt threw her head back.

"I'm in hell."

Whit laughed, the barest wisp of something compassionate escaping through his nose.

"Only I could tell, I promise."

She looked at him then, and he gave her a gentle smile whose meaning was illegible.

He fucks his grad students.

"Well," she sighed, "that's good, I guess. God, that Ian man is annoying."

"A wretched human being," Whit agreed. "These days, at least. We used to be friends, and he used to be all right. A little snooty, but in a funny way, and it didn't matter as much because he didn't have the fame to back it up. It's harder to overlook haughtiness when there's an actual reason for it."

He scanned the darkness in front of them. Was he being respectful? Avoiding her glance? Was he worried he'd catch some sort of disease from her?

Oh, she was embarrassed. He was embarrassed, too, it seemed. She gripped the warm mug in her hands, a lifeline, and then said the horrible thing out loud.

"We weren't just fucking." She winced. "I *hate* when people use that word like that. But that's not what it was. We were in love. Or I was at least. God."

She winced again.

"That sounds pathetic. He would probably say I threw myself at him or something, when really, he went after me."

She was saying too much. She looked at Whit and immediately found she could not bear the weight of his soft, sweet glare.

"I just mean, it meant something to me, and then I realized what I was becoming when I was around him, and so I ended it."

Merritt had not actually told anyone this. People seemed to assume Graydon had broken things off with her, and she had been so desperate to put it all behind her that she hadn't bothered to correct them. What did it matter in the end? They were done. She was out of his life. But now this book had dragged her back in.

"I ended things because I didn't want to be the person he was turning me into." She was repeating herself. "He was this magnanimous man, invested in me and my career, and he would say things about the importance of women's voices and my voice in particular, but it was all hollow. He just wanted me around and said what he needed to keep me there."

Rambling, she thought, *you're rambling.*

"And then he went and did *this*."

Merritt raised her hands, at a loss.

Whit looked at her then. She watched his white teeth push into his now-beardless lower lip, and she was struck by the thickness of his mustache, the fullness of his lips and eyebrows.

"Merritt," he said at last, and her name coming from his mouth was like a bell piercing the silence of a church service. He pulled her mug from her grasp—her emotional support mug!—and set it on his other side. Then he turned on the step so that his knees touched hers, and her hands, which felt like they were flailing wildly, looking for something to grasp, were taken into his.

"You don't have to explain yourself."

The words did not immediately compute.

"Yes, I do," she said. "Ian said that—"

"Ian is one of the most socially inept people you'll ever meet. Nothing he says should be taken seriously."

Merritt's heart was pounding; she felt the places his skin touched hers with a sharp keenness, as though her other senses had dulled themselves to focus her energy on only those points of contact. It was really getting cold, but their fingers folded over one another like tiny cords of warmth.

She found herself speaking without really meaning to.

"But he was right, Whit. Apparently, this is just something Graydon does with people like me, and I was too stupid to realize—"

"Why are you defending him?"

"I'm not defending anyone, I'm just—"

"Putting yourself down?"

She pulled her hands from his to push her fingers through her hair.

"I don't know, Whit. It's just . . . he . . ."

Whit reached up for her hands again and pulled them down, slowly and carefully.

"So the book is about you," he said, all frankness.

"Yes. I think so."

Merritt felt her head dip low, pulled by shame. It hurt to hear him say it.

Whit's hands slipped from hers—God, he felt the shame, too—but then he leaned forward slightly, so he could look her directly in the eye. "Who gives a shit."

He enunciated each word so that they sounded like pebbles dropped one after another.

"That's easy for you to say." Merritt said this, not because she necessarily believed it, but because his face was close to hers and the heat from his body was palpable, a blanket of Whit-ness, and she needed to speak to avoid complete brain shutdown.

"It is easy, you're right," he said, still looking at her head-on.

She felt his leg push against hers. Her hands were back in his.

"But it's also the truth. Ian Hoult is a bonehead, and Graydon Lyons sounds like a real dick. He took your private life—the life you trusted him with—and made it into some lurid story that he knew would get him attention? Whatever. That's ruthless, Merritt. It's gross."

Finally, *finally*, Whit moved a few inches away, relinquishing her hands in the process. She found her entire torso turned his way, all on its own.

"But it doesn't say *anything* about you, because *you* are . . ."

And here at last the confidence he'd been pulsing with seemed to falter.

"You're . . ." he said again, and Merritt realized that their faces were closer together than they had been before. She could smell the wine on his breath, and beneath that, the old-fashioneds he'd had earlier, and beneath that, something like cedar and mint.

The idea returned to her with force that perhaps this night *was* something more than the casual, low-key thing she'd convinced herself it was. Whit's river stone eyes were heavy with emotion as he took a breath, and then they dropped to—it couldn't be—but they did, they dropped to her lips, and her eyes dropped to his.

She watched as he dampened them, and then they were moving, slightly open, in her direction. Merritt took a deep breath, feeling as though she was smelling all of him.

The door to the house opened.

"Dad," a voice called, and Whit slid several more inches away from Merritt.

There was Annie, dressed as Velma from *Scooby-Doo.* Willa and Adrienne's son—a twelve-year-old Beetlejuice—was standing behind her.

Annie looked intrigued at finding the two of them on the porch, confused even, but then her mind clearly turned to more important things.

"Can you come inside? Albie and I want to ask you something."

Whit shot a look at Merritt, both wary and apologetic, before turning back to his daughter.

"Sure thing."

Whit's face was still turned away from her, but Merritt could see the anxiousness in his body. She felt it in her own. What had Annie seen?

"Hurry," Annie said rapidly, and Merritt forced a smile at her childish desperation.

Slowly Whit looked back to Merritt, his eyes wide and jaw clenched in barely contained worry.

"Coming, sweetheart," he said, not turning from her. *Sorry*, he mouthed.

Merritt lifted a hand jerkily, as if controlling it with a spotty remote control, and waved dismissively.

Go, she said with her face. *Of course you should go.*

She sat outside for a minute longer, finishing her wine, nearly consumed by a buzzy feeling in her chest. Then she grabbed Whit's now-cool mug and—what the heck—threw it back as well. Almost instantly, the buzziness subsided into a warm vibration.

He had been about to kiss her. There was no doubt about it. She had been thinking about this moment, or something like it, and here, tonight, it had almost happened. Whit Longacre had felt what she felt, and he had been *this close* to doing something about it. And yes, Annie had almost seen them, and he had not liked that, but Merritt . . . she was pretty certain that he did like her.

She grinned, gripped a clear glass mug in both hands, and stood to her feet. Instantly, wooziness swirled in her head, like the shaken contents of a snow globe, and she steadied herself against an oversized terra-cotta pot. As she waited for the feeling to pass, a wisp of chilly uncertainty met the warmth inside her.

He was her new boss. This was her big break. She was going to be a writer.

What was she *doing*?

She went inside, deposited the mugs in the sink, and made for the front door, abandoning her lost top hat. It was time to go home.

*

Whit could not find Merritt anywhere.

The thing Annie had needed to ask him was about a picture she'd found with Albie, of the four parents, several years younger: Willa, Adrienne, Whit, and Helen, dressed as *Lord of the Rings* characters. Whit was, embarrassingly, a sad sexless imitation of

Aragorn, and Helen was resplendent in a blond wig, a pregnant Galadriel.

It hadn't really made sense to have a baby just then. They were two struggling writers. Whit had an agent and a manuscript on submission with publishers, and he was writing the occasional piece for regional travel magazines about local flavor—things he didn't have to actually travel to do. Helen was writing trade manuals by day, hating every second of it, and by night completing what would become *The Door in the Garden Wall.* They felt their pennilessness all the time, but they believed in each other so much, and then along came this baby, a girl, like they had wanted—and they were very, very happy. Helen looked so lovely.

"Albie said that's me in there."

"It is," Whit had said, resting his hand on the top of her head. "Your first Halloween. Do you think you dressed up in there?"

Annie had laughed. "In her belly?"

"Yeah," Whit said, smiling back. "Maybe you had a tiny little goblin or vampire costume."

"*Dad.*" She took the picture frame back. "Can I keep it?"

Her face was eager and hopeful and, Whit realized with a pang, a little bit sad.

Whit looked to Albie, who was in seventh grade, as if asking his permission—but of course, it was the other way around.

"I'm sure Willa won't mind," he said.

Annie beamed and clasped the frame to her chest, giving it one last look before handing it back to her dad.

"Will you hold it for me?"

"I will."

"Thanks, Dad." She dabbed at one eye with a rapid hand and then ran off with Albie to join the other kids upstairs.

Whit looked at the picture, their youthful faces, remembering what it had been like before Helen was a *New York Times* bestselling author and he was a *New York Times* bestselling author's husband. A relic from a different time. Something wriggled in his chest, and he let himself feel it for a moment: the grief and the longing for the woman he had only had for ten short years. But as he focused his eyes to assess his own face, it felt like part of him split in two. The Whit in the picture was exuberant, and the Whit of the present day felt a kinship with him that would have been impossible a month ago.

He missed his wife terribly. And he had tried to kiss Merritt tonight. Both things were somehow true.

But now he'd probably lost Merritt as well. He had looked for her all over Willa's house for at least fifteen minutes, and then his text—Where'd you run off to?—had gone unanswered. Whit could play dumb only for so long before he had to face the obvious truth: he had scared her away. The almost kiss, out there on the porch, was born from a swell of feeling that seemed to have filled his whole body, and he'd acted rashly. He'd known it then, in the moment, known he was being stupid, unprofessional, presumptuous, and now he was reaping the cost.

When he was sure she was no longer inside, Whit wound his way to the front door. It was pointless, he knew, and yet still he peeked into the lane before him. It was empty but for a spiral of dead leaves floating on the wind.

Whit closed the door and pressed his forehead against the wood, trying to ignore the sound of laughter and the faint strains of the Kidz Bop version of "The Monster Mash" filtering down from where the children played above.

God he hated parties.

CHAPTER FIFTEEN

When Merritt woke up, she thought she was back in Texas. In the split second before her eyes cracked open, she pictured the clean, white studio apartment she'd shared with Mrs. Robinson, an elderly shelter cat. Mrs. Robinson and the graduate student—adorable at the time, perhaps slightly unsettling in hindsight. Then she remembered that Mrs. Robinson had died of some horrible worm disease, and she had dropped out, and now she was here, in a high wrought-iron bed in her mother's guest room. The walls were painted a yellow Merritt found simultaneously infantilizing and suggestive of a nursing home. There was a whatnot full of knickknacks, and her bed had a crocheted quilt that had been made by a great-somebody in the past. But there was a window seat, beyond which was a grassy, tree-lined park where people sat on benches and played with their dogs and watched fireworks from blankets on the Fourth of July, and that was nice.

Merritt moved from her bed to sit by the window, allowing herself to feel like this was an accomplishment after the night she'd had. She brought Whit's novel, *The Hour of Matins*, with her, though she didn't feel like reading it, and eventually she found herself scrolling her phone.

After a half hour or so, she FaceTimed her friend Bebe—since last March, her sole confidant in the *Serious Games* nightmare—to regale her with the story of Willa's party. As she waited for her to pick up, Merritt felt only slightly horrified by the unbrushed, unwashed person reflected in her phone, knowing Bebe wouldn't care. But Bebe didn't answer. As Merritt wondered whether her friend was in class or off at some literary conference (the kind of thing you did when you were still in an MFA program), she felt even lonelier.

The knock at her door interrupting her loneliness was not necessarily welcome.

"Hi, honey," her mom said from the doorway. Kathleen Pryor wore a Foothills Craft Club T-shirt and cargo shorts: her gardening outfit. "Want to come help me in the yard?"

Merritt opened her mouth to respond, but then let her reclining, bedraggled state speak for her. Kathleen laughed and moved forward to sit on the bed.

"You came home sooner than I expected you to last night," she said in what Merritt recognized as her *treading lightly* voice. When she had explained to her mother that she was joining Whit for a party, Kathleen had resorted to the practice she'd maintained since Merritt was in high school: she bit her tongue, but made a great show of doing it, so Merritt knew exactly what was going on in her head.

Now her mother sat waiting on the bed for an explanation, and Merritt, who every day made a concerted effort to distinguish her current existence from her adolescence, chose to give her one.

"The party, um, took a turn."

Kathleen raised her eyebrows, and Merritt spent a moment ordering her thoughts. There were multiple ways in which this was true, but which "turn" should she expound on? It took only a few seconds to determine that, no, she would not be mentioning Ian Hoult and his investigation into the truth behind the novel, because Merritt and Kathleen had never yet discussed *Serious Games*—though she was sure her librarian mother was aware of its existence and had put two and two together. In classic Kathleen style, however, she had not mentioned it.

Instead, Merritt groaned, pushed her head back into a throw pillow, and then sat up to tell the story of Willa's party. After sharing a few well-chosen details about the beginning of the evening, she explained to Kathleen that eventually she had stepped outside for air, waiting for Whit, who eventually came.

"And we almost, well . . ."

"Uh-oh . . ."

". . . *kissed.*"

"Oh, darling, no. A fate worse than death."

"Don't joke."

Kathleen made a stern face and saluted her daughter. "Roger that. Why did you only *almost* kiss? Did he chicken out? Did *you*?"

"*No*," Merritt protested, "Annie interrupted us."

"Oh, poor thing."

"Her or me?"

Kathleen considered this. "Mostly her. But you, too, of course."

Merritt laughed. "I don't think she saw much. It was just, you know, immediately awkward, and I realized how stupid it was to kiss my brand-new boss."

"But you didn't kiss him."

"Well, no, but—"

"Maybe you should have. He's very cute."

"His wife just died."

Kathleen nodded, then added gently, "It *has* been over a year."

"But he's still sad, I think. And he has a daughter, and I just *know* she's still sad. How could she not be?"

"Poor thing," Kathleen said again, then waited a few beats. "These things do happen, though."

"That doesn't mean they're a good idea."

"It doesn't mean they're no—"

"I still need to work with him, Mom," Merritt interrupted. "Or maybe I don't. Maybe I should quit—"

"No," Kathleen said, shaking her head. "Anyway, he's the one who needs to work with *you*, from everything you've told me."

Merritt smiled at that. She knew her mom was right. Kathleen straightened up. She had always had a knack for knowing when to move on from conversations like this.

"All right, Merritt, you stay here and fret."

"Mom!"

"*Justifiably* fret. I'm going to work in the garden, but . . ." Kathleen raised her index finger. "You can't control when things like this happen—no, *don't* object. Listen to me: you don't get to choose how these things go. They just go, and maybe you go with them. Maybe you don't, but it's up to you."

Merritt smiled, begrudgingly.

"I feel like there's more."

Kathleen nodded. "There is: I will not allow you to quit working with him. If he makes you feel weird about last night, you remind him what you're made of, *just* in case he somehow forgets. All right?"

"All right, Mom."

Kathleen stood. "And I'd still welcome your help in the garden, when you regain the vigor required to get up and out of bed."

"I'm out of bed!"

"You're very much recumbent, dear," Kathleen called back, having already left the room.

Merritt laughed. She lay back against the wall and looked out her mother's window, down at her mother's low-fenced autumn garden, barely visible around the building's far corner. She had a good mom, and it had been good talking to her. Talking like two adults, at that. Except Kathleen had reminded her of one horrible truth: she and Whit still had to write a book together.

Oh joy.

*

Whit's parents had divorced when he was in ninth grade. The signs had been visible long in advance, and he and Evie, who was three years younger, had developed strategies to avoid the unpleasantness of their parents' slowly crumbling relationship. Whenever the cold war between Ned and Maureen Longacre bubbled up into full-scale aggression, the siblings would ride their bikes to the convenience store or the nearby playground. When the divorce was finalized, the back-and-forth between their parents' houses felt, to Whit, like he and Evie were soldiers on the move, constantly deployed and redeployed to familiar spaces with slightly different objectives: support Mom, cheer up Dad.

Evie was better at both missions. She could see where their mother's path needed easing ("Let's clean the kitchen before Mom gets home from her meeting") and sensed her dad's impending depressive episodes ("Star Wars marathon tonight?"). Whit had been happy to follow his sister's lead, despite being the older of the two, but it was his torn ACL in eleventh grade that really cemented her role as Emotionally Intelligent Surrogate Parent. Evie was the one who'd come to his room when he called out for help in that first week after surgery, and she was the one who made sure he remembered his PT appointments, regardless of which house they were at for the week. She was the one who'd always ask, "You okay, Bubba?"

She'd been checking on him ever since. So when Whit called Evie this time, she answered immediately.

"Whit? Are you okay?"

He laughed. "I'm fine."

She waited.

"Okay, that's a lie. But everything's all right."

"Annie—?"

"—is fine."

"Mom and Dad—?"

"—are alive and well. Seriously."

"Ok-*ay*," Evie said, her voice rich with restrained anticipation.

Whit clenched his jaw for a moment.

"It's just . . ." He rubbed his forehead. "I don't know."

Whit sighed. He was sitting on the back terrace, looking out over the wide lawn, on the other side of which he could see the woods through which he and Merritt had hiked. Behind the woods the land continued to rise into a hill, and beyond that was the sea.

"I am *worried* about Annie."

This was not the only thing that had compelled him to call his sister, but it had been where his mind landed after the party. He both did and did not want to talk about the mistake he'd made with Merritt, and the image of *Lord of the Rings* Helen was hanging like haze before his eyes, twisting his humiliation over Merritt into something more complicated.

But when he squeezed those thoughts out of his head, his memories returned to the dull feeling that had wormed its way into him as he held the picture frame and then looked at Annie's hopeful face. He'd focused on his daughter.

"I don't know what to do about her. She seems . . . most of the time she seems really okay, but the other day she was clearly upset after school, and then later I found her crying in bed, and she wouldn't tell me why. Even after I pressed. I've asked her a few times since, too, and she won't budge."

"Oh, Whit," Evie said, and unlike the irritation Whit normally felt at her displays of sympathy, the gentleness in her words nearly broke him. He felt like he had at age twenty when he called home after being dumped at college. The sound of his mother's voice, her chipper hello, had sliced through him then, and his next words had come out all weepy.

Whit did not cry now, but he did take a deep, settling breath.

"I know," he said at last. "It's pathetic."

"Shut up," Evie scolded. The intensity of her drive to protect her older brother, even from his own harsh self-critiques, made him laugh.

He told her then about the party and Annie finding the picture.

"Wait," Evie interrupted, "who's Merritt?"

"What?"

Whit hadn't even realized he'd said her name.

"You said you were on the back steps with Merritt when Annie showed up. Who's Merritt?"

Whit's free hand clenched the bench beneath him for reasons unknown. Fine, half-known. Okay, reasons fully known.

"She's the one who's helping me," he said after too many seconds. "With Helen's book."

The silence on the other end of the line suggested that his voice had done something weird. And just when he'd been desperately trying to make it sound normal, too.

"And now she's coming to parties with you?"

Whit let out a huff of exasperation. "Yes. Don't."

"Okay," Evie said, trying and failing to sound casual.

"That is not why I'm calling, Evie."

"I didn't say it was."

"But you're implying—"

"How can I be implying anything, Whit? I asked two questions and then said '*Okay.*'"

Whit, the writer of the two of them, did not have the words to respond to that.

"Fine. Whatever." A weak defense. Whit rubbed a hand down his whole face.

"But if I were . . ." Evie began.

Whit laughed despite himself.

"No, it's not like that," he said, fully aware that he was lying. It was at least partially like that, though speaking it aloud felt impossible. He wanted to ask Evie, *Am I evil for even thinking of kissing another woman? Would Helen be horrified? Am I going to ruin Annie's life? Should I be shunned?*

"But," he said instead, "Annie found this picture of Helen. And she begged me to keep it, and she was so happy to have found it, but I could tell she was sad, too. And she just won't talk to me about it or anything, and I don't know what to do."

He paused. He sensed her waiting for him to say more, so then he added, "That's all."

"Of course you don't know what to do," Evie said, slowly, measuredly. "No one tells you how to parent a child who's lost her mother."

"Well," he mused, "there are books."

She laughed.

"Has it gotten that bad? Are you reading the grief books Mom sent you?"

Whit smiled, too. "It has not gotten *that* bad."

He stood up. He hardly ever sat still while talking on the phone, and he was feeling a bit more like himself now. Whit leaned against the stone wall that limned the back terrace, comfortable in the silence.

"I think this is all normal," Evie said eventually. "Everyone processes loss in their own way, including kids, and—I'm about to give you unsolicited advice, so brace yourself—but I think the thing to do is just to be there for her, and be patient with her, and let her know that her feelings, whatever they are, are allowed. She knows she's safe with you. When she's ready, she'll talk. So don't freak out."

"I'm not freaked out."

Evie laughed at that, and even over the phone, Whit had the sense she was laughing in his face.

"Whit, you called me. To talk about your feelings. Two things that are enough to make me consider the possibility that you have been *body-snatched*."

Whit was pacing in the grass now. He paused to look at the popcornlike clouds above him.

"Tough but fair," he said through a sigh.

"Anyway," Evie said, with an air of finality, "I need to go, but I have a couple of things to say to you, and I'm trying to figure out what order to say them in."

Whit began pacing again, suddenly wary.

"Okay. Maybe do the less painful one first."

He could almost hear her eye roll. "Neither one is painful, but you might be annoyed with me. Okay, fine, the first one is this: I am not going to press, but I am signaling to you my interest in this Merritt woman—that's it, end of statement. I am interested."

Whit's mouth hung open slightly, unsure of what to say, until finally he went with, "Okay. Statement acknowledged."

Evie laughed. "All right, and the second thing is . . . listen, Whit, I know you are essentially fine, because you are always fine."

Whit waited.

Evie waited.

"Okay," he said eventually.

"And I really do think you have the Annie stuff under control. But . . . okay, don't take this the wrong way. I am not judging or critiquing you or anything like that."

She trailed off, and Whit predicted, accurately, what she was going to say next.

"I just wonder if it might be good for you both if I came to stay with you for a bit."

"Evie—"

"Don't be defensive, it's just a thought. Édouard is neck-deep in some case, and he hardly has time for me anyway, and you know I can work from anywhere, and—"

"Evie," Whit said, surprising even himself, "I think that would be great."

The pause on the other end of the line was so pronounced that Whit repeated himself.

"Did you hear me? I said I think that would be great."

"I heard you all right," Evie said, her grin audible. "I'm just seriously, *seriously* weighing the body-snatcher possibility, that's all."

"If you annoy me, I will change my mind."

"It's too late," Evie laughed. "I've already started packing."

CHAPTER SIXTEEN

Evie didn't mess around. The next morning, a Sunday, she texted to say she had bought a plane ticket and would be landing in Boston Monday at noon. He felt the pinch in his chest that he often experienced when he got something he more or less wanted and then immediately second-guessed both the wanting and the thing itself.

He had been cheered by the thought of Evie in the house for however long (a week? two weeks? a month?), playing board games with Annie, helping with carpool, and noticing whatever ghastly household things he'd let go before setting them to rights again in her capable, attentive way. Why, then, did he feel something that wasn't quite dread but certainly wasn't excitement, either?

Sitting on the freshly made guest-room bed, he ignored that thought in order to text Merritt.

Hey Merritt. My sister is flying in tomorrow as a last-minute thing, and I don't think we'll make it back from the airport until time to pick Annie up. Then I have my writing group Tuesday. See you Wednesday?

He headed down to the refrigerator, which he planned to clean out to avoid the silent shaming Evie was destined to give him when she discovered four separate weeks-old takeout containers hiding in the back.

No worries, Merritt texted as he stood there, head in the fridge like Robin Williams in *Mrs. Doubtfire*.

That was it. *No worries.*

No "See you then," no "Oh, that's nice."

For the first time, he felt defensive. He had tried to kiss her, yes. That was stupid. Misguided. Deranged even. But it had felt right in the moment, and they had had a good time when he arrived, and he had also valiantly saved her from Ian Hoult—oh. Ian Hoult.

Whit retraced what had happened back there with Ian Hoult and Merritt. First, Ian's grandstanding about his class and autofiction and his next *Atlantic* piece, and Merritt on the back porch, offering him a confession. Vouchsafing a true and painful thing to him. *We were in love.* And then he'd gone and tried to kiss her, and they hadn't spoken again about what she'd revealed to him.

His mind flinched at the thought and changed gears as he purposefully turned to the fact that she was apparently the inspiration for a popular novelist's juicy new book. He tried to imagine how he would feel if Helen had put him in one of her novels, or how Helen would feel if he'd done the same to her. Sharing with the world even the most glowing portrayal of someone he knew felt taboo, yet here was Graydon Lyons dropping Merritt into some sort of vengeful takedown dressed up as high art.

The face Merritt had made, explaining things to him on that cold step, had been one of deepest shame and regret. Why hadn't he worked harder to prove that he wasn't the kind of person around whom she needed to feel those things . . . instead of *trying to kiss her*? He was someone who had spent much of his early life being embarrassed by most parts of himself. These days it wasn't shame that disgusted him but the lack of it in the Lyonses and Hoults of the world. Why hadn't he said that out there on Willa's porch? Maybe she would be justified in thinking he was no better than them.

Should he text her again?

No, he would wait until Wednesday, when he would be radically normal in her presence, not at all like a crush-stricken teen, and then he'd bring it up only if the opportunity presented itself with undeniable clarity. He would say something to let her know how things stood for him, and how he saw her no differently from before, and how really, to love someone was the brave thing to do—

The phone buzzed again, and thank God.

It was Merritt.

Actually, I'm taking my mom to a doctor's appointment on Wednesday. Thursday okay?

Fine then. Radical normalness could wait until Thursday.

*

Whit did what he always did, which was to arrive at the airport far earlier than any sane person would think necessary. He felt this was excusable when he was the departing traveler, but he wasn't. He was here to pick up his sister, and he now had an hour and a half to kill, so he found himself doing the other thing he normally did in situations like this one: driving around, today in the Seaport District, looking for a bookstore that also sold coffee. He settled on a place that was more industrial than he preferred, with lots of tall glass windows and dark steel beams, but at least the music was ambient and soothing, and the Americano he now sipped as he walked the aisles was hot and strong.

Whit's most prosaic I-am-a-writer feature was his ability to spend hours and hours at a bookstore and never be bored. In a normal year, he was a regular at Goodenough back in Whelk Harbor. He'd become fast friends with Moishe, the nice older gentleman who worked there, while mostly ignoring the nosy questions Diana asked whenever she spotted him. But he hadn't left the house much at all lately, and this was his first trip out of Whelk Harbor in some time. Now here he was, alone, surrounded by stories and possibility. *This*, he thought to himself, *is nice.*

The coffee bar was at the rear of the shop. Holding his cup and *The Remains of the Day*, Whit slowly made his way through the

FICTION section toward the front, where the NEW RELEASES were. The Ishiguro book was an old favorite, and he'd been wanting to reread it, but his copy had gone missing. When he reached the MYSTERY subsection, he hesitated for a long beat, then shrugged and made the turn into the little enclave. His eyes scanned the shelves for the Ls, and there it was: his life's work. There were several copies of *The Hour of Matins*, his first book, and then a smattering of the later works, with more copies of his last release, *The One Keeping Vigil*, already in paperback. His agent would want him to alert the booksellers of his presence so he could sign the merchandise, then post about it online—"If you're in the Seaport District, there are signed copies at . . ." But Whit was feeling very satisfied in his silent aloneness today, and so he merely dragged a finger across the spines and then made his way to the CHILDREN's section, hardly thinking about what he was doing.

There was an entire Greenwood Castle shelf, with the four extant novels and the companion texts, plus stuffed animals, journals, sticker sets, pins like the one Merritt wore on her Foothills School lanyard—the whole kit and caboodle. Atop the shelf was a cardboard cutout with enlarged illustrations of the books' three main characters. Whit could have found this depressing: the sharp contrast in the degree of fanfare for his books and his late wife's. Instead, he felt a warm sense of pride. How many people could say they'd made something like this before they died? And how many others could say they knew someone like that?

The glow quickly faded, however, when his eyes wandered over to another shelf in annoyingly close proximity to the Albright Longacre section. There a handwritten chalkboard sign read: SERIES TO HELP YOU SURVIVE THE WAIT FOR GREENWOOD CASTLE 5.

Whit gripped his Ishiguro and sighed. Then he looked back at the veritable altar dedicated to his wife and resumed his trudge toward NEW RELEASES. There was a Claire Keegan book he'd been meaning to buy and a new Ann Patchett, and, oh God, there it was. The new Graydon Lyons, in between a Min Jin Lee and an Emily St. John Mandel. Whit caught himself looking over his shoulders before picking up a copy, then shaking his head at himself. No one would catch him in the act here.

He held the book in his hands, feeling a bit like someone with an issue of *Hustler* out in public. It did feel indecent to be holding it now that he knew it was definitely about Merritt. It felt like a betrayal, too, but then something in Whit—perhaps the devil on his other shoulder—told him that was silly. Books were books. Anyone could read anything. To behave otherwise was to get dangerously close to aligning with the book-banning idiots of the world, and anyway, Merritt hadn't said he *couldn't* read it, had she? And who was he to be told anything anyway?

Whit lowered his stack of books to his waist and shook his head again. He was, of course, full of shit. He wanted to read it, and his conscience could be confronted later. Right now, he needed to be heading in the direction of the airport. (Evie's flight would land in a mere forty-five minutes!) He hefted his books—Ishiguro, Keegan, Patchett, Lyons—and headed to the register.

*

Evie was nowhere to be seen on his first lap around the pickup lane; nor could she be spotted on his second lap, or the fourth, but by the fifth time around she was standing there smiling, with her light brown hair in a ponytail poking out the back of a Yankees cap, and the rest of her covered by sunglasses, a fawn-colored tweed trench coat, white sneakers, and jeans.

Evie waved enthusiastically as he pulled to a stop, and she gave him an enormous hug when he reached her to help with her two bags.

"Hi, Bubba," she said.

"Hi, Evelyn."

She gave him a light shove because she, like Willa, hated her full name.

"How was your flight?" he asked as they loaded her luggage into the back of the Range Rover.

"Fine. How was your drive? Did you get here at 6 a.m.?"

"Ha-ha," he said, closing the trunk and moving to the driver's seat. Once they were both seated and buckled in, he looked at Evie. "Thanks for coming."

She beamed at him. "Seriously. I'm so happy to. And excited to get out of the city for a bit."

Whit pulled the car away from the curb. "Aren't you sad about leaving Édouard?"

Evie laughed.

"I'll survive. He's the one you should worry about. He's hopelessly in love with me. And he'll have no one to show his fancy little outfits to with me gone."

She had stowed her trench coat in the backseat and he could see that she was wearing a designer sweatshirt underneath. Evie had been wildly popular in high school and college, and she now enjoyed a minor degree of fame, thanks to Édouard's former hockey career and his enduring reputation as one of the best-dressed players in the game.

"You're one to talk, dressed like the wife of a professional athlete."

Evie made a face at him. "Don't be rude."

"How can stating a fact be rude? You are the wife of a professional athlete."

"*Former* professional athlete, and you used a tone."

"Yes, that is one of the requirements for producing speech."

"Can you turn around? I'd like to go home now."

Whit laughed, and they spent the remainder of the drive alternating between teasing each other and catching up. Evie asked about Merritt only once, and he explained their working arrangement before redirecting the conversation to focus on the actual logistics of finishing Helen's book. Evie let him.

He was really very glad she was here.

But not nearly as glad as Annie.

"Evie!" she squealed when the back door opened in the carpool line at the Foothills School.

"Annie!" Evie said, matching her niece's enthusiasm.

Annie scrambled over the console to squeeze her aunt while Whit scanned the carpool line for Noel. When he found him, Noel saw him, too, but rather than approaching the car, he only waved meekly. Whit almost grinned, wishing that Merritt were here to see this.

"So," Evie said as they drove away, "how's third grade? Tell me everything."

Annie hardly needed the invitation. Within fifteen minutes, Whit had learned more about the inner workings of Annie's life than he had in the past two months—who her new friends were, what her teacher was like, math concepts she was finding especially hard to learn. And then, in response to a single question of Evie's, she spilled her guts about what had been bothering her. She had been crying herself to sleep over some drama between her, her friend Liza, and a new girl at school, but the issues had been resolved and things were now back to normal.

Whit felt shame folding over him, like a thick quilt stitched through with worry. Why hadn't Annie been able to tell him this? How much else had he and Annie not talked about? How many things had he forgotten to ask?

"And," she said from the backseat as they rounded the turn to the house, "today was library day, and Dad, I got another Lois Lowry book."

She was rummaging through her backpack as she spoke, until she came up with a copy of *Number the Stars* in her hands.

"Oh," Whit said, "that's one of my favorites—but I didn't read it until I was nine or ten."

Annie grinned at the rearview mirror. "Mrs. Pryor told me she thought my reading was advanced enough."

Whit caught a glance from Evie out of the corner of his eyes and grinned back, proud. "I'm sure it is."

"And she said it's one of Merritt's favorites. Will you tell her I got it?"

Whit felt his eyebrows rise and cursed them for the betrayal. Evie's throat made a little sound, and if Whit hadn't been driving, he would have closed his eyes rather than bear the weight of her now full-on glare.

"Definitely," was all he said, resolutely ignoring the giddy, villainous way Evie was tapping her extended fingertips against one another.

*

After dinner, Evie volunteered to read with Annie before bed while Whit cleaned up the pizza night debris in the kitchen. When Evie came back downstairs, she was looking mischievously at him.

"I've been exceedingly good, Whit."

Whit finished wiping crumbs from the counter into his hand before he stood up and looked at her.

"I do not like where this is going."

Evie placed her phone on the counter and leaned against the fridge, arms crossed and feet bare. She was wearing sweatpants and a huge Montréal Carabins T-shirt that was clearly Édouard's from college. Whit felt like they were back in one of their parents' kitchens.

"You have a young woman coming into your house—"

"She's basically my age."

"—writing Helen's book for you—"

"*With* me."

"—and Annie tells me that she's picking her up in the carpool line and that, by the way, she's cool and has cool green-framed glasses—those are hard to pull off—and also she asked me if you two were boyfriend and girlfriend."

Whit felt his mouth open, close, and open again. He leaned back against the counter and crossed his own arms.

"She did?"

"She did."

"And you said . . ."

"I said, *Oh, I don't know, your dad doesn't tell me anything, so let's find out together.*"

His eyes widened. Evie shook her head and rolled her eyes to show she was kidding.

"I said you two were coworkers, and that lots of times boys and girls are just friends."

Whit sighed. The two lapsed into silence.

"Do you want some tea?"

Evie jabbed a finger at him. "Don't stall."

"I am not stalling, there is nothing to stall about."

"*Are* you just friends, or do you like this similarly aged woman?"

"What kind of question is that?"

"Literally the only question anyone else would ask in this situation."

Whit started walking toward the living room, and Evie followed.

"You're not answering me, Whit. And what about the tea?"

Whit stopped, dropping his head back for a moment before turning to look at his sister.

"Evie." He sighed. "Do you know why I asked you to come here?"

She gave him an incredulous look.

"I offered, actually. But yes?"

He nodded.

"Right. We lost Helen. And you're here to help us. Because we're having a hard time."

He shrugged, refusing to feel guilty about these words because they were true. Annie's question had meant that they were all he could think about right now.

Evie's incredulity softened, and she gave a solemn nod and disappointed sigh.

"All right, fine, Whit. I'm sorry."

"Don't be sorry. But definitely do chill out on the . . . whatever that line of questioning is called."

Evie looked like she was about to say one last thing before thinking better of it and changing direction.

"Of course."

He smiled, and then left the room, choosing not to interrogate why exactly the end of this conversation felt less like a victorious walk-off and more like a retreat.

CHAPTER SEVENTEEN

Merritt had been lying, of course. Kathleen did have a doctor's appointment, but not the kind she needed a ride to. Some small part of Merritt felt a twinge of guilt, trotting out her mother in this way and implying that she was older and more fragile than she was, but as she typed out the text message Merritt had been mainly focusing her energy on making sense of her own choices. She had delayed seeing Whit because of her confession about Graydon and because of the almost-kiss. Everything suddenly felt complicated.

Now, on Tuesday, Whit was at his writing group, and she was an hour away from finishing her long shift at Goodenough Books. It was the actual day of Halloween, and she had chosen manual labor in an effort to exhaust herself too much to worry about how she had put her wonderful new job at risk. She had unloaded boxes, rearranged the furniture by the fireplace, and, in the break room, organized the boxes to which decorations would be returned tomorrow, on November 1. She'd also brought the "General Fall" decoration crate out of storage and sifted through it to arrange its insides by type: turkey-based, cornucopian, vaguely pilgrim, leafy. Now she was reshelving books, dusting as she went, and intermittently helping customers while Huong worked the register.

When the bell above the door rang as she was crouching behind a shelf of manga, she had a vision of Whit entering with his sister. Merritt imagined her to be a beardless, more prototypically feminine version of her brother, and she wondered what he'd told her. In Merritt's mind, Whit had been the one about to do the kissing, but with the passage of time since the party, things felt fuzzier. What would the sister think? That Merritt was making a move on her grieving, single-dad brother? Or worse, what if Whit hadn't mentioned her at all? She was annoyed by how embarrassed the thought made her, and she scolded herself into remaining cautious and holding her chin high in defiance.

"There you are," said a man who was not Whit.

Ian Hoult, dressed today in a gray sweater with chartreuse stripes and faded green corduroys that clashed horribly.

"I knew I recognized you from somewhere," he continued as he walked in her direction, "but I couldn't put my finger on what it was until I got home and slept on it. Isn't that the way of things?"

Ian leaned on the chest-high shelf Merritt stood behind, peering at her with a troubling level of interest.

"Merritt, isn't it?"

"Yes. And your name was . . . ?"

He let only the vaguest look of surprise trace itself over his face.

"Ian Hoult. You have some of my books over there."

He nodded nonchalantly toward the FICTION section.

"Oh," Merritt said in her falsely cheerful customer service tone, "do we have some books on hold for you? I can grab them from the back, and then Huong will get you checked out."

She pointed over his shoulder, and Huong, who had been openly watching the interaction, raised her hand in a gleeful wave.

"I—well, no, I'm actually a novelist."

"*Oh*," Merritt said, as if perplexed. "I thought you wrote for, um, was it *Newsweek*? And I think you said you were an adjunct somewhere?"

Ian's eyes bulged as if he'd been shocked.

"For the *Atlantic*," he corrected her, his voice clipped. Then he seemed to remember himself. "And yes, I was also *invited* to teach some courses at Plymouth College. But my primary *thing* is fiction."

Merritt nodded like she would if Ian were a child announcing grand, unrealistic plans for when he grew up.

"How neat."

Again, Ian looked physically pained. "Yes. Neat. Well."

He stood up straight.

"Well, I'm actually here on a mission," he said, as if Merritt were the one keeping him talking. "I think I told you I'm writing an exposé about Graydon Lyons and his newest book, *Serious Games*?"

An electric bolt shot out from Merritt's gut to the end of each extremity. He had figured it out. This was the final moment before she was exposed once and for all.

"Yes," she said, softly.

"Well, I realized something."

Merritt's body was one large heartbeat.

"Yes?"

"I have misplaced all my copies of Lyons's earlier works, and I can't write about this new book unless I also reckon with his backlist."

He shrugged in a way he must have thought was endearing—and in that moment, it almost was. The weight on Merritt dissipated, and she nearly laughed. She was safe.

"Oh, okay. Did you want to see what we have available?"

"That would be lovely."

Merritt felt positively aerodynamic as she guided him through the store.

"So," she explained without looking back at Ian, "in most bookstores, including ours, the FICTION section is organized alphabetically by author."

"Yes," he said, his voice once again clipped, "I am aware."

"Oh, I just thought, since you seemed to need . . . well, anyway, here's the section with the *L*'s. And here are the Lyonses."

Merritt pointed to a row of books, mentally checking them off in her head: *Mission*, the revisionist history of the Alamo; *Saint Joseph*, which imagined that the bullets meant to kill Joseph Smith missed, turning the man into a proto–Billy Graham and reshaping the next century of American religion; *Blanche & Buck*, about two lesser-known members of the Bonnie and Clyde gang. There were others, along with the few stray copies of *Serious Games* that had not fit on the special dais, and looking at them together made her angry more than anything else. She had loved these books, had read *Mission* even before meeting Graydon, and the man had ruined those memories, like all those directors and producers whose films had been tainted by their loathsome treatment of women. Graydon was not Harvey Weinstein, not even close, but she didn't hate the idea of him doing a stint in prison.

Ian *hmm*-ed.

"I don't believe I see his short story collection here—the first thing he published?"

This was starting to feel like déjà vu. Merritt knew the book: *Down in Texas with the Rodeo*, its title taken from lyrics in a Bob Dylan song she'd listened to only once, and then only to say she'd heard it. But she played dumb now rather than further reveal her intimate knowledge of the man in question.

"Oh, is that right? Let's go see if we can order it for you."

"No," Ian said, shaking his head. "I'll need it faster than that."

"It'll only take a week at most."

Ian clicked his tongue, as if deeply regretful. "No, it looks like I'll have to resort to the dreaded Amazon."

He waved his fingers next to his face, as if describing a scary monster.

"Ah," Merritt said, "well, if you need it that badly."

"I do, I do. But these"—he held up a stack of Graydon's other books—"I'll purchase here."

"How generous of you," Merritt said, under her breath.

"What was that?"

"Huong will help you."

"Ah, yes."

Ian lingered where he stood.

"One more question for you, Merritt, although this one is a little more *fun*."

Oh God. From the look in his eyes, she knew what was coming.

"I was actually wondering whether you'd like to—"

A crash interrupted Ian, causing both of them to turn toward the register. On the floor in front of the desk lay the rotating display stand that normally stood on the counter. Complimentary bookmarks were scattered all over the floor.

"Oh *shoot*," Huong said in an exaggerated tone Merritt had never heard her use before. "I am such a klutz."

"Oh *gosh*," Merritt said as she walked toward the front of the store. "Here, let me help you with that. In fact, why don't I clean it up while you get Ian here sorted."

Merritt dropped to her knees and began slowly gathering bookmarks. She sensed Ian move behind her to hand his books over to Huong, who immediately began talking at a rapid clip about how she'd overheard him mentioning Amazon, and was he *sure* he didn't want her to place the order for him here? It would only take a minute, and he'd be supporting his local bookstore rather than a mega-capitalistic enterprise bent on denying its warehouse workers basic rights.

She jabbered on in that way until the man left with a haphazard "Thank you." Merritt made short work of the remaining bookmarks and popped up to look at Huong.

"You saved my life."

Huong laughed aloud—a rare occurrence.

"You had suffered enough."

"Seriously." Merritt stared up at the ceiling. "I think he was about to ask me out."

"Not on my watch."

Merritt smiled gratefully at Huong before she returned to the cart with the go-backs, thinking about the difference between Graydon and this man. His barely hidden condescension made picturing his classes at the college easy. She took pleasure in imagining the course catalog listing classes with names like "Cormac McCarthy and Friends" and "Norman Mailer Was Good Actually." Graydon, on the other hand, exuded natural, authentic modesty and championed the work of women and minority writers, whether they were his students or authors whose books were to be used as mentor texts. It was a quality that had *kept* Merritt in love with him, even when the cracks (his self-centeredness, his wandering eye, the way he mocked her when she mentioned the possibility of writing a children's book) began to show. Standing in SCIENCE FICTION now with an Octavia Butler book in her hands, she felt the familiar pang of shame for her blind spots. At least Ian was transparent in his efforts to turn her life into content and profit.

She shook away her thoughts and moved with the empty cart back to the register, where Huong was packing up.

"Where are you headed after work?" Merritt asked, more to distract herself than because she thought Huong would have an interesting answer. "Some fun Halloween party?"

"I'm taking an art class. At the Whelk Harbor Art Collective."

"Oh," Merritt said, then immediately realized her mistake. Of course the girl somehow looking cool in an overall dress and tights was on her way somewhere noteworthy.

"What?"

"Nothing, I just—"

Huong narrowed her eyes.

"Do you want to come?"

Merritt smiled, appreciative, as an idea solidified in her mind.

"No," she said, "but thank you. I have something else I need to do."

But Huong wouldn't let her off that easy. The bell tinkled at the entrance of Moishe, their evening replacement, and after their hellos, he walked off to drop his things in the break room, and Huong still waited.

"Well?" she said. "What is it?"

"What?"

"The something else?"

"Oh," Merritt said, now packing her own bag in the space where Huong had stood. "You've inspired me. I'm going to go write."

"With that sad dad you work for?"

"*No*," Merritt said, a little too intensely. She softened her tone. "With myself. For myself."

Huong smiled.

"Good."

"Yeah. It is."

*

From where Merritt sat writing in Carafe, she could see the street slowly begin to fill with costumed kids and their parents, all on their way, she knew, to trick-or-treat. She wondered if Whit and Annie were out there, with his sister, and then she went back to typing.

The document she was working in was so old that she'd almost expected moths to scatter from behind the file name after she double-clicked it. It was her unfinished manuscript. The words came surprisingly easily after so many stagnant months of doing things that were decidedly not writing. Writing with Whit, she realized, had been good practice.

As she wrote now and sipped her decaf coffee, she felt herself opening up, like a stubbornly coiled peony that has finally agreed to bloom. Whatever else had happened or not happened, this was who she was. A writer. And though Graydon had nearly crushed this part of her, and she had nearly let him, and though she had no idea what was next for her in nearly any category of importance, she was writing. For herself. And she was happier than she'd been in weeks, happier even than in those first days with Whit.

And another strange thing happened: writing like this, on her own, made her want to go back to writing with Whit again. To remind him that she was good, that he needed her, and that no amount of chemistry or the awkwardness it generated could change that.

She pulled out her phone.

Hey Whit. My mom's friend offered to take her to the doctor. See you tomorrow?

The man texted back with uncharacteristic alacrity.

Great, he said. Looking forward to it.

Merritt flipped her phone face down on the table.

She smiled to herself.

Me too.

CHAPTER EIGHTEEN

Merritt drove with purpose. She felt like the main character in a network TV series about a strong, smart professional woman who doesn't need a man to complete her. Something like righteous determination was animating her, giving every pump of the gas, every turn of the wheel, an edge of significance. She and Whit had almost kissed, and that was perhaps unfortunate, but she wouldn't let it derail this huge career opportunity. ("Huge career opportunity" was something they said on those TV shows.)

Today she was going to be *so* cool. The consummate professional.

She parked in her usual spot and allowed herself thirty seconds of staring at the house through narrowed eyes, nodding along to the Cranberries song playing from her car speakers. The opening credits were winding down. It was time to go in.

As she walked to the door, the song still played in her head, alongside the thought *What would Dolores O'Riordan do?* She would probably not have had as many scruples as Merritt did about eating in front of people (a quirk that had led Merritt, in her singularly focused state, to have lunch before leaving the bookstore), but that didn't matter. Today Merritt was devil-may-care. She was rock 'n' roll. She was—

She was staring at the open front door, which now framed one of the most beautiful women Merritt had seen in her life. Suddenly the last five minutes of her thought life became deeply embarrassing. This woman must never know she had mentally used the words "rock 'n' roll" to describe herself. She was wearing a light brown, ribbed mock-turtleneck tucked into jeans, which as a sentence was offensive to Merritt but in the present moment was somehow the chicest thing she'd ever seen.

"Hi," the woman said warmly. She had lips and eyebrows that were impossibly yet naturally full. "I'm Evie. You must be Merritt. I've heard a lot about you."

What an absolutely terrifying statement. A vision flashed before Merritt's eyes of grabbing this woman by the shoulders and begging her, "*What has he told you?*" Instead, Merritt smiled what felt like an incredibly stupid smile.

"Hi. I've heard a lot about you, too," she said, which was essentially a lie. *A lot? Really?*

"Come in," Evie said with a nod. "Whit ran out to get some tea, which he seemed to think was suddenly urgent, but he should be back any minute. It sounds like you've fully saved his life."

Evie had moved seamlessly from one subject to the next, but at these words, Merritt hesitated. In response, Evie halted on her track to the living room.

"He said that?"

"Maybe not in those exact words," Evie said, "but I got the picture."

"When?"

Her voice had gone all squeaky and, well, there went playing it cool. The presence of this woman had made Merritt short-circuit.

"What do you mean?" Evie asked. Merritt had expected her to look confused, but instead she and her perfectly threaded eyebrows seemed interested, almost excited.

"Sorry, just wondering if he said that today or last week or what."

"Why? Did something happen?" The eyebrows were arching now.

Merritt—*stupid, stupid*—scrambled for a lie. "No, nothing like that. It felt like we were hitting a wall last week. Not getting anywhere. I just wanted to make sure he was still happy with me. With the work we're doing, I mean."

Sure, Merritt, overexplain, that will help.

"Oh," Evie said, squinting toward the ceiling and demonstrating a remarkable gameness for this round of twenty questions. "He said you've been . . . I think the words were 'exceptionally helpful,' but it could have been 'astonishingly helpful.' Though that sounds a little more gushing than the Whit we both know. And that would have been Sunday, I'm pretty certain."

Relief caused Merritt to take too long a pause.

Evie leaned her head toward Merritt, as if trying to hear someone through mumbles. "There's something you're not telling me, which is fine because we met thirty seconds ago, but I think maybe you could use a cup of coffee?"

Merritt said that she could, and the two women small-talked while Evie fiddled with the kettle and the French press. She asked Evie about her freelance work, and Evie asked Merritt about her job at the bookstore and the Samantha Irby book they had both recently read. Merritt immediately liked this woman.

"Now," Evie said, handing Merritt a mug of deep black coffee, "drink that, while I tell you embarrassing stories from Whit's childhood."

Merritt laughed harder than she expected.

"Well," a voice said from the doorway. "This is a harrowing sight."

It was Whit, holding a now unnecessary box of tea. His voice flipped a switch in Merritt, her fuzzy uncertainty returning at speed. She set her jaw.

"What did you hear?" Evie demanded, jutting out an accusatory finger.

"Just threatening laughter, that's all."

"*Good,*" she said, and that made both her and Merritt laugh again.

Whit looked genuinely frightened. He stood a little stupidly for a moment before finally speaking up again.

"Well, should we get to work?"

Merritt looked to Evie, who was clearly crestfallen at having lost the chance to divulge juicy details about her brother's past.

She sighed.

"Okay. If we must."

*

Things were off today, and Whit chastised himself. He had been so focused on Annie and on Evie being in town, and then when the time came, he'd been nervous about his sister meeting Merritt—so nervous that he'd made up the false pretense of going out for more tea in order to avoid bumbling through their initial meeting. Driving back from the store, he'd imagined that maybe somehow they could go straight back to normal, but then he'd had to watch as Merritt's face went from laughing naturally with Evie to a strained, toothy grin at the sight of him.

Merritt sat there typing at the kitchen table, and even the sound of her keystrokes seemed unusually upbeat.

"What?" he said, thinking she'd spoken.

She looked up, her eyes too wide and her smile too polite. "Hm?"

"I thought . . ."

"I didn't say anything."

"Oh."

He tried to turn his wince into a smile. *God, if you wanted to take me now, you could.*

More silence. This was stupid. He should just acknowledge what happened. He geared himself up to speak, but when he opened his mouth, his lips rebelled, flopping around uselessly like the jowls of a bloodhound.

Mercifully, Evie appeared.

"I'm going to do some errands before I pick up Annie," she said from the archway that connected the breakfast room to the hall. "Do you need anything?"

Whit tried not to look like a puppy being left at the pound.

"I'm good," he said, hesitantly. "Do you?"

"All good here!" Merritt said, her voice chipper in a way he usually associated with cartoon chipmunks.

Evie stared for a moment at the trainwreck before her, then turned her gaze to Whit.

"Actually, I need you to show me how to drive the Range Rover."

Whit paused. "How to—"

"I don't have a car," Evie explained to Merritt, before her eyes went back to searing into Whit's. "And the Range Rover is so *fancy*, please come show me all of its bells and whistles so I don't drive into a ditch."

The words came out with such increasing speed and intensity that Whit was already on his feet before she finished.

In the garage, she turned on him.

"What on *earth*—"

Whit flinched.

"Oh, please don't start."

"*Something* happened, you little liar!"

"*Lower your voice.*"

"*Okay*," she hissed. "But you are being a real weirdo in there. Both of you. She was much more normal before you showed up."

"Thank you so much for pointing that out. Helpful as always. And now you've pulled me in here on the dumbest possible pretext, and I get to walk back in and tell Merritt, sorry, my sister is just really scared of cars."

"Of Range Rovers," she corrected.

"I'm going to *kill* you."

Evie watched him, and when he didn't speak again, she sighed.

"Fine, be that way. But when I get back, we will be having a *big* debrief."

"There is nothing to—"

"*Whit*," she said, raising her voice and looking pointedly at the door to the house. "*When I get back, you are going to tell me*—"

Suddenly ten years old again, Whit pressed his hand against her mouth. She pulled away laughing, but looked ready to yell again.

"*Okay*," he whisper-yelled.

"Thank you," she said in her own cutesy, falsely chipper way, before getting in the car and starting it, literally, with her eyes closed.

Whit trudged back inside and found Merritt sitting with her arms crossed and a smirk on her face.

After a moment, he asked, "What did you hear?"

Merritt pretended to think. "I believe the phrase was 'you little liar,' followed by 'you are going to tell me' . . ."

Whit threw his head back. "God."

Now Merritt grinned openly.

"I'm sorry about that," Whit said. The tone of the room had shifted for the better, and he found he could suddenly speak naturally. "And I'm sorry for what happened at the party. You were telling me something really vulnerable and difficult, and I ruined it by getting carried away in the moment."

Merritt pulled back just slightly but relaxed immediately now that the silence was broken.

"It's not your fault," she said. "Or not only your fault."

"I was pretty tipsy."

"And I had just been accosted by your friend Ian."

"*Former* friend," he said. His whole body felt suddenly light again. "Anyway, it was stupid."

"We'd been drinking," she agreed. "We were at a party."

"All kinds of silly things happen at parties."

Merritt was smiling, too, happy to be pushing through. "Exactly."

It felt as if the windows had been opened and a light breeze had whisked away their former awkwardness.

She squinted at his face for a moment.

"I must have been pretty tipsy myself," she said.

"Oh? Why's that?"

Another beaming smile. "Normally, I would have fled at the sight of that mustache."

"I am going to ignore that low blow," he said, turning toward the kitchen, "and make us some tea."

"Great," Merritt said. "I'll have my usual."

CHAPTER NINETEEN

They were working quickly now, perfecting their arcane, slightly persnickety system of outlining and revising and writing and rewriting. Evie was an enormous help, picking up Annie from school or the nanny share most days and often taking her off on adventures—to the library, the seaside, a whale museum. Whit and Merritt were able to spend more and more time writing each day. They worked from lunchtime on, sometimes writing through dinner or, if Merritt was wanted back at the bookstore, until the absolute last minute before she could leave and expect to make it to work on time. There were endless pots of tea and several more chilly walks in the woods. The fire was always going, and Merritt seemed to be getting comfortable—with Whit, yes, but also with Evie and Annie, with taking a blanket from the antique wooden crate at the end of the couch or finding a snack to munch on in the kitchen. Never, never did they bring up the kiss that wasn't, and Whit was glad of it.

The first weeks of November passed, and as the days grew colder and a little gloomier, the forest completed its transition into an autumn coat. One day during the week leading up to Thanksgiving, before Whit and Merritt began work in earnest, she made an announcement over her bowl of Italian wedding soup.

"I finished the book last night."

Whit's immediate reaction was one of bewilderment and surprise.

"What? Without me?"

He felt none of the relief he expected himself to feel at this moment, and he was more than a little hurt.

Merritt covered her lips with one hand, laughing through a mouthful of food.

"Sorry, I finished *your* book last night. *The Hour of Matins.*"

"Oh!" Whit said, understanding cracking over his mind like an egg. Then came the realization of what this announcement implied. "*Oh.* Should I be concerned it took you a full month?"

Merritt smiled gently and shook her head. "*I* should be embarrassed. I'm just so tired when I finally get a moment to relax."

"I blame the bookstore. It can't be *this* that's exhausting you."

He spread his hands out, including the room around them in his statement, and Merritt sniffed out a laugh.

"No." She paused, chewing on a thought and a piece of the sourdough she'd been dipping in her soup. Eventually she explained, her voice more tentative than usual.

"I've been making myself write a little, after work. For me."

Whit's grin was entirely natural. "That's great! Your old manuscript? Or something else?"

"A little bit of both. Fiddling with the old stuff and trying some new things, too."

"That's excellent," Whit said, leaning against the kitchen counter. He downed his cup of tea then spoke again. "But wait, you're writing *more* after the work we do here?"

She shrugged. "Yeah."

"I can't fathom it," he said, shaking his head. "I've been trying to start the next Sister Marguerite book, but writing alone isn't like writing with you. It's like the tank is empty at the end of the day. I keep expecting my agent to call any moment and ask when the new manuscript will be finished, and then I try not to be hopelessly offended when she doesn't."

Merritt gave him a gracious smile, then wiped her mouth with a napkin. "Well, I'll read it whenever it comes out. Once I finish, what is it, *A Liturgy for Mourning*?"

Whit flinched, keeping one eye closed for protection. "Yes."

"Oh, stop," Merritt said, standing up. "I really enjoyed *The Hour of Matins*. Sister Marguerite is great, and I love the whole 'How would Father Brown *really* feel about all these murders in his parish?' thing. Surely that man should be having more crises of faith."

Whit shrugged. "That is sort of the driving question . . . hey, wait."

Merritt hunched her shoulders slightly, looking like she might know what he was about to say next.

"How much is left to write in your manuscript?"

She turned to walk toward the living room and spoke with her back to him. "I don't know, not much. Just the ending, really."

"Nearly finished!"

She nodded, still not looking. "I'm struggling with it a bit, but I'll figure it out."

"You know what could help . . . are you trying to run away right now?"

She finally turned back. "Yes, Whit. I'm not enjoying talking about this."

"We were *just* talking about my book."

Merritt crossed her arms. "Which has been published. After it was gone over a dozen times by your editor and agent and whoever else. It's not the same thing."

She was walking now, trying to retreat to her chair.

"Merritt," he said more loudly.

"What?"

She turned back. Whit did not have a plan for what to say next. He looked around the room. On the coffee table were the remnants of a game of war between Evie and Annie.

"I'll play you for it."

"For what?"

"For your book. If you win, the manuscript can remain hidden from the world indefinitely. And if I win, I get to read it."

Merritt deliberated, then smiled. "Fine," she said, with a scheming look on her face, "but I get to pick the game."

Now Whit considered. "Fine. What are we playing?"

"Nertz," she said, scooping up the cards and walking back to the kitchen. "Do you have another deck of cards?"

"What's Nertz?" he asked once they had procured a second deck and were seated again at the kitchen table.

His ignorance visibly thrilled Merritt. With her shoulders pushed back as she shuffled, almost in shimmying territory, she was suddenly looking very superior.

"Oh, it's not hard."

"I feel like you're lying."

"I'm not lying. The rules are straightforward. I'm just very good."

She began to explain the game. Each person got thirteen cards—their Nertz pile—and laid out four other cards next to it, face up and side by side.

"Then, when we say 'Go,' you flip the top card on your Nertz pile—"

Whit listened, nodding along as she explained that each player essentially played solitaire on their four cards, except for their aces, which they placed in the middle, where they were free game for anyone to play cards of the same suit in numerical order. All this time, Whit nodded along, squinting as if overwhelmed by her quick explanation of the rules.

"Ready?" she asked, barely able to contain her glee at the onslaught that was about to occur.

"I guess."

Then, with no preamble, she said, "Go!" and they were off.

Whit watched her for a moment as she flipped cards, three at a time, from the deck in her hands and moved with an easy grace to place a black ten on a red jack, a red three on a black four. Then the ace of clubs appeared, and she slid it fluidly to the middle.

"Aren't you going to go?" she asked, not looking up.

"Yep," he said, and then he was off, too.

He did not move with the same elegance, but he did have the speed. A red queen on a black king, a whole run (jack, ten, nine, eight) over to that pile. The ace of hearts, and the two of hearts, and the three, then Merritt's ace of clubs covered in a flash.

"What—" she started, but Whit played on steadily and in silence.

The truth was that, from the moment she'd mentioned the "Nertz pile," he'd known what was what. He'd grown up playing a similar game, with a few tweaks to the rules. Some people called it Dutch Blitz. The Longacres called it Hell, and they were vicious.

"Hell!" Whit shouted at last, slamming the final card from his pile of thirteen onto a stack of spades in the middle. "I mean, Nertz."

Merritt made a noise like a cut-off gasp, then gave him a fiery look.

"You little shit."

He grinned back at her. "I know. I'm sorry."

But he was not sorry.

"You can email me the manuscript whenever. And I'm sure it will be wonderful."

Merritt stewed in the reality of Whit's deception for a moment before she spoke.

"Okay, whatever. But you should know—"

He waved her words away with a hand.

"Don't," he said. "Just receive the compliment. I mean it. I'm really looking forward to reading it."

"Fine. I'll email it to you today. But if it's really bad, I want you to simply send me a text message firing me and asking never to see me again, because I won't be able to show my face here after that."

"It won't be really bad!"

She gave him a stern just-you-wait-and-see look, and Whit laughed again. He was laughing a lot these days.

"And what if it's only a little bit bad?" he joked.

She shrugged. "Then your feedback would be . . . helpful. I *suppose*."

"And if it's really good?"

Merritt had clearly had enough. She swatted the air, moving to stand up. "Let's not get ahead of ourselves."

"Hey, wait."

She looked at him as though he might be about to deliver some sort of meaningful statement.

"Yes?"

He nodded at the cards. "Don't you want to play again?"

She rolled her eyes, then relaxed. "Actually, I do."

They played four more games, but after the first, they forgot to keep score.

*

In fact, it took her days to hold up her end of the deal. She typed the message, attached the incomplete doc, the whole thing, but the email sat unsent for at least seventy-two hours.

This was stupid, of course. She'd spent the first year of her MFA building up the calloused skin necessary to endure criticism, especially the brutal, unfiltered kind that came from those students most willing to demolish their peers to get a leg up themselves. Still, Whit was Whit. This was risky, like jeopardizing her standing in his eyes; she was inviting him to judge her. What if giving him access to her work—the book of her heart—what if that somehow proved, once and for all, that she wasn't cut out to be an author in her own right?

It took another hike, another morning spent staring at the same misty pond—its trees now leafless and black against the pinkish dawn light—before she was ready. *I am going to be a writer*, she reminded herself, then pulled out her phone and released the email from the confines of her drafts folder.

Immediate regret. That was her first emotion. Then, after taking two deep breaths and stretching her arms to their fullest extent, she felt relief. It was done now, and anyway, things were going well. For the first time in—what was it? a year?—Merritt felt like she awoke each day with a purpose. It reminded her of those early months of grad school, when she was visited by a total certainty that she had made the right decision, that she was right where she should be, that her future would work out in the right way. She had written so freely and fearlessly back then. She'd been prolific and inventive. Now as then, she felt in control, like each day she was choosing to do the things that mattered, writing with Whit by daylight and then, in the hours before bed, writing at the little desk in her room while the sun set over the park beyond her window.

She loved writing with Whit—loved both being with Whit and doing the work itself. The two of them were good partners, making something she felt proud of, and even if she was a little confused about where things stood between them, she was allowing herself to enjoy the time she spent at the Longacre house. And it wasn't just that. Her work at the bookstore felt more fulfilling, and her own writing was compelling again in a way that hadn't been true since Graydon had called writing for children "trite and easy." She was feeling early-in-a-project momentum, but here she was, almost finished with the manuscript.

Things *were* going well. Really well. And people were starting to notice.

"There's my *radiant* daughter," Kathleen said one morning. She liked to do this—to pretend she and Merritt were the cheesy mother-daughter duo in a bad Netflix movie.

Sometimes Merritt would play along, but today she was too focused on reading Whit's third book as she waited for water to boil in the kitchen. (She had flown through *A Liturgy for Mourning*, and Whit, it turned out, had been right: the books did get better as she went on.)

When Kathleen, standing in the arched doorway, spotted the oatmeal packet in Merritt's hand, she pointed as if it were a shocking wound.

"Yuck. It's Saturday. Let's go get breakfast instead."

Merritt was not hard to convince. She switched off the burner, and in ten minutes, two of which were spent debating over wearing a scarf, they were walking down Cork Street. Other people were out, too, as the morning was mild and the farmers' market would be happening on the village green. Watching kids in beanies holding their parents' hands and noting the steam rising from people's coffee cups, Merritt liked how fully *fall* it all felt. Her feet continually found crunchy leaves to step on, and her hair lifted gently in the perfectly cool breeze. A couple approached them, holding hands, and Merritt and her mother naturally split to give way to them.

"You know," Kathleen said, as she and Merritt rejoined each other farther down the sidewalk, "you are in a markedly better mood than I've seen you in weeks. I was joking about you being radiant, but it's also true."

Merritt felt the blush in her neck and cheeks, and she wished she'd worn the scarf. She could feel her mother looking at her as a dozen ways of answering the implied question stacked up in her mind. Kathleen knew about Whit and the kiss that wasn't, and she knew about Graydon—not everything, but enough to hate the man and rejoice at Merritt's freedom. She knew a bit less about Merritt's dashed writing dreams, at least from the source, but Merritt realized that her mother had probably intuited quite a lot.

After too long, Kathleen spoke again.

"Well, now you're just being obvious, dear."

"*Mom.*"

Kathleen finally looked away. "I'm just saying, a quick, short response could have forestalled me, but you look as if you're playing 20 Questions with yourself."

Merritt sighed and looked across the street, where people were standing in line for doughnuts.

"No, you know what you look like? Sherlock Holmes when he's thinking through all the possibilities. Please, Merritt, answer me, you look like a cocaine-addled Victorian detective."

"Speaking of, did you finish your book?" Merritt asked, leaning heavily on the barest trace of a segue—from general nineteenth-century detective fiction to the specific nineteenth-century political novel her mother had been reading.

"I did," Kathleen said. "I loved it in the end, as is my way. But I will not be diverted."

Merritt sighed again, hating the petulance rising up in her. "Mom, please."

"I am just happy that you're happy. Because you are happy, yes?"

It was a simple question, but of course, it opened a chasm in the sidewalk that Merritt felt herself peering into. A month ago, she would have said *no*. Or, she would have said *yes, of course*, and been lying. A year and a half ago, she'd have replied, *Yes, yes, I'm deliriously happy!*, but now, in hindsight, that felt false, too. Perhaps she *was* deliriously happy, "deliriously" being the operative word.

Maybe now she should just say yes and spare her mother from fretting. For all of Kathleen's discernment and keen insights, there were times when Merritt thought her mother's primary desire was to assuage her own worries about her daughter—the only person she had left to worry about—as quickly and easily as possible.

"I'm in a good place, Mom," she said, nudging her with her shoulder. "Really."

Kathleen smiled at that, easily pleased, and then Merritt's hopes that she had put a stop to this line of questioning were immediately deflated.

"I'm so glad, Merritt. Truly. And may I ask *why* you're in such a good place?"

Internally, Merritt bristled at both the question and the addition of the word "such," which pushed the description she'd applied to herself into the realm of exaggeration.

Outwardly, Merritt lifted her hands. "I like my job, Mom. Jobs. I'm finding them fulfilling right now."

Kathleen nodded, as if this information were obvious. "But which job in particular, dear?"

"The *writing* one, obviously. Because I'm getting paid to write."

"Which you've always wanted."

"Yes."

"And I suppose you've forgiven Whit for almost kissing you?"

Merritt nodded.

"Nothing to forgive. It was dumb of him, and he knows it."

"My favorite kind of man."

Merritt laughed. They paused their conversation for a few steps. They could see the bistro now, and she hoped this landmark would provide a natural endpoint to the conversation. It did not.

"Though maybe it wasn't *that* dumb of him—"

"Mom," Merritt groaned, stopping right there on the sidewalk. "I told you. We agreed to move on, and we haven't talked about it since. It would be stupid to ruin things."

"Yes, but something must have happened. You were so high-strung and serious after that party, and now, look at you." She shrugged at her daughter with her whole upper body. "Radiant, like I said."

Merritt allowed her feet to begin moving again, primarily because Kathleen had only slowed rather than stopping completely, and Merritt refused to revert to anything resembling the strategies of an adolescent temper tantrum.

The door to the bistro was ten paces away when Merritt said, "I don't know, Mom. He apologized, and it was nice. I think he really respects my position and my contributions. And that just feels . . . good."

"Well, good," Kathleen said, pausing with her hand on the door pull. "And you know I abhor violence, darling, but I do need to tell you that the world will be down one mystery novelist if Whit Longacre fucks this up."

"Mom!"

Kathleen grinned, shrugged again, then opened the door.

"Table for two, please," she told the host, and it was several seconds before Merritt recovered enough from her mother's threat of violence, and what must have been her first use of the F-word in the last twenty years, to follow her to the table.

*

Over a breakfast of pecan coffee, crusty rye toast with strawberry-sumac jam, peppery bacon, and eggs Benedict, Merritt's mother mercifully relented. Instead of Whit, they discussed Thanksgiving, which was the following Thursday.

Merritt had spent the holiday in Texas the year prior, helping Graydon host an elaborate dinner party that would go down as one of the most stressful evenings of her life. Besides several professors and local authors, Graydon's teenage daughters were also in attendance, as was his ex-wife, Leonora, and her boyfriend, a man ten years older than Graydon.

"It's the holidays," Graydon had said, as if this explained the unconventional guest list, and Merritt had of course understood about the twins. But she had never met Leonora, who scared her a bit.

Merritt did very little in the way of cooking, as Graydon had the day catered by the same operation he apparently used annually. She did make her mother's citrusy cranberry sauce, which made her feel a little less guilty about leaving Kathleen alone in cold New England, and she watched eagerly during the meal to see which guests enjoyed it. In the end, she felt it was woefully neglected in favor of a prosaic brown gravy.

Before the meal, however, she had finally met Leonora, and that went even worse than expected. Horribly, the woman was *nice*. She seemed perfectly unfazed by Merritt's existence, entirely unthreatened, and she was funny, much to Merritt's dismay. And Graydon laughed at her jokes incessantly, and he touched her frequently, on the elbow, the shoulder, and once with a jaunty little hip-to-hip movement she'd never seen him do before.

It was miserable. Merritt was *on* the whole time, desperate to impress the Orange Prize and Lambda Award winners, to be cool in front of the twins, and to make Leonora like her, at the same time that she was pathetically, heartbreakingly desperate to feel like Graydon was even slightly aware of her presence.

She missed her mother terribly the whole time, and even worse, she missed her late father, who loved Thanksgiving and would have hated Graydon. As it turned out, that evening had been the beginning of the end for them. Merritt confronted Graydon afterwards, while washing dishes as he put away leftovers and finished off the wine. She had started obliquely at first.

"It's nice that you and Leonora get along so well."

He put down his wineglass and crossed his arms in a deliberate motion.

"Don't start," he said, and Merritt felt stupid and small, like a jealous tween girl whose boyfriend had been spotted talking to someone else between classes.

"I'm just saying—"

"We had a life together," he interrupted. "*Have* a life, but it's all very mature and friendly."

"I could tell."

"Don't be jealous." It had been a command. He was still in his sport coat and button-down, while she had changed into sweatpants and a T-shirt. Stupid mistake. She was unarmed.

"Did you have to *touch* her so much?"

"I've done quite a bit more than *touch* her, sweetheart."

Merritt turned back to the sink then, showing her disgust at both the faux pet name and the unnecessary, unhelpful allusion. Two plates later, though, she turned back around. He was waiting, smirking, and she hated him then.

"You barely spoke to me all night," she said, pointing with a soapy silver ladle.

"Our friends were here."

"Your friends."

"Sweetheart, please," he said again, leaving the kitchen to gather more leftovers from the dining room, "you're embarrassing yourself."

Merritt finished the dishes in silence, refusing to turn around again. She knew that Graydon probably felt victorious, that she had been appropriately shamed, but the truth was that her working hands were fueled by rage. It was there in Graydon's kitchen that she had first seen, with glaring clarity, what this all was. What she was to him. She had read scenes like this in books, and she knew this should be her Nora Helmer moment. Instead, she was doing the dishes, because this was not a three-act play, and Graydon wasn't Torvald, and this wasn't even her house.

The next morning Graydon had halfway apologized for being distracted by the guests—she knew, didn't she, how much he cared about things like this going well?—and Merritt accepted that apology. She did not wait for him to mention Leonora because she knew, instinctively, that he would never apologize for whatever happened with her.

Now, looking back, Merritt wished she had left the dirty dishes and the house and never returned, but she did return. They, too, had built a little life together, and there was always the chance she was being unreasonable. Graydon was the kind of man who seemed to have some secret knowledge about the way things really were, and so she had stayed, and she'd spent Christmas with him, too, and then the day before Valentine's Day, which a man like him hardly deigned to acknowledge anyway, she was in the department mail room and decided to do the kind thing of checking Graydon's box for him. On top was a red envelope addressed in an unfamiliar script, but a hunch told her to check the outgoing box for interdepartmental mail and there was a similar envelope, addressed in his cramped, hypermasculine handwriting to *Leonora Benbrook, Religious Studies*. Valentine's cards, after all these years.

Back then, she did not think Graydon and Leonora were sleeping together, and she still didn't think so. But Merritt did realize in that moment that whatever this man felt for his ex-wife was not what he felt for her, was not something he could ever feel for someone like her. She went home to her studio apartment, which she loved, and took stock: of her day and the days before it, of the recent writing she was doing and despising, of the tepid feedback she'd begun to receive in workshops and from professors, and she thought, of course, of that Thanksgiving dinner and Leonora's wine-drenched laugh. She let herself feel small again for a moment, aware of her passive role in this smallness, and then she drove to Graydon's house and ended things.

He put up an enervated fight for the first half hour, but the encounter ended with the same cold dismissiveness he'd shown her in November. Merritt remained calm, a fact she was proud of even today, as she told the man about himself:

"You fool a lot of people, and you fooled me for a while, but what's so depressing is how boringly predictable you ended up being. This whole thing—going after a grad student and treating her like shit, dismissing her the moment she stops propping up your fragile ego. It's just like every sleazy professor in every bad, gossipy story, and *God*, it makes me feel stupid for having ever thought you were interesting or kind or good. You're not. You're condescending and cruel, and you've diminished me—as a person and a student and a writer—and yes, fine, I am partly to blame for that. But now I'm through."

That stopped him short because, knowing him as she did, she was certain he planned to say something about how she herself was responsible for any feelings of weakness or insignificance, but she'd beaten him to it. She was also proud of having given him a small, cold smile in this moment of bewilderment, and the way she'd walked away from him then. She did get the last word.

At least until the book came out.

"So anyway," her mother was saying while signing the check, "what do you think about going to a B&B on Wednesday and staying for a day or two? There's one here in town, but I found a quaint little place on the coast that does a whole big Thanksgiving meal. That way we won't have to cook, and we won't feel so pathetic about it being just the two of us."

Merritt watched her mom, who watched the ceiling. Merritt waited until Kathleen looked her way, then rolled her eyes, drawing a laugh from her mother.

"You know I could never feel pathetic about that, Mom."

CHAPTER TWENTY

Evie was clearly succeeding at the job she had assigned herself. There was no other way to explain why Whit was currently walking with her toward the farmers' market with Annie skipping giddily between them. Whit had no problem with farmers' markets, but they were exactly the sort of thing he never seemed to have energy for these days.

Today, though, he was glad he had listened to his sister. The morning was pleasantly cool, and Annie was over the moon to be out and about. Whit caught Evie's eye over his daughter's head and gave her an appreciative nod. She beamed back.

"You're going to *love* the farmers' market, Evie," Annie bubbled, talking at the frantic pace eight-year-olds are accustomed to. "It's *so* cute in the fall."

"I believe it," Evie said. "Is it all pumpkins and scarecrows, or has Christmas already started taking over?"

"*No*," Annie said gravely, before immediately jumping back to full speed. "November is for *Thanksgiving*, and Christmas has to wait until afterwards."

"You take this very seriously."

Annie shrugged. "My mom did. She always hated that people skipped over being thankful and jumped right into wanting presents."

Whit looked at Evie again, who smiled once more, this time sympathetically.

"I remember that," she said lightly, in a voice Whit had used frequently himself: a cheerful acknowledgment that responded to the spirit of Annie's statement. So often people allowed any mention of Helen to drastically alter their tone or mood, but Annie wasn't speaking from grief, just memory, and Evie recognized that. She was a good aunt.

"So," she added after a moment, "pumpkins it is, then?"

"*So* many pumpkins," Annie gushed.

"I can't wait to see it."

They had not parked far from the green, so Evie did not have to wait long. As with Cork Street, "cute" really was the only word for the Whelk Harbor village green. Brick-lined paths spread like spokes from the fountain at the center of the big grassy space, watched over by old-fashioned lampposts; at the far end was a bandstand crowded with piles of gourds and draped in burlap bunting. Tiny collections of trees—red maples, sycamores, white pines, balsam firs—popped in bursts of flint corn colors. And then, of course, there were the booths selling slender French green beans, squashes in every geometric shape, hairy sweet potatoes, intimidating kohlrabi, and exceptionally phallic daikon radishes. Representatives from the nearest orchards were there, surrounded by open barrels of apples, quinces, pomegranates, persimmons, pears. There were two coffee roasters offering pour-overs and Americanos and one vendor doling out paper cups of cider, hot chocolate, and wassail. Under tents were representatives from the bakery selling warm loaves of bread and giant cinnamon rolls as well as the florist and various local artists selling pottery, jewelry, and landscape paintings. Next to displays of elk jerky were quilts and woodworks, and several places were offering cartons of brown and light blue eggs. And everywhere they turned were so, so many pumpkins.

"*See?*" Annie said.

"I do," Evie said enthusiastically. "It's lovely."

She gave Whit a knowing look and was rewarded by him mouthing the words *I kind of hate this!*

Live a little, she mouthed back, squeezing Annie's shoulders.

"DAD, CAN WE GET HOT CHOCOLATE?"

"WE CAN GET HOT CHOCOLATE!" Whit said, matching Annie's hyperactive tone. She laughed.

After stopping for drinks (spiked with Kahlua for the adults), Whit let Annie lead. She filled their Goodenough Books tote with purple lavender soap and vanilla-scented candles they absolutely did not need, as well as sour belts and muffins and, while Whit distracted Evie, a handcrafted ceramic mug she wanted her aunt to have for Christmas.

"Okay," Whit said eventually, after they took a break to sit on the lip of the fountain and eat from paper cones of roasted nuts. "While we're here, I do actually want to get some fruits and vegetables for the week."

"Boring," Annie sighed, but she quickly cheered up: nearly every produce vendor also had a smattering of pumpkins available. While Evie did the shopping, Whit slowly morphed into a man whose entire torso seemed to be made up of decorative gourds.

"Please, it's too much, they are *squashing* me," he was saying in an exaggerated whine when a familiar voice broke through the noise of the crowd.

"Sir, could you save some for the rest of us?"

"Mrs. Pryor!" Annie rushed to her, throwing her arms around Kathleen's shawled and beaded body.

"Merritt!" Another hug, this time for Merritt, who grinned a little sheepishly in her mustard yellow sweater and jeans.

"Hi," Whit said from behind his tower. It was a general "hi," but Annie was introducing Evie to her librarian, whom Evie was engaging with conspicuous focus, and so he and Merritt found themselves in a private pocket of conversation. Something crackled in Whit's chest as they smiled back and forth.

"Hi," she said. "Here, let me help."

She moved toward him and delicately relocated the pumpkins and gourds from his arms to the nearest park bench.

"Thank you. I wonder if I could convince people to let me drive the car in here to pick them up."

"It is a shocking number."

Whit laughed. She had a brown paper gift bag in one hand.

"Candle?"

"Lemon verbena soap."

"Ah, they got you, too."

"I can never resist artisanal soaps."

They were small-talking, bantering—why? What was different here, in this public space, away from the comforts of his living room?

"Oh," Whit said, trying to discuss something real, "I'm enjoying your manuscript."

Merritt's eyes widened in immediate dread.

"Oh God."

"No, seriously. It is, as the book blurbs say, *compulsively readable*."

He had been sitting up late, reading from his laptop and making notes. He had seen many first drafts in his time, and he was serious when he said hers was a good one.

"I'm sweating."

"And," he added, ignoring her, "you're great at world-building, which I find to be *so* difficult. I feel like all my stories take place in empty towns and blank rooms."

"That's absurd, you have the nunnery and the church and there's that scene in Venice."

"Yes, but those are all things people can imagine for themselves. You're creating an entire magical kingdom—"

"Seriously, Whit," Merritt urged, stepping toward him, "could you lower your voice? I know you're a real-life professional novelist and this all comes easily to you, but talking about this in public makes me want to throw up."

Whit laughed.

"I mean, to be fair," he said, "talking about *your* work is easy, but never, ever my own."

"Well, let's go easy on ourselves then," Merritt said, smiling and looking around as if someone might have overheard the word "manuscript." But beneath that embarrassment, he could also make out a layer of pride. He was learning to read her.

"For instance," she said, "I could talk about how I finished your second Sister Marguerite book and am hurtling through the third, but I wouldn't do that to you here, in front of your family."

"Oh, you're so merciful."

"I am. I really am."

They were standing close now, their faux-clandestine conversation having unconsciously drawn them nearer and nearer to each other. After Merritt spoke, they seemed to take this fact in together, but neither one moved away. Whit could smell the scents he now associated with her: the unparsable blend of things that made up her shampoo; gardenia, which he could only name from having seen the label on the lotion she used; Ivory soap; and amber oil. He found himself looking from her light brown eyes to her lips and back, feeling her nearness with his mind and some previously dormant sixth sense.

He felt compelled to speak—to say something funny or cute or disarming, but instead he heard the words, "Oh, that is so sweet."

The thing between him and Merritt broke, and the two of them turned swiftly toward Kathleen's voice. Whit was mortified that she might be talking about whatever she thought she was watching happen to her daughter, but Kathleen's eyes were trained on Evie with her hand clutching the younger woman's.

"Merritt, what do you think?"

Merritt took a step back, and Whit felt like a quilt had slipped from his bed in the night.

"About what? Sorry, I didn't hear . . ."

"Evie has invited us to do Thanksgiving—"

"Has she?" Whit asked.

"—with the Longacres and, I'm sorry, who else did you say, dear?"

"The Barrett-Linds."

"That's Albie and Willa and Adrienne," Annie filled in.

Merritt's and Whit's eyes found each other, both knowing that the other was asking permission or forgiveness or something similar, all of which was granted instantly.

"Oh," was all Merritt seemed able to say.

"We'd never want to impose," Kathleen was saying, but Whit was looking only at Merritt.

"You wouldn't be," he explained eagerly. "Of course you wouldn't, we'd love to have you. And anyone else—the more the merrier."

Kathleen laughed at that. "I don't have anyone I'd like to invite, although Merritt might. Someone from the bookstore, perhaps?"

Merritt's eyes widened. "*No.* Definitely not."

Now Whit laughed, imagining what it would be like if Diana showed up in her nosiest state.

"Well?" Evie said, looking from Kathleen to Merritt to Whit. "What do you say?"

"*Please* come," Annie begged, yanking at Kathleen's sleeve.

Again, Merritt looked to him. He gave what he hoped was a small, serious, meaningful nod, holding her eyes with his.

"Please come," he said.

Merritt shrugged, a small smile clearly constraining a much bigger grin beneath it.

"Sure," she said. "We'd love to."

*

On the walk home, Merritt and her mother talked about what a cute kid Annie Longacre was, and Evie Longacre's gorgeous hair, and the crispness of the weather, and the crisp they planned to make with their apples and quinces.

They did not discuss Thanksgiving or the now-forgotten B&B.

They did not discuss how handsome and alive Whit Longacre was looking these days, with his well-trimmed beard and his strong posture and those shining white teeth. With his eyes that held your gaze like hands gently cupping a fresh egg. With his broad shoulders and warm cheeky grin.

They did not—thank God—discuss the way Merritt herself was grinning, nor the fact that she didn't stop grinning for one second all the way back to her mother's house.

CHAPTER TWENTY-ONE

With Thanksgiving three days away, Merritt and Whit were on a roll. They had recently passed the halfway point of the novel—they were deep within the murky middle, the part every writer hated, and they were stomping through it like fearless, well-seasoned explorers intuiting the proper paths to take. They had crafted a comfortable, habitual world for themselves, communicating often through looks and *hmm*s and glances at the clock. Merritt started bringing new teas for them to try, and she had left one of her sweatshirts hanging on the coatrack for days when the house felt drafty. She had a favorite mug and a favorite blanket; the chair nearest the fire was hers in the early hours of their work, and the spot on the rug in the patch of sun was where she moved as dinnertime approached. Annie, now on break from school, would swan in and out of the living room, "bothering" Merritt, who loved it. She would talk with the eight-year-old about books and TV shows and what she wanted for Christmas.

Merritt was really happy. Scrolling on her phone from the cracked red leather chair during a break at the bookstore, she was thinking about just how happy she was: the kind of state, she would later think, virtually guaranteed to result in bad news. Thus, the text from Bebe shouldn't have come as a shock, though of course it did. Things like this were impossible to take in stride.

Forwarded you an email you need to see, Bebe wrote. I didn't respond, and as far as I know, no one else did either. The faculty have asked us not to. Call me if you want to talk.

Merritt's stomach looped itself into a Möbius strip as she navigated to her email and opened the top forwarded message.

To Whom It May Concern:

My name is Ian Hoult. You may have read some of my books—at least I hope you have! (If not, they are available for purchase at this link.)

I'm currently writing a story for *The Atlantic* about Graydon Lyons and his latest book, *Serious Games*. For this piece, an investigation of the rumors that the work is a *roman à clef* or something similar, I'm trawling the depths for any true-to-life details that might grant me the *clef* to this *roman*.

I write this with an e-wink and an e-nudge, but I'm sure you'll understand the obstacles I face. People are often reticent to speak up about a beloved mentor or to speculate about the *meaning* of a work of literature. As such, I am reaching out to ask that question burning in each of our minds: *What's the true story of Graydon Lyons? What is he really like? What's fiction? What's fact?*

Perhaps you know, perhaps you don't. Perhaps you know someone who knows someone. Perhaps you've heard something, however frivolous, you think would be worth sharing. I can promise you a listening ear and a discreet pen, not to mention my immense gratitude. Please feel free to email or give me a call at your earliest convenience.

Cheers,
Ian Hoult

"*Fuck*," Merritt hissed. The tangle in her stomach seemed to have doubled in weight as cold tingles crisscrossed her skin. She scrolled up, frantic, and skimmed the email addresses in the forwarded email. Ian had done the mental math necessary to send this missive to all the third years and, she thought, to the last three or four graduating classes.

"Shit, fuck, *fuck*."

"Goodness," said Diana, looking up from the display where she was micromanaging Huong's arrangement of various fall cookbooks. "Is everything all right?"

Her ivory-colored hair was in a ponytail today that swayed as she surveyed Merritt. There was a hint of eagerness in her eyes, and Merritt was sure her mind had wandered up the hill to Whit's house.

"Um," Merritt said, looking to Huong, who was intrigued herself but without all the indecent eye-work. "It's nothing."

Diana and Huong narrowed their eyes in unison.

"It's just something with an ex."

Merritt wanted to stand, to put distance between herself and the now-oppressive heat of the fireplace, but that would look like retreating from the scrutiny of her coworkers' eyes. That would look like this was a big deal.

She shrugged instead, clearly unconvincingly, because Huong laughed at her, while Diana very nearly scampered over to perch herself on the armrest of the mismatched Edwardian sofa.

"Well," Diana said, and Merritt could tell she was excited about the word she was going to use next. "*Dish*."

"No, I don't think I will," Merritt said, straightening up as if about to stand. "It's fine."

Huong, with her eyes trained on the cookbooks, muttered, "You said 'fuck' three times."

Merritt pressed her head against the chair. She did not have to tell these women anything. She did not owe it to them.

But Ian's email had not been about her, not really. It had been about Graydon and what he was *really* like. What he was really like was a man who performed progressiveness in order to mask his serial womanizing. Merritt had been fooled by this behavior, but that did not make her the fool. And anyway, Diana had been surprisingly restrained about Merritt's working relationship with Whit after their car ride, while Huong, she sensed, would be on team Screw Graydon Always and Forever.

Right. Screw Graydon, then.

"Okay," she said, before tumbling into a short version of the story: boyfriend, breakup, book.

Diana, paying rapt attention, raised her eyebrows as high as her recent Botox treatment would allow. Even Huong detached herself from her arrangements and came to join their boss on the sofa somewhere around the part where Merritt was explaining Graydon's jokey promise that he'd never write about her and Bebe telling her about the draft he'd shared in workshop. By the time she read the email aloud, both women were shaking their heads in angry solidarity.

"I never liked him," Diana said.

"Graydon? You know him?"

"No, Ian Hoult. A cold-blooded striver, if you ask me."

The older woman shrugged demurely, as if they might scold her for saying the truth, then she smoothed the creases on the silk scarf tied at her neck and returned her hands to her lap.

"I know he's supposed to be a good writer—he *and* Lyons—but I find it all so boring."

"Well."

Merritt's mind was divided: Graydon's books at least were good, and yet the thrill of having spotted a fellow hater in the wild was powerful. Though she suspected that Diana was putting on an exaggerated show of solidarity, it was nice regardless.

"Do you think your friend is right?" Huong asked seriously.

"Bebe?"

"Yeah. Do you think she's right that no one will respond to him?"

Merritt heaved a deep breath from her lungs. "No. I don't know. She's just being kind, probably. People love gossip, and it's not hard to send an email and ask to be kept anonymous."

Huong nodded. Diana shook her head.

"Pigs, they're all pigs."

"Ian's just doing his job," Merritt said, mostly to fill space. "He's not targeting *me*."

"Fuck that," Huong said. "If he read the book, he knows he's doing a hit job."

The sweat on Merritt's neck and back was immediate.

"What? Have you read the book?"

"Yes," Huong said flatly, as if it were obvious.

"Is it awful?"

"The book or the grad student part?"

"Both."

Huong exhaled, then looked at the fire before finally forcing her eyes back to meet Merritt's.

"The book is unfortunately good. And it's not nice. The character, Isabel, she becomes pretty unsympathetic. And by the end, it's clear that she's been fooling everyone about her talents and that she's actually more or less insubstantial as a writer. And there are some gratuitous descriptions of her boobs and ass and 'curvy hips' and comparatively few mentions of the professor's presumably flabby old-man body."

Merritt clenched the armrests while Huong continued.

"And if Ian Hoult knows that, then he knows that revealing the source material isn't going to do that person any favors."

"But . . ." Merritt had to force herself to say it. "Does she seem . . . like me? Is it obvious?"

Huong actually closed her eyes to think. She hesitated.

"Be honest," Merritt urged.

Huong sighed. "Yeah, a little. She looks like you, and there are elements of the plot that sound like the story you just told. She approaches him at a party. On one of their trips to London, the professor tells her she'd make a great protagonist for his next novel. At the end, she drops out and moves home with her parents."

For the first time in their acquaintance, Huong offered her a look of pained sympathy. Merritt hardly noticed.

"Fuck," she said again.

Diana nodded. "Fuck *him*."

"Diana!"

Even Huong laughed at that. The older woman shrugged again.

"Fuck them both. Pigs."

"If Ian comes around here again," Huong said, "we'll just lay him out. It wouldn't be hard to push a bookshelf onto him."

"*Don't*," Merritt said, managing to laugh. "Then he'd just know he was on to something."

The bell above the door rang, and all three women's heads whipped around to see Moishe arriving for his shift.

"Don't mind me," he said. "I know a coven meeting when I see one."

He doffed his messenger cap and moved quickly into the break room.

That meant Merritt's shift was over, and anyway, the spell was broken. The three women stood, and Diana briefly put a hand on Merritt's shoulder.

"Maybe nothing will come of it."

"Maybe," Merritt said, nodding her thanks with a small, hollow smile.

*

Well, this was a new experience. Whit's phone was ringing. The name on his screen said JOAN EATON—WORK. Yet Whit was not panicking. In fact, he was *excited*.

"Hi, Joan," he said, surprising even himself by answering the agent's call, despite his mental goal to unplug, as he usually did while walking by the stream in the woods behind his house.

Joan sounded surprised, too. "Whit! Hi. I'm glad I caught you. How are you?"

"I'm good," he said, actually smiling.

"Really?'

"Really. I'm good. How are you? Any big plans for tomorrow?"

"Well, yes, actually," Joan said, and Whit could hear noise in the background. "I'm on the train headed in your direction."

For the space of a breath, Whit did panic at the thought that she was coming to find him, to threaten him with physical violence if he didn't have a draft ready, but Joan kept talking.

"My family lives in Plymouth, and as you can imagine, Thanksgiving is a big deal there."

Relaxed now, Whit smiled. "Does everyone wear lace collars and buckle shoes?'

"Sort of," Joan said, laughing. "There's a parade, of course. Several reenactments, you get the picture."

Whit laughed, too, realizing in the back of his brain that this was perhaps the first time he and Joan had done sustained, pleasant small talk since Helen died.

"So listen," she said eventually. "I just wanted to check in before the holidays get into full swing—"

"We're halfway there, Joan. A little more than, actually. And moving swiftly."

He winced and crunched a dry leaf with his duck boot in the space of silence that followed. The *we* had come out of him without thinking, but then Joan didn't take it the way he'd meant it.

"We *are*?" she said, in the same tone a child would use upon learning she was taking a surprise trip to Disney World. *Close one.*

"Yes," Whit said, and the ability to say that word and mean it filled him with a light easiness he hadn't ever felt when talking to Joan before.

"Oh, Whit, that's great. That's great. Do you think, by January, you'll . . ."

"I really do."

He was nodding vigorously, more to himself than to her. They were really going to do this thing. The Monumental Task had been chipped and chiseled away at like the ominous face of a Greek sculpture worn down by the centuries. It wasn't scary anymore—it just was—and if it weren't so cold out, he might have been tempted to grab the beanie off his head and toss it in the air like Mary Tyler Moore. They were going to make it after all.

*

It took a lot to take Ian Hoult's vile little email off Merritt's mind, but the sight of the Longacre homestead glowing like a dollhouse against the overcast November day did the trick. Her fondness for the place had grown over the last two months or so, in spite of its neglected single-father-slash-widower state. Inside, it had been at turns gloomy and cozy, and the cozy was mostly to do with its fireplace and what it meant for Merritt, and yes, its inhabitants. Annie, Evie, Whit.

Whit.

On Thanksgiving Day, however, the house was cozy on its own terms. Evie had met Merritt and her mother at the door wearing a bright white bodysuit top, jeans, and a light pink apron at her waist. Her hair was pulled back in a copious high ponytail but was as glamorous as ever, and Merritt had immediately second-guessed her own outfit, which, just half an hour earlier, she had felt was quite chic: a smocked, long-sleeved black maxi dress. She had even put earrings in—little gold fan-shaped ones that had made her lobes bleed at first. And then, there was her signature indigo coat and the bulky crocheted scarf and, oh God, she had thought, do I look like a teacher on Back to School Night? A minister's wife? And why am I suddenly so *freaking* nervous?

These thoughts passed in an instant as Evie pulled first her and then Kathleen into hugs before stepping back to welcome them into what amounted to a brand-new house. Lamps were on in every room, and candles burned, in both the squat scented and skinny white beeswax varieties. Curtains that were usually drawn had been pulled pack; the Vince Guaraldi Trio played in the background; and the kitchen, which in Merritt's experience had only ever been used to make tea, was emanating oven heat and noise and the smells of a dozen delicious seasonal dishes.

Willa and Adrienne were here, as was Albie, and more hugs were exchanged. Annie was in the living room, streaming the Macy's parade, and a very, very handsome and fashionable man in a ribbed black turtleneck rolled up to the elbows sat on the couch beside her.

"This is my uncle Édouard," Annie explained when Merritt stopped to say hi, now without her coat or scarf. "This is Dad's friend Merritt."

The man was long-limbed and broad-shouldered, with olive skin, pond-green eyes, and a dark, elegantly trimmed beard. He quickly came to his feet and held out a hand to shake, revealing veiny arms and a tattoo in French just below the inner crook of his elbow.

"Hello," he said in a slight accent, as she shook his wide, moisturized hand. "Pleased to meet you."

"Hello," Merritt said, trying to ignore the flustered feeling fluttering in her chest. God, he was handsome.

"You're the hockey player?" she asked, because she felt a desperate need to say something to keep from staring at his eyes, his arms, the thighs that seemed to be testing the durability of his designer jeans.

"Former," he offered with a shrug, before explaining that he was working *somewhere* doing *some* kind of law, though the details went unheard as all of Merritt's attention had now centered itself on the man's sharp jawline and enticing accent, the Frenchness with which he'd said the words *Montréal* and *liaison*.

"Is this your second Thanksgiving then?" Merritt asked, when she realized he'd finished speaking. "Isn't Canadian Thanksgiving in October?"

He smiled, as if proud of her trivial Canadian knowledge, and her heart fluttered a bit faster.

"Yes, but Evie and I don't make a big to-do about it. My family are terrible, and we 'ave more fun at this one, anyway."

Merritt laughed far harder than was warranted, and Whit appeared in the room, as if drawn by the sound. He wore a crisp blue button-down tucked into dark jeans, and his hair was styled just slightly more than usual. The fluttering bird in Merritt's chest became a warm, affectionate cat at the sight at him.

"Hi," Whit said, looking from Merritt to Édouard with—what was that?—was that *nervousness*? Merritt suppressed a smirk.

"Hi," she said back. "Édouard was just telling me a bit about himself. He's quite fascinating."

She patted playfully at the Canadian's bare forearm and watched as Whit's eyes widened slightly.

"Yes, Éd is certainly something."

Édouard smiled, oblivious to whatever this was playing out before him, until Evie called to him from the kitchen and Whit noticeably relaxed.

"He is incredibly handsome," Merritt said in a quick, low voice she knew Annie wouldn't register over the sound of the parade.

Whit nodded, as if it would be impossible to disagree.

"Like, *incredibly* handsome."

"Yes, that is correct."

"You did not tell me you were related to someone so handsome."

"I don't often go around talking about it."

"You should really warn people."

"All right," he said, with some finality.

Merritt let her smirk come out. "What, are you jealous?"

She was taking a chance.

Whit narrowed his eyes at her. Playfully.

"Jealous? Of the winner of the number-three spot in *La Semaine*'s Sexiest Quebecois Professionals for the second year running?"

"Is that real?" Merritt asked.

Whit shrugged.

"And who on earth beat him out for first and second? Hold on, I need to google something."

He rolled his eyes. "This is how it always goes."

They were close enough for her to touch him, so she did. She pressed his elbow, gently, and said, as if comforting him, "You look very nice."

He grinned, clearly choosing to take the compliment genuinely. "That's what I was going to say—about you. But you ruined it by fawning all over my brother-in-law."

"I did not *fawn* over him."

"You came pretty close."

"Well, he . . . I'm sorry, my hands were tied."

He rolled his eyes again, then smiled at her. "You really do look nice. I like your hair that way."

She had done her hair—had lightly curled it—and he had noticed.

*

Whit looked around the dining room table. Typically covered in laundry and Annie's schoolwork, it was now draped in a deep green tablecloth and elegantly appointed by his sister, who'd found the china he and Helen had registered for but never actually used. Evie handwashed each plate, hand-selected the greenery and pine cones arranged up and down a muted gold runner, and handmade each dish now weighting down the long, sturdy table. Around him were his friends, his family, his daughter's librarian, and Merritt.

Kathleen sat between them at the midafternoon meal, and Adrienne and Willa sat across from them, asking Kathleen about books and book bans and rehashing memories of Thanksgivings past. Whit didn't mind. He liked just being near Merritt, liked watching her interact with his friends and her mother, liked how Evie laughed at her jokes and how Annie listened when she spoke. He liked . . .

He liked her.

He *liked* her. There it was.

And of course, beneath the self-loathing he felt at having used such a silly phrase to describe his feelings—*I like her*—those words had an echo, and that echo was the name *Helen*. This was his and Annie's second Thanksgiving with her gone, and that was still a tender thing. The day felt different without her, the family felt incomplete, and if he allowed himself to dwell on it for too long, he could feel himself slipping into a kind of yearning—to hear her voice, to smell the pies she always made, to laugh at her parade commentary.

He had taken a walk early that morning and thought of all these things, and though he would never hear Helen's voice again, Evie had made the pies, and Édouard had made Annie laugh at the parade floats, and Merritt was here. That felt different, too, but an okay different. A happy different, in fact. He liked her.

As they ate, he watched Annie, who really did seem all right. Occasionally, a cloud would pass over her face, and he wished for the millionth time that he could read her mind, that he knew how to break down the tough walls she'd inherited from her often enigmatic mother. Was she worse off than him, one more holiday into a life without Helen? Was she better? She seemed to be watching Merritt and thinking, and no matter how hard he tried, he could not decipher what the look on her face might mean.

He would talk to her, he decided, at bedtime. For now, there was turkey and cranberry sauce and a sweet potato casserole he would have happily paid $18 for at the bistro on Cork Street.

After the meal, Whit said he'd do the dishes and Merritt offered to help. In seconds, Adrienne and Kathleen decided they'd go on a walk, while Willa joined Édouard as he explained the rules of a complicated card game to Annie, Albie, and a very competitive Evie. Whit had the distinct sense that people were deliberately leaving Merritt and him alone, but who cared. That was what he wanted.

"Evie is a really good cook," Merritt said, as she moved around the dining room table making stacks of empty plates.

Whit was pouring unfinished glasses of wine and water into a used pitcher. "Yup," he said. "Self-taught. Our mom was awful."

"Mine, too. Or really, she just doesn't like it. She'll bake occasionally, but that's mostly because she loves desserts. My dad was the big cook in the family."

"Mine too," Whit said. "Before my folks split up, he'd lock us out of the kitchen and make these huge spreads. That was probably the worst part of the divorce. We very quickly became a Hamburger Helper family half the time."

Whit said it as a joke, and Merritt smiled softly. "That was probably kind of a sad reminder, though. Sitting down to dinner each night."

Whit considered her words and shrugged. "Sort of, yeah," he said. Then, realizing something: "Oh God."

"What?"

"No, it's fine."

Merritt set her stack of plates on the table corner so she could really look at him. She did not seem convinced.

"Really," he said. "It's fine, I just didn't think I'd find myself in the same position. Poor Annie, stuck with my bad cooking."

Merritt's smile returned, sad this time.

"I'm sorry, Whit."

He let out a puff of a laugh. "It's fine. Helen wasn't actually a very good cook, either."

Merritt waited, thinking, then spoke. "I'm pretty good."

"Are you?"

"I am, actually. I've been lazy lately, letting my mom order takeout or whatever, because I guess that's what you do when you stay at your parent's house."

"I grab a drink from the fridge every time I leave my mom's."

"Exactly."

She started stacking plates again.

"But maybe I could teach you a few dishes—just some stand-bys I think Annie would like."

Her head was down as she talked.

"I don't want to intrude or overstep—"

"I would love that," Whit said, looking at her from across the table.

She looked up at him. She smiled. She had a very nice smile. And a very nice not-smile, for that matter. He just liked looking at her, whatever state her face was in.

They continued cleaning to the sounds of clinking glass and metal, until Merritt spoke up again.

"Whit, listen," she said, in a tone that made Whit feel a bit like he'd expected solid ground where a hole turned out to be. What came next felt very important.

"I've been thinking," she said, pausing again, and Whit's hand found the table below him for support. Should he interrupt her?

Should he insist that he already knew, that he felt it, too, that he agreed?

Merritt looked to the ceiling, steeling herself, then shrugged as she said, "I think Ursula needs to die."

What?

Oh. Oh, she was talking shop. He was thinking about her, and she was thinking about *the book*.

"What?" he said, buying time.

"I know," Merritt said, moving toward the kitchen with the plates. He followed.

"It sounds crazy, and I don't really like the idea of killing off one of the two female leads, but we still have Christabel, and I just think it sort of makes sense with her character arc. I think she should die saving Christabel and Rupert, in a final act of her own agency."

Whit was struggling to catch up, but that didn't inhibit his ability to tell that Merritt was making sense. She really got these books.

"You're really good at this," he said, and here he was, thinking about *her* again.

She twisted the hot water handle at the sink and turned back toward him, surprised.

"Thank you?"

He stopped walking. They were perhaps three feet apart. He shrugged.

"You just are. And I think you're probably right. That makes sense—it feels real. It feels true to the story."

"It will be really sad," Merritt said, her voice suddenly soft. Her eyes were searching his.

Whit nodded slowly and purposefully. "Sometimes sad is good."

There was an apple pie in the oven and the smell was powerful. Steam from the sink was filling the air, and from beyond the kitchen, Whit could hear the sounds of a football game on TV and laughter from the card game.

Merritt shrugged. "True. I thought I might have to persuade you to do it."

Whit cocked his head, and she kept talking.

"It's just a big choice, you know, killing off one of the three core characters. There could be backlash, I don't know. I thought you might need some convincing."

"Merritt," he said, his voice slightly hushed, "I don't think you know how good you are. If it's your idea, I like it."

"Unless it's a fairy tale allusion."

Whit rolled his eyes, and she smirked. He took a single step forward. He could see her swallow.

"I mean it," he said. "I trust you."

"That's nice, but I can be wrong—"

"Of course you can. But you're usually not. You're right about most things. You're just good."

He was trying to talk about the book. He really was. But Merritt kept cropping up in each sentence, each implication.

He took a breath. She took a breath. He could almost feel the heat of her body in the air between them.

Whit forced himself to speak.

"Can I—"

She leaned forward and kissed him, and he felt it from his lips to the back of his head, as if the kiss had gone through him. He leaned into it, so she'd know he was kissing her back. His hands cupped her face on either side, with hers moving to his ribs, and they stood that way, their bodies linked together in something warm and safe, until they both seemed to sense something at the same time, and they pulled apart.

She grinned. He grinned.

"We should—"

"There are people—"

They laughed. Merritt patted at her dress, as if to unruffle it, and Whit, needing to do something, reached for the ladle on the stove's spoon rest before delivering it to the sink. He turned off the water and looked out the window, then glanced at the breakfast table, listening, before turning back to Merritt. She was waiting to see what he'd do—and what he did was grab her hand and kiss her once more on the lips as he squeezed that hand, hoping to intimate what he couldn't say right now. *I like you. I like this.*

When they pulled away, they were both laughing.

"Well," she said.

"Well."

She took a deep breath. "We should finish cleaning up."

He did a mock bow by way of assent.

"If it's your idea, I like it."

Merritt pointed at him. "Don't get cheesy on me, Longacre."

Whit smiled. "I'll try my best."

CHAPTER TWENTY-TWO

Act normal, act normal, act normal, Whit told himself as the party stood in the entry hall, saying their goodbyes. Kathleen was cupping Annie by the chin, looking down at her like a good witch uttering a blessing. The Barrett-Linds had left earlier to pop in on Adrienne's cousins a town over, and Édouard had taken on washing the dessert dishes in the kitchen, but Evie was there, saying goodbye to Merritt while keeping one eye trained on Whit. He was stewing in his awkwardness as he tried desperately to tamp down the frenetic energy he felt in all of him.

They had kissed. They had actually kissed, and something had passed between them, and then they hadn't been able to talk about it. Annie had come looking for them, wanting to show them Édouard's game, right as Adrienne and Kathleen were returning from their walk. So Whit had spent the next several hours playing cards, eating pie, and finally, half-watching their first Christmas movie of the season (*A Muppet Christmas Carol*, Annie's choice), when all he'd wanted to be doing was *talking to Merritt about how they had just kissed.*

Now he was waiting to say goodbye while his sister lurked in the distance with a sinister smirk on her face. And here was Merritt.

"See you Monday?" she asked.

"Sure," he said, wondering if his voice always sounded this vibratey. "Unless—"

"Yes?" Merritt said quickly.

"Well, I was kind of thinking about working tomorrow, if—"

"I'd love to," she said, even more quickly.

"Great."

"Great. Okay. See you then."

"Okay."

They hugged. It was a sad, pained, stiff-armed thing (their first hug), and then the hall was empty but for him and Evie. And he was thinking a stupid thing (that he missed Merritt and wanted to call her) when he heard Evie clear her throat.

He turned to her, and she was on him in a flash.

"*Something* happened."

"What?"

Her eyes were glowing. "I know it did, something happened between you two."

"I don't know what you're talking about."

"Oh my God, look at your face. You *kissed*, didn't you?"

"*Shh!*" Whit hissed, conscious that his daughter had just gone upstairs.

"Didn't you? They probably just got into their car, I can just go out there and ask her if you—"

"Yes, fine, yes, we kissed. Now *shut up*."

Evie clapped her hands together above her head and then raised them even higher, as if she were someone praying dramatically in an opera.

"Thank you, God. Thank you."

Whit let himself laugh. "Oh, shut up."

*

Merritt spent the car ride home urging herself to *act normal, act normal, act normal*. Kathleen did most of the talking, going on about what a lovely job Evie had done with the food and the house, and how it must be good for Whit and Annie to have her around, and then they talked about Édouard, and Merritt did contribute then because, as she'd told Whit, it was hard not to fawn over him, and because he had done that rare thing of being both handsome and perfectly unobjectionable all night long. He had been *funny*, even, over their pie à la mode. A perfectly nice man who also happened to be shockingly enjoyable to look at.

That was one reason Merritt knew she had it bad: she was daydreaming about a world in which a man like Édouard was a *side character*. The whole day felt tremendously normal, natural, and then she had kissed Whit, and he'd kissed her back, and here she was, having to act unfazed as her mom pulled into her garage.

"I think I'll go on a walk," she said when they walked into the kitchen.

"It's after eight and in the forties," her mother said, surprised. "And dark."

"I'll bundle up."

Merritt quickly donned some long johns, and as soon as her booted foot hit the sidewalk, she knew she'd made the right decision. The brick-lined streets glowed orange in the light of the lampposts and set her mind to imagining this village a hundred, two hundred years ago, lit up then by actual flames brought by men with long, curved sticks, when women like her would be inside, fast asleep, or perhaps writing furiously by the light of their candles. Playing whist—whatever that was—or sitting at the pianoforte. And yes, these were just things heroines did in novels by Jane Austen and the Brontës, and who knew whether the same was true of old New Englanders. The point was that the walking was expelling the live-wire energy roiling in her body, and thinking about nineteenth-century ladies and horse-drawn carriages was taking her mind away from Whit Longacre—until her phone buzzed and it was him.

To her mind, there were two opposing possibilities: either he was merely calling because they'd failed to set a time to meet up tomorrow, or he was calling with regret, with anger, with great grief and a sense that he'd betrayed his late wife. Merritt felt an urge to answer and spit out an apology before he even spoke, but he was too quick.

"I'm sorry—"

There it was. Already.

"—for calling so soon," he continued. "Maybe it's more, I don't know, *smooth* to wait a bit, but I just needed to talk to you."

Oh.

"Are you okay?" he said, surprising her again. "I mean, was that okay? Do you feel okay about what happened?"

"Do you?"

She winced as she waited the space of a breath for him to respond.

"Yes. I do."

"You do?"

"I do!"

He was smiling, she could tell. He was happy.

Oh, she was happy, too.

"So do I," she said at last. "I feel . . . I've wanted . . . but, I didn't know if you would—"

"I didn't know I would, either."

Merritt laughed, and she thought to herself that it was really more of a giggle, and that that was allowed. This was the sort of thing you giggled over. There were so many factors at play—Whit had a daughter, he was a widower, they worked together—that the whole thing felt secretive and a bit high-school-ish. It felt thrilling and difficult to talk about in complete sentences.

"Listen," he said, after they'd laughed a bit more about their awkwardness. "Evie and Édouard are leaving in two days. After that, we should get dinner—not a working dinner, but a real dinner. A date."

She liked that he called it a date. She liked that it was his idea.

That he was letting her know where things stood. Goodness, it was refreshing.

"I'd love that," she said. "It's a date."

"It certainly is."

They hung up, and here she was, back where she started: her body full of electricity and her mind full of Whit. She walked for another hour before finally going home to lie awake in bed, resisting the urge to pick up her phone and text him to say good night.

CHAPTER TWENTY-THREE

Whit had called Merritt after carrying Annie to her bed. She had fallen asleep watching *The Santa Clause*, her second Christmas movie of the season, and Whit had felt momentarily crestfallen at failing in his plan to talk to her. But she looked so sweet and content that he allowed himself to be convinced she'd had a good day.

After a shower, he'd gotten into bed with his laptop, more eager than ever to read Merritt's manuscript, which he'd been ingesting in large doses over the last few days. But within a minute of opening it, he thought, *screw it*, and called up the real thing. Only after the call had he let himself be satisfied with reading her words.

Now it was Friday, and they were writing again. Evie and Édouard had made the insane choice to bring Annie along with them for Black Friday shopping, so Whit and Merritt had the house entirely to themselves. They usually had it to themselves, but today there was potential in the space, as if what had happened was a secret and the house was waiting for them to slip up and spill the beans.

Whit had greeted her at the door, and Merritt had laughed at him, telling him he looked serious. She extended her hand as if expecting him to kiss it and said, "How do you do?" He shook it as if they were business partners, and she laughed at him again. But then she, too, had settled into a business-as-usual groove, and the two of them wrote and wrote all morning. Finally, Merritt cleared her throat.

"Okay," she said, taking off her glasses to rub her eyes. She was sitting in her spot by the fire, with her legs tucked up under her, laptop balanced on the armrest, and she was cradling a cup of steaming tea in both hands.

"Okay?"

"I think it's time," she said, "to kill Ursula."

"Oh," Whit said, and despite his assurances of his trust in Merritt the day before, he did find himself hesitating.

"You're hesitating."

"I know. I am."

"It is a big deal."

"Exactly."

Merritt took a deep breath, and Whit smiled at the way her bangs swooped up when she exhaled, and the indentation her teeth made on her bottom lip. He had always noticed these kinds of things about her, but now he was allowing himself to enjoy them.

"Does it feel," she asked, "a little bit like killing someone else's child?"

"Goodness, that's dark."

"You know what I mean. Helen *created* her, and now we're . . . *un*-creating her."

Whit shrugged. "The story has to go somewhere. That's what stories do."

"Okay, Mary Oliver."

Whit laughed, and Merritt did, too. She looked out the window, her eyes glinting for a moment in the sunlight.

"I just wish there was a way to know whether Helen would've approved," Merritt said.

"I can assure you, there's not. I've looked everywhere."

Merritt nodded, unsatisfied. Whit thought about Helen's study high at the top of the house. He hadn't disturbed it in months and months, but now he had an idea. He briefly wondered whether it was a betrayal, and then he wondered whether that mattered, whether such things could even be betrayals when the person to be betrayed was gone. But he had kissed this woman. He had already taken the first step in whatever direction they were going. Had already taken many steps, in fact.

He decided.

"Would it make you feel better to look around?"

Merritt's eyes zipped to his. "What?"

"In her study. Upstairs."

Whit watched Merritt's face open up with what could only be described as obvious appetite. Her eyes were wide, and her mouth hung open slightly. He almost laughed.

"I don't know, Whit, would that be an invasion . . ."

"Of what? Her privacy?"

Merritt shrugged.

Whit thought. Would it?

"She left me the book. It's mine to finish. *Ours* now. I think it's our right. I think it's what she would have expected."

"But, you would be bringing another . . . bringing someone else into her space, and—"

"—and finishing the book. I think that's the main thing."

Whit was less sure than he sounded, but more sure than he would have been two months ago. This moment was internally tense, and there was something compelling about that. Tension meant he was feeling something, two somethings even, and being pulled between them. Tension meant he was alive. He stood up, signaling his resolution.

"Listen," he said, his voice soft and full, "the only reason the book is in the state it is—the only reason the end is in sight—is *you*."

"That's not true, Whit—"

"It *is* true, and you know it. You have saved this book, and you're as entitled as anyone to do what we have to do as we search for the proper ending. Let's go have a look."

Merritt smiled, holding his eyes in hers. When she stood up in agreement, he grabbed her hand, pulled, and they kissed again. A gentle, comfortable thing, her soft lips against his, as he took in the smell of her hair and the Ivory soap and amber oil on her skin. And still his belly dropped, and his head felt light and airy.

When she pulled away, she was smiling. "Whit, please, I'm working."

He nodded.

"Come on. The ivory tower awaits."

*

Merritt's heart rate increased as she followed Whit up two flights of stairs, the first one wide with a well-trod oxblood runner down its center, the second narrower, like the passageway to servants' quarters in a period drama. She was nervous. She had anticipated something like this, an almost forbidden glimpse behind the curtain, all those weeks ago when she and Whit had spoken over their meal at the bistro. She was going to see, finally, where Helen had worked. Where she had crafted the books that had saved Merritt in more ways than one, had made her into a writer with a dream.

And here they were, at a wooden door painted the gray-blue color of a raincloud, and there was a golden emblem like a door knocker about where a peephole might have been: a kestrel with a spoon in its beak. Just like the necklaces, worn by the characters Ursula, Rupert, and Christabel, that had become the symbol of the Greenwood Castle books in the real world as well.

This was it. The inner sanctum.

Merritt took a deep breath and tried to hide it.

Inside was a square room, perhaps fifteen feet by fifteen feet, with windows all around, like a lighthouse. The ceiling was peaked and paneled with wood slats; on either side of the doorway and along the right and left walls were low bookshelves that went from floor to window. A built-in desk lined much of the far wall, and the space in the middle was covered by a rug patterned in emerald and seafoam and sage greens. It was cold up here, and Merritt noted the quilt draped over the back of the desk chair and the space heater at its feet.

It was like stepping into a keepsake box. The room was lovely, exactly the kind of place Merritt would've liked to write in, but it was also sad in its disuse, its emptiness, its bygoneness. She spun slowly in a circle and looked through the windows, where she could see the hillside, a strip of the sea, and the peaks of the buildings in the village. So this was what Helen had seen as she thought and imagined and wrote and revised.

"Oh," Merritt said, in a quiet church voice. She resisted the urge to wipe her eyes.

Whit gave her a kind, appreciative smile.

"Yeah," he said, dropping his eyes. She wondered what he was thinking, and what it was like for him to have her here. "Let's have a look around. You can have the desk. I'll start with the bookshelves."

"Okay," she said. He turned to the nearest set of books, and she walked across the room, feeling like a trespasser.

But then he said, "Here," and she saw on the shelf a small, table-top record player she hadn't noticed before. In a few seconds, the room was filled with the sounds of Fleetwood Mac's *Mirage* album.

"Because you like Stevie Nicks," he said, reminding her of Halloween. She smiled, and the two of them set to work. Merritt chose not to sit in Helen's seat, showing the same respect she might show a Victorian novelist's writing chair in the British Library.

The desk was a mess, which Merritt found refreshing. Helen's laptop still sat on the leather-top, and around it were stacks of papers: copies of old publishing documents, a handwritten draft of a speech for the American Library Association, and many, many fan letters. Merritt got hung up on those for a time, reading from young people who asked questions about warlocks and elves, or who wanted help with school projects, or who just wanted Helen Albright Longacre to know that they, too, were going to be a writer someday. Merritt felt wistful for these kids who had probably felt the loss of their favorite author rather deeply, and she wondered whether Helen had gotten the chance to respond to any of them.

Then there was the sticky note: lime green, with a phrase written in Sharpie.

Check baby giant story??

This was the note Whit had found, two months before, that had driven him to the bookstore looking for her help. She was grateful for this note, for a multitude of reasons, though she hadn't thought of it since. Now it caught her eye. Did it mean something? What was Helen going to check the story for? And was there a copy of that story somewhere—perhaps an early, pre-auction draft?

Crouching now, she started opening drawers, this imaginary draft on her mind, and was surprised to find them mostly vacant but for a half-empty package of pistachios, an old Luna Bar, a gray woolen glove, and a pair of scissors. In the central drawer, beneath which Helen's legs would have sat, there were only paper clips and an unused Moleskine. Merritt glanced back at Whit, who was absorbed in a book, then padded her fingers around inside the drawers, searching blindly, idiotically, for the kind of hidden compartment you might see in an old film caper. No such luck.

"There's nothing over here," she said, and Whit nodded, unsurprised but unannoyed. "I did find this, though."

She held the sticky note up between two fingers, and Whit laughed.

"A fateful note, in the end."

"I still wish we knew what it meant," she said.

He nodded again. "I think we just have to be okay not knowing."

They paused for a moment, then Merritt turned back to the desk and patted the laptop.

"Anything on this?"

"Yes," Whit said, with his eyes back on the open book. "The most organized, least informative stuff you can imagine. There are notes for each book, which I spent the early days reading—but they're bare outlines, lists of possible names for characters and places and things, which is sort of fun but not super-helpful, and I think maybe an early explanation of the books' magic system. I searched and searched for any information that seemed to gesture toward something in the final book, but I came up empty. You're welcome to look if you want. I'm checking the books for notes between the pages."

Merritt *did* want to look. But it felt like the kind of thing she'd want to do on her own.

"I'll help with that first," she said.

She lowered herself to sit on the rug and began pulling volumes from the shelf. Within a few minutes, she found a bookmark in one text, which was briefly exciting, but it was in a book on German philosophy, with nothing obviously relevant on the page. Two dozen books later, there was still nothing to show for her efforts. Whit flipped the Fleetwood Mac record, and on they worked, singing along to "Hold Me" in mumbly voices.

"Here's something," Whit said, holding up a book of fairy tales. "The page on Sleeping Beauty is dog-eared."

"Oh." Merritt watched Whit as he skimmed the page. Then he looked up to her with a face that was all sweetness and humility.

"So you were right about that. The allusion I thought she wouldn't be making. You were right."

Merritt wasn't sure what to say.

"We don't know that for certain" was what she settled on. There was something like vindication pulsing in her (she *had* been right!) but it was faint, and in this moment it didn't matter as much anymore. "She might have folded that corner twenty years ago."

Whit smiled at her. "I suppose it's not important. We're writing the story now."

Now Merritt really didn't know what to say. She had been the proponent for alluding to Sleeping Beauty, but she had been treating the book like a puzzle then, with missing pieces to be filled in. These days, she wasn't so sure that metaphor was apt. Whit seemed to think they might never find the right pieces, and it was their job to fill in the blanks in their own way. And maybe he was right. Helen might have intended to use any number of allusions in the final book, but Merritt and Whit would never be able to write the story in precisely her way. That way was lost now, and they were always going to be making something different, putting themselves into the story, designing the final fraction of the tale as an approximation at best.

Merritt thought of the semester she'd studied abroad in Italy, where she'd learned that restorers repairing ancient frescoes often left gaps in place rather than try to repaint what had been lost to memory. It was a way of honoring the old masters and acknowledging the power of passing time. She and Whit, however, had no such luxury. The end of the story, if Helen had ever finished conceiving it, was lost, and they had to splash some paint across the plaster and hope it worked out okay. There was no other way of doing it.

Whit put the book back on the shelf.

"All right," Merritt said, trying to will herself into agreement. She returned to the books, thinking about Sleeping Beauty and the baby giant, too. If they were to honor (what they assumed to be) Helen's wishes by weaving allusions to the fairy tale or the cryptic note into the plot, they would have to unravel much of the winding story they'd settled on, unmaking some of the magic she and Whit had managed to create, and who knew what would be lost in the process. *We just have to be okay not knowing.*

"Can I ask something that might seem invasive?" she said, sitting on the ground with her back against the desk.

Whit looked up from a book on the language of flowers. He pretended to think with squinted eyes, and then nodded firmly.

"Yes."

"How did she *leave* the book to you?"

"What do you mean?"

"How did you know she'd done it? Did you talk about it?"

Whit, who was also seated on the floor, shook his head quickly. "Oh, no. It was a complete surprise. There wasn't a reading of the will like they do in the movies, because nobody expected any bombshells. I knew everything was going to me and Annie, and it more or less did. She left some money for a scholarship at Annie's school, and she gave some to the creative writing program at our alma mater, and we all thought that was going to be that."

Whit shrugged. He was looking up at the windows, and his eyes shone in the midday light. Merritt could tell he was remembering with the lucidity that came with big, life-changing moments.

"Then the lawyer—this elderly man straight out of central casting, with the exact voice you think of when you hear 'elderly man'—called me into his office and told me there had been a late addendum, or whatever you call it in legalese, and he looked at me, and I won't say I *knew* what he was about to say, but this great sense of foreboding washed over me."

"Had you thought about it?"

"About what?"

Merritt considered her words before speaking. "About how there was still one book left to be written? That someone would have to do something, or else leave the series unfinished?"

"Honestly? No. I think—I *know*—that's what most of her fans would have thought about—"

Merritt blushed, despite the fact that Whit was neither looking at her nor speaking with any unkindness about "fans" like her.

"—but I think I was still in shock. Even when you know it's coming . . ."

He trailed off, cleared his throat.

"And I was mostly worrying about Annie all the time."

Merritt closed her eyes for a moment, feeling these words like a physical rebuke.

"Of course you were," she said, and Whit gave her a quick, appreciative smile before drawing his eyes back to the light.

"Anyway, the lawyer read off what she had written. I could find it somewhere, but I remember it pretty well. 'In addition to the management of my estate (including all existing social media handles, all future editions, the approval of film rights, and so on and so forth), I leave the completion of the fifth and final novel in the Greenwood Castle Saga to my husband, Whitman Howard Longacre, using whatever means he deems necessary and appropriate.' Something like that. The real legal force has to do with her contract, which says her estate will decide who completes the book in the event of her death. And you're looking at her estate."

Merritt felt relief whistle through her limbs. "She said that, though, about 'whatever means'?"

Whit nodded. "Yup."

"So we could use AI?"

Whit narrowed his eyes. "I do *not* deem that necessary and appropriate."

They laughed together for a moment, and then Whit rubbed his brows.

"Is it hard," Merritt asked, "being up here?"

Whit looked around more thoroughly before he spoke.

"I think it's not as hard as it could be. I almost never came in here when she was alive, she was so private. It'd be like if she had been an accountant and I had to collect her things from her office or something after. I don't know that it would affect me very much. It's more the *things* themselves. That quilt. Her aunt made her that for her college dorm room."

He nodded at the desk behind Merritt.

"There's a pen over there that she loved—always those G2-10s, which I find to be so runny and messy, but she loved them."

He smiled a soft smile, looking down at his hands as they touched the ground.

"I remember her picking out this rug. Things like that."

Whit nodded to himself, and Merritt felt a little guilty about being here in this room with him, which she had not forced him to enter but which he had entered on her behalf nonetheless. But then, he turned to Merritt with a look that felt layered in meaning, like he was trying to comfort *her*, like he was seeing her, fully, in spite of all this talk and in spite of where they were, and he said something that felt sharp and soft, like a knife and a blanket at once.

"She would have liked you."

"Oh. Oh?"

"Yeah," Whit said easily, with a quick raise of the shoulders. "You have the sort of humor she enjoyed, and you're kind, which was what she valued most. And she would've liked your work."

Merritt felt warm all over.

"You can't know that."

"Of course I can."

Whit stood up and extended a hand, which Merritt took.

"Grab that," he said, nodding at the laptop. "Have a look around tonight. The password is just capital-*A Annie*."

"Are you sure? I mean about me looking at it?"

Whit nodded, then continued his thought from before.

"I don't know how she would have felt about what we're doing with the book—I think she knew she couldn't have an opinion at this point anyway. Hence the 'whatever means he deems necessary' business. But if we could somehow remove what you've done from the context of it being *her* series, she would have liked it. And I *know* she would have liked your own manuscript, which, by the way, cuts off at a very cliffhanger-y moment. I can't wait to read the end."

He had deliberately shifted away from her as he said this, and Merritt's laptop-free hand shot out, unbidden, and yanked him back by the shoulder. He was laughing as he turned to look at her.

"You *what*?"

"I finished it. What you have anyway. I have some notes—almost entirely positive—but—"

"Shut up, you read it. And you waited until now to tell me? When did you finish?"

"Late last night after you left."

"Last *night*?"

He was turning away again, walking toward the door and down the narrow stairs, giving Merritt the opportunity to storm after him.

"And you didn't call or text to tell me?"

He held his hands up, as if saying, *What do you want from me?*

"Oh my God," she said, mildly frustrated. Then she stopped midway down the stairs and said again, in a new, fearful tone, "Oh my God. You hated it, didn't you?"

Whit stopped, too, and turned back to look at her. "What?"

"You hated it. Otherwise you would've told me—"

"I've just told you. *And* I explicitly said Helen would have liked it."

She held up her pointer finger. "Exactly. And you have also explicitly said you did not like Helen's books—"

"Hey now," he said, holding up his own pointer finger. "I said they weren't for me, there's a difference."

"But *my* manuscript *would* have been *Helen's* kind of thing."

"*You* are *using* a *lot* of *emphasis*," he joked. "But it would have been her thing, yes." Then he let out a heavy sigh and leaned against the wall of the stairway for support.

"And you . . ."

He trailed off.

"What?"

He bit his lip, eyes on the ceiling as he spoke.

"You are about to force me to say something that makes me feel very guilty, but I am going to say it anyway."

"Oh God, just get it over—"

"I liked it," he interrupted, "more than I liked Helen's stuff."

He winced.

Merritt was aware that her eyes had gone wide and that her mouth now hung open, but a great hollowness also seemed to have filled her skull, from ear to ear. She felt lightheaded.

"I'm not the best judge of kid lit," he said. "So who cares what I like. But you've done something with this story—the reverse Narnia aspect, the people on the other side of the portal—that's subversive and interesting, but it still feels like the sort of thing Annie would read, and I think that's really impressive."

Her face burned with the most pleasant heat she could ever remember feeling.

"But what really matters," he continued, "is that the writing be undeniably *good*. And Merritt, it's *really* good. You are a *good* writer."

He said these words in a tone that left her incapable of disbelieving him. Then he squeezed her hands once and released them. Merritt waited, a bit thunderstruck.

"And now, you must promise me you will never again be surprised when someone tells you something like that, okay?"

Merritt tried to think.

"I . . ."

He smiled.

"Fine, be surprised all you want, but know this: you're going to be hearing it a lot, and one day you'll get used to it."

He smiled, a beautiful, proud smile, and then turned and walked away, leaving her stunned on the staircase.

CHAPTER TWENTY-FOUR

After that, their work had stalled out for the day. The next thing to do was write the death scene, and Whit could tell that Merritt was still waiting for some sign from Helen that this would be okay.

Instead, they took a walk along the trails behind the house, bundled up and mostly in companionable silence. Whit was sure that he and Merritt were both thinking about the same thing: how good all this was. He was somewhat surprised, almost perplexed, by his own feelings on the matter. He really was at ease about it all—killing off a main character, making the book their own, what had happened between him and Merritt the day before, and what he hoped would happen again. Merritt walked in front today, and he watched her as he thought. He liked the way the occasional bursts of sun through the clouds seemed to brighten her hair first, turning it a shade lighter than it looked up in the house, and he liked her purposeful stride and her quiet, unconscious humming.

They walked for a little over a mile, until Whit said they should turn back. Annie would be home soon. On the return, they walked side by side, and Whit reached out, tentative and sure at once, to take Merritt's gloved hand in his. It surprised her, clearly, and she looked at him, a little stricken, until her face softened into a smile.

"Sorry, I'm such a weirdo."

He laughed. "You're not."

"It's just that I've been trying very hard to *not* do this."

"What?"

"*Like* you," she said, giving his hand a squeeze. "Have any feelings for you whatsoever."

"Oh, I've made it very hard, have I?"

She rolled her eyes but didn't release his hand.

"Don't get cocky." She paused. "But oddly enough, yes."

"You must have a thing for borderline depressed dads who need therapy and a good shave."

"Everyone needs therapy," Merritt said casually. "As for the rest, maybe I do. The heart wants, et cetera."

Whit stopped, pulling Merritt's hand until she did the same.

"What?" she said.

"I don't want you to think . . ."

He could see the worry descend on her face, and he jumped to find the right words.

"It's not like you've been languishing in your feelings for me all alone."

"I object to 'languishing,' but go on."

She waited, clearly unsure where he was going.

"I . . ." He puffed up his cheeks and let out a long breath. "It's complicated, being a . . . widower. I hate that word. Anyway, I'm not very self-aware when it comes to my own feelings. I'm trying to be, but it's still hard, even without all the grief and guilt. Lately, though, when I *do* have any nameable feelings, it's like they're plants in a terrarium, and I know they're there, but I have to break through to get to them."

He looked down and stepped on a dead leaf.

"Not always, but often, and so anything I've felt for you—and I've felt a lot for you, from the beginning, from the moment you got that book stuck in the book drop—but I had to let myself *get* to it first, if that makes sense. And I don't want to always talk about Helen, really, I'm sorry about that, but I think that's just going to be part of this. Part of me, and—"

Merritt brought her other hand forward so that his hand was wrapped in both of hers.

"Whit," she said, interrupting him, "you know how you said I'm not allowed to be surprised when people say my writing is good?"

She said this directly without a single quiver of self-doubt.

"Yes?"

"Right. Well, you are not allowed to apologize for grieving. The guilt is another story—it's natural, I know that from when my dad died, even if it's not logical or fair to yourself—but you can't change the grief, and you can't feel bad about it. That, or talking about Helen. Okay?"

Whit started to speak, then stopped himself, waiting, letting himself feel Merritt's words. And the feeling came. In the early months after Helen's death, he had tried to push through, for Annie, and he had lived more or less on autopilot, going through each day without being really conscious of any decision he made. The soft parts of himself were buried far within, unreachable except sometimes, when something unexpected would breach all his protective layers: discovering one of Helen's earrings in the couch cushions, or a song they'd both liked coming on the radio. Or once—he remembered this specifically—he'd been sitting in the optometrist's chair, and the technician, who was adjusting the refractor against Whit's eyes, barely grazed his cheekbones with his fingertips at the very same moment he asked, "So how have you been?" and Whit had felt a shudder roll through him, and his eyes had filled with tears. He'd apologized, explaining that his wife had just died.

He felt much the same now as Merritt gave those soft parts permission to be, and as she told him in so many words that feeling these things for her did not lessen his love for Helen. And he did not cry, and he did not apologize, but he wrapped his other hand around hers for the second time that day.

"Okay," he said softly. "Thank you."

Merritt nodded.

"And," she said, "just a point of clarification: *I* did not get the book stuck in the book drop. I got the book unstuck, thank you very much."

Whit smiled.

"Of course. I must have forgotten."

"Well, don't do it again," she said, pulling her hands free as she continued to walk. "I'm the hero of that story."

"Yes," Whit said, "you are."

*

Once they were back in the house, they unbundled, and Whit made tea while Merritt stoked the fire back to life. He popped a mixed berry pie left over from the day before into the microwave, and the two of them sat in the living room, warming themselves and feeling, Merritt thought, simply happy. She assessed the sensation, because she'd felt it so infrequently lately. The truth was that everything in her immediate vicinity was right and good, and that rare impression was casting a warm, fuzzy glow over the rest of her life. She was glad, she realized, to be living in Whelk Harbor, glad to be spending time with her mother in a place that wasn't Texas or her childhood home in Virginia. She was more and more confident in the book she and Whit were crafting. She believed in it. And then there was Whit. She has happy with Whit.

When the front door opened and slammed in rapid succession, it shook both of them from their quiet reverie. Annie shot through the room in a blur, and then the back door opened and shut in the same way, letting in a wave of cold air from both sides.

Whit and Merritt looked at each other, perplexed and worried, and then Evie and Édouard came in through the front door.

"I told her we're going home on Sunday," Evie said.

"Whit mentioned that," Merritt said. "You'll be missed."

Evie turned to her and nodded with a somber smile. "I figured I'd fly back with Édouard. We're having Christmas with my dad in the Cayman Islands this year, and I want to spend some time at home before we go. Plus, Édouard misses me desperately."

"It's true, I am despondent," he said, crouching dramatically to rest his head on her shoulder. "I can hardly function."

He said "hardly" like *'ard-lee*, and Merritt felt herself grinning at him like a schoolgirl. Whit cleared his throat, and she laughed.

"I gather Annie didn't take it very well," Merritt said, returning to the business at hand.

Evie *hmm*-ed and inclined her head in response.

"I'll go talk to her," Whit said, standing up.

Once he'd left the room, the other three adults moved to the window and watched as Whit called for Annie, who turned to him from the edge of the woods. She waited for him to approach, then fell into him, and he scooped her up and held her to his chest while she cried.

"Oh," Merritt and Evie said in unison, and then Evie nudged her with her shoulder.

Later that night, when Merritt was home, trying to read on her window seat, she thought about what she'd seen. About the way Whit hadn't said much, had just held his daughter and let her cry. She thought about how, several minutes later, a puffy-eyed Annie had come back inside and run to Evie, hugged her tightly, and whispered, "I'm just going to miss you so much," and about how Whit had clearly helped her sort out her feelings just by being her dad whom she loved and trusted. Merritt felt such affection for him that she couldn't help grinning. And there was Evie's nudge, which was hard to interpret. Was it a proud-sister-of-a-brother thing, or something more sororal, a look-at-your-man moment? Whatever it meant, Evie had made Merritt feel good, at the end of an afternoon of feeling good.

Now her phone buzzed. Whit.

Find anything on the laptop?

Merritt sniffed out a laugh. She had felt *so* good that she'd forgotten all about her mission. Within a minute, she was back on the window seat, her book shoved to the side and the computer on her lap.

She opened it, and the lock screen presented her with a picture of slightly younger Longacres. Annie looked to be about five, and the three of them were bundled up in snow gear, squeezing each other next to a leaning snowman. They looked happy, and it tugged at Merritt a little, but also made her smile.

Are you watching me? she silently asked the redheaded woman in a tasseled beanie. Helen's smile was inscrutable—of course it was, she wasn't going to speak from the computer screen—and Merritt thought for the hundredth time how strange it was that her days were filled with this woman's work and now her husband. Two years ago, she would have given anything to meet her; now she almost felt like she knew her, and the thought made her both thankful and sad.

She typed in the password—*A-n-n-i-e*—and was met by an entirely empty desktop. She'd never seen anything like it. Helen was either extremely organized or she'd been in the CIA. Merritt started to click around. It didn't take long to find the folder of Greenwood Castle documents, but Whit was right: all she found was a smattering of bare outlines and four files with titles like "GC 1–TDITGW Final."

Merritt let her mouse hover over the last file for a moment before closing the folder. To open those, she felt, would be like intruding on Helen *as* she wrote, like barging into her study at the top of the Longacre house. Merritt knew it didn't make sense, but it's how she felt, and she decided to respect that feeling, and Helen in the process.

As she clicked around the rest of the laptop, going everywhere she could think of, she found again that Whit was right. There was nothing. Nothing in the Trash folder, nothing in the folders with names like "Household" and "Miscellaneous." Merritt even opened a browser to find that Helen was still logged into Google, but her drive was empty. She would not check the email, but she did make a mental note to ask Whit if he had done so, despite being sure that he had.

So there was nothing. Really, truly nothing. And nothing in Helen's desk. Nothing in her study. Whit had gone through her things, too, after she'd died—her closet, her car—but had nothing to show for it.

The only possibility, to Merritt's mind, was that Helen Albright Longacre was a genius with a magical, encyclopedic brain. That was all there was to it.

Nothing, she texted Whit, who sent back a shrugging emoji that felt like an *I told you so*. She rolled her eyes.

Eventually, Merritt got out her own laptop and went through her usual ritual. First, she set a ten-minute timer. She would check her email, then do the Mini Crossword on the *New York Times* website, and then, with whatever time remained, scan the news headlines, opening tabs for the articles she wanted to read later. When the timer went off, she'd write until she reached a thousand words, maybe more.

At least, that was how things usually went. Because usually the email part went quickly. Usually, there was nothing exciting waiting in her inbox.

But today, amid the newsletters and notifications of flash sales, there was a message with a subject line that made Merritt's throat seize up.

> Interview Request for The Atlantic (Graydon Lyons's SERIOUS GAMES)

It was from Ian Hoult.

Merritt shut her laptop without clicking it. She would not be writing tonight after all.

CHAPTER TWENTY-FIVE

That Sunday morning, Whit was doing a rare thing: he was still in bed, with a book. He had spent the day before with his sister, brother-in-law, and daughter, visiting a pumpkin patch before it closed for the season and then watching both of the good *Home Alone*s. He and Merritt had texted intermittently, but she was busy most of the day helping her mom do yard and housework. In the evening, he and Evie had planned the following day—it would be her last morning with them, and so she would wake up early and make Annie breakfast. Now Annie and Édouard were playing one last round of his card game while Evie finished packing her things. Meaning Whit could have a slow morning for once, in his pajamas with coffee and a book.

Evie came in and leaned against his dresser.

"I need something to read for my flight."

Whit told her to check his study, and she was back in a few minutes with a stack. She set them on the dresser and gestured to them like a *Price Is Right* model.

"Which one will I like?"

Evie did this often, deferring to Whit's judgment on books just as he often deferred to her judgment on clothes and TV shows and, back when he and Helen traveled, places worth visiting. He always loved being asked about books. He could almost physically feel something click into life in his brain as he leaned forward to examine the stack more closely—until he saw the one at the bottom.

Serious Games. He'd totally forgotten buying it. The moment they had returned from picking up Annie at school on the day of Evie's arrival, he'd quickly stowed these books on the large shelf in his study.

"Um," he said through the sudden throbbing in his neck.

Evie seemed to clock his gaze and turned back to the books, misreading his apprehensions.

"Some of these were still in a shopping bag—do you want to hold on to them? I can just get one at the airport—"

"Don't," Whit said, shaking himself into normalcy. "They're always so picked over. Sorry, I just forgot I had those. Take whatever you want."

"Okay," she said, clearly choosing not to press Whit on his strange reaction. Then he watched in mild horror as she drew her finger down the stack of spines to land on the one with a royal blue cover.

He thought about stopping her. But then he'd have to explain. And anyway, it'd be good to be rid of it.

"Is this one okay?" Evie asked, understandably hesitant.

"That's great, yeah," he said, too eagerly. "I hope you like it."

*

There were many tears at lunchtime as Annie said goodbye to Evie and Édouard, hugging them both and crying into their shirts. Evie was never the type to get emotional, but her husband certainly was, and she and Whit exchanged several pained, slightly impatient glances as a kneeling Édouard held both of Annie's hands and cried through utterances of "*ma puce*" and "*mon petit chou*." Finally, they were out the door, dropping off Annie at her friend Liza's on their way to the airport.

Once they were parked in the departures lane, Édouard went in first to begin checking their bags, while Evie lingered with Whit on the sidewalk.

Whit took a deep breath, leaning on the still-open passenger door.

"Well. Thank you."

Evie shrugged. "Anytime."

"No, seriously. Sincerely. Thank you. You helped get me out of my rut, and Annie loved having you here. And you cleaned the house and hosted Thanksgiving and picked Annie up from school, and a million other things I can't ever repay you for."

Evie paused from pretending to wave to an applauding crowd in order to offer him a judgmental glare.

"Siblings don't *repay* each other."

"Some do. Probably."

"Well, not us. And anyway, I'm not so sure I'm the one who got you out of that rut."

Whit looked at the oncoming cars and remained silent.

"No, seriously," she said. "Don't mess it up, okay?"

He shrugged dramatically.

"I make no promises. I am, as you know, an idiot."

She nodded with mock solemnity.

"I do know that."

She paused for a moment before speaking again. This time she was the one watching the traffic. Finally, she said:

"I'm very proud of you, Whit."

Whit didn't know what to say. She was his younger sister, and they didn't often talk like this, but she kept going, her face all affection.

"A really horrible thing happened to you, and you had a hard time with it, because of course you did, but you're doing okay. You're a good dad, and you've figured out a way to do the really difficult thing Helen wanted you to do, and you seem like you're actually happy again. Maybe not all the time, but enough of the time. I'm proud of you."

He gave her a humble, frowny smile.

"Thanks." He nodded. "Really."

She shrugged.

Whit closed the passenger door.

"All right. Safe flight. Love you."

Evie moved to him in a quick burst, giving him a brief hug before pulling away.

"Love you, too, Bubba. Drive safe."

He watched until she was inside, and then he drove home buoyed by an unfamiliar lightness.

*

Darkness had descended on Merritt, and not just metaphorically: on the same evening that *Serious Games* had finally caught up with her, a wide, long rainstorm had engulfed much of the Northeast. Merritt moved groggily through her shift at Goodenough Books the following morning, a change noticed by Huong as well as Moishe, who were both now working double shifts in order to accommodate the holiday rush.

Merritt felt a little guilty, as she herself was working at the rate of half a person, despite the fact that the store was indeed more bustling than usual.

"Are you all right, dear?" Moishe had asked when he found her kneeling in the BIOGRAPHY section long after the go-backs had been returned to their shelves. She had lied, saying something about being tired with a headache.

"Hello, are you alive, there's basically a line out the door," Huong had said, less generously, when she found Merritt sitting in the break room with her hands on her knees and a blank look on her face. She hadn't even bothered lying then. "Sorry," she'd said, and then returned to the floor, which in reality featured a line of only three people.

The end of her shift could not have come soon enough, and

then she didn't even bother to say goodbye, simply slipping out the door and into the pouring rain. A deceitful break in the storm earlier that morning had led her to leave her anorak and umbrella at home. After driving to Whit's on autopilot, she ran from the car through the mud and now stood on the porch, pinching her cheeks and willing herself to feel peppy or focused or at the very least *awake*.

Whit opened the door before she accomplished any of the above.

"Hi," he said warmly, bouncily, until he noticed her face. "What's wrong?"

"Nothing," she said, walking past him. "Sorry about the mud."

She tried wiping her glasses with her jacket, but the wet fabric merely moved the rainwater around. She groaned, shaking her glasses slightly, before replacing them on her nose.

Whit watched her, and she tried to seem calm, unshaken. But his eyes found hers, and she broke then, folding her arms across her chest and looking away.

"Oh," she moaned in a voice that immediately drew Whit toward her.

He placed his hands gently on her elbows, correctly sensing she did not want a hug, and waited until she finally spoke.

"Ian Hoult figured it out," she said at last, once she knew she wouldn't cry. "He figured *me* out. He emailed me Friday night."

"Oh God, Merritt, I'm so sorry. Why didn't you say sooner?"

She shrugged. "It was your last weekend with Evie. And I didn't really want to talk about it anyway."

He nodded. "What did he say? Did you respond?"

Merritt let out a full-body sigh and began to pull out her phone.

"No," Whit said. "Don't do that yet. Here."

He took off her sodden coat and demanded that she wait for him in the living room while he made a cup of tea. She obeyed, and minutes later he met her at her chair by the fire with a mug of steaming, cinnamony tea and a hand towel. She placed the former on the small side table and used the latter to dab at her hair and glasses. They did not speak until she had pulled her favorite blanket over her knees and drunk half of the tea.

"Now," Whit said, ever so gently from the couch, "what did he say?"

She pulled out her phone slowly, its weight like an antique iron in her hand, and she began to read.

> Dear Ms. Pryor,
>
> I hope this email finds you well.

She stopped immediately. "It does *not*."

She took a breath and read further.

> You'll remember me, I think, from our brief interaction at Willa Barrett-Lind's charming Halloween party. And, if I recall correctly, you have also been of service at our local bookshop.

Merritt pursed her lips in the slightest of smiles. "He totally remembers me helping him, I was deliberately rude." She continued to read.

> I'm currently writing a story for *The Atlantic* about Graydon Lyons's SERIOUS GAMES. After months of reporting, I have confirmed my suspicions that this work is a *roman à clef*. Furthermore, it has been insinuated to me that, of the many graduate students with whom Mr. Lyons has liaised, the most likely source for the novel's main character is—and I'm sorry there isn't a more polite way of putting this—well, *you*.

"*Jackass*," Whit hissed.

Would you be willing to discuss this discovery with me? I understand, of course, the sensitive nature of this request, and I do apologize. But such is the world of journalism, which in this case, intersects with the world of literary fiction. I can assure you that, had I known that this Venn diagram would encompass our own little town, I never would have accepted the call of what was once an enticing literary mystery, and which has necessarily transfigured itself into something local, personal, and just a bit *icky*.

Now we come to the most delicate point, which is that, to our mutual chagrin, I'm sure, the publication of this article is a foregone conclusion. As such, I can offer you two options: the first and easiest is to go on the record, telling your side of the story in your own words. I understand you're a bit of a writer yourself, so I can imagine the appeal this narrative control might offer you. The second option, which brings me no pleasure to mention, is *not* to participate, and thereby let the tale of Graydon Lyons be told by classmates, acquaintances, and the man himself should he deign to respond to my interview request.

I would apologize again, but I predict such protestations will grow tedious. Should you wish to discuss the matter further, and I certainly hope you will, Merritt, I can be reached via any of the methods in my email signature. In any case, I remain

Your friend and advocate,
Ian Hoult

Whit had made the full range of angry and incredulous noises during this reading, but Merritt hardly noticed. She knew she had grown pale while reading; her skin felt cold and clammy, sweat beading across her upper lip and a deadened ringing in her ears. She was not prepared, though, to look up and see Whit so red-faced, stone-jawed, fuming.

"I know where he lives," Whit said, standing up. He was wearing duck boots, and she felt a sudden fear he would run out the door before she could stop him.

"Whit, don't."

"I'm serious," he said, raising his hands and stretching out his fingers, as if preparing to strangle something. "We can go over there—*I* can go over there and tell him to stop."

"No, we can't."

"Why not? We can make him see reason. And if that doesn't work, I can punch him in his greasy little face. I can punch him many times."

Merritt smiled, glad of the distraction. "Have you ever punched anyone, Whit?"

"Craig Peterson, junior year. Used a homophobic slur about my friend. And Howie Garner in college, also for using a homophobic slur to describe me when I dropped out of pledgeship."

"You were almost a frat boy?"

"Yes, very nearly."

"The world is full of so many surprises and delights."

"*Merritt.* This is serious."

She gave him an ugly look. "Trust me, Whit, I know that."

Cowed, Whit sat back down on the couch.

"God, I'm so sorry," he said after a moment. "I can't believe him."

"Can't you? It's a good story. Everyone loves a reveal. That's why people like that singing show where people wear those costumes—"

"*The Masked Singer.*"

Merritt raised an eyebrow.

"*Annie* likes it. Don't."

"Sure."

Merritt sat thinking, absent-mindedly rubbing her half-full, still-warm mug with one hand. The point of the article was to expose Graydon for his philandering, but she would be exposed, too, in the crossfire. And people would read the story—she knew that—just as she would read a story revealing the identity of Banksy or D. B. Cooper. She wouldn't be able to blame people for being curious, even those who hadn't read or heard of the book. In fact, the article would probably boost Graydon's sales. How humiliating. Insult and injury both.

And who had been Ian's source? There were dozens of possibilities, really: students, professors, fellow authors, former friends. Anyone who'd ever seen her tagged with him in an Instagram photo, or who put two and two together at a reading. Knowing that she'd never be able to find out who it was irked her, yes, but the real question was, what *kind* of person would do that? Who would so cavalierly tell a story that made her into collateral damage, and worse, tell it to someone who planned to splash that revelation across the pages of a nationally read magazine? The answer was depressing: so many people, she knew, would do that sort of thing.

She sighed, pressing her head back against the chair.

"What do I do?" she asked.

She looked at Whit, whom she suspected was trying to be a good listener rather than leap to problem-solving. He was smiling patiently and compassionately, and Merritt sort of wanted to kiss him.

"I'm really asking," she explained.

Whit immediately jumped to his feet again.

"Let's think," he said, energized. "Let's strategize."

They went over the options Ian had laid out once more. Talk. Don't talk.

"There's a third possibility," Whit said, pacing the small area before the fire.

"What?"

"Speak to him, but do it anonymously. 'An anonymous source.' 'A close friend of the woman who inspired the main character.' Whatever."

"And say what? 'Actually, Merritt's a really nice person and Graydon sucks'? I'd just be confirming that it's me in the book."

Whit shrugged an apologetic shrug. "I think that ship has sailed. Unless . . ."

He wagged a finger in the air, thinking. Then he turned back to the couch and began digging through his cushions. When he came back up, he held his cell phone aloft and was already dialing. Merritt waited.

Who are you calling? she mouthed.

Whit held up his finger again, and then the call must have been picked up.

"Édouard, hi," he said.

Merritt's mind raced to make sense of things. Whit was smiling at her perplexed face as he spoke.

"Yes, that's it," he said, with a quick laugh. "I missed you *so* much, I just needed to hear your voice. Listen, I have a legal question for you."

Oh, Merritt thought. *Oh!*

"But I need you not to mention it to Evie. Yes, top secret. Exactly."

Whit smiled at Merritt, then asked his question of Édouard the lawyer.

"What do you know about sending a cease-and-desist letter?"

When he hung up, Merritt did kiss him. Gently, at first, and then the kiss grew deeper and more urgent. Eventually, they paused to breathe, and she met Whit's eyes, which were both soft and bright with an unspoken question. He must have seen the answer reflected in her own, because he stood and took her hand. She walked beside him as they went upstairs, abandoning her tea to slowly grow cold.

CHAPTER TWENTY-SIX

The next day, Whit was waiting for her in the driveway with an eagerness that made her grin.

"You're obsessed with me," she joked, after they'd kissed beside her car.

"Wow, okay," he said, turning to walk up the porch.

"It's going to be hard for you to focus today, I can tell."

But in the end, it was Merritt who had trouble. For an hour at least, she tried to write the death scene. She was still waiting for something to click, to have some indication that Ursula's creator would've approved of her impulse to kill off the half-fairy. She'd asked Whit whether he had checked Helen's email for clues, and of course he had: the inbox, the sent folder, the drafts, the trash, all of it. There was nothing.

They spent some time reading back over the last four or so chapters they'd written, wondering whether the story could possibly lead in a different direction, waiting for a different narrative thread to tug at them both. They drank more tea, they watched the rain, they kissed again. Then it was time to go and get Annie from the nanny share.

"Why don't you come?" Whit said. "She'd be happy to see you, and we can keep talking about Ursula."

Merritt did not need much convincing. She suggested they make a tumbler of hot chocolate for Annie on this dreary day.

"Let's take the jeep," she said, once they were in the garage.

"It's raining."

"Oh, I'm sorry, is this one of those famous two-wheel-drive jeeps everyone's always talking about?"

He rolled his eyes. "No, but it gets kind of cold—"

"Whit," she said, placing a hand on his upper arm. He looked at her. He smiled.

"Live a little?" he asked.

"Exactly."

So they took the jeep and listened to the National as Merritt watched the rain toss about the branches of trees, which were now almost entirely bare.

"Surprise," Whit said when Annie popped into the backseat. Merritt twisted around.

"We brought you hot chocolate."

Annie's eyes grew wide and excited, then narrowed.

"Any marshmallows?"

"Just say thank you, please," Whit laughed.

Merritt laughed, too, and Annie buzzed from the back, chattering about the day's miniature dramas, and for a moment Merritt felt like she had slipped outside herself, pulling away from the doom and gloom of Ian Hoult and the strange twists and turns in her life. And again, she realized, she was happy. The car was warm, the windows were pleasantly fogged. Annie was joyful. Whit was good. And she was a part of it.

*

Whit was content as he drove home, Merritt in the passenger seat, Annie leaning over the console with the hot chocolate tumbler in both hands. Mostly Merritt and Annie talked, rehashing the plot of the latest Kate DiCamillo book, which Kathleen Pryor had pressed into Annie's hands, and which she had read in less than twenty-four hours.

"Is your car broken down again?" Annie asked eventually.

They were nearing the house now, and it was getting close to dark, especially with all the rain.

"What?"

"Is your car broken down again? Like the last time you picked me up?"

"Oh," Merritt said with a laugh. "No. Your dad and I were trying to figure something out about the book, and we figured we could talk about it on the way to getting you. Although we didn't actually talk about it, did we?"

"Not a word," Whit said, but his brain had hooked on Annie's question. He needed to talk to her about him and Merritt, but he dreaded the idea. How much had she pieced together already? Evie had told Annie that they were just friends, but that was weeks ago. It *had* been true at the time. But now . . .

"What are you trying to figure out?" Annie asked.

Whit glanced at her in the rearview mirror. They hadn't spoken much about what it was he and Merritt were doing, though he knew she understood. She had not yet read the Greenwood Castle Saga—Helen had insisted that Annie wait until she was ten or eleven to do so—but she was familiar with the world of the books, as most kids were.

"Well," he said, realizing that Merritt was deferring to him, "we're almost finished with the story, and there's a character whom we think—well, we think it might be best for the story if that character died."

Annie's eyes went big.

Oh God. Was she thinking about death? About Helen's death? *Oh God.*

But then her face turned playfully angry.

"Aw, that's *mean*, Dad."

Whit laughed. "Yes, it sort of is. But it seems like the right thing."

"Is that what Mom wanted to happen?"

They were on the driveway now. Whit sighed and slowed the car to a stop before answering. He turned around to look at Annie, noting the way Merritt sat tactfully still.

"Well, sweetie, we don't really know. We just have to do our best and make the smartest guesses we can, because Mom didn't leave anything behind saying what she wanted."

He wasn't sure how these words would affect Annie, who sat straight and eager, her reddish hair down, looking longer than he could remember it ever looking before. In the instant before she responded, he was struck by the knowledge that she was getting older all the time. She looked so big.

The face she did end up making was not what he had expected. Her eyebrows furrowed, and her scrunched-up cheeks made her eyes go squinty. She was surprised, maybe even indignant.

"Yes, she did," Annie said, with a little spice in her voice.

Ah, Whit thought, *indignant it is*.

Then her words caught up to him.

"What?" he said, more loudly than he'd meant to. "What do you mean?"

"Yeah," Annie said brightly now. "I'll show you."

She got out of the car, and Whit looked to Merritt, whose face was curious. But nothing like the cold shadow that passed over and into Whit. He got out of the car and followed Annie into the house. Upstairs he went, with Merritt close behind him.

Then they were in Annie's lavender room, standing amid the round paper lanterns and several discarded items of dirty clothes flung across the wood floor. Annie walked directly to the Larkin secretary desk where she kept her mother's knickknacks and the picture from the Halloween party. For the first time in Whit's presence, she lowered the drop-front panel—the part that actually made the shelf into a desk. Then she stepped aside.

"See?"

Whit moved forward, feeling his heart beat with every step. The weight of the cold shadow seemed to double.

At the desk, he reached out his hand to rub the spines of ten or so Moleskine journals, all in different colors, worn and lined up like—well, like exactly what he and Merritt had been looking for. He grabbed one at random—a red one—and held it in his hands, turning it over without opening it.

And suddenly he knew the truth he'd been avoiding for over two months: he didn't want these to exist. That first year after Helen died, he would have given anything to find this treasure trove. It would have made everything so much easier. Finding them now was like rebuilding a car engine through trial and error only to learn that you lived next door to a world-class mechanic. This collection of journals was the *I Ching*, the Key to All Mythologies. This was it.

But ever since he'd met Merritt he'd been okay with the possibility that there was no such store of answers. He'd been glad—grateful to do this with *her*, to build this story with Merritt. He had thought he needed notes or guideposts, when in fact he only needed her.

But now . . . now it was all here, and it had been here all along. He felt a hot streak of anger sear through him, filling his chest, his shoulders, his arms and legs. He was angry that these journals existed, and angry that he hadn't known about it. Angry at Annie, angry at Helen, at himself. Why hadn't he thought to look here? Why had he been so complacent and stupid?

"Have you read these?" he asked.

"Only a little. It's a lot of stuff about her books. Did I do something wrong? I know Mom said I couldn't read the books until I was ten, but you said I could take whatever I wanted—"

"No," Whit said urgently, feeling the anger begin to leave him like air from a punctured balloon. "No, no, honey. Of course not. I'm so glad you have these things."

He pulled her close to him, gazing at Merritt over her head.

She looked stunned. Not quite stricken, as he felt, but flabbergasted. And she was smiling. It was a soft, noncommittal thing, but it was certainly a smile.

"Thank you for showing me these," Whit said after a while. "I'm going to take them for a bit, if that's all right, but you can have them back after. Sound good?"

Annie nodded, though she clearly was still worried that she'd made a misstep. Whit hugged her again, this time fiercely, until the flash of anger he'd felt finished burning itself out.

*

Now the Moleskines stood in three wonky stacks on the kitchen table, with Whit and Merritt staring at them from chairs on either side. In the windows, the sky had gotten very dark.

"What do we do with them?" Whit asked, feeling suddenly childlike.

"You read them," Merritt said immediately.

"I do?"

"Of course you do. Isn't this what we've been looking for?"

"I guess so—"

"I'm sure she expected you to. And now you can look for any indication that Helen might have been okay with killing off Ursula. Or if not Ursula, Christabel or Rupert. Just some sign that it was on her mind. Or maybe evidence that it was *really not*. Both work, right?"

Whit nodded.

"All right," he said. "Yeah." Then, "I think I better . . ."

"Of course," Merritt said, grinning almost too widely as she stood. "Let me know . . ."

She trailed off. Whit understood.

"I'll let you know what I find. See you tomorrow?"

"Yeah," Merritt said, still wearing that stage smile. "See you then."

It took the closing of the front door for Whit to realize that he'd dropped his eyes back to the journals and Merritt had slipped out, unnoticed.

*

As she drove home through the heavy rain, Merritt cried. She cried and cried.

*

Whit started at the end. The last journal, the only one that was incomplete.

The first page said simply:

Book V
The Plan

The pages that followed were filled with several sections of disorganized lists and graphic brainstorming efforts and then, finally, a twenty-page, highly detailed outline, all in Helen's achingly familiar handwriting.

Whit read this, spellbound, and found himself smiling, laughing, and letting out short sounds of approval and admiration. Even just in outline form, the last three pages made him cry.

When he finished, he set the journal down and looked around the kitchen.

"Dear God," he said aloud. "We got it all wrong."

CHAPTER TWENTY-SEVEN

Merritt lay on her bed, fully clothed. Her hair was wet once more from the rain, and her hands were chilled, and she thought she really might die. She felt as though a twister had entered her bloodstream and turned her entire body into a disaster zone. Her thoughts were a mangled mess, making vast jumps from subject to subject and feeling to feeling. She was happy for Whit, because he had found something meaningful; she was frustrated with Helen, for not mentioning the existence of the journals when she was alive; she was perplexed by Whit, who had somehow not known that his wife kept writing notebooks for years. And oh, oh, she was worried about what this could mean for the thing she had dedicated her working hours and her resting thoughts to for weeks upon weeks. Writing this fifth installment of the series had been the most difficult and rewarding thing she'd ever done. Doing it with Whit had meant something wonderful, yes, but she had also proven so much to herself. Until Annie (sweet, darling Annie) had pulled the rug out from under them.

Merritt was fairly certain that she knew what this meant. It was the end of her hard work. How could it be anything else? How could they keep up this sham effort when Helen's own wishes had been discovered in black and white?

"I feel sick," she said out loud to herself.

She also felt generally damp, which was not pleasant. Slowly, she roused herself. She took a warming shower, put on her pajamas, and returned to the high bed with her laptop. She'd decided in the bathroom, under the pulsing rhythm of steaming water, that she would read through what she and Whit had written. She owed the work that much at least. She owed herself that much.

She read for a long, long time.

*

Whit held it together through the night. He took two melatonin and listened to a podcast about the Supreme Court and its failings until he fell asleep. And he held it together the next morning on the way to the Foothills School, driving through the endless rain and listening to Annie's hopes and dreams for her school's upcoming holiday party (apple cider, the Rankin/Bass *Rudolph* movie, Liza's mom's homemade chocolate fudge). He made it through the drop-off line and pretty far down the storm-slicked road, but when his initial turn came at the THICKLY SETTLED sign, he passed the bowered lane to his house and drove, aimlessly at first, then with a destination in mind: the sea. Not *into* the sea, though he did make a private joke to himself about how What's-Her-Name at the end of *The Awakening* probably would have liked to have a Range Rover to speed things along. But no. He wasn't suicidal, had never been suicidal. He was just—and this should not have come as the shock it did—extraordinarily sad.

His wife was dead. Time had betrayed him, and he was unable to fulfill her final wishes, and in spite of everything, he was suddenly very much alone.

For over a year, the stress of Helen's final task had filled every space, like the gases Whit learned about in science class, except that this gas had left room for nothing else, and the liquid feeling of grief had mostly trickled away. Then, the book was actually happening; the crushing worry had begun to retreat, and there was Merritt, who had cracked the seal on the cryogenic vault where he kept his feelings imprisoned, and all of it had begun to thaw. But now . . .

Whit was feeling now, all on his own. He drove to the pier and parked. He turned off his headlights and watched the rain hit the misty gray waves. He sat for a moment, a man on autopilot staring at the sea, and then he dropped his head to his steering wheel.

People say that grief is something that gnaws, but this wasn't like that. This grief had teeth, and those teeth had latched onto Whit from the inside. The feeling was sharp and deep at once, and it gripped all of Whit, he felt it everywhere, it was all there was. A sob jumped from his throat, and Whit realized this was what people meant when they talked about weeping. He shook, he gasped for air, he felt his eyes grow sore and tired, and he did all of it in the Range Rover P615, which he'd never wanted but which Helen had convinced him would be safer than his old jeep. It had been an easy sacrifice to make for Helen. She had, after all, started putting the silverware upright when she loaded the dishwasher. For him. And he had folded clothes the way she liked, and they had bought the couch he wanted, and they had sent Annie to the school Helen liked. They had pleased each other like this, in small and big ways in the beginning, offering little gifts, surrendering their preferences when they could. Whit had gone to bed earlier than he would have liked, just because Helen liked for him to be in bed with her, and Helen had gone to see more than one post-punk revival band with him in concert. The house was Helen's idea, and he'd ended up loving that house.

And here was the truth: Just before she died, they were fine. They were not unhappy. They did not often argue. But they had stopped giving these gifts to each other. Things had changed, and some days they hardly spoke. Life was all Annie and their careers, and what made Whit feel ill now was that he had been okay with that. He had been okay just existing in his wife's proximity, and with her in his, never thinking that one day that would be impossible, and that she would leave him with an impossible task that he had been stupid to believe would ever grow less impossible. He had tried to bring in someone else to fix his problem for him, a choice he now felt had only ever been a slap in the face to Helen—how could it have been anything else? And he had thought he was somehow making it all up to her, as though, by finishing her life's work, he was undoing those last months or years of accepting that things were only *fine*, but he wasn't. He simply could not do it. It would never be done.

And now Helen was gone, and he had failed her, and he felt it everywhere.

*

"Well," Merritt said later that day, "what do they say?"

They were standing at the kitchen table, Whit having skipped his writing group for the journal emergency. Whit had them arranged on the table when Merritt arrived, and she tried not to read into what she saw as a less cozy, more clinical setting than their usual armchairs and blankets.

Whit tapped his fingers on the table before selecting a plum-colored journal from the stack.

"This one," he said, holding it up like a preacher might hold a Bible, "has a full outline. All of book 5 just laid out for us."

"Oh my God," Merritt said in disbelief. All this time.

"Yeah."

Whit dropped his eyes. He had hardly looked at her since she arrived. The previous day's downpour had abated into a drizzle, but the clouds were as dark and heavy as ever, and the temperature was just above freezing. When Merritt had peeked into the living room, she noticed that Whit had forgotten to start the fire.

"So," she said, slowly, feeling her heart dribble more quickly against her ribs.

Whit leaned on a chairback and looked to his side.

"So."

"Seriously, Whit," she said, in an attempt at lightness, "you're scaring me a little. What do we do?"

Now he looked at her. His eyes held pure astonishment.

"What do you mean? What else can we do?"

Merritt's neck was hot, her throat was pounding, her eyes felt shadowy.

"What do you mean?" she said, feeling dumb for repeating the phrase back to Whit.

He narrowed his eyes at her, really and truly in disbelief.

"We have to start over."

She had mostly expected this. She had known it would come to some version of this, and still the words were a metal rod through her chest.

"Whit, wait a minute. The book is due in a month. We're already cutting it close as it is. I'm not sure starting over is—"

"Merritt, please."

He looked deeply troubled. Sad. Her heart dropped.

"We were wrong," he said. "We were so wrong. She—Helen imagined it all differently. New and different characters, different conflicts and revelations. It's all so different."

Merritt bobbed her head from side to side as if deliberating.

"I mean, of course it is, Whit," she said after a moment. "We always knew that was probably true."

"No, but now we know it's *actually* true."

He was leaning his hands on the table now, so that his head was lower than before. More like a cornered animal that might pounce out of desperation.

"Right, but Whit—"

"*What?*"

Merritt took an involuntary step back. His voice was harsher than she'd ever heard it before.

No, she told herself, remembering what she'd felt the night before. She straightened her spine, pushed her shoulders back, and spoke in a level, self-assured voice.

"I read it over last night," she explained. "I reread everything we've written."

She shrugged.

"I don't know what to say, Whit, other than that it's really good. It's . . . it's a perfect ending to the series. It *will* be a perfect ending, when we finish it, and I think we *have* to finish it. Even apart from the deadline, it just . . . it deserves to be finished. To be published. It's good. It's the right ending to the story."

Whit looked to the ceiling and shook his head.

"How can you say that? It's not what she wanted."

"But our story is—"

"It's not *our* story, Merritt, that's what I'm trying to tell you. It's her story. It's been hers all along. You and I have just been playing pretend. Writing fan fiction. We haven't made anything *real*."

The last word came as a slap.

An echo of an echo reminded her that this man was grieving. These journals had reopened the cuts he'd been healing from. She knew that.

But her work deserved more than this.

"Whit," she said, moving away from the table, "I know how you're feeling—"

"You don't."

She took the response in stride. "You're right. I just mean, I understand. This feels like it changes everything, and of course, it affects what we've done. But it doesn't change that we've written something wonderful, something we should be proud of, and something I really believe Helen would be proud of, too."

She knew the final words were wrong as she said them.

"How could you possibly know that, Merritt?"

He had been cold and burdened, and now he looked beaten

down, a shell of the man she'd met back in her mother's library. He slumped into a kitchen chair at last as Merritt spoke again.

"I just feel like, knowing what I know about her, that—"

"But that's just it, Merritt. You don't know her. You might know her books, but you didn't know her."

How did he keep finding new words to sting her with?

"This was the last thing she asked me to do, and you're asking me to betray that wish. When I think about what she would have thought if she knew . . ."

"Knew what?"

"Knew that I asked *you* to come and help me make up this bastardized version of what she wanted."

Merritt winced but quickly crossed her arms, refusing to show any feeling but indignation.

"So that's it?"

Whit looked up.

"What do you mean?"

"We're just supposed to throw out everything we've done. Everything we . . ."

Merritt trailed off when she felt her voice begin to falter. She would not do it this way. She waited to see what Whit had to say next.

He pressed on his eyes with his fingertips.

"I don't know," he said, sounding completely exhausted. "I don't know what to do, Merritt. I'm back where I started."

"But you have me now." Merritt was pacing as she spoke, ignoring the personal pronoun he'd chosen. "Let's call the publisher. Call your agent, whatever, I don't know how it works. Let's ask for more time. We can try to blend Helen's vision with ours, maybe, and—"

"Merritt."

He was grasping her wrist in his hand and looking at her from his seat. His ocean blue eyes seemed deep and yawning. He was giving up.

"What?"

She waited, dreading his answer.

"We can't."

She pulled her hand away.

"Whit—"

"We have to start over from the beginning—"

"No," she said. "No, I'm not doing that."

Whit's eyebrows crinkled. Now he was the one who looked like he'd been slapped.

"What do you mean?"

The thought shot across her mind, like a meteor streaking across the sky: If she said these next words, that would be it. The job would be over. The money that had changed her life and made it possible to imagine herself writing full-time would disappear. She said them anyway.

"I'm not writing someone else's story."

"What? We were always writing someone else's story—"

"You know what I mean. I won't do it. I'm not doing some paint-by-numbers novel. I never would have agreed to do that."

"Merritt, don't be silly—"

"Don't call me silly. I am a *writer*, Whit. A good one. You said it yourself."

"Of course I did. But Merritt . . ."

She could see Whit preparing his next statement. An explanation of some sort. But she had already chosen a direction and said her piece. She would not choose another person's story over her own—not again—not even if that person was Helen. Not even if that person was Whit.

She spoke first.

"I think I should go."

Whit stood.

"Merritt, don't."

But she was already gathering her bags. The Tupperware container holding her uneaten lunch banged against her leg as she lifted her tote.

"I'm sorry, Whit, but I can't do that. I can't do this if that's what you want."

As she looked at him guilt and anger crisscrossed within her chest. She had given up on her writing for a man once before. Not intentionally, not because he'd asked her to, but she had done so nonetheless.

And Whit was not the same man. And he had every reason to ask what he was asking. But the only person she could answer to in this moment was herself.

"What are you saying?"

"I don't know, Whit. I don't know. But I don't think I can help you write your wife's book anymore."

The sentence hurt as she said it, and again Whit looked as though he'd been struck. His shoulders sagged. He opened his mouth to speak, then bit his lower lip and looked away.

"All right," he said finally.

"All right?"

He nodded slowly.

"All right."

So he'd made his choice then, too. And he hadn't chosen her.

"All right, fine," she said, using all her restraint to keep the contempt and pain out of her voice. She turned to hide her eyes from him.

"Goodbye then, Whit."

For the second time in two days, she left without waiting for him to say goodbye.

CHAPTER TWENTY-EIGHT

"Hi, Joan."

Whit's own literary agent hardly ever called, preferring to email him back three to six weeks after he reached out. But dear old Joan was used to frying bigger fish than Whit Longacre, and so she had been able to sneak-attack him at this particularly low moment.

He was lying on the floor of his bedroom, partially because his back had been hurting (injury) and partially because he felt like pure shit, undeserving of a bed or couch (insult). Annie was at school, thankfully, and thus unable to witness this choice bit of self-abasement.

It had been a week since Merritt walked out on him. It had taken hearing her car on the gravel road to shake him from his state, and he had hurried to the door in hopes of flagging her down, apologizing, saying, "Let's work something out." And it had taken his hand hitting the doorknob for a second, stronger impulse to overpower him. Merritt had made herself clear. Helen had made *herself* clear. There was nothing more to be done.

For a week now he had tried not to think about Merritt while muscling through a task that had once again become monumental and overwhelming. He had been reading and rereading Helen's journals and trying to Rumpelstiltskin them into something literary and lovely. And he had failed. Abjectly.

It was as if Peter Jackson had handed him a script and said, *Go, good luck*, and then Whit had tried to make *The Lord of the Rings* in his backyard with a 1980s camcorder. Everything he wrote felt lifeless and hollow. Helen's intentions were so clear, and his inability to shape something from them was making him more insecure than he'd been in years. Had she been the master and he the pretender? What was he even doing in this career?

He found himself once again spending his days in excruciating inactivity, watching clips of singing competitions and falling prey to more than one *Vanderpump Rules* marathon. He learned, too, that there were entire spin-off series, and their siren call was very strong indeed. He skipped his writing group for the second time in two weeks, which he hated almost as much as he hated having to tell Willa *why* he was missing it.

Even Annie noticed something was off.

"Where's Merritt?" she asked one morning over waffles. Whit was rushing from room to room, looking for her shoes and backpack and the folder where they were supposed to be keeping track of her daily reading minutes, for which he usually just made up numbers that sounded about right.

"What?" he called back from the living room, stalling for time.

"*Where's Merritt?*" she said in the drawn-out voice she always used when she had to repeat herself.

Whit snagged a second sneaker from under the couch and stared at it. Well.

He walked back into the kitchen and dropped the pair of shoes at Annie's feet, before pulling a chair out for himself. They were just going to have to be late to school today.

"I don't Merritt think will be coming around here much anymore."

Annie's face fell with her fork. "What?"

Whit shrugged. He was determined to be honest in this already belated conversation. Annie deserved that.

"We aren't working together anymore. We had a disagreement, and—"

"But you're still *together*, right?"

The words sped like arrows through his chest.

"What?"

Annie gave him the most grown-up look he'd ever seen her make.

"You two are together. I know Evie said you weren't, but you are."

Whit made a noise almost like a laugh.

"You're right. We were. Um . . . how did you feel about that?"

Annie ignored his question to ask one of her own. "So you aren't together anymore?"

"No, sweetie," he said gently, unsure what this news would mean to her.

Annie stared at her plate. She poked at a triangle of waffle and then slid it around in syrup before dropping it and sliding the plate away from her. She looked at the empty table as she spoke.

"Is it my fault?"

"No," Whit said instantly. "I'm glad you showed me Mom's journals."

"*No*," Annie said, dismissing his last sentence. "Is it my fault she's not your girlfriend anymore?"

Whit pulled back slightly, confused. "Why would it be—"

"Sometimes you act like I'm sad," she said forcefully, "and you're weird about Merritt."

"Are you sad?" he asked, ignoring the "weird" comment.

Annie looked away, scrunching up her face like she did when she was about to cry.

"*Yes*," she said tersely. "Sometimes. I miss Mom."

Whit got up and moved to kneel next to her, holding her hand in his.

"That's okay," he said, and she was crying now, her forehead on his shoulder. He brushed hair from her face, rubbed her back, and his own tears came then. "I miss her, too. And it's okay to be sad. It's good. It means Mom was special to you. It means she was a good mom."

Whit let them both cry for a moment, then asked the question that had been bothering him in vague and not-so-vague ways for months.

"Did Merritt ever make you sad about Mom?"

Why had he waited so long to state it plainly? Was he a terrible father?

Annie sniffed and looked at him. She really thought about her answer, and he felt an unexpected surge of pride in her then.

"Um," she started, still thinking carefully, "I don't know."

"It's probably kind of hard to see your dad with someone who isn't Mom. Right?"

She shrugged. "Yeah. But I like her, too."

"And that's confusing."

She gave a single hearty nod, and then her face twisted once again.

"And now she's gone?"

Her voice went up at the end, and the hope he heard in the question—hope that she was mistaken—nearly broke him. Now they were *both* gone.

"She's not gone," Whit said, his voice quavering. "She's just . . . we're just not together anymore. And it's no one's fault. It's just over now."

Annie nodded again, but he could see that she was not finished feeling. She pulled her plate back toward her and ate, somberly and thoughtfully, and Whit was *this* close to calling Evie and pleading with her to come back right that instant. He probably would have done it, too, except that Christmas was in less than two weeks (God help him), and he had (idiotically) agreed to their father's absurd, bachelor-in-his-early-sixties plan to spend the holidays in the Cayman Islands. Evie would be there, of course, and another trip to Whelk Harbor was simply too much to ask when he and Annie would be seeing her again so soon.

At drop-off, he told her, "I love you more than ice cream."

"I know," was her only response.

When Joan called later that day, she was enthusiastic and warm and all the other qualities Whit knew he did not deserve to be met with. "How are you? How's Annie? How was your Thanksgiving?"

Whit answered the latter two questions with the same canned responses he would have used with Wet-Looking Curly Hair Woman and Woman with the Extensive Neck Scarf Collection at Annie's school. He hardly knew what he was saying, but Joan seemed satisfied, as well as blithely unaware that he had avoided the first question—*how are you?*—entirely.

"That's great," she said, "that's really great. Well, I'm sure you know why I'm calling. Just wanted to check in on how things are going. We're about to close up shop for the holidays, and you know how publishing is—everyone will go radio silent until at least a week after the New Year. Then that January deadline is going to come *fast*."

"Mm-hmm, time flies," Whit said, wondering if he sounded like a man who was speaking from the depths of despair while lying prone on the floor of his bedroom.

Joan let out a fake laugh, obviously filling the silence. Whit willed himself to speak.

"It's—it's good, yeah. It's good. It's really close to being finished. I think late January should be no problem."

What the fuck, you moron?

"What about January 15? That's the deadline, on paper I mean."

"January 15, no problem."

What the fuck?!

"Oh, that's great. That is so good to hear."

Joan's relief was palpable. And worse, it threw Whit's misery into sharp contrast. He was a disaster. He was doomed, and a damned liar.

Joan hung up shortly after, as if she were trying to escape before the people from a television prank show could bang on her office door and say, *Psych! Whit Longacre is a pathetic joke, and you should be embarrassed for believing in him!*

Whit stayed there on the floor, half-dozing, for a full hour more, only getting up when the cold wood had chilled him enough to make a batch of hot tea an absolute necessity. It was only after the kettle was boiling that he remembered he needed just enough water for one cup.

*

Despite her now-free afternoons, Merritt's days were as regimented as ever. She worked every morning at the bookshop, taking up extra shifts on the weekend, ostensibly to help Diana manage the holiday shoppers but in actuality trying, impossibly, to make up the money she'd lost when she quit working for Whit. She had gone back to eating lunch in her car, usually listening to an audiobook or watching a mindless half-hour comedy on her phone. She would check *The Atlantic*'s website, just to make sure the cease-and-desist letter that Édouard had sent was still doing its work. Then she drove to Carafe, where she wrote feverishly—except on Tuesdays, when she knew Whit's writing group met there. She did not acknowledge this even to herself, choosing instead to believe that Tuesdays could be a perfectly normal day of rest for the nonreligious.

She wrote reams and reams. The words surged out of her now, and occasionally, she *did* think of Whit, wishing he could help her once more with her pacing and plotting. But then she would craft something, a little gem of a phrase, an image that seemed to pull at her heart from within the computer screen, and she would think, *Forget him*, and stumble onward.

Merritt was invigorated. She was writing, for the first time, entirely for herself, according to a private purpose. She did not spare a thought for what people like Graydon Lyons or her writing professors might think. She did not consider agents, editors, or publishers. She did not paint by numbers, and she did not waste time missing Whit.

Her writing was all hers.

She felt alive again.

*

Whit's time in the Cayman Islands, to put it mildly, blew. They stayed at an all-inclusive resort that had seen better days. Whit's father, who greeted his children and granddaughter in the hotel lobby wearing a white Tony Soprano–style shirt, told them he had "a surprise" for them. That surprise was named Sherry Hatzilakos, a bleached-blond, wire-thin woman whom Ned Longacre had met in the waiting room at the dermatologist's office four months earlier. She wore a floral wrap dress with a plunging neckline, and when she held out her left engagement-ring-ed hand for them to shake, Evie's throat made a guttural warning noise that would have brought tears to the eyes of the person who did sound mixing for the *Predator* film franchise.

Things did not get better. Their rooms were cramped and felt constantly damp. The food was plentiful but mediocre. The drinks were weak. And they spent their days on a beach that, it turned out, was really more suited for launching boats full of scuba divers than for swimming with an eight-year-old. Meanwhile, Ned and Sherry, who sold crystals on Facebook Marketplace, giggled and canoodled like teenagers.

Whit was furious with his father for springing a surprise stepmom and stepgrandmother on them, and that made him grumpy around everyone else. Édouard got food poisoning on the first night, so Evie was busy tending to him for forty-eight hours, while Whit, somehow depressed and antsy and lethargic all at once, alternated between watching Annie swim alone in the ocean and watching Annie swim alone in the pool.

The worst part came after Annie was asleep, when Whit would slide open their glass balcony door with meticulous, squeak-avoidant slowness, then step out to sit on the world's most uncomfortable patio furniture. His goal every night was to write, but he was sun-tired and irritable, and usually he ended up watching the ocean and thinking about how much he wished Merritt was there. She would have made the Sherry situation funny. She would have delighted Annie with conversations about books and, he imagined, really good sandcastles and games to play in the surf. She would have been helpful to Evie during Édouard's illness, she would have charmed Ned Longacre's socks off, and she would have been kind to Sherry, toward whom Whit could not help but be cold.

Merritt would have helped him finish the book, too, but he thought of that only once and then not again.

*

On the fourth day of their six-day trip, Evie and Édouard were finally back in commission. Evie and Whit were alone at the beach, lounging under two umbrellas, while Édouard and Annie attempted to snorkel.

After a long-time-coming and utterly brutal debrief about their dad's idiocy, with a deep dive into Sherry's crystal-centric Facebook posts, Evie began to needle her brother.

"Anything you want to tell me?"

She was watching the waves, but still it felt as though she was glaring at him.

"Something tells me you already know."

She nodded. "I have a source on the inside."

"How did she seem to you?" he asked, meaning Annie.

Evie understood. "She's okay. She'll be just fine."

"Okay," Whit sighed, saying no more.

"So it's just over then?" Evie continued. "Professionally and romantically?"

"It is."

He explained about the journals and the disagreement, impossible to be surmounted.

Evie sighed, clearly disappointed. "I'm sorry, Whit. What are you going to do?"

"About the book?" he asked. "I really don't know."

"Well, allow me to change the subject. Here's this."

Evie reached in her bag and tossed Whit something. His stomach dropped. *Serious Games* stared up at him from his lap, its book jacket a little worse for wear.

"What did you think?"

"Well." Whit couldn't see Evie's eyes behind her big round sunglasses, and he waited eagerly for her next words. "From the first page, I was prepared for it to be some joyless, humorless, crude thing with an insufferably stupid narrator, and honestly, it sort of is some of those things."

Whit found that he was smiling.

"But then—"

Oh.

"—I don't know, it just sort of won me over. It's really funny, and the narrator is stupid on purpose. Every character is like the last person you'd ever want to hang out with in real life, but it's satirical, I think, and it's really hard to put down."

"I didn't think you'd like it so much."

She shrugged.

"I did. And if I can enjoy it over the sound of Édouard's retching, it must be pretty good."

Later that night, on the balcony, Whit kept the overhead light off for Annie's sake as she slept, but he did pull out his phone flashlight.

He began to read.

CHAPTER TWENTY-NINE

Kathleen Pryor always made holiday gift bags for her colleagues. They were little cellophane-wrapped bundles of homemade chocolates and hard candies with miniature mason jars full of butterscotch sauce and ready-made packets of hot chocolate. And to her daughter's annual delight, she always made more than enough, so they spent the days leading up to Christmas snacking on leftovers as well as indulging themselves with the smorgasbord of student gifts: cookies from Italy, boxes of Läderach chocolates and Vosges truffles, candied nuts, not one but two genuine English fruitcakes, more than one bottle of fine wine, and a batch of specialty coffee from Yemen. They caught up on reading, completed two jigsaw puzzles, and watched their favorite Christmas movies—*It's a Wonderful Life*, *White Christmas*, *Meet Me in St. Louis*, and *You've Got Mail* (it counts!).

It was a pleasant, quiet time, apart from one necessary conversation with Kathleen about the end of her and Whit, and the end of their cowriting days.

"Well," Kathleen had said, "I hope he regrets it."

"Mom, it wasn't—"

"I *hope*," she said, with finality, "he regrets it. And I hope you don't give up on yourself again."

That had stung slightly, but it had also been the end of it. Afterwards, Merritt found that she was able to turn off her brain. From December 21 to December 24, she did not think of Whit, she did not think of the book, she did not even attempt to write. It wasn't until Christmas Eve, during an a capella rendition of "O Come,

O Come, Emmanuel" at the candlelit service at the Episcopal church her mother occasionally attended, that something seemed to bend inside of Merritt, and she thought, *I do miss him*.

She tried to bury this feeling on the following day, but every Christmas song seemed to make her feel sad, doing the washing up after a pleasant holiday meal with her mother made her think of Whit, and their blustery post-dessert walk made her long for the trails behind his house.

She knew what to do. On December 26, she turned her brain back on. In the murky, amorphous stretch between Christmas and New Year's, normally reserved for lounging and puttering and dozing, she threw herself back into her writing, knocking out chapter after chapter. For New Year's Eve, she humored her mother by going with her to a party of old and retired teachers, but she slipped out at 9 p.m. and returned home to write, typing as the sounds of fireworks popped overhead, even as someone in the park beyond her window blasted "Auld Lang Syne" from a speaker.

She wrote and wrote and wrote for days, and then, on January 5, she sent two text messages. One to Willa Barrett-Lind, and one to Ian Hoult.

*

Whit had started reading *Serious Games* because of two contradictory impulses. First and foremost, he was driven by disdain, perversely excited to hate-read something he felt predestined to find offensive. Excited to hate the man whom Merritt thought so little of. But also—and this impulse felt complicated, messy, embarrassing—because he missed Merritt. Every idle thought sprinted in her direction, and that hurt. But still he hoped he might find in these chapters some semblance of the woman whom both he and Graydon Lyons had known.

That first night, on the balcony, he'd started the book by looking at Graydon Lyons's author photo on the back flap. The man was, irritatingly, quite handsome. Salt-and-pepper hair and a sharp jaw, silvery blue eyes that made him seem like a creature from folklore. He looked like the kind of person you'd find yourself eager to impress.

Well, he thought, *we'll see about that.*

Evie was right about the narrator, a stupid man who might have been played by Steve Carrell in an adaptation. But Graydon knew what he was up to. Allowances had been made for the white, male professor throughout his professional life, and he had nimbly slipped through the cracks of accountability. He believed himself to be a hack, and yet those around him were continually impressed by his spare, straightforward writing. He brought nothing to the table, yet he was impossible to hate because he was funny and hapless and moved through a world that was silly enough to constantly laud him.

And then there was Isabel, the grad student writing heady, stream-of-consciousness prose that captivated her peers and professors alike. She was silver-tongued and quietly, ferociously ambitious. You knew from their first interaction that the professor didn't stand a chance, even if she hadn't been beautiful, sensual, and attuned to his every desire in a way that appeared natural to him but read, to the reader, as calculated. The novel seemed to be saying something smart about men's susceptibility to flattery, and the ease with which two hacks can dupe an insular community—until the smoke screen of Isabel's talent disappeared, provoking her twisted revenge, and leaving the professor more revered than when the novel started.

It was annoyingly good. Whit was so carried along by it that he almost didn't pick up on the familiar details until they began piling up. Isabel was from Virginia, her father had died (when she was in high school, but still), and she secretly loved young adult and children's lit (despite the graphic sex in her own writing). The presentation of this last trait as a reflection of Isabel's underlying immaturity, in both character and craft, broke the book's spell and was also a strangely pleasing reminder for Whit: underneath the book's layers of camp and irony was a real woman known to both him and Graydon. An absurdly talented woman who, on the page, was unapologetic about her excellence. This detail was unfamiliar to Whit, and yet, through this book, he could *see* the truth of how Merritt once was—and would be again, he hoped. In fact, the woman in the book, Isabel, had a kind of energy and sharpness and wit that, in a different kind of story, would have made her an iconic heroine instead of the obvious villain.

Looking at *Serious Games* with a critical eye, taking a scalpel to it and peeling back the layers of disdain and parody, revealed a vibrant, funny, beautiful woman. Graydon had seen the same Merritt that Whit saw, had in fact seen a version of her more alive and more attuned to her own brilliance, and he had tried to squash that. He had made Merritt feel small, and then he had created this caricature as revenge.

Whit felt awful for Merritt, but he also found himself pitying Graydon, who had missed so much and lost something so dear.

When they landed in Boston, Whit shoved the book into a Dunkin' Donuts trash can before he and Annie even left the terminal.

*

Merritt sat at the bistro, waiting. When she had agreed to meet with Ian, her one condition had been that he wait until she was ready. Graydon's book was still a *New York Times* bestseller. The editors at *The Atlantic* were growing antsy, he'd told her, but the promise of more and juicier information had persuaded them to wait.

Now she was almost ready. But that meeting would come later.

The door opened, and a cold wave of air filled the room. Merritt smiled.

"Hi," Willa said as she crossed the room after hanging her long puffy coat on the coat rack and stuffing her quilted beanie into one of its pockets.

"Hi," Merritt said warmly.

Willa sat down and adjusted the place setting before her. Her hair was in long box braids now, and she wore a flowy white blouse tucked into an equally flowy maroon skirt, patterned with little paisley shapes. Merritt watched her look around the room, which was cast in a coppery light in contrast to the dreary day outside. Whelk Harbor was still stuck in the foggy gloom that had descended just before Christmastime.

Willa seemed happy to see her, but somewhat tentative. Merritt knew she was thinking about Whit and what Merritt might want from her as it related to him. She was about to put her at ease when Willa spoke first.

"I'm sorry things didn't work out with Whit."

Merritt waved her hands before her. She did not want to talk about this.

"It's okay. This has nothing to do with that. Not really."

Merritt felt herself make some kind of face, and Willa laughed.

"Well, okay. What are you getting?"

They discussed the menu, small-talked about the holidays, and ordered wine and food.

"Okay," Merritt said once they were waiting to be served. "I've finished the manuscript I started back when I was in an MFA program."

Willa's eyes widened, excited.

"Can I read it?"

"What?"

"Do you need a beta reader?"

"What?" Merritt said again.

"Let me read it, give you some feedback, and then maybe I can connect you to my agent."

Merritt was floored. She wanted to leap across the table and hug this woman, but she felt frozen, too, overwhelmed by her generosity.

"I was just going to ask you what you thought I should do next," she said, stumbling a bit with her words. "You don't have to . . . I didn't mean to—"

"You didn't. I'm offering. I'm answering your question. What you should do next is let me read it—I'm a really fast reader—"

"It's kid lit," Merritt said, as if offering a warning.

Willa shrugged. "Sounds great. I love kids' books."

Merritt's eyes were stinging. Something like joy, or maybe shock, prickled across her skin.

"But," she said, her voice dropping and her words tripping over themselves again, "but what if it's bad?"

Willa's attitude shifted. The exuberance and excitement on her face softened into compassion.

"Oh, Merritt. Do you think Whit didn't talk about you? Do you think he hasn't told me all the wonderful things there were to say about your writing?"

Merritt swallowed, willing the swell of emotion to stay within her rather than pouring forth right here and now.

"Besides," Willa continued, "I don't know much about you, but I do know one thing. You've got something to say. You need to believe in yourself enough to say it."

Merritt thought of the promise she'd been urged to make, about not being surprised by compliments. Well, she was glad she hadn't made it. She hoped this feeling never went away.

CHAPTER THIRTY

And then on January 14, Joan called again. Whit was in Helen's office, hoping the *genius loci* would possess him. He had written fifty or so pages, but then, he would not call what he was doing writing. He was transposing, taking Helen's notes and writing them out in grammatically correct, well-punctuated sentences. He was Helen's posthumous amanuensis, and he was bad, bad, bad at the job.

Writing this without Merritt felt like taking the band on tour after the lead singer had died. And—*and!*—every part of him ached without her. It wasn't the same grief of losing Helen. That had felt heavy and cold and final. Losing Merritt, when Merritt was still out there . . . losing Merritt when he could clearly trace the cause of her departure back to himself, to his hang-ups, to a duty he felt he'd never be relieved of . . . that filled every cell of him with unmet, unmeetable yearning.

"Hi, Joan," he said, leaning back in Helen's desk chair.

How was your Christmas. Oh, the Cayman Islands, how fun. Does Annie still believe in Santa Claus? Yes, they are so sweet at that age.

"Joan," Whit said at last, cutting through the chitchat and preempting the coming question. "Joan, I can't do it."

"You what?"

"I can't finish the book. I've tried it, and I failed."

"Oh, goodness."

The conversation was brief, and Joan masked her irritation well. It felt to him as if she already suspected what he would be telling her, but still her sympathy was strained. He told her, finally, about Merritt, and about the journals. She told him about another children's fantasy author the publisher already had in mind. This author was known for their unceasing productivity and, most appealingly, for their speed. She asked if she could make arrangements to get the journals to the publisher for their benefit, and Whit agreed. Finally, she explained how the royalties would work, though Whit could not have cared less.

At that point, it seemed she was ready to get off the phone.

Okay, Whit told her. He understood.

When they hung up, Whit reached behind the chair to grab Helen's old blanket and then sat very still, watching the wet snow drop into piles in his backyard and slowly melt away.

*

And then on January 17, someone knocked on his door.

Only after he'd answered it and found her there did he realize what he looked like: matted hair, wearing a white T-shirt and gray sweatpants under a maroon-striped robe that looked like it had come from a high school theater program's costume closet. His beard was scragglier than ever; his eyes, he thought, were probably a little bloodshot from drinking too much and sleeping too poorly.

But here was Merritt, standing tall in her indigo coat, full of confidence and warmth. Her hair was down, looking extra shiny in the presence of Whit's greasiness, and she had brought the sun with her after days of rain and gloom.

"Merritt," he said, surprised and embarrassed and, in some small pocket of himself, thrilled. *Merritt!*

"Hi," she said. Her voice was soft, as though she might scare him off. Her face was polite, and maybe a little concerned. She kept one hand on the straps of the tote bag she had slung over her shoulder. He wanted—*oh*, how he wanted—to pull her into his arms.

No, he wanted *her* to pull him into her arms. He needed her.

"Can we talk?"

Talk? Whit thought. *No*, he thought, *let's skip all that!*

"Yes, of course. Come in. Take your coat? Cup of tea?"

"That's all right," she said, standing in the entryway. "I don't need to stay long."

"Oh." The warmth that had begun to rise in his chest tumbled downward like fog rolling over a mountain peak.

"It's just . . ." she said, trailing off as she reached into her tote bag.

When her hand came up, it was holding a sheaf of papers bound by a large black binder clip.

"I finished it," she said, "and I wanted to know what you think."

She handed the manuscript over, and as Whit looked at it in his hand, he registered, first, that she had come up with a title for her previously unfinished work. Then his eyes processed the words at the center of the front page.

THE FAIRY IN THE HIGH TOWER
The Final Installment of the Greenwood Castle Saga
by
Whit Longacre and Merritt Pryor
in the style of
Helen Albright Longacre

"What?"

His voice felt paper thin. The manuscript was suddenly heavy, his arms suddenly weak. The sounds in his ears seemed muffled.

"I finished it," she said again. "I finished my own manuscript first, and then this."

He was stunned.

"You did . . . you did *both*? How is that possible?"

She shrugged. Then smiled in a way that suddenly seemed very like Isabel Abbott's trademark smirk. He felt awed and immediately powerless. He wondered if he had been an impediment, if he had been an unnecessary part of the thing they'd made together. He should have gotten out of the way far sooner. Had Merritt enjoyed writing without him? He felt stupid. He felt territorial, relieved, and then . . . oh.

"But," he said slowly, "Merritt, there's no point."

She pulled her head back.

"What?"

"The deadline, it's passed."

"What do you mean? It's still January."

Whit felt incredibly tired.

"The deadline was two days ago."

Her eyes widened.

"Joan called," he explained. "I told her everything. She said they already have someone lined up anyway. It's over, Merritt."

Her eyes narrowed.

"I'm sorry," he said. God, he was sorry.

Merritt's face began to scrunch up, but then she seemed to set her jaw and harden her eyes.

"Whit, no."

He wanted to hold her. He wanted to lie down.

"I know," he said softly. "But . . . but I'll read this. Of course I will. I want to know how it ends."

He gave her a weak smile, but she was shaking her head. She was angry.

"Whit," she said again, "*no.* We can't just give up. I finished it for us—"

He closed his eyes halfway.

"Merritt, we talked about this. Helen—"

"Helen wrote some stuff down in some journals, yeah, I know, Whit."

His eyes shot open.

"Wow," he said. He could not believe her.

"But she also wanted *you* to write the book. *That's* what she put in the will. Nothing about the journals. Nothing about how the book was supposed to end. She just wanted *you* to do it, 'by any means you deem necessary.'"

"Merritt—"

"No, Whit," she said. Her hands flew to either side of her head, then she stepped forward and actually grabbed him by the lapels of his robe. "Whit, don't you get it? She *gave* her life's work to *you*. Because she loved you and she believed in you and she thought . . . when she realized she couldn't finish her story herself . . . you were the person she thought of."

The words hit Whit like a battering ram against the sides of an iron ship: hard, but dull.

Merritt gave the lapels a tug.

"Do you hear me, Whit? She gave the story to you, and now you're letting it go, so some *stranger* can swoop in and make God knows what of her life's work. All because of a deadline? A deadline that passed *two days* ago?"

Exhaustion. That was Whit's primary feeling, his central thought. He was exhausted. *This* was exhausting. The story was out of his hands now, and that had devastated him, but it had also freed him of an unrelenting burden. And letting it go had meant letting Merritt go, too, but now she was here, trying to storm back into the picture, to force their story over the transom of the publisher's locked and barred door.

"Merritt, they don't want me. You don't know what it's been like. They're glad to be rid of me. They have no reason to listen—"

"Then we make them listen, Whit. Honestly, do you hear yourself?"

He closed his eyes again, weary, weary, weary.

"I do. Merritt, I think you should go."

She was crying now, shaking her head and biting her lip. She slipped her fingertips under her glasses to rub at her eyes, then gave a big, final sniff.

"I got you so wrong."

She swallowed.

Whit didn't know what to say.

Without another word, she walked out the door, leaving Whit standing there, the manuscript still in his hand.

*

In the car, Merritt checked her hair in the mirror, reapplied a layer of sensible lipstick, and took one deep, steadying breath. Then she texted Ian Hoult a second time. A simple three-word text.

I'm ready now.

CHAPTER THIRTY-ONE

That evening Merritt sat in a booth beneath a window overlooking the harbor. The village was situated so that the sea was largely out of view from the shops and cafés that formed its heart. The harbor was reserved for restaurants and bars like the one she was in now, sipping on a dry martini, which she had decided was a respectable drink (if a little boring).

She had chosen the bar, the Blue Mollusk, because, though she'd heard of it, she had never heard of anyone she knew actually going there. Unlike the crab shacks and dives that dotted the street on either side of it, the Blue Mollusk had recently been redecorated and now featured striking Prussian blue walls, a copper-topped bar, and velvety cushioned booths. In the cloudy, refracted light of the coast, it was a good place for a clandestine meeting with an author–turned–investigative reporter.

When Ian arrived, Merritt suppressed an eye roll. Under his coat, he wore baggy khakis and a baggy gray button-up, and she wondered whether he had prepared for this meeting by googling "What do journalists wear?"

"Merritt Pryor," he said, too loud, from the doorway, before gesturing at the bar in an I'm-going-to-get-a-drink way.

Merritt nodded back and resisted checking her phone. She'd almost brought a book to read but had thought better of it, worried that it might make its way into Ian's article. It seemed wiser not to give Ian a chance to describe her in a way that invited readers to close-read her literary choices. As he stood at the bar now, waiting to order, Merritt went over her plan.

She was going to take control of her story. She'd start by admitting to having dated Graydon Lyons. There was no shame in that. On the subject of the book, she had a line prepared: *You know, I haven't read the book, so it's really impossible for me to say whether Isabel is based off of me or one of the many grad students it turns out Graydon has been with over the years.*

She was proud of that line. It gave the impression of taking the high road, of being unbothered, while also focusing on the truth that had been unjustly ignored by everyone but Ian—that Graydon Lyons had skeletons in his own closet.

Then—and this was the part she was so eager for—she was going to shift the conversation to her own writing. To what, in the end, Graydon had not been able to take from her. Always, she had planned to do this, but the exhilarating new kicker was that, three days prior, Merritt had signed a contract to be represented by someone at the agency where Willa's literary agent worked. They'd spoken on the phone twice now, and the woman loved her work. She had the most wonderful ideas for revisions and thought they would be able to take Merritt's manuscript to editors in the next two months or so.

After signing, Merritt had emailed her new agent about Ian Hoult's article and her impending conversation with him. Though she had new ulterior motives for the conversation, she kept them to herself, and her agent had agreed with her initial plan: she would tell Ian about the book, in hopes of stirring up interest in the publishing world.

Merritt smiled to herself as she watched the bartender slide Ian his Manhattan. She had heard Graydon talk about other writers he knew, people he felt had leveraged their relationships with him to land book deals, speaking gigs, professorships. He spoke of these people with contempt, but only ever privately, always conscious of the need to maintain his image as an evolved, generous human male.

A year or two from now, Graydon might find some other young woman, whom he would tell about Merritt. He might make up some story about her using his name to climb the ladder, never mind the fact that he'd used her whole identity. But at least Merritt would have a voice.

"I have to say," Ian said, setting his drink down before lowering his body into his seat, "I was surprised to get your text after that very serious cease-and-desist letter from the French lawyer."

"French Canadian," she corrected.

"Ah," he said. "Well, and then after the text, I was beginning to doubt you'd ever agree to actually meet."

Merritt attempted a warm smile, remembering that this man had very nearly asked her on a date the last time she saw him. She did not care how Ian felt about her, but she was conscious of his power in this situation. She needed to be *likable*—gross—but she was determined to be strong and self-possessed as well.

"No one likes talking about their bad exes," she said, lifting her glass, "especially in print. But I think this will help. Should we drink to Graydon Lyons and his little book?"

Ian's eyes widened, delighted, and a wicked grin spread across his face. He clearly thought he was going to enjoy this.

"Here, here," he said, clinking his glass against hers. After a sip, he pulled a notepad and his phone out of the front pocket on his shirt. "Do you mind if I record?"

"Sure, but there's just one thing."

This was the first step of the plan, and it was a crucial one.

"Yes?"

"Can I speak off the record? For a minute or so, tops?"

Ian waited, holding his phone a few inches from his chest and looking a little caught off guard. Merritt reminded herself he was not quite a real journalist. This might be his first off-the-record experience.

“Fine,” he said, putting his phone face down on the table. “Yes, sure.”

Merritt smiled. She sipped her martini, then put it carefully back on the table before folding her hands together and taking a big breath.

“All right,” she said, slowly, firmly, likably. “If I’m going to do this, I’m going to need one thing from you.”

“Scheming and making deals, Merritt Pryor, I didn’t know you had it in you.”

“You don’t know me at all.”

Ian’s eyebrows went up, but one coy smile seemed to bring them back to their resting state.

“Oh,” he smirked, “how very mysterious.”

“Yes. And I will remain a mystery to you unless I have your word about what I’m about to ask you. Are we clear?”

Ian thought for a long moment. He leaned back in his seat dramatically and took a sip of his Manhattan before putting his glass firmly on the table with a *clack*.

“Okay,” he said, once he’d made her wait what must have been a pleasurably long amount of time for him. “What is it you have to ask me?”

*

When Merritt left his house, Whit had put his energy into anything he could come up with that didn’t require thought or feeling. He took a shower first, then trimmed his beard. He cut his fingernails and toenails. He cleaned the house, paid some bills, and ordered the Valentines Annie wanted to give her classmates next month.

He picked up Annie, using all the energy he had to be chipper and interested, asking her questions about the day and playing the music she requested in the car, and they had pizza in the living room while watching a movie, and when Annie went to bed, he went to his bedroom, turned on the lamp on his bedside table, and pulled out a stack of papers.

The Fairy in the High Tower. How had she decided on that title?

It didn't matter. None of this mattered. And yet—well, here he was.

He decided to start at the beginning.

CHAPTER THIRTY-TWO

Annie was annoyed with him. They were running late, and it was his fault. He had slept in, like a teenager who'd stayed up playing video games, except he was a thirty-seven-year-old man who had stayed up reading a book he had mostly cowritten. A crazy thing had happened to him as he read: he found that he could not put the book down. Never, *never* had he felt something like this rereading one of his own books. This creation of his and Merritt's was lightning in a bottle. It was clearly written for younger readers, and yet it called to him and moved him. He loved it.

And then Merritt's ending—the bits she'd written herself—*God*, they were good. He found himself crying during the death scene and grinning goofily, unselfconsciously, as he reached the book's resolution. It was magical, joyful, and touching, the polar opposite of cheesy or didactic, and yet it actually said something about what it meant to be a human, to be loved, to do good in the world.

When he had fallen asleep around 4 a.m., his thoughts were a blurry mix of elves and giants (including, near the end of the book, a baby one), of dragons and warlocks, and of Merritt . . . so much Merritt.

Now he drove like a maniac in the blue jeep, desperate to drop Annie off and hustle over to the bookshop to tell Merritt he had loved it. He could have called her, but he had to see her face to face, to tell her about how wonderful this thing they made had turned out to be. More than that, he had to tell her she had been right and he had been wrong. Screw the deadline, forget the journals. They had to do this.

"I love you, Annie," he called as she walked into the school. "More than ice cream."

Annie waved in a you're-embarrassing-me way, but she grinned.

Whit was grinning, too. He made it from the school to Goodenough Books in record time and opened the door with such gusto that he worried the bell overhead might swing off its hinge.

"Whoa," said Huong, whom Whit did not actually know but whom Merritt had sometimes talked about. Today she wore a blue Dickies jumpsuit and oversized hoop earrings. She stared at him from behind the counter.

"Hi. Is Merritt here?"

Huong looked at him coldly and crossed her arms.

What had Merritt told her about him?

"No," she said.

"Doesn't she work in the mornings?"

"Usually," the woman said, her voice flat and uninterested.

"But today . . ."

Huong shrugged. "Not here."

"Okay," he said. "You've been very helpful, thank you."

She gave him a sarcastic smile and turned her eyes to the computer.

On the sidewalk outside the store, Whit pulled out his phone and texted Merritt. He waited thirty seconds for a reply before calling, but his call went straight to voicemail.

She's ignoring me, he thought. *Or worse—she blocked me.*

He had to talk to her, though. Had to.

He thought, pacing the space outside the bookstore door.

Why wouldn't Merritt be at work? Where else could she be?

He stopped abruptly, snapping his fingers.

Of course, he realized. She was back where this all began.

*

"So you're telling me," Whit said to Wet-Looking Curly Hair Woman, "that Mrs. Pryor is here today? Merritt isn't subbing for her?"

"Sorry, who's Merritt again?"

"Her daughter," Woman with the Extensive Neck Scarf Collection said. She looked intrigued. "You know," she explained, "she subbed when Kathleen was out on medical leave last semester. Cute girl, green glasses."

"*Oh*," Wet-Looking Curly Hair said, nodding eagerly. "Yup. A pretty girl, isn't she, Mr. Longacre?"

Whit nearly groaned. From Goodenough Books, he had driven back to the Foothills School, speeding once again and going so far as to cut through the parking lot of an under-construction building to beat the wait at a red light.

"Can I *please* have a visitor pass?"

"What?" the ladies said together, confused.

"I need to talk to Kathleen. If that's okay."

Adding the last part pained him, but these ladies seemed to need a gentler touch than he was currently capable of giving.

"Well," Extensive Neck Scarf Collection said slowly, sharing a look with her colleague, "I think she's with a class right now, and I'd hate for her to be interrupted."

Whit closed his eyes just briefly, then said, with all the sad-widower-ness he could muster, "I really need her help. It's an emergency. *Please?*"

The two women clocked his change in tone and posture, and their faces fell in unison.

"Oh, well, if it's an emergency," Wet-Looking Curly Hair said with what could only be described as rapacious pity.

Extensive Neck Scarf Collection began scrambling for a pass. "Yes," she said, "if it's an emergency, I suppose . . ."

Whit snatched the pass from her hands.

"It is. Thank you."

And he tore down the hall.

*

Kathleen Pryor was halfway through reading *Everybody in the Red Brick Building* to a first-grade class. She sat in a gold-painted rocking chair beneath the tree made of construction paper and felt, and fifteen or so kids listened from the beanbag chairs and floor pillows that surrounded her. It was a quaint scene until Whit burst through the doors and every head snapped to look in his direction.

"Mr. Longacre," Kathleen said, half-surprised, half-admonishing. "Is everything all right?"

Whit's cheeks burned a bit under the gaze of so many six-year-olds and their very intrigued teacher leaning against a nearby shelf. In an instant, he remembered the last time he'd been in this room, weighed down with an unspeakable weariness and a sense of failure that seemed like a self-fulfilling prophecy. But then he had met Merritt, and so much had happened, and now he stood here, huffing and puffing, invigorated.

"Yes," he said, ignoring Kathleen's tone and the universal attention that felt like the heat of a spotlight. "No . . . I don't know. I need to talk to Merritt, but she's not at work, and she's not answering her phone, but I need . . . I need her."

Kathleen's eyes opened wide.

"Whit," she said, a little more softly, a little more gently, "if you'll just wait fifteen minutes—"

"Kath—Mrs. Pryor, please, I can't wait."

Kathleen looked at the students around her, then at her watch. From the shelf, the first-graders' teacher cleared her throat impatiently. Kathleen sighed.

"She's not here. She left for New York late last night—"

"*New York?*"

"Whit, please, if you'll just give me fifteen minutes—"

"She's *gone*?"

The teacher cleared her throat again. Kathleen set her jaw.

"Yes, dear, she left for New York—"

More throat-clearing.

"Do you need a cough drop, Ms. Santo?"

"Mm-mm," the woman said, shaking her head with a false smile, "all good."

Whit did not have time for this. He turned to leave.

"Where are you going, Mr. Longacre?" Kathleen called. "Whit?"

"New York," Whit answered.

He did not look back.

CHAPTER THIRTY-THREE

He did not look back, but he did look down—at his phone to buy a plane ticket, and then again, minutes later, at the nail in his now-flat front tire.

"Dammit," he shouted, in a voice that echoed across the parking lot, drawing looks from a group of moms unloading Valentine's Day decorations from a Yukon XL.

Whit's hands were on top of his head as he turned back and forth, cursing himself for cutting through that construction zone. He already had his phone out, having called Willa to ask if she could pick up Annie after school and let her spend the night. When she'd asked why, he'd simply answered "Merritt—" and Willa had said, "Say no more."

But now this. He dialed Merritt's number again, thinking perhaps she'd landed by now and he could talk to her about, well, *something* rather than behaving in this reckless way. Once again his call went straight to voicemail. He checked how long it would take a Lyft to pick him up, and at the sight of "30 minutes," the electric charge that had animated him from the inception of this plan (talk to Merritt, fix things) faltered.

For the first time that morning he paused to think about what he was chasing. What did he mean by *fix things*?

He had to tell Merritt he'd been wrong. That was part of it. She was right about the book. The book was incredible. And she'd been right about Helen—how could she not be right? How could Helen, had she been able to read this thing he and Merritt made, want the story to go any other way, to be handed off to some stranger? This was the only way things could go, in the end, it just *was*, and—

A sigh overtook Whit. He placed his hands on the car and lowered his head to the cold metal of its roof.

All of that was true, but what he was really chasing was Merritt. He had lost her, and over what? A mistake. A misguided belief. Fear and grief. Merritt had been an antidote to that fear and a reprieve from grief. She had liked him, perhaps even loved him, despite his sorry state, and she had helped him break the terrarium that housed his feelings—the good ones, the bad ones, the mourning, the joy. He wanted to be close to her all the time. He wanted to kiss her, to hold her, to sit with her at dinner while they asked Annie how her day was. He wanted Merritt in his space, to take up her space. He wanted to hold her hand.

He tapped his forehead against the car, just once, holding back the urge to cry.

"Whit? Are you all right?"

Oh no. Oh no, no, no.

Whit waited, closing his eyes as he considered his options, which, it turned out, were either speak to this person or duck into his immobilized jeep and hide like a kid behind a too-narrow tree.

He sighed.

"Hi, Noel. I'm fine."

Noel Pendergrass chuckled. (*The nerve.*)

"Oh, ha-ha, Whit. You are clearly *not* fine."

Whit finally looked at the man, opening his mouth to speak but at a loss for how to explain himself. He raised his hands weakly and then gave a wild shrug.

"I'm not, no, you're right."

Noel nodded.

"Rowan forgot his lunch," Noel said. "So that's why *I'm* here . . ."

The man waited, his eyes magnified slightly by his hexagonal glasses. He pulled a handkerchief from the front pocket on his Patagonia vest and wiped his runny nose, but still he waited.

"Um," Whit said. He gestured to the flat tire to stall for time.

"Ah," Noel said. "Need help putting on the spare?"

Whit balked at the suggestion that he might not know how to change a flat, then shook his head.

"No, I can do it, I just don't have time if I'm going to make my flight."

A light flicked to life in Noel's eyes, and the genuine compassion that had shaped his face curled just a fraction into something more complicated.

Noel smiled. "I could take you . . ."

Whit felt dread well up in him like water seeping through the sole of a worn-out boot.

". . . but, oh, well, I hate to ask this, but could you do me a favor in return?"

Whit waited, cringing.

"It's just that I need someone to cover carpool duty next week. Greg and I are taking the boys to the Poconos to ski, and well . . ."

There were flights nearly every hour, from Boston to New York. Whit knew that. He could wait for a Lyft and get to Logan in two hours. He could take a train, rent a car, there was a shuttle—except every nerve, every synapse within him pulsed with longing. He needed to find and speak to Merritt. He needed to do this reckless, stupid thing, no matter the mental cost.

"Fine, Noel, I will help you with carpool duty."

The man's face lit up like a bottle rocket.

"Wonderful. Then *to* the *airport* we *gooo*."

Noel spoke in a singsong voice that almost made Whit back out. But his Tesla was parked right next to the blue jeep, and within a minute Whit had set out on the hour-plus drive to the airport, with only Noel and several Imagine Dragons–heavy playlists for company.

*

Whit had gone through security, boarded the plane, and finally buckled his seat belt before he came to his senses. He did not know why Merritt had left Whelk Harbor. He did not know what she was doing now that she was in New York—which, he told himself as the plane began to taxi, was, you know, kind of a big place—and he didn't know how he intended to find her. He didn't even know if she'd be willing to speak to him. And still, he had spent the last eighty-five minutes in a car with Noel Pendergrass, who vacillated between talking about his and his husband's most recent renovation of their cabin in the Poconos ("We call it 'the cabin' affectionately, but it's very much a house"), describing the various leadership roles Whit could take on with the carpool team ("Social Chair Whit Longacre has a nice ring to it"), and, worst of all, singing along to every Imagine Dragons song he'd ever heard and several he certainly had not.

"Should we play Two Truths and a Lie?" Noel had asked around the time the Boston skyline first became visible, but Whit chose that time to make a phone call to Willa to update her.

Now the plane was making its ascent, and Whit felt like a helium balloon that had whizzed away with force, enthusiasm, and whimsy until it had suddenly become snagged on the top of a chain-link fence.

Oh God. This was a mistake. More than that, it was a supremely embarrassing and misguided grand gesture. Most grand gestures involved some degree of certainty. When Harry sprints across the city to spill his guts to Sally, he knows exactly where her New Year's Eve party is. When Meg Ryan decides to leave Bill Pullman and shoot her shot with Tom Hanks, she knows there's at least a possibility he'll be at the top of the Empire State Building. Flying to New York without a plan wasn't romantic or exciting. It was just stupid.

He had left on such a whim and arrived at the airport so close to his departure time (a personal nightmare) that he did not have a book and had been far too stressed to stop at a Hudson News to get one. It was lunchtime, more or less, and his stomach was rumbling. And he had a middle seat.

Stupid, stupid, stupid.

He tried reading the in-flight magazine, but it reminded him of the writing he used to do before his first book deal. So instead he turned his attention to his fellow passengers. The suited man in the aisle seat was clearly traveling for business. As Whit watched him poring over spreadsheets and Microsoft Teams messages on his laptop, he did think, for a moment, *Well, things could be worse for me.* He turned to the woman in the window seat, who was poring over an e-reader. She seemed to be in her early twenties and wore large noise-canceling headphones over a beanie he suspected was homemade. This woman looked entirely content, enjoying a book in her own world, and Whit felt a kind of affection for her that only grew when he noticed the black line tattoo peeking out of the bottom of her sleeve.

He must have been gawking, because the woman suddenly pulled away from him and slipped off her headphones.

"Can I help you?" she said, clearly on the defensive.

Whit shook himself from his stare and laughed apologetically.

"No, I'm sorry, I just . . . I noticed your tattoo of the kestrel and spoon. The Sign of the Scout."

The woman glanced down at her upper arm, touching it with the fingers of the opposite hand.

"Oh," she said, more mildly, "are you a fan?"

Normally, Whit would have just said, "Yes." In the past, in moments like this one, he had occasionally said, "My wife's a big fan," which had always made him laugh.

Today he told the truth.

"My wife wrote those books."

The woman started. Whit could feel her really looking at him.

"That sounds made up, I know," he said, "but Helen Albright Longacre was my wife."

He wasn't sure why he did it, but he pulled out his phone and swiped quickly back to a picture of him with Helen and Annie. They were crouching together by a snowman, laughing.

"Oh my God." The woman spoke in a gentle tone that contrasted with her powerful words. Then she remembered.

"Oh," she said, "I'm so sorry for your loss."

Her hand moved from the armrest to touch the back of Whit's hand, for less than a second.

Whit had imagined this kind of interaction. It felt like everyone he had spoken to for the last year had known him and Helen personally, before her death. Everyone except Merritt. This was only the second time someone had learned who he was and then, owing to his wife's fame and her vibrant fan base, realized what that meant. He had been prepared for something nebulously gross. He'd thought fans like this woman, like Merritt, would ask invasive questions or overwhelm him with their sympathy or their secondhand grief, but that simply was not what had happened.

The woman was really seeing him, and she wasn't ogling him or quizzing him. This woman who loved his wife's stories enough to permanently ink a memento from them onto her skin was looking at him like he was a person.

"Thank you," Whit said after a beat. "I guess you really liked her books?"

The woman's mouth opened slightly. She touched her tattoo again, this time keeping her hand there.

"Do you know the character Christabel? Of course you do."

Whit laughed.

"In the third book, when her brother dies . . ."

She clicked off the e-reader that had been resting on her lap, then touched her lips with her thumb.

"My brother died," she said finally.

"I'm sorry."

She nodded.

"He died, and then I read that book, and there's a part where she talks about how she's fighting for him now, you know, in her journey to the castle beneath the waterfall. And she says, 'I don't know if the dead can feel pride, but I'm not taking any chances.'"

Whit nodded, letting her speak. The woman did a miniature shrug, lifting her hands from her lap slightly.

"It just meant something to me. I don't know what I think about God or heaven or whatever, but most days I try to live in a way where I think my brother would be proud of me."

She touched her tattoo once again and added, "She gave me that. Your wife."

Whit looked at her.

"What was your brother's name?"

"Ethan."

Whit nodded.

"Thank you for sharing that with me."

"Thanks for asking. I like talking about him."

He smiled. "I like talking about her, too. Listen, can I ask you something else?"

The woman's eyes brightened. "Sure," she said with enthusiasm.

"How do you think the series ends?"

She seemed confused, so Whit kept speaking.

"I mean, do you have a feeling about what should happen? When all is said and done? Am I making sense?"

"Yes," she said quickly. "I just don't know what my answer should be. I mean, in the end, it's a story about the things we do for the people we love. Isn't it? Whatever else happens, I think that would be the point."

She waited, as if wondering whether she'd said the correct thing.

"What do you think?" she asked.

He had spent the last fifteen months trying to write this book for Helen, whom he loved. It had been such a burden at first, coterminous with his grief. But then something had changed, and it wasn't just Merritt. The book had sort of saved him, he realized. It had helped him write again; it had given him something vital to accomplish. And Helen, who loved him, who thought of him even as she was dying, had given him that.

"I think you're right," he said, smiling again. "I think you're exactly right."

*

Whit's first stop in the city was to grab food at a Pret, a sad, soggy premade chicken salad sandwich that he ate while wandering around the Upper West Side. He was there, ostensibly, because that was where Evie and Édouard lived, and where he'd probably be sleeping that night. If it happened to be where the main characters of *You've Got Mail* also lived, and if he happened to know that Merritt loved that movie, well, that was incidental. He did feel near to her there, which made him feel dumb. But he felt it nonetheless.

His conversation on the plane had left him feeling buoyed, but now, as he walked into Riverside Park in the late afternoon, he was weighed down once again by the magnitude of his powerlessness. Whit felt more than just moronic now. Aware of how pathetic and pitiful this had all been, Whit was startled when, at last, his phone rang and he glanced at the caller ID.

"Merritt?"

"Whit, goodness. Are you okay? Why do I have seven missed calls from you?"

"Um." Whit felt suddenly sheepish. "Why weren't you answering?"

He braced himself for her to remind him that she did not actually have to answer.

"I lost my phone for a bit," she said instead. "Are you okay?"

"I'm fine. Where are you?"

"What?"

"You're in New York, aren't you?"

There was a pause on the other end of the line.

"How did you know that?"

Whit was approaching the 91st Street Garden now. Behind its black name placard and wrought-iron fence, the flowerbeds were in a muted winter state. It had snowed in New York the previous week, and the plants looked like they were still recovering, trying to poke out from beneath the remaining layer of dirty gray slush.

"I came looking for you," Whit explained, leaning with his free hand on the fence. He pulled away immediately, wishing he'd thought to grab gloves from his car back in Whelk Harbor. "I thought you might be subbing for your mom, but she told me you were here, and so I just—"

He paused, realizing what he had just revealed.

"Sorry," Merritt said on the phone, "did you say *here*? As in you're *in* New York?"

He took a breath.

"Yes. I'm at Riverside Park."

"Oh, Whit," Merritt said, and her tone made him cringe at his foolhardiness.

"I know. I don't know what to say."

"No, Whit," she said, with an apology in her tone, "I just got back to Whelk Harbor."

Whit's voice stopped midway up his throat, until he forced out words.

"You what?"

CHAPTER THIRTY-FOUR

About Eight Hours Earlier

Merritt stared at the building, feeling like a slightly lost ingenue at the beginning of a Golden Age movie musical. Willa had assured her that this was the right place. She had also mandated that Merritt not mention her name at any point during this reckless mission, but Merritt tried not to think about that now.

When she had arrived in New York the previous evening, she'd gone to pull out her phone, only to realize that she'd left it in the seat pocket on the airplane. She felt a brief moment of panic, but then remembered her mother's insistence when she dropped Merritt off in the departures lane that she tell her Evie and Édouard's address, just in case. After visiting the customer service desk to file a claim for her phone, she used the landline to call her mother, who told her the address and as much as said, without saying it, *Aren't you glad you have a mother who takes such prudent precautions?*

Two weeks ago, she had planned to tell Ian Hoult some of the truth and to jump-start her own writing career in the process, but this second step was a spur-of-the-moment move. When the pieces clicked into place in her mind, she had called Willa and Evie in quick succession. Both had expressed skepticism about her plan but had nonetheless agreed to maintain silence on the matter should they speak to Whit within the next forty-eight hours.

This morning, following a cozy dinner with Evie and Édouard

and a night of restless sleep, Merritt joined her hosts for breakfast. Evie took one look at Merritt's proposed outfit of black jeans and black sweater and gasped.

"No," she had said. "I'm sorry, but no." After a protracted argument over coffee and yogurt, Merritt had been talked into borrowing a pair of high-waisted trousers paired with a silky green tie-neck blouse, as well as Evie's fawn-colored tweed trench coat.

Now, standing on the city street with this intimidating building before her, she wished she hadn't also let Evie bully her into trading her public radio tote for a big designer bag. She would have liked to use the old thing as a security blanket.

"Just walk in confidently," Willa had said the day before. "Wear your sunglasses—"

"I don't wear sunglasses. I wear regular glasses."

"*Act* like you're wearing sunglasses, and then ask to speak to Shreya. Tell her you're with legal."

When Édouard heard about this plan over dinner, he had simply said, "*Non.*"

"What?"

"*Non*, it will not do. You need a real lawyer."

"I don't have a real lawyer."

"Merritt," Evie said. She set down her red wine. "Édouard is a real lawyer. Whit's lawyer."

"And I would be honored to assist you."

Merritt fought a blush, though she refused to interrogate whether the source was her forgetfulness or the full force of Édouard's gaze.

"How?"

"I will go with you to this place and get you in."

"I don't know, I don't want to get you in some sort of trouble," Merritt lied. Inwardly she was thrilled by the prospect of not doing this part alone.

"*Non*," Édouard said again. "Nonsense."

Then he held his hand out and spoke in a voice of mock ceremony: "Merritt Pryor, would you do me the honor of being my client?"

She suppressed a giggle and shook his smooth, strong hand for the second time.

Now she stood on the sidewalk, waiting for him. From everything Whit had told her, publishing people did not seem like the type to get to the office early, and so Édouard had headed into work first for meetings. But now he was approaching her, in his Stoffa raglan coat, Loewe suit, and shining oxfords. The wind tossed his coat and hair with cinematic chicness.

"Thank you again for doing this," Merritt said.

"Of course. Now listen."

He set his briefcase down against his leg, straightened his clothes, and took both of Merritt's hands in his. A luxury watch glimmered in the midmorning light.

"You must be confident and at ease, and per'aps a little bit rude until we get past the front desk. This I do all the time."

Merritt sighed, her breath appearing in a puff that fogged her glasses. She straightened her spine as they approached the rotating door and were met by a warm blanket of air that fogged her glasses yet again. She had worried that they might have to charm a security guard, but before them was a wide stone-tiled lobby lined with well-lit bookshelves. At the far end of the room was a reception desk, where two people in white shirts and black doorman-like jackets sat.

Édouard led the way. Merritt pictured her favorite TV lawyers—Christine Baranksi, Viola Davis—and channeled that energy as they approached the desk.

"We're here to see Shreya Ramanathan," Édouard said in a tone at once forceful and bored, so unlike his normal speaking voice.

"Okay," the woman said hesitantly. "Is she expecting you?"

"She *should* be," Édouard said, as if offended by the question. "I'm with Mulryan, Martineau, and Poore. I called ahead."

This was a lie, but Édouard had warned her of the trick in advance. It gave the appearance of certainty and set the other party scrambling, afraid that something had fallen through the cracks on their end.

"I represent Whit Longacre and his late wife, Helen Albright Longacre," Édouard went on, sliding a business card across the table. "The author of *those*," he continued, pointing at the Greenwood Castle books displayed in the bookshelves across the room.

The woman's eyes widened, but she turned to Merritt. "And you are?"

"Merritt Pryor," she said with a smoothness she was proud of. "An associate of Mr. Longacre's."

"Fine," the woman said, as if growing bored. She cradled a black phone against her ear and called an extension. As they listened to her repeat Édouard's words to the faceless person on the other end of the line, Merritt tried to look serious and fully at ease but also a little impatient.

"He said they're with . . ." The woman put her hand to the receiver. "Sorry, what was the firm?"

Édouard shot Merritt a performative can-you-believe-this look. "Mulryan, Martineau, and *Poore*."

"Mulryan, Martineau, and Poore. They represent Helen Albright Longacre and—"

"Her husband."

"Her husband."

Merritt nodded approvingly.

"Mm-hmm," said the woman. "Yes, I think so . . . No . . . No . . . All right, thank you."

She hung up the phone.

"If I could just see your IDs, please, we'll get you upstairs."

As the woman fiddled with their cards, Édouard shot Merritt

a conspiratorial wink, which she would have returned had she not been close to fainting from relief.

*

In her daydreams, and occasionally her real dreams, Merritt had pictured herself being escorted into the offices of an imprint at one of the country's most prestigious publishing houses. It had looked about like this. There were books and bookish people everywhere, as well as trinkets and statuettes from canonical and not-so-canonical texts. But it had not felt like this. In her dreams, she was an author going to meet her editor or on her way to approve potential book covers or meet audiobook performers.

Instead, she was now on a covert mission. As merely Whit's associate, for all anyone knew, she sat in a glass-walled conference room, waiting, occasionally catching people in the open offices beyond looking her way with curiosity. What did they think of her? What had they heard?

"Look more confident," Édouard admonished, and Merritt sat up straighter, earning a nod of approval. She tried not to appear like she was doing mindfulness exercises, which were in fact what she had turned to for support. Deep breathing, feeling the ground holding her feet, sending a kind wish to the Shreya woman—humiliating stuff, and none of it working. Her heart beat like a bouncy ball in a contained space. Her upper lip was sweaty and the small of her back, too, and she kept crossing and uncrossing her legs. Not very Christine Baranski–like behavior.

When the door opened, she was surprised to see two people: a forty-something South Asian woman in a black dress and red spherical earrings and a dowdy, square-shaped white man with patches of curly gray hair on the sides of his head and glasses that could have been borrowed from a trunk labeled "Senior Citizen Props."

"Mr. Marchand? Ms. Pryor?" the woman said, extending her hand. "I'm Shreya Ramanathan."

Merritt stood to shake the editor's hand, ignoring how intimidatingly perfect her silky chin-length hair was and how Merritt's own had more of a panicked-and-also-it's-wintertime vibe.

"And this is Alan Binford. He's a member of our legal team."

Alan, who was wiping his glasses with a microfiber cloth, held out his hand and missed the mark so spectacularly that Édouard had to take a large step to his left to shake it.

Merritt yearned to say, "Nice to meet you," but she followed Édouard's serious, disinterested lead and sat silently opposite them at the table.

"I apologize for being caught a bit off guard," Shreya said, through a polite smile, "but I don't think I knew you were coming in today."

Merritt sighed. She had talked with Édouard and Evie the night before about what they would do if they made it this far. Édouard had given her oodles of examples of the language he could use to make his case and threaten this woman into capitulation. But now that she was here, Merritt realized that getting in was the complicated part. Now it was best to go down the path of least resistance.

She placed a hand on Édouard's forearm to stop him from speaking first.

"Please don't apologize," she said. "I appreciate you meeting with us."

Alan had pulled a notepad from an old leather briefcase and had not looked up since, but Shreya was staring, her expression unreadable.

"And may I ask *why* you wanted to meet me?"

"Well, I'm not just an associate of Whit's. I'm his coauthor."

Shreya's eyes went wide, and Merritt could sense her wariness. Even Alan looked up from his notes. Merritt reached into Evie's designer bag and slid the finished manuscript across the table. Shreya took it gingerly and began to flip through its early pages. Then she let the manuscript pages fall back into a stack.

"Whit told Joan he had no manuscript," she said in a clipped voice that Merritt might have used herself if she were being confronted by a clearly delusional stranger.

"Yes, I know that. But that's not true. He and I wrote this together."

"Then why . . ."

"He had a crisis of confidence." She was massaging the truth, but what choice did she have? "He doesn't consider himself a fantasy writer, and he convinced himself that what we'd written together wouldn't be . . . right for the series. But I'm here because I know it is, and I think you might agree. When you read it."

Shreya remained suspicious, but an intrigued look had crept across her face. Merritt wondered whether Helen's agent had mentioned that Whit had brought on a coauthor. It would explain why she wasn't treating Merritt as if she were *completely* insane. Merritt kept talking.

"Ask Joan. She's been checking in on Whit and knows we'd been making progress. And you and I both know Helen left the completion of the manuscript to Whit in her will, and well, here it is. Completed."

"Yes, there is *a* manuscript here," Shreya said, curt once again. "But Whit himself said he could not complete it, and we are in the process of amending the contract in light of the estate's failure to deliver. Another writer has already been signed to write the book, and we now have access to Helen's journals and plans for the final installment. We are in a position to complete this *quickly*, and in a manner that best suits the interests of the series and the publisher."

"Even if it means ignoring what Helen wanted."

Shreya's face darkened at that. She pushed her hair behind her ears and leaned forward.

"Listen. Helen wasn't just my author. She was a good friend. It pains me that this is how things have ended up. Really. To lose her, first of all, and then to lose her before she could complete her . . . well, her masterpiece. I hate this, truly. It's been so awful."

"Awful for Whit, too, as I'm sure you can imagine."

Shreya nodded, genuine compassion in her eyes, and Merritt was relieved to see that this woman did indeed have a soul.

"So there's nothing you can do? Even with the completed manuscript sitting *right* in front of you?"

"I wish—"

Alan cleared his throat, drawing Shreya's eyes his way. She turned back to Merritt just as her eyes finished rolling at her colleague.

"No" was all she said.

Édouard cleared his throat in a way that might possibly have been meant to mock Alan. "And you think this decision will hold up to legal scrutiny."

Alan smirked. "I can assure you, Mr. Marchand, that it will."

Merritt and Shreya sat silent for a moment. Alan seemed to be losing interest, so Merritt pulled out the first weapon in her arsenal.

"Fine. Let me ask you this then, Shreya. How do you think Helen's fans will respond when they find out you've given the book away, against Helen's *final* wishes? That you've chosen, for the sake of efficiency, some ghostwriter over Helen's husband—the person she *hand-selected* to shepherd this beloved series to its conclusion?"

Shreya made a face, as if this were a distasteful thing to say, but when she spoke, her tone was measured.

"Merritt, I can understand how disappointing this must be for you. I'm sure this"—she gestured to the manuscript—"must have taken a lot of time and effort. From both of you. But as I said, we have the journals."

"The journals are just journals. *This* is a finished manuscript, completed by Whit, like Helen hoped. She left it to *him* to complete, using"—Merritt repeated what Whit had told her about the will with far more certainty than she felt—"whatever means he deemed necessary and appropriate."

Shreya clenched her jaw for a moment. "We had no choice, Merritt. We gave Whit as much leeway as we could, but he missed multiple deadlines, not just the final one. We knew it was difficult for him, but we needed him to deliver, and he couldn't. As for how the fans will respond, I highly doubt that our publisher is going to be motivated by empty threats."

Merritt narrowed her eyes.

"Empty?"

Shreya cocked her head in a pitying way. She was visibly ready for this meeting to be over.

"So you really won't consider Whit's version? No matter what?"

Shreya gave her a sad smile and shook her head.

Merritt took a deep breath and rolled her shoulders back.

"I see. And nothing I can say will make a difference?"

"I'm afraid not."

Merritt nodded once, then stood, extending her arm. Édouard looked at her in confusion.

"Well," she said, taking first Shreya's hand and then that of the slowly standing Alan, "I'm sorry for wasting your time."

"Well," Shreya said flatly. She shrugged, as if not knowing what to say, and Alan made a noise that seemed to lament the lost minutes.

"Thanks," Merritt said then, her voice suddenly meek as she straightened up to go.

She turned to the door, then stopped and turned back.

"Oh, sorry, just two more quick things I forgot to mention."

"*Yes?*" Shreya's annoyance was fully visible now. Alan fiddled with his briefcase, and Édouard watched her, enrapt, as if she were an actress in a play.

"Whit inherited all of Helen's social media," Merritt said, speaking like someone remembering a temporarily forgotten piece of information, "and as of when I checked last night, that amounts to around four million followers across platforms."

Alan looked up from beneath his Martin Scorsese eyebrows, then at Shreya, who seemed pained in her attempts to wear a neutral face.

"I have a sort of strong feeling that any video or thread Whit makes about this will go *pretty* viral."

Shreya narrowed her eyes. "Yes. If *Whit* were to do that, it would probably go 'pretty viral.' And the second thing?"

"The second thing," Merritt said, smiling, "is that Ian Hoult, the writer who sometimes publishes pieces with *The Atlantic*—"

"We know who Ian Hoult is," Alan said irritably.

"Oh, good, that's helpful." Merritt's voice, she knew, was gratingly chipper. "Anyway, Ian is interested in interviewing us for an article—about how corporate greed can be so great that it supersedes even the dying wishes of one of the brightest lights in children's literature: an author who, some might say, had been carrying this publishing house *on her back* for the last decade, and whose death has revealed not grief, not respect, but an overly fussy commitment to arbitrary deadlines and a deep and abiding love for, above all else, the bottom line."

Merritt needed to take a breath after that.

Alan stood up straight, clearly incensed, but Shreya put a hand on his arm to keep him from speaking.

"You make two very interesting points, Merritt."

Was that a small smile on her face?

"Do you mind waiting here, just a bit longer, while I have a chat with my colleagues?"

"Not at all," Merritt said, retaking her seat.

"Great. I'll be right back."

Shreya left quickly, effectively dragging Alan with her as he scowled all the way out the door.

Édouard turned his lovely eyes and curling smile on her when they were gone.

"Very good. Very, very good."

Merritt felt glowy and warm for the next fifteen minutes—until Shreya returned. Alone.

"Can you get this to me as a doc?" she asked, placing her hand on the formerly forgotten manuscript.

"What?"

"Can you?"

"Yes, of course. Does that mean . . ."

"It *only* means," Shreya interrupted, patting the manuscript as she spoke, "that I will read this with an open mind and get back to you and Whit."

Merritt's hands flew to her cheeks, and tears threatened to spill from her eyes.

"Oh my God." Merritt was hardly able to hear her own voice.

"*Fuck yeah*," Édouard hissed, delightfully out of character.

"I know," Shreya said. She picked up the manuscript and walked back toward the door. "Now, I don't mean to be rude, but I think you two should probably leave before Alan calls security."

"Yes, of course," Merritt said, standing up instantly. "Thank you. Thank you so much."

"Don't thank me yet."

Shreya began to walk away, but then she paused and looked back at Merritt.

"Or rather," she said, holding up the manuscript slightly, "thank yourself."

CHAPTER THIRTY-FIVE

Just . . . can you just stay there?" Whit said into the phone, breaking into a jog as he ran in the direction of the 96th Street station. "Just stay there. I'm coming."

"Whit," Merritt said on the other end of the line, "I have things to tell you."

"And so do I," he said, crossing Riverside Drive, "and I can't say them over the phone. I have to say them to your face. I'll be there in, I don't know, four hours? Five? Just stay there, okay? Don't run away again."

Merritt paused. Whit waited.

"Okay," she said at last.

"Okay," Whit said.

*

Merritt tried to nap as she waited for Whit. The meeting had ended at 10 a.m., and afterward, she and Édouard had gone to meet Evie at the law offices to share the news. After changing out of her borrowed clothes, Merritt allowed Evie to order and pay for a celebratory Lyft to the airport, where she picked up her now-dead phone from customer service. Four hours later she was back in Boston, and one slow Whelk Harbor Shuttle ride after that, she'd made it back to her mother's home.

Now she was pacing her room, stopping herself, over and over again, from grabbing her phone and shooting off texts. She wanted to tell Willa it had more or less worked; she wanted to tell

Whit what had happened, before he could say what he had to say. She was bursting with pride in herself, and part of her was eager to prove to Whit that he'd been wrong and she'd been right.

But then, after washing and folding all of her trip clothes, and while rearranging and then un-rearranging the furniture in her bedroom, she began to wonder how Whit would take her news. She had gotten Shreya to agree to read the manuscript, but it was the manuscript they'd made together. What if he was still hung up on Helen's journals? She couldn't blame him. And then what?

"Goodness, you *are* a mess, aren't you?"

Merritt looked up from reorganizing her mother's ancient, untouched CD catalog, which usually filled the built-in cabinets beneath the TV in the living room. Kathleen was staring at her while holding two bags of Chinese takeout.

Merritt waited for a follow-up and got in return, "What's up with you?"

No good fibs sprang to mind.

"I'm waiting for Whit."

Kathleen gave one reflective nod.

"What'd you get?" Merritt asked.

"Egg rolls, crab Rangoon, wonton soup, and sesame chicken. Why are you organizing my CDs?"

"Just . . ." Merritt struggled again for a believable lie. "Bored."

Not believable.

Another laborious nod from Kathleen.

"Mom, what do you want?"

"You fly to New York for this man. He flies to New York for you. Now he's coming here . . ."

"I did not fly to New York for him, I flew for the book. And me."

Kathleen's pauses were maddening.

"Mom."

"Well, there's no denying that *he* flew there for you. And I let him."

She added the last part with a wicked smirk that then shifted to something more earnest. "If you could have seen him in the library, Merritt, he just—"

"Mom, I don't want this right now."

Merritt stood up but stopped short of storming off to her room like a moody sophomore.

"What time is he getting here?"

"I'm not sure."

"Hopefully soon. You're running out of CDs."

"Mom."

Kathleen sighed.

"I'm going to eat some of this. Do you want some?"

She raised the bags. Merritt nodded, and her mother nodded back.

"All right. And then I'm going to walk across the street to check in on Peggy Stafford."

Peggy was an octogenarian neighbor whom Kathleen had never once visited in the last five months.

Merritt groaned.

"Mom, seriously, don't—"

"*I am going to eat some of this and then go check in on Peggy, all right?*"

Merritt took her glasses off to rub her eyes.

"Do whatever you want, Mom."

When she replaced them, Kathleen was smiling at her in a soft, amused way.

"Oh, Merritt. I think you love that man."

Merritt opened her mouth to protest, but Kathleen spoke first.

"Actually, I'm really only in the mood for soup. I'll take it with me to Peggy's, and the rest is yours. Sound good?"

Merritt dropped into her mother's favorite armchair.

"Sounds good, Mom. Thanks."

And once again, Merritt was alone.

*

It was 9 o'clock when an Uber driver named Stan in a Honda Odyssey pulled away from the Pryor house. Whit looked down at himself as he stood on the sleet-wet pavement. Under the light of the old-fashioned streetlight, he felt a bit sad and dumpy in his jeans, dove gray T-shirt, and Carhartt jacket. His body seemed to be covered in a travel-born film of stickiness.

The yellow Victorian before him glowed like a jewel on the somber, wintry street, with each of its windows lit from within. Behind one of them, Whit felt rather than saw, was Merritt.

*

Merritt leaned against the kitchen counter, which now smelled like lemon and shone like the surface of a lake. The house was sparkling, the trash taken out, the CDs were alphabetized. As Merritt considered whether deep cleaning the oven was worth her time, there came a knock on the door.

Crap, Merritt thought, looking down at herself. She had had time to scrub the sink with baking soda and hot water but hadn't thought to change out of her sweat-shorts and the long-sleeve Foothills School T-shirt she had on permanent loan from her mom.

Who cared, anyway. She wasn't trying to impress Whit anymore—only to tell him she'd saved the book. Her main concern should have been whether he would actually be pleased with this news, but as she padded in her sock feet toward the front door, something aching and broad filled her from shoulders to knees.

Whit was behind that door. She had hardly seen him in a month. Sad, sweet, stuck Whit, who was also smart and funny and compassionate. And good. She missed him. Desperately.

Merritt stopped in the entryway and closed her eyes tight.

No, she told herself. *No.*

She gave her head a shake and, before she could think about it much more, yanked open the door.

*

The light from inside spilled onto the dark, cold porch where Whit stood, and there was Merritt.

She looked like a fond memory.

She looked like home.

*

He was standing there, the same old Whit, in the Carhartt jacket she loved, and he looked tired, or rather like someone waking up. At the sight of her, his eyes grew wider and bluer, and for a moment it felt almost like he was having to hold himself back, but she chastised herself, because surely she was just confused by her own deep well of longing. She wanted to go to him, to hold him and smell the cedary, minty smell of his skin. And there *was* something behind his eyes, too, something soft yet determined that had not been there before.

"Hi," she said.

"Hi," he said, and it came out in a cloud of white.

"It's freezing, come in."

"Thanks," Whit said, and his hesitance sent a pang through her—a sharp shot that cut through the ache.

"Can I take your coat?" she said in the entryway.

"Yes, please."

"Tea?" she offered.

He smiled, sheepish. "Sure."

Merritt swiped Kathleen's copper kettle from the stove and

turned toward the sink, but as she extended it toward the faucet, Whit put his hand gently on her forearm.

"Merritt." His voice was soft and stretched.

When she looked at him, she saw that his eyes were full of something painful.

"Whit . . ." she started. She hadn't told him about the book yet. She hadn't explained what had happened with Shreya and the manuscript—*their* manuscript—and whatever he was going to say next, she felt that she needed to explain those things, because what if that changed everything again, and what if—

"Merritt," Whit said once more, turning her and gently cupping her cheek in his hand. The rest of the words died in her throat. His face was beautiful to her.

"Merritt, I love you."

She stood with her mouth slightly open.

"I love you," he said again, "and I'm sorry. I was so wrong . . . the book, our book, it's just . . . *perfect*, and that's because of you, and I should never have thrown that all away, and more than that, I just . . . I can't believe I was willing to let *you* get away over, God, I don't know, my own sense of impossibility—and I think I was mad because all this would have been so much easier if I had just known about the journals, but then . . ."

Whit shook his head. She still held the kettle in one hand, but his fingers on her face were hot water bottles that filled her whole body with warmth.

"But then I wouldn't have met you, and I wouldn't have realized that I *can* do it, and that Helen loved me enough to *let* me do it. I think I was afraid, because this is all messy and complicated, and I do have Annie to think about. But when you were gone . . . when I thought you'd maybe moved away to New York, I realized this is worth whatever messy complications there are. *You* are worth it."

Merritt tried to speak, but he continued, his next words spilling out rapidly, tripping over each other in an angry sprint.

"And then—I'm sorry, Merritt, but I missed you so much, so I read that stupid Lyons book—and I realized that there is no version of the story where you're the bad guy. You're the heroine. In all of it. And you saved me, too."

He paused, swallowed, and tenderly stroked her cheek. "I love you, Merritt, and I don't care about any of the rest. I love you."

Merritt stood, stunned, as the ache in her body moved up her throat and prickled all around her head, transformed into something fizzy and buzzing. She looked at the kettle in her hand as if it were an alien object, until Whit deftly slipped it from her fingers and set it, blindly, on the counter behind him. His hands reached for hers, but she pulled them away and up, up toward his face. His beard was bristly against her palms, and his eyes latched onto hers.

"Oh Whit, I love you," she said, and the words came out almost perfunctorily, because of course, *of course* she did. "I've been lying to myself about it since that first day I came to your house."

He looked so surprised that she laughed.

"What, then? I was a mess."

"'Was'?"

He pretended to pull away, offended, but she held his face straight.

"You brought my back to myself, Whit. You saw me when I couldn't, and I've loved you all along."

She pulled him toward her. Their bodies pressed together, his hands spread across her back, and they fell into a long kiss that felt like hope.

*

Later, as they sat by the crackling fireplace, drinking tea out of mugs that said "World's Best Librarian" and "I Read Banned Books," Merritt broke the companionable silence.

"I have to tell you something."

"What?" Whit asked, looking at her like whatever she said could only bring comfort and peace.

She set down her empty mug.

"It's big."

He shrugged, as if it would be impossible to move him out of his current harmonious state.

Merritt leaned toward him, took a breath, and said, "I convinced Helen's editor to read the manuscript."

Whit's jaw fell open.

"You what?"

Merritt raised her hands semi-triumphantly.

"I got some information about the publishing house from Willa—"

"Willa knew?"

Merritt nodded.

"And Édouard came with me—"

"*What?*" Whit said again.

"Well, I called Evie, and they let me stay over, and then the three of us sort of strategized. Édouard insisted that he would come along and tell them he represented both of us."

He let out a little gasp. "*Deception!*"

"I know."

She looked at him, as if asking for permission for this thing she had already done, and he nodded so that she'd go on.

"And anyway, Édouard got us into the building—"

"It's those eyes."

"Or the extreme confidence. Anyway, they let us meet with Shreya—"

"Seriously?"

"Yes, Shreya, and this awful lawyer man, and then I told them who I was and what we had done. I slid a copy of the manuscript across the table like I was a businessperson making an offer in a movie, and I reminded them of Helen's rabid fan base, and I suggested that to take this project away from her husband in direct violation of her wishes was pretty bad optics. I remembered you mentioning in passing that the will put you in control of her social media accounts, so I threw that in as a threat."

Whit nodded, clearly impressed and maybe a little bit awed.

"And *then* I told them that I had Ian Hoult from *The Atlantic* ready to write a piece if they didn't listen—"

"Sorry, you *what*?"

Whit froze. Merritt grinned.

"That's a pretty huge bluff, Merritt."

"It wasn't a bluff. Ian told me he'd do it."

Whit's hand flew to the top of his head.

"How did you get him to—"

"I gave him an interview. About Graydon and his book, but I made him promise to help me with this if I needed it. The article hasn't run yet, but it will."

Whit dragged his hand down his face, as if trying to wake himself up.

"You did all that—for me?"

Merritt laughed.

"No, Whit. I did it for both of us. And just for me, too, if that makes sense. I gave Ian the interview in the first place because I realized I didn't want to let Graydon be the only one telling my story. And anyway, the truth is pretty damning for him. But I made it a condition of my cooperation that Ian let me drop his name as one of my intimidation tactics, and anyway, Whit, what I'm trying to say is that it *worked*. I scared them, and they have agreed to read your version. Our version."

"Oh, Merritt," Whit said, looking into the fire. A stab of doubt hit her chest.

"I hope that's okay," she said quickly. "Maybe it was overstepping, but I couldn't bear the thought of our work meaning nothing and of them giving it all away to some random person. That's not what Helen wanted, and—"

Whit reached out to place a hand on her elbow. A log split in the fireplace as a charge crackled up her arm.

"No, Merritt," he said. "That's not what I meant. I mean . . . *thank you*. You're right. We have made a wonderful thing together, and they will love it. They *will* publish it."

The sharpness in Merritt's chest and stomach dissolved.

"You really think so?"

"I know it." He shrugged and let his fingers travel the length of her arm before taking her hand in both of his. "I get the books now. I get them in a way I never did before. All anyone wants from this story is to see how far the characters will go for each other. It's all about the things we do for the people we love, and we figured that out. It took me a while, but I figured it out, too. Really, what else can you ask for?"

*

"I can't believe you thought I moved to New York," Merritt said as they walked in Kathleen's neighborhood. After they both agreed that Merritt's mother could not possibly stay at Peggy's house past 10:30 and that they'd rather not be home when she returned, Merritt had found Whit a knit cap and one of her dad's old coats.

Now they walked the slick streets, and Whit kept one bare hand in his coat pocket, and one wrapped around Merritt's gloved fingers.

"I thought it was a *possibility*. I was not existing in a rational state at the time—"

"And you flew to see me at the drop of a hat—"

"And to see my sister."

Merritt scoffed.

"Okay, for you," Whit admitted.

"Just very dramatic of you, is all I'm saying."

Whit sighed and out came a misty puff of mock agitation.

"You love me," she reminded him, and he nodded. "Also, I have to ask, were you going to Riverside Park because of—"

"*You've Got Mail*, yes. I thought you might be there. It's a lot less romantic in January, just so you know."

"Well," Merritt said, bobbing her head a bit, "that's still pretty romantic. And a pretty good guess. But to fly all the way to New York on so little information . . ."

"I went to the bookshop looking for you first, and your coworker was very unhelpful—"

"Huong," Merritt said affectionately.

"Yes. But you weren't working, so I decided you must be subbing, and I interrupted your mom while she was reading—"

"I bet she hated that."

"You bet correctly. And she told me you were gone." He paused to consider. "She probably could've been clearer about what that meant if she wanted to."

"She absolutely could have," Merritt agreed with a laugh.

"Anyway, I bought a plane ticket immediately, but then I had a flat tire, and so I got a ride with Noel Pendergrass, but I had to—"

"Stop," Merritt said, rounding on him. "You rode from Whelk Harbor to Boston with Noel Pendergrass? For me?"

Whit smirked.

"I did. And I cannot overstate how awful it was. And also, I had to agree to help with carpool duty."

Merritt beamed.

"You did that for me?"

"I did. And I will do almost anything else for you, too, but not *that*, not ever again."

"That's fair," Merritt said, dropping her head to his shoulder as they continued their late-night stroll. "That's very, very fair."

They walked on into town, passing the village green, the bistro, the bookstore, until eventually they got too cold, and together they headed back home.

EPILOGUE

When the book was published, several months later, there was a single dedication:

For Helen

Helen's name was also on the cover in large letters, as:

THE FAIRY IN THE HIGH TOWER

The Final Installment of the Greenwood Castle Saga, begun by

Helen Albright Longacre

Beneath, in much smaller but still clearly legible letters, were two names. They were Merritt Pryor and Whit Longacre. In that order.

ACKNOWLEDGMENTS

I think it is so cool and professional when authors keep their acknowledgments short and sweet, and that is just not going to be the case here.

Thank you first to my wonderful agent, Elizabeth Harding, who has stuck with me for so long. Thank you for talking me off many ledges, for always being calm and collected, and for looking the other way when my emails begin to sound especially unhinged. Thank you also to my editor, Laura Schreiber: you were the perfect person to find this book, and I am so grateful to you for believing in it and for loving it as much as I do. To the whole team at HarperCollins/Avon: Catherine Hay, Cynthia Buck, Jeanie Lee, and others I haven't met who work behind the scenes, thank you for shepherding this book into existence and answering my questions without making me feel like the dumbest boy in school. Thank you, also, to Holly Ovenden for the beautiful cover art. I love it.

Sarah Gerton, you've read hundreds of thousands of my words through the years, always taking them and me seriously, and I'm so grateful for the ways you made me a better writer. Thank you to Katie Herman: your insights on this manuscript were invaluable and gave me much needed early belief in the project. Alex Kiester, Anne Wynter, and Ashley Winstead, you've happily answered newbie author questions and given me sound advice.

Thank you to my early readers, particularly Alex Toney, who has gone over every piece of fiction I've written since I was twenty-five and only mocked me in the marginal notes when I really deserved it. This book might still exist without you, but it would be a whole lot worse. Thanks are also owed to: Fabs Harford and Mary Tucker, who helped me work out some kinks and made me feel like a million bucks; cheerers-on and readers of other manuscripts, including Zach Barnett, Lori Ann Stephens, Kate Boswell, and Carly Schneider; and Jeanette Horn, Susannah Frishman-Phillips, and Alejandro Puyana, who all make very good food and also good suggestions.

I wrote most of this book while teaching at St. Andrew's Episcopal School in Austin, and I owe a great debt to my friends there, particularly in the English department: Amy Skinner, Kimberly Horne, Anna Konradi, Heather Tone, Claire Canavan, Elizabeth Doss, Jennifer Tollefson, Nitya Rayapati, and Matt Kelly. Your encouragement and excitement on my behalf have meant the world, and our students (hi, guys) are so lucky to have you. Thanks, also, to Alice Nezzer, for encouraging me to "go and write" (I hope you enjoy listening to this on your commute), and to Chad Fulton, who will be insufferable if I leave him out.

Thank you to Meg Ryan, Tom Hanks, the late Nora Ephron—honestly the entire cast and crew of *You've Got Mail.* Where would I be without you? And to Ethan Clark, Ryan Graney, and Austin Sailsbury, for being good friends and, more importantly, very funny people.

In fourth grade, my language arts teacher made me believe I was a good writer, and she did so with whimsy, warmth, and humor. Thank you, Mrs. Sally Riddile. I think of you often. You changed my life.

Most worthy of thanks are my family, who have cheered me on for decades. To all the Staffords, but particularly Jim and Linda, the best in-laws and grandparents imaginable—thank you for all you've done for us. To the Sheltons: thanks for celebrating me so well. And to my parents, Ellen and Larry Forrester; my sisters, Amy Forrester and Emily Lacy; and my brother-in-law, Jake

Lacy: I am so fortunate to have had you in my corner all this time. Can you believe it? Also sorry, Mom, for all the bad words.

Lastly, thank you to my own little family—to James, Winnie, Peter, and William, for being yourselves. I am very lucky to be your dad. And to Megan, whom I love: you're just the best thing to ever happen to me. Thanks for everything, always.

ABOUT THE AUTHOR

Andrew Forrester is a writer and former English teacher whose work has appeared in McSweeney's Internet Tendency and *Parents* magazine. He holds a PhD in nineteenth-century British literature and lives in Austin, Texas, with his family. *How the Story Goes* is his first novel.